KT-449-084

0135574856

STARSHINE

Like so many other men in 1914, Jim Hickman
and Bertie Murphy are plunged into the
nightmare of WW1. Loyal friends, the pair had
done everything together since they became
neighbours as children, from falling in love with
the same girl to enlisting as soon as the war
began. Now, they must become closer than ever
to ensure they both survive the countless,
gruelling battles at the front line. As the war
progresses, Jim receives honour after honour,
whilst loveable Bertie struggles to deal with the
mindless slaughter around him. And meanwhile,
back in Birmingham, their beloved girl Polly
must choose between the two men.

STARSHINE

STARSHINE

by

John Wilcox

WARWICKSHIRE
COUNTY LIBRARY

CONTROL No.

Magna Large Print Books
Long Preston, North Yorkshire,
BD23 4ND, England.

British Library Cataloguing in Publication Data.

Wilcox, John
    Starshine.

    A catalogue record of this book is
    available from the British Library

    ISBN 978-0-7505-3792-6

First published in Great Britain by Allison & Busby in 2012

Copyright © 2012 by John Wilcox

Cover illustration by arrangement with Allison & Busby Ltd.

The moral right of the author is hereby asserted in accordance with
the Copyright, Designs and Patents Act, 1988

Published in Large Print 2013 by arrangement with
Allison & Busby Limited

All Rights reserved. No part of this publication may be reproduced,
stored in a retrieval system, or transmitted in any form or by any
means, electronic, mechanical, photocopying, recording or otherwise
without the prior permission of the Copyright owner.

Magna Large Print is an imprint of Library Magna Books Ltd.

Printed and bound in Great Britain by
T.J. (International) Ltd., Cornwall, PL28 8RW

All characters and events in this publication, other than those clearly in the public domain, are fictitious and any resemblance to actual persons, living or dead, is purely coincidental.

*For my dear friend Jim Farrand,
whose pacifistic views influenced
the writing of this novel.*

CHAPTER ONE

October 1914, France.

The bugle call sounded loud, clear and as intrusive as a douche of spring water, for the bugler stood in the predawn merely a few paces from where they all lay wrapped in groundsheets by the railway sidings, just outside Boulogne. A gentle rain was falling and it was cold, damned cold.

Jim Hickman shivered, threw aside his greatcoat and groundsheet and looked across at Bertie. True to form, Private Bertram Murphy, of King George V's Territorial Force, continued to sleep, only his curly red hair peeping out from his turned-up coat collar, completely impervious both to the hardness of the ground on which he lay and the bustle all around him.

'Get your mate up, or I'll 'ave 'im on a charge as soon as you can say Kaiser Bill.' The corporal emphasised his words by prodding Murphy with his boot.

'Don't worry, Corp, he'll be up.' Jim bent down and shook his friend. 'Come on, Bertie. Rise and shine. Time to fight the Germans, mate.'

One sleepy eye, as blue as his mother's best china, regarded him. 'In France, then, are we, Jimmy?' The muffled voice was mellifluously Irish and came from deep beneath the groundsheet. There was no sign of movement. 'I think I'll sleep

11

on a bit, if it's all the same to you, son. I've only just got comfortable enough to close me eyes, see. Give me another shout in a minute or two, there's a feller.'

Hickman reached down, seized the end of his friend's groundsheet and pulled, unrolling Murphy like a pork sausage from its wrapping.

The simile remained, however, for the Irishman lay inert on the wet ground, still, it seemed, sleeping.

'For God's sake, Bertie, get up.' He pulled his friend to his feet and shook him. 'We're on the way to the front now, man. This bugler's in the army, not the bleedin' band. Come on, now. Smarten up.'

He flicked away a piece of mud that was attached to Murphy's ear and jerked the rumpled tunic downwards in an attempt to straighten it. The Irishman regarded him with a happy smile and knuckled his eyes. In truth, the figure he cut was not soldierly. At just over five feet five inches, his rotund build made him seem much smaller than Hickman's lean six feet, and his face was round and rosy. A dimple cut into his chin and his eyelashes were long and fair. He had somehow managed to button up his tunic haphazardly, so that it was lopsided. The binding of his puttees had come undone and one end trailed in the mud. The lace of his right boot draped over the toecap.

'Am I not the very model of a modern British soldier, James?' he dreamily enquired of his friend. 'Just what you'd want to fight the savage foe, eh?'

'You two.' The corporal's voice thundered. 'If you're not fallen in line within five seconds you'll be on fatigues for a week. Move your bloody selves. NOW!'

There was no breakfast, no water to wash in or make tea and they waited gloomily, some two hundred of them, for the train that eventually trundled into view. The euphoria that had accompanied their crossing of the Channel from Folkestone – they had sung all the way – had lingered on when they landed on French soil. Girls had flung flowers at them and they had been offered glasses of wine as they marched through the streets of Boulogne, under the surly gaze of a troop of French soldiers who looked like something from a musical comedy with their long rifles and in their kepis, dark-blue frock coats curled back at the thighs, red pantaloons and white spats.

'Toy soldiers, that's what they are,' growled a sergeant. 'The Boche walked all over 'em in the seventies an' they're doing it again now. Let's 'ope we can get 'em out of the mess they're in.'

The euphoria had died quickly, however, as they reached the railway station at Boulogne to find no train waiting to take them to ... where? Rumour fuelled the speculation: they were destined for a big counter-attack below Mons, where the French had sustained a great defeat, only saved from rout, it was said, because the tiny British Expeditionary Force had stemmed the German advance; or Paris itself, to where the Boche had advanced dangerously close; or perhaps Belgium, which the uhlans had ridden

13

through contemptuously, spearing babies, it was said, on the end of their long lances. Wherever it was, there was no train to take them there and they were forced to wait on the platform and then march outside the town to the sidings where they camped in the open – and the rain began.

Now, however, as dawn began to seep through the pewter-coloured clouds, an aged locomotive was wheezing into sight, pulling a line of open cattle trucks.

Bertie's eyes widened. 'Surely the King is not himself sending us to war in these things,' he cried. 'I'll get me stuff all dirty, I will.'

He and Jim filed on board and made themselves as comfortable as they could on the damp straw at the bottom of the truck, easing the large packs on their backs so that they could sit upright, and balancing their rifles so that the bolt mechanism was protected against the soft rain.

The sergeant who had spoken so disparagingly about the French army squeezed himself next to Hickman and took a puzzled gaze at his rifle.

'Blimey,' he said. 'What's that thing?'

'It's me rifle, Sergeant.'

'I can see that, yer bloody fool. But what sort?'

'Er ... it's a Mark I Lee-Metford.'

'Ah. Single shot, eh?'

'Yes, Sarge.'

The sergeant sniffed. 'You must be Territorials. I didn't think Lord Kitchener wanted you lot over 'ere.'

Bertie, bright-eyed, leant over to join the conversation. 'No, Sarge, he doesn't. For some

14

reason, y'see, he doesn't like us and kept most of us back home to defend England's green an' pleasant land, although with respect, sorr, it ain't so green and pleasant as Ireland, although to be true it's bin years since I seen the place meself, see.'

The sergeant flicked the rain from the end of his long moustaches. 'Wot's 'e on about?'

'He's Irish, Sarge,' said Jim, 'although he's really from Brum, like me. But we both wanted to fight and not stay at home, see, so we took the ... what's it called?... Ah, the imperial service obligation, that's it, which allows Terriers to fight abroad, like.'

'Humph. Well,' the sergeant gestured to their rifles, 'you won't do much fighting with them things. They're well outdated. You won't last long with single shots. When the Huns come at yer in their 'undreds, as they do, you need rapid fire to 'old 'em. You just won't 'ave time to pop single cartridges into the breech. They'll be on yer before you can scratch yer arse. You've got to 'ave rapid fire and you've got to pump the bolt till yer 'ands bleed. I know...' He paused. 'I was at Mons, yer see. There were only a few of us there – cooks, clerks, grooms, the scrapings of the battalion thrown in to support the few Regulars like me that was left. To fill in the 'oles, so to speak.'

Jim and Bertie leant forward transfixed, their eyes on the leathery face at their side. But the sergeant now seemed almost unaware of their presence.

'There seemed millions of 'em,' he continued, staring at the strange assortment of soldiers squatting around him but seeing none of them. 'Grey 'ordes of 'em, comin' over massed together, their bayonets glintin'. We couldn't miss at that range. We'd got no machine guns and we just pumped bullets in as fast as we could.'

He seemed to rejoin the present and turned his head back to Hickman and Riley. 'They do say as 'ow the Germans thought we'd got Maxim guns, so fast was our firin'.' His momentary elation quickly disappeared, however, and he sighed. 'Now it looks as if we've got to do it all over again.'

A silence fell. Then: 'Any idea where we're going, Sarge?' asked Jim.

'The captain says it's a little town over the Belgian border called Wipers, or somethin' like that. I 'ear that things are desperate, 'cos we're outnumbered, with little artillery an' lots of their 'eavy stuff comin' over. It's another rescue job. This lot is a ragtag and bobtail get-together of everything that could be thrown into the line.'

He indicated the men lining the walls of the truck and sitting awkwardly in the middle. 'None o' these is regulars. They're mainly Reservists who've just arrived, with clerks, sanitary orderlies an' so on from the back lines about 'ere who can be spared. If you're from Birmingham, you won't be joinin' any Warwicks, as far as I know. An' if you take my advice, you should get rid o' those bleeding so-called rifles they've given you.' He glanced sharply at them. 'But don't just lose 'em – that's a court martial offence. At your first chance, stick mud in the breech, or something like that, so you get reissued with proper Lee-

Enfields. But don't say I said so.'

'Thanks, Sarge.' A glum silence descended on the group, to be broken with a half cheer as, eventually, the trucks shuddered into life and began to clunk forward.

Bertie bent his head towards his friend and whispered. 'Just as well we're the two best shots in the whole of the British army, then, Jimmy. Trouble is, if my hands are as cold as this when the Germans' lads come at us, I'll never get a single round into the bloody gun, that's for sure. I'll just have to throw mud at the bastards or take down me breeches an' fart at 'em.' He gave his great face-splitting smile. 'That'll put 'em off, so it will.'

If the situation at their destination was desperate, then the driver of the locomotive seemed to be unaware of it. The trucks juddered together regularly as the train slowed down and then picked up speed with seeming difficulty, as though the cargo was too heavy for its capacity. The men in the trucks were continually being thrown together violently as the staccato journey continued. Black smoke belched from the funnel of the engine and hung low over them to add to their misery and the rain slipped down like a damp shroud.

At mid afternoon, after a journey of what the sergeant estimated to be only some fifteen miles, the train halted and they disembarked to be met at the rail side by the welcome sight of cooks handing out mugs of tea and sandwiches. As they stood munching and drinking, a darkly moustached major, dapper despite the rain, called them to gather around him. Ominously, as he spoke they could hear the rumble of guns from the north-east.

'I'm sorry the journey is uncomfortable and slow,' he said, 'but there were no proper passenger carriages to be found for love nor money and this bloody loco has as much puff as George Robey's whistle.' They all laughed dutifully. 'Now, men, we are going to a little town called Ypres, just over the border into Belgium. The Boche are attacking it strongly and have pushed us, the French and the Belgians right back, virtually to the walls of the town. They dominate us with their guns from the slopes that surround the place to the east and they know that, once they take Ypres, the Channel ports are open to them. And we can't have that, of course.'

He looked around at them. 'Well, they are not going to take Ypres because you lot will arrive in time to prevent that.' An ironic cheer broke out. 'Nevertheless, the situation is critical. If the Hun breaks through, then he will stream down the coastal plain, take the Channel ports, break our supply lines and turn our and the French lines. He has to be stopped.'

He coughed and took a sip of his tea. 'I came down from there two days ago and I can tell you that it is not pleasant. You will be under constant shelling and the blighters outnumber us strongly. At the rate this loco is going we won't be there until after nightfall, but I'm afraid there will be no time for rest. You will be issued with basic rations and ammunition and undertake a night march to go straight into the line. I am sorry that

18

you will almost certainly not be fighting with your own regiments but I know that I can rely on you to show the Kaiser just what strength the British army has in its Reservists.'

Another ragged cheer followed and the major held up his hand. 'Right, get back on board now. Make sure your weapons are dry because you will have to fight with them.' He looked up at the sky. 'At least this damned rain has stopped. Good luck, lads.'

'Now there's a nice enough feller, don't you think?' asked Bertie, as the pair settled down together again in their truck.

'Oh, lovely. He's just told us that we're almost certainly going to be shot or blown to hell. Lovely feller.' Jim indicated his friend's rifle. 'Wrap your hankie around the breech bolt and block. It may only fire one shot at a time but it's all we've got and we don't want the bloody things to rust up.'

'Ah, right you are, Jimmy lad.'

Dusk was creeping down when they wheezed into a station marked Poperinghe. The only lights to be seen were lanterns held by NCOs who rapidly segregated the men into groups of about thirty each. Shellfire thundered near to them, it seemed, and the sky to the east was lit sporadically by flashes of scarlet, although these grew less frequent as the night closed in. In the semi-darkness, gaunt-faced quartermasters gave them sealed packs of field rations and water bottles containing, they were told, also a 'wee drop of rum'. Each man was issued with seventy rounds of ammunition and then, under the command of a sergeant major whose uniform was smeared with mud, they set off.

Their march took them through the town of Ypres and, in the dim light, Jim Hickman could see that this was a fine town, with solid and lofty architecture. But there were no lights in the streets and the artillery flashes in the near distance had now died away and were occasionally replaced by the flashes of Very lights. No one was about and it seemed a ghost city. Soon darkness had completely descended and they were ordered to march in single file, with one hand on the shoulder of the man in front. Heads down and hearts pounding, they stumbled over broken ground and a strange smell assailed them.

'I know what it is,' said Bertie. 'It's tobacco and beetroot, so it is. It must be grown round here.'

'Quiet at the back,' hissed the warrant officer.

'I think we're marchin' into hell, Jim lad,' murmured Bertie. 'Let's keep together whatever happens.'

'Don't worry,' answered Jim over his shoulder. 'I'm never going to lose you, I'll promise you that. We'll stay together.'

Together. They had been together almost as long as both could remember, living in the same street with only one house in between them since Bertie and his Irish road labourer or 'navvy' father – his mother had died at childbirth – had moved in at the turn of the century. Together they had joined the Territorials, for they offered exciting camps on Salisbury Plain and the chance to 'play soldiers', as Bertie called it. Together, too, they had answered the call to arms on August 4th when war had been declared on Germany.

The year was 1914, one which had begun so well for them both, with their beloved Aston Villa, whose huge, bright red brick stadium loomed large just down the road from them, finishing second in the first division that season for the third successive year. Jim had begun the fourth year of his apprenticeship as a diamond mounter in the little business where his father laboured in the heart of the jewellery quarter in Hockley and he had managed to get Bertie a job there, too, sweeping, making tea and becoming universally popular, just by being his cheerful, happy self. It was a good time to be eighteen and they had both enjoyed the blissful summer of that year, playing football and cricket in Aston Park and, of course, taking Polly rowing on the lake in Handsworth Park.

Polly was exactly their age and she lived in the terrace house between them at number 64, Turners Lane, Aston. Neither of them could remember a time when the girl had not been at their side. They had formed an inseparable trio, going everywhere together. As children, when the boys played their way home from school by rolling marlies in the gutter, Polly came too, jumping, skipping alongside and talking continually. As they grew older, Polly quietened a little but stayed close, doing what they did, insisting – to their embarrassment – on holding their hands as they walked, bowling at them at cricket and keeping goal in the park kickabout.

She grew to be tall, slender and pretty in an unconventional way, with soft brown hair, high cheekbones and strange, green eyes that seemed to shine in the dark. As the boys went through their teenage years, growing tall (less so in Bertie's case) and filling out, Polly appeared to segue almost imperceptibly from tomboy into striking young woman. She remained unusual, however, in spurning the friendship of her own sex and the approaches of other boys and staying one of the trio, joining Jim and Bertie as they in-puffed their first Woodbines and heroically matching them as they drained their first pints of mild beer.

She had seen them off at the station when they had enlisted, but now it was mid-October and the boys had to concede that the war that was to be over by Christmas perhaps was going to take a little longer. The two and a half months that had passed since they had enlisted had been marked by major setbacks to the Allied cause. The Germans had marched through Belgium, despite valiant resistance by the little Belgian army, and the French army had been forced to retreat from Mons, under cover of a last-ditch stand by the British, and Jim had read that only an heroic victory by the French at the Battle of the Marne had saved Paris itself from being taken by the enemy. Now the British Expeditionary Force – the largest army that Britain had ever sent abroad, but still tiny compared to the force facing it and depleted by the bitter fighting at Mons – had been redeployed to the north-west to take its position on the left flank of the mighty French army, now swollen to more than four million men. The British, then, occupied a key position between the French and the Belgians in a line that extended some thirty-five miles in a curve to the east of Ypres, against eleven German infantry divisions and eight cavalry divisions.

The long file of men were now approaching the front and a smell very different to that which Bertie had recognised earlier now assailed them. It was an odour sweet and sickly and came from the bloated corpses of mules and horses that emerged starkly from the darkness every time a star shell illumined the sky ahead of them. They no longer walked in a straight line, but threaded their way between shell holes half filled with water that reflected the light of the flares.

'Hey, Jimmy,' whispered Bertie hoarsely, 'it's not just horses that are dead. There are bodies in them holes.'

'Quiet!' The sergeant major's urgent whisper came from the front.

On they went, now in pitch darkness that was only occasionally lit by a flare or, even less frequently, the flash of cannon fire. It was impossible to see even the man in front, and the track that had once been firm was now uneven and spongy, causing them to stumble and curse and grope for the shoulder ahead. There was no smoking and no conversation. Jim Hickman felt that they were a ghost army advancing to ... what?

Eventually they halted, just as the clouds above receded to reveal a watery moon. A sergeant whom they recognised as the veteran from the cattle truck strode along the line touching each one and giving them a whispered number. Hickman was the last to be numbered and Jim caught the NCO's arm.

'My mate's behind me, Sarge,' he said urgently. 'Don't part us, there's a good bloke. We've always been together and I sort of look after him, see.'

For a moment the sergeant paused, then he nodded. He pulled out the man in front of Jim and pushed him into the line behind Bertie. Then he gestured to the numbered men to fall out and join him and a corporal who was waiting at the beginning of what had once been a sunken road, although shellfire had brought its sides tumbling down, leaving it merely a depression in the ground.

The sergeant gestured for them to sit, then addressed them in low, urgent monotones. 'Right, lads. I am Sergeant Jones. I'm goin' to be your platoon sergeant. Corporal Mackenzie 'ere is goin' to guide us up to the front. But from what 'e tells me it ain't much of a front. There's very little cover up there – just scooped-out trenches only about three feet 'igh, sort of joining up with shell 'oles.' He sniffed. 'Seems everyone's waiting for the bloody sandbags to be shipped over from England. But never mind that.

'Now listen. Jerry doesn't shell much at night but 'e knows exactly where these support trenches an' tracks go up to the line, because 'e's up there on the 'eights ahead of us and can see 'em all during the day. So, whatever you do, don't show a light otherwise we'll 'ave bloody great Jack Johnsons – those are 'is 'eaviest shells – down on us like a ton o' bricks. So definitely no smokin'. We've got about 'alf a mile to go an' we'll soon be in sniper country. They operate at night, even if the artillery doesn't. So no noise, keep yer 'eads down an' freeze when the star shells go up, 'cos that's when the Jerry snipers will be lookin' down their sights. Understood?'

Everyone nodded. Bertie held up a muddy hand. 'Where are we goin' to exactly, Sarge?'

Jones sighed. 'If I told you Piccadilly Circus, lad, it wouldn't make much bloody difference, would it?'

'Oh yes. Piccadilly's in London, isn't it, Sarge? Me father told me that, anyway.'

'All right, then, sonny. So as not to confuse your father, I'll tell you that we're 'eading for a place that we call Nun's Wood, although it's summat unpronounceable in Flemish. It's almost up on the top of the ridge ahead of us. The Germans 'ave pushed us down that 'ill to this wood – although there ain't many trees left I'm told – an' we're 'angin' on by our eyelids. A mixed bag up there trying to 'old the line: Jocks, Service Corps blokes, an' dishwashers. Not many rifles to go round and the corporal tells me that we pushed back the last attack by swingin' picks and shovels. So the lads there are waitin' for us to 'elp 'em an' that's what we're goin' to do.'

He fell silent and stayed still as a green light soared into the sky behind him, leaving his silhouette – broad shoulders, rifle pointing to the sky and soft peaked cap, jammed squarely onto his head – gradually fading as the flare dropped and died.

'Right. Just one more thing. There are twenty-five of us. 'Ow many Reservists?' Everyone but Jim and Bertie raised a hand.

'Ah yes, our two Terriers with their bloody muskets, last used at the Battle of Waterloo. Well the rest of you at least are trained soldiers, who have seen service, even if it was a year or two ago. Who's seen active service, though?'

Three hands rose.

'Where?'

'Boer War, Sergeant. All three of us.'

'Right. Well I know that was no picnic because I was there too. I survived the Kop. But I've got a feeling, lads, that this one is goin' to be a bit different. A bloody sight worse, in fact, because of the guns the Jerries 'ave got: heavy stuff an' machine guns. Even so, we'll beat the buggers, but remember – from now on, 'eads down and no talkin'. Lead on, Corporal.'

They plodded on and Jim realised that they were beginning to climb – up a gentle slope, of course, to where the Germans looked down on them. As they neared the front line, or what was left of it, they all became aware of sharp flashes that penetrated the darkness ahead sporadically and then the rattle of a machine gun. As if on cue at this, the corporal peeled off to the right and took with him the leading half of the column, who disappeared into the darkness. Sergeant Jones waved his arm and the remainder followed him, walking at a crouch until they were able to

26

slip into a communications half-trench, which zigzagged up the slope and whose walls, about four feet high, offered protection of a sort.

Three minutes later an officer loomed out of the darkness and held a whispered conversation with the sergeant. Jones turned and waved his men towards him.

'Right,' he said. 'We're whispering because the enemy is only just about one 'undred and twenty yards ahead of us, up by what's left of them trees up ahead – NO, don't look now, you duffers! You'll get a bullet in yer 'ead. A couple of corporals will be along in a minute to take you along the line and deposit you in the gaps. I'll come on afterwards and settle you in and make sure you're nice an' comfortable.'

Then the jocularity died. 'Listen. You'll be sprawled up there without much cover, so dig in as much as you can while it's dark. I'm told that trenches 'ardly exist, so it's a case of finding what cover you can. Rations are due up soon so you should get something to eat before daylight comes. I know that you're tired but don't sleep. DIG!

'The Jerries will almost certainly come at us at daybreak so make sure that your rifles are clean and oiled and fix your bayonets at dawn. You'll probably need 'em. Ah, the corporals are 'ere. Off you go – and good luck, lads. Now then, where are the Brummie Terriers?'

Jim and Bertie raised their hands – but only as far as their shoulders.

'Good. You two come with me.'

They crawled behind the sergeant, for by now

the trench had given way to little more than a de-
clivity in the ground and the occasional swathe
of the German machine gun was obviously firing
on a fixed traverse, aiming to hit anyone who had
the temerity to stand in what was left of the
British lines.

And, indeed, it soon became clear that the line
hardly existed. Jim and Bertie were deposited
into a shell crater, some seven feet deep, occupied by five men, who were sprawled on the
German side of the crater fast asleep, their rifles
at their side, while a sixth kept watch.

A trench of sorts had been scraped out from
either side of the shell hole and the sound of
digging came from it.

'Get in there. You,' he indicated Jim, 'go to the
right and Paddy to the left and see if you can
relieve the diggers. They've all been at it for
forty-eight hours or more with little rest, so they
could do with a spell.'

'Sure, Sergeant,' said Bertie, 'but, bless you,
we've no shovels or spades, see.'

'Use what they're usin', which I expect is
bayonets and their 'ands. Get on with it and be
thankful it's not rainin'. I'll be back later with
any luck.'

The two sloughed off their heavy packs and
ammunition webbing, drew their bayonets and
split up, right and left. Hickman found that his
so-called trench was, again, only about three
feet deep, but it was wide enough to accommo-
date his long legs if, when facing the enemy, he
knelt. Now, however, he found himself facing
the ample bottom of a soldier who was hurling

28

soil over his left shoulder to form a low barrier and so raise the wall on the enemy side of the trench.

He put his hand on the man's buttocks and suddenly found a bayonet at his throat.

'For Gawdsakes, son,' exclaimed the soldier, 'don't do that. I thought you was a Jerry.'

'Sorry, mate. I've come to relieve you. Is there a spade or something?'

'Blimey, no. This ain't the Ritz. You've got to use your sticker. This clay is an absolute bleeding bitch. Thing to do is to cut it out in lumps with your bayonet and then claw it out with your 'and and toss it on top. See? But keep your 'ead down. That machine gun comes round every sixteen minutes, I've timed it. Waste of bullets. Stupid, but he'll get you if you forget 'cos he skims the top of the trench like.'

'Strewth!'

The soldier, thin-faced, with dark bags under his eyes, hitched up his braces and looked sharply at Jim. 'New at the front, lad?'

'Yes. Just arrived.'

He sighed. 'It's bad 'ere. So keep your wits about you. We've been pushed down this bloody slope for days now. We're just about 'angin' on, but they do say that reinforcements are coming soon to give us an 'and, so if we can keep the buggers out for a few more days, we might be all right. Now, there's only room for one to work 'ere so I'll be off. Thanks for relievin' me. See if you can join this ditch up with the shell 'ole up ahead, there ... ooh, watch out, 'ere 'e comes again.'

29

They both ducked their heads as the machine gun began its chatter and, true enough, bullets clipped the tops of the turned earth, pinging away with a high-pitched whine as they hit stones.

'All right now, son.' The older man squeezed his way past Hickman. 'We've got a rota. I'll see that you're relieved in two hours. Keep diggin', lad.'

Jim set to with a will. The work was constricting, particularly for someone of his height, for he had to work kneeling, but he was fit and strong and, despite the fact that he had had virtually no sleep for twenty hours, he almost enjoyed the labour. He too began timing the machine gun's traverse with his wristwatch and found that the swing began exactly every sixteen minutes. How stupid! He had heard that the Germans were methodical but this was ridiculous. Perhaps there was no one behind the gun; perhaps it was set to go off, like an alarm clock, every sixteen minutes. If this was war, it was strange. Nothing like the manoeuvres on Salisbury Plain when they had marched, countermarched, flung themselves down, fired and then charged an imaginary enemy. That was stirring stuff, real soldiering. This scraping away on hands and knees waiting to be shot at every sixteen minutes was ridiculous. He felt no fear of the morrow. It would be good to stand up and face a real German and fight properly!

Nevertheless, it was a relief when his turn came to crawl back into the crater. There, he found Bertie in conversation with Sergeant Jones. The

NCO had brought two of the modern Lee-Enfield rifles.

'Ah, good, you're back. These are dead men's rifles, but it can't be 'elped. There's no time to instruct you properly with them but it's better that you 'ave them before Jerry pays a visit in a couple of hours' time. Now listen. The main difference is that they're shorter than the Lee-Metford, so they're much easier to 'andle in trenches. Your sword bayonets will fit just the same. Best thing, though, is that they're magazine guns, see, 'ere.'

He slapped the magazine protruding in front of the trigger guard. 'This means you can load with ten shots, instead of one at a time. Difference between life or death when you're just a few feet away from the enemy – like now.' He pulled back the bolt. 'Just stick a couple o' clips of five rounds each down there. The firin' ejects the spent cartridge case, an' the workin' of the bolt, like this, pushes a new round up the spout. When you really get used to it you can let off about forty rounds a minute. It's a great little gun. You got your oil and pull-through?'

They nodded, holding the rifles admiringly.

'Good. Well give 'em a good clean now, while you've got the chance. I 'ope you 'ave better luck with 'em than their last owners.'

'Thanks, Sarge,' said Jim.

'Very kind of you, sorr,' added Bertie.

'You don't "sir" me, lad. I'm only a poor bloody sergeant. Now, clean the rifles and try and get your 'eads down. You might be able to 'ave about two hours' shut-eye before we 'ave

31

visitors.' He paused. ''Ang on.' He looked at his wristwatch. 'Noticed anything?'

The boys stood, silently listening. 'No, Sarge.'

'That fixed machine gun's stopped firing. It could mean that it's a night attack, but I doubt it.' The sergeant crept up to the watchman at the lip of the crater and lay there, his head just above the edge scanning the darkness ahead. He ducked momentarily as a blue Very light shot up from the British lines, then resumed his vigil. Eventually, he slipped down again and rejoined them.

'Seems okay. Get some sleep. I'll be back just before stand-to at dawn.'

'Thanks, Sergeant.'

'Nice bloke,' said Bertie, as they saw Jones's back disappear down the communications trench. 'He's looking after us.'

'Yes. I like the look of these things.' Jim held up the rifle admiringly. 'We're in the twentieth century now, Bertie. Proper rifles, for the killing of Germans. Come on, let's oil 'em and try and get a bit of shut-eye.'

Hickman had no intention of sleeping, for he was on edge with the thought of what was to come in the morning and he wanted to be completely ready. He had carefully oiled the breech mechanism of his rifle, pulled a small square of cloth through the barrel several times to clean it, fixed his bayonet, and it seemed that he had only just closed his eyes for a moment of relaxation when he was being shaken awake.

'Come on, lad, stand to. The good news is that grub's up.' It was his friend from the digging. He was handing him a hot mug of tea and a sandwich of bread and jam. 'Get this down you quick 'cos it'll be light soon.'

Jim took the mug and the sandwich gratefully and began gulping down the tea and the bread and jam in successive mouthfuls. He looked across to find Bertie and winced as he saw that the little man had gone to sleep again, curled up on the soil of the crater edge, his mug and sandwich by his side.

He crawled across. 'For God's sake, Bertie. Wake up or you'll be shot. Come on, man.'

The blue eyes opened and beamed at him. 'Good morning, Jimmy boy. Holy Mary. Is that tea you've got there?'

'Stand to, men.' The sergeant had miraculously appeared. 'Lookout – any sign?'

'No, Sarge. Nothing moving as far as I can see.'

'Right. Get that grub down you quickly, all of you, and then man the edge of the crater. You two Terriers, get out on the trench at the side there. You two,' he gestured to two men who were hurriedly buckling on their equipment, 'don't let me see you taking off your belts at night again. The next time it'll be a charge. Now get out on the trench on the left. Put a cartridge up the spout. Move now.'

The sergeant turned to greet a young subaltern who had slipped into the crater. It was obvious from the mud that clung to the young man's boots and riding breeches that he was attempting to work his way along the line. 'Morning, sir.'

'Morning, Jones. Everything all right?'

'Yessir. Ready and waiting.'

'Now, men,' he addressed them all in a low monotone. 'We've held 'em off so far. There's to be no more retreating, so we have to hold out here to the end. Understood?'

There was a low murmur of assent.

'Very good. Rapid firing when they come. Good luck.'

Hickman and Murphy crawled their way along the ditch that Jim had helped excavate during the night. A soft light began to illuminate them all. Bertie threw away his last crust and took a peek over the edge towards the German lines. He called back to the sergeant.

'How many men would there be in the German army, then, Sarge?' he asked.

'What? Oh, about seven million. Why, for God's sake?'

'Well, they're all standing up now just across there and starting to come towards us.'

'Stand to! Lookout, what the hell's wrong with you?' The sergeant scrambled to the lip of the crater and pulled back the inert form of the lookout who had a small black hole in the middle of his forehead. Jones's voice rose to a shriek. 'Man the lip of the shell hole and trenches. Rapid fire at enemy in front. FIRE!'

Jim, on his knees, levelled his rifle and looking down its unfamiliarly short barrel found himself gazing at a grey mass of uniformed men marching stolidly towards him, a frighteningly short distance away. At the same moment the British line exploded into a crackle of gunfire.

He pulled the trigger and saw his target collapse and fall. He groped with his hand to find a replacement cartridge and realised, with a curse, that the action was unnecessary and a waste of precious time, for he did not need to feed the breech with single cartridges; he could just keep firing. He did so, hardly bothering to take aim now, pumping the bolt as fast as he could and blessing the fact that he had cleaned the rifle, for it was firing fast and smoothly. His ten rounds were soon spent and he fumbled to put two more clips into the magazine, flipping away the clip holders with his thumb, and recommenced firing.

The enemy were falling all across the line, for they were tightly bunched together and presenting an unmissable target to the British rifles. Yet they still marched on with great courage into that devastating fire. The front rank were near enough now to break into a lumbering trot, their bayonets presented to the front and the rising sun glinting on their strange, spike-topped pickelhaube helmets.

'Bloody 'ell, Jimmy boy,' Jim heard Bertie cry. 'They'll be on us in a minute.'

'Keep firing,' hissed Jim. 'When they're a few yards away climb out back, away from the trench and get behind me. They'll have to reach across the trench to get to us.'

'I'll not be fightin' behind yer, lad, that's for sure. But I'll be awful glad if you'll stay with me...'

But these desperate measures were not needed. Within some ten yards of the flimsy entrenchments the grey line suddenly seemed to pause, stop and then turn and run back up the slope, leaving behind it groups of bodies, some of them still moving and emitting a low moan of men in pain. A faint cheer ran along the British line.

'Keep firing, don't stop, bugger it!' The sergeant's voice rang out from the shell hole to the left of the two men. 'You're allowed to shoot the bastards in the back if they run away. Rapid fire still!'

Hickman kept sighting down the barrel of his Lee-Enfield, firing and banging the bolt down until his hand felt bruised and perspiration ran down his forehead and into his eyes, affecting his aim. He looked across at Bertie. The little Irishman's head was lying, cheek down on the soil to the side of his rifle. A surge of fear ran through Jim.

'Bertie! Have you been hit?'

The familiar round face turned slowly and regarded him. 'No, but I'm fair knackered, Jimmy. And, I don't mind confessin', more than a touch shit scared, darlin' boy. I thought we were done for.' The grin came back. 'Think of it, Jimmy boy, our first battle and killed in it in the first mornin'. Now that wouldn't have been fair, would it? Gone without a sniff of the altar cloth. Snuffed out with no chance of enjoyin' it all and gettin' medals and stuff like that. Eh?'

Hickman grinned back. Then he half rose and looked at the dead men in heaps before them. The smile disappeared. 'Well, I'm right glad, Bertie, that you took a look over the top. Otherwise we'd probably have been done for. Strange we didn't hear the bullet that got the lookout, poor bugger. Must have been a sniper.'

He indicated the bodies. 'We shot well, though, didn't we?'

'Couldn't miss at that range. Lucky we'd got the new rifles, though, eh?'

The sergeant's voice called from their left. 'You Terriers all right?'

'Yes, Sarge.'

'Good shooting. You knew what you were doing.'

'Ah well.' Bertie's voice had pride in it. 'We was both marksmen with them long rifles, Lee-Whatsits, but it was even easier with these new little darlin's.'

'Will they attack again, Sarge?' asked Jim.

'Oh yes. But I can't understand why we weren't shelled first. We'll probably get it now. Use your bayonets to scoop out 'oles in the side of the trench and crawl into 'em when the shelling starts. At least they won't attack when we're being shelled. Well done, lads.'

The two removed their bayonets, laid down their rifles and began scraping away at the side of the trench. As if to give their efforts urgency, the German guns began to boom and they felt for the first time the fear that comes from being shelled and knowing that there was absolutely nothing at all that they could do about it. They were lying virtually out in the open, like rabbits sprung from the last vestige of corn as a field is harvested – except that the rabbits could run. Here, all the two men could do was to press into the slight depressions they had made in the

37

trench wall, put their hands to their ears and pray.

At first, the shells exploded behind them, further down the slope towards Ypres. Ah, thought Jim, they're targeting the support tracks and trenches, to stop reinforcements coming forward to the line. Clever bastards! Then the explosions began to creep nearer until they seemed to be all around them, landing everywhere and sending clouds of soil, rock and steel fragments into the air to rain down onto the trench. The hiss as the shells soared down, and then the crash and crump as they landed, were deafening and caused Hickman's tongue to cleave to the roof of his dry mouth.

As he pressed, foetus-like, into the scraping he had made, Jim thought of the German wounded, lying even less protected, out in the open the other side of the low parapet. Would the gunners think of them? Would they lift their sights to avoid killing their own kind?

They did not. The shells continued to rain down, exploding with less ferocity as they landed among the soft bodies of the fallen, sending remnants of what had been living men high into the air. An arm, torn from its body, landed at Hickman's side as he crouched. He noticed with disgust that a watch was still fixed to the wrist. He wrinkled his nose and shuddered. None of the wounded could have survived that. If this was modern warfare, then it was disgusting!

'Are you all right, Bertie?' he called.

'No. I'd rather be somewhere else, Jim boy.'

He had no idea how long the bombardment

had lasted but suddenly it ceased. Immediately, the sergeant's voice came from the shell hole to their left. 'They'll come at us again now. Fix bayonets and man the edges, but keep your heads down. I'll shout when you have to fire.'

'Oh, bloody hell, Jim,' said Bertie. 'You'd have thought that they would have had enough–'

He was interrupted by the arrival of a young Gordon Highlander, his knees grimed and his kilt filthy. 'Move up, boys,' he said. 'Sergeant's sent me to give a hand. We've had reinforcements, the noo. All four of 'em. Very crowded in our shell hole.'

'Stand to!' The sergeant's voice was high and it cracked now. 'Rapid fire!'

The three men immediately thrust their rifles above the rim of the trench, resting them on the soil piled there. 'Blimey,' exclaimed the Scotsman. 'They're coming over as thick as before. Stupid. They should be in open order, yer ken. If only we'd got a machine gun.'

Jim realised that he had not heard a machine gun fired from the British lines and, for a brief moment, he wondered why. Did the British Expeditionary Force in France not possess the things? But the thought was soon replaced with a mixture of twin emotions: fear and a new kind of elation as, through his sights, he saw the grey mass dissolve into a line of individuals as they neared – men, like himself, except that they wore funny hats and grey coats. They were coming once again to kill him and he must kill them. He squinted down the barrel, fired, worked the bolt and fired again, as the fragmented British line sprang into life in a blaze of yellow flashes.

The German attack this time, however, was a little more sophisticated. Its front line fell – some men, indeed, as casualties as a result of the British fire, but others because they intended to do so. They fell, levelled their long rifles and delivered a volley at the British lines, reloaded and then fired again. It became apparent that the second line had been kept further back, for it now stepped through its supine comrades and charged ahead, bayonets levelled.

That volley had had its effect, because, as bullets thudded into the turfed mound and whined overhead, Jim, Bertie and the Highlander instinctively ducked their heads. As they lifted them again, the German line was closer, considerably closer.

'Bloody hell,' shouted the Scotsman. 'Rapid fire, boys. Rapid fire.'

The fire was effective but not completely so, for six men bounded ahead of the German line and were within ten feet of the three men kneeling in the trench when the bullets of the defenders caught three of them and brought them down. The other three, however, presented their long bayonets low and came on, so close that Jim could hear the sound of their heavy breathing.

'Out and back, Bertie,' he shouted, scrambling to his feet and climbing up the trench wall behind him. Immediately, he found the little Irishman beside him. But the Highlander was too late. The leading German's bayonet caught him in the shoulder as he attempted to rise to his feet and he spun round, to be bayoneted again in the chest. Bertie jerked back his bolt and fired, catching the German in the breast, so that he toppled into the trench in front of his comrades.

This gave a moment of precious respite to the two Territorials who worked their bolts and fired again, bringing down both men. They had no time, however, to do anything more than present their bayonets to the next two Germans, who jumped down onto the bodies of their fallen compatriots and thrust upwards at them, stabbing fiercely at their ankles and calves, forcing them back.

Hickman swung his own bayonet downwards, locked it onto the steel of his opponent and swung up and to the side, allowing him to bring the butt of his rifle into the man's face. He had time to mark the look of surprise in the German's eyes – blue and staring – before he swung the bayonet back again and plunged it into the man's neck. He withdrew it, remembering instinctively the drill of 'twisting and pulling', and then, turning, he thrust it deeply into the back of Bertie's opponent. The man fell without a sound.

For a moment, Jim and Bertie stood facing each other, gasping across the bodies of the two men slain. Then they turned to face what was next to come – to find the Germans retreating once more, leaving a new line of bodies, like seaweed detritus on a beach after high tide had receded.

'Mother of God bless us,' exclaimed Bertie, wiping his brow. 'That was close. Thank you,

Jimmy. He was a bit big for me and I don't think I could have taken him. God bless you, boy.'

Hickman stayed for a moment staring into the eyes of his friend, then he switched his gaze to the end of his bayonet, which was dripping with blood. He felt suddenly sick. Plunging a blade into straw effigies of Germans on the training ground, urged on by the instructors screaming, 'Go on, stick the pigs, kill 'em,' had been one thing. This was very, very different. With both thrusts he had felt his bayonet scrape against bone – someone's bone, the bone of a man of flesh and blood. The bone of a man he had killed. He shuddered and turned away.

He felt Bertie's hand on his shoulder. 'It had to be done, Jimmy. I'm feeling, sonny, that this is a terrible war, so it is.'

'Get down, you bloody idiots.' The sergeant's voice rang out just in time, for as they half jumped, half fell on top of the bodies in the trench, the machine gun began its chatter; not on a fixed traverse this time, but aimed at them, for the bullets thudded into the soil just above their heads.

Hickman turned to the Gordon Highlander, but the man was quite dead, his face contorted into an expression of wounded surprise, his eyes staring. The Germans, too, were dead and they realised that they were kneeling on corpses.

'Ugh,' exclaimed Jim. 'I think we'd better throw 'em up on the top, if we can. But keep your head down.'

Somehow they were able to lever and then push the bodies up above the side of the trench and then give them a push so that they rolled away, but only a few inches.

'Jesus,' said Murphy. 'I don't fancy resting me rifle on their arses.'

'Here,' muttered Hickman. 'Give me a hand to drag the Jock into the shell hole. There's no room for the poor devil here.'

Together they pulled and pushed the Scotsman the few yards into the crater where the sergeant was kneeling over a wounded Tommie, applying a dressing to his stomach. The man was groaning and three others lay dead, spread-eagled, their faces half buried in the soil, having slipped back from the rim. Of the original seven men, plus the four reinforcements, who had defended the crater, only six were left.

The survivors lay sprawled along the walls of the shell hole, still breathing heavily, their rifles with their fixed bayonets in their hands.

The sergeant looked up, perspiration running down into his moustaches. 'Gawd, you two know how to look after yourselves, I'll say that for you,' he said. 'You, Lofty,' he nodded to Hickman, 'take post as lookout. When the shell-in' starts again, you take what cover you can. They won't attack then. You, Paddy, go back down the line and try and find company head-quarters. It's down that so-called communi-cations trench leading down the 'ill, though I doubt if there's much left of it after that shellin'. Tell the major that I doubt if we can 'old on if they attack again unless we get reinforcements. Oh,' he nodded to the wounded man, 'find stretcher-bearers and tell 'em we've got a bad one 'ere.'

'Very good, sorr... Sergeant.'

'Come back, you bloody fool.'

'Sorr?'

'Take yer rifle with you. Never move without it when you're in the line. Oh, and see if you can scrounge a couple of spades while you're gone – and sonny...?'

'Sorr?'

'Don't call me "sir".'

'No, sorr.' And Bertie crawled away, one long strip of his puttees trailing behind him.

Hickman took up his post, removing his cap and showing only a few inches of his face above the rim, a few seconds at a time. He also moved his position along the edge so that he did not offer a set target for a sniper. He became aware that Sergeant Jones was at his side.

'Sarge?'

'You're doin' well, lad. Seen you movin'. You've got sense. 'Ow long 'ave you been in the Terriers?'

'Oh, only about ten months. We joined at seventeen.'

'Well, if you stay alive, you'll make a bloody good soldier.' His voice dropped slightly. 'Better'n these Regulars 'ere, who just can't think for themselves. Look – what's your name again?'

'Hickman.'

'Right, Hickman. If I cop it when they come over again and we don't get reinforcements, take charge of this little lot. Make sure they spread out along the top of the crater and don't present a bunched-up target. Get a report on ammu-

44

nition. If there's not enough left, then take 'em back down the line. You can't 'ang on without bullets. 'Ow many 'ave you got?'

'About forty rounds.'

'Good. The others 'ave got about twenty-five or so each. Just about enough to defend this bloody 'ole. Below two apiece move out. Now, I'm just goin' along the line to see what's either side of us. 'Aven't 'ad a chance yet. With any luck I'll be back in about ten minutes. If the lieutenant comes, explain to him. Right?'

'Right, Sarge.'

The weathered face broke into a smile. 'Good lad.' He moved away and as he did so, Jim noticed that he was limping and a thin trail of blood, dried now, had dripped down from a tear in his trousers at the thigh. Hickman looked round at the men in the crater. Everyone was now sleeping, except for the wounded man, who lay softly moaning. He could see no regimental badges but he sensed that they were a mixed bag, made up from different battalions, including probably some service troops, drivers, clerks and the like. He gulped. He had been in the front line, in action, for less than twenty-four hours and already he had his first command, of a sort. He closed his eyes and hoped that the Germans would not attack again while the sergeant was away. Then he opened them again when he realised that the alternative was probably worse: shelling.

He was moving himself along the rim, with great caution, when a crisp voice called up, 'Where's Sergeant Jones?'

'He's gone along the line, sir,' Jim called down, 'to make contact with the blokes on our left.'

The young lieutenant looked even older in daylight, for his face was lined and his cheeks and chin were covered in stubble. 'Right.' The young man looked at the bodies. He bent down and shook awake two of the sleeping men. 'You two. Get up and put the bodies out of the shell hole. Tip them over the front, on the enemy's side, and they will help to protect the lip. Can't bury them, I'm afraid. There's no time and nowhere to put them anyway. Lookout...'

'Sir?'

'Has someone gone to find bearers for this wounded man?'

'Yes, sir. My mate's gone.'

'Good.' He looked around again. 'You've done well. I'll see if we can reinforce you but we are very thin on the ground. Hang on here. It's vital that you do. So far the line has held and it's important that it does. There's nothing between here and Ypres, so it's backs to the wall, chaps. Take it in turns to sleep. I don't think they'll come over again today, but the fact that they're not shelling means that they might. Good luck.'

He raised a languid finger to his cap and was gone.

The Germans did not come again that day, for their attacks across open ground had cost them dearly. The machine gun remained active, as did the snipers, but the little redoubt sustained no more casualties and, for some reason, the shelling did not recommence. The sergeant returned to say that a company of Bedfords were holding the shell holes and ditches to the left 'in good order', so that flank seemed to be soundly covered. To Jim's relief, Bertie returned after about an hour, carrying two shovels and bringing with him two stretcher-bearers, who gently loaded the wounded man and disappeared with him, at a crouch, down the hill.

'Where's the battalion of Grenadier Guards that I asked you to bring back with you?' demanded the sergeant.

'Well,' said Bertie, 'I did find an officer and gave him your message, sorr, but he told me to fuck off, so I thought I'd better. Mind you, I pinched two shovels when his back was turned so it served him right to be rude. You know, it never pays to be rude, sorr, it never does.'

Sergeant Jones sighed. 'Don't call me ... oh, never mind.' He threw the shovels at two men, half asleep. 'Here, you men, deepen the trenches either side. Get crackin' before the shellin' starts again.' He turned back to the two Terriers. 'Get some rest, both of you. It'll soon be dark.'

Later, having taken their turn with the shovels, the two friends curled up together in the trench in which they had fought earlier. They lay silently at first. Then Bertie spoke, in a half whisper.

'Have you thought about Polly since we landed, then, Jimmy?'

'Hmmm.'

'Have you thought often about her, I mean?'

'All the bloody time, if you must know. Have you?'

'All the time, like you.'

The silence returned, to be broken by a crack

as a Very cartridge broke into light above them, to deter any night patrols in no man's land. Then:

'I think I love Polly, Jimmy. Do you?'

'Yes, I do.'

'Is it all right for us both to love her, then, d'yer think, Jim?'

'Course it is.'

'But I'd like to marry her, yer see. Wouldn't you?'

'Yes, but not yet.'

'Right. But we can't *both* marry her, now can we?'

'No. But p'raps she wouldn't have either of us, so it wouldn't come up, would it?'

'Ah, sure you're wrong there, darlin' boy. She loves us both. I know she does.'

Jim rolled over. 'Well, the way this war is turning out, it's not very likely, Bert, that we'll both survive, or even one of us. Blimey, we've only been here a day and we've both nearly got the chop. So we won't have to bother about it, I should think. Now get some sleep.'

'Yes, Jimmy. Perhaps you're right. You always are. Goodnight.'

CHAPTER TWO

For the next three days, the line was quiet except for desultory shelling during the day and some sniping and machine-gun fire from the German lines. Relief for the men in the shell hole came with the arrival of reinforcements in the shape of newly arrived Reservists, enabling work to begin – mainly after dark – on establishing proper defences. Trenches were dug between the shell holes, deep enough at seven feet to offer protection from anything but a direct hit by shell or mortar. Precious duckboards were brought up from the rear to lay on the floor of the trenches, where mud was beginning to ooze through, despite the absence of recent rain. Timbers arrived, too, to shore up the sides and, under the directions of Sergeant Jones, proper fire steps were cut to give firing height and a base for the lookouts.

More heartening, on the fourth day, the first hessian sandbags appeared and, with them, Sappers to erect wire during the hours of darkness. Wire, but only sufficient to fix a single strand in front of the trench lip.

It seemed that the Royal Artillery was also facing economies. When asked why the British gunners were not replying to the salvoes of German shells that still peppered the lines and the communications systems in the rear, Sergeant Jones snorted.

'The lieutenant says that the British Expeditionary Force 'as only got fifty-four 'eavy guns,' he explained. 'An' all our gunners are short of shells – only eighteen rounds per battery is all they're allowed to fire each day. We're outgunned, son, an' that's the truth of it.'

Bertie listened to this and watched the nocturnal efforts of the Sappers with interest.

'Well bugger it, Jim,' he said. 'The British Government must be very hard up, you know, what with short rations, no rifle oil, no shells and now sending up Engineers to the front line to stretch out one single bloody strand of barbed wire which is the only single bloody strand in the whole of France and Belgium and which a bloody giraffe could get up and walk under.'

Jim nodded solemnly. 'So it seems, Bertie. So it seems.'

For the last three days he had been anxiously scanning the British positions and the terrain, as best he could analysing it from the trench and from what he could pick up from Lieutenant Yates, the young man who was their platoon commander. It was becoming clear to Jim that the British lines had been thrust forward from the little town of Ypres – vital to protect the Channel ports only a few miles to its rear – in a sweeping line that curved from north to south, but which occupied a far from ideal position. He explained it to Bertie by extending his right hand and cupping it.

'You see, Wipers is here, just in front of the ball of the thumb. Got it, Bertie?'

The Irishman frowned and nodded.

'So we're all spread in a great curving line along the cup of my hand, with the Jerries up here on high ground on the base of my fingers. Look up there, up front to the ridges. Their guns are all up there, looking down on us, with the plain behind us. So, from their observation posts, they can see everything we do on the plain. They can see and shell all the movements out of the town. They can spot all the supplies and re-inforcements coming up the line, which means we have to bring everything up by night. But they can fix firing lines on all the tracks and roads by day and shell 'em by night, even when they can't see.'

'I see, I see. Ah, Jimmy lad, you'd make a fine general, so you would.'

'Well I don't know about that. But I know enough to see that this bulge we're in – it's called a salient, I think – means that we can be fired on from three sides, which is a fair old bugger, I would say. And if we attack, we will have to go uphill, up to this ridge up ahead.'

'So we will. So we will.'

They were interrupted by the arrival of Sergeant Jones. 'Hickman, I want a word.'

'Sergeant?'

'You're getting a stripe, lad. Lance corporal.'

'Blimey!'

'Don't let it go to yer 'ead. It's dead man's shoes – like your rifles, so to speak. We've lost so many men that we 'ave to plug the 'oles, even with a Terrier. But you deserve it. As I said, you've shown more nouse than most of these Regulars that are left. Get down be'ind the lines

51

and find the quartermaster at Regimental HQ. Say the lieutenant sent yer. They know about it. Draw your stripe and get it sewn on smartly. Well done, lad. Off you go now.'

It was clear that some order had been restored to the British line by the arrival of the reinforcements from home, but it was also clear that the original BEF, consisting of some 96,000 Regulars in twelve divisions and arguably the most efficient army ever to have left British shores, had been terribly mauled by the fierce fighting at Mons and now in what was being called the Battle of Ypres. The superior artillery of the Germans and the sheer numbers of their troops had made themselves felt, and only the disciplined rifle fire of the British in the centre above Ypres, plus the bravery of the Belgians on their left and of the French on their right, had saved the town from being taken and the Channel ports falling. However, it was still touch and go – as the little band on the ridge below Nun's Wood now experienced.

Jim had hardly time to sew on his single stripe when the Germans recommenced their attack.

It was presaged, as usual, by an artillery barrage, complemented by short-range bombardment from *minenwerfers* fired from trench mortars, cylindrical bombs some eighteen inches long which whirled up high and tumbled down to explode, unleashing a deadly cargo of shrapnel splinters that killed and maimed.

The two comrades crouched on the firing steps, close to the buttress provided by the zigzag in the trench, their rifles, bayonets fixed, in their hands, their cloth caps pulled down and the collars of their greatcoats pulled up in a pathetic attempt to provide protection from the shell splinters. Bertie put down his rifle and pulled out a rosary and began fingering it, murmuring to himself.

'Your rifle will do you more good than that thing,' yelled Jim.

The Irishman shook his head. 'No, lad. No. Me trust is in the Almighty. God save us both. This is dreadful.'

'Stand to! Here they come.'

The cry came as soon as the barrage had lifted and the men in the trenches sprang on to the firing step and levelled their rifles. Once again, Jim squinted through his sights and saw the edge of the stunted trees that was all that was left of the wood ahead of him up the slope come to life as bodies rose in a mass and began their grim advance. This time, two Vickers machine guns began to stutter into life from the British lines and the grey figures fell, as though reaped by some mighty sickle. The attack was stillborn before it had a chance to get under way, for the British rifle fire, supplemented by the Maxims, was deadly at that short range.

A whistle blew and the cry rose: 'Cease fire. Save your ammunition.'

Jim reached out his hand to clutch his friend's shoulder. 'Well, thank the good Lord for that,' grinned Bertie, a touch shamefacedly. 'Though I don't much fancy this killin' business at long range, I prefer it to doin' it up close when I've got a bayonet pointed at me belly.'

'Aye,' nodded Jim. 'But I'd rather have both than just lying here, shittin' meself when the big guns start.'

'Corporal Hickman.' The cry came from Sergeant Jones, conferring with Lieutenant Yates. 'Bring your section up 'ere, at the double.'

Hickman stepped down from the fire step, nodded to Bertie and the five other men who made up his section and they ran to where the sergeant waited.

Yates – Jim noticed that a third pip was now fixed to his shoulder and forearm, making him a captain – looked around and counted. 'Right,' he said. 'This company is moving quickly. Get your reserve ammo and entrenching tools and follow me and the sergeant.'

'Where are we going, sir?' Bertie's blue eyes were wide.

Yates pointed to the right, to the south-east. 'There's a crossroads up there, on the ridge, a little village called Geluveld. It's important because it's the last observation post we hold up on that ridge. Or at least, we did hold. We've been pushed back and out of the village. It's vital we get it back. We are going to join the counter-attack. No more talking now. Get your things at the double. GO!'

They all ran and returned within a minute and followed Yates and Jones, down the zigzagged support trench, trotting as best they could in the crowded, narrow trench, about a hundred of them. Jim noticed that Sergeant Jones was limping and that his uniform was still torn and the line of blood remained congealed, running down to his puttees. He maintained the pace, however, biting his moustache as he trotted. Was this worse for him, Jim wondered, than when he crouched in that shallow trench at Spion Kop, being raked by the Boer sharpshooters?

All around them shells were falling and they were forced to stop several times as debris rained down upon them. But dusk was falling also, and the shelling began to die down and then ceased altogether. They emerged, about a quarter of a mile behind the line, and formed up, a makeshift company, in the semi-darkness at the side of what had obviously been a main road. Now, however, it was cratered and potholed and, from what they could discern in the dusk, lined by the bodies of animals and the wreckage of carts.

'The Menin Road,' mouthed Jim to Bertie. 'Blimey, I hope we are not going to be marching up here.'

But they were.

Captain Yates had been joined by a short, stout major, who now addressed them. 'We've got just over a mile at the most to go,' he said in a low voice. 'The Hun probably knows we're here but there's a chance that he doesn't. So we don't want to do anything to attract his fire. No smoking, no lights and – particularly as we start to climb the ridge – no talking. There will probably be a bit of shelling on fixed sights when we start but that should die out as we near Geluveld, where our lads are preparing for a counter-attack at dawn. So we've got to get a move on to be with them. Right. Let's go.'

The major was right about the shelling. Although the night was moonless and black, the German gunners seemed to know that they were there, for immediately the big guns began to boom. The range was approximate but near enough to cause extreme discomfort and fear. The whine of the shells approaching caused the men to hurl themselves down and then regain their feet to stumble onwards as the crump of the explosions followed to the rear and either side of them.

The company was not the only unit on the march up the Menin to reach Geluveld. They passed strings of mules, heavily laden with supplies and ammunition, being urged along by frantic muleteers, anxious to get close enough to the crossroads up ahead to escape the long-range shelling. Not all succeeded. The company heard screams ahead of them after one explosion and, heads down, on the trot, they passed the remains of one train: dismembered mules and horses sprayed across what was left of the track, and bodies of men, some of them crying for help, among the carnage.

'Don't stop,' cried the major. 'We must keep going. The bearers will come for these poor chaps.'

'But I don't think they will, Jim,' puffed Bertie. 'We're a long way from the bearer posts. We should stop and help them, for mercy's sake. Holy Mother of God! What sort of war is this, then?'

'Well, it ain't the Boer war, mate, that's for sure.' Hickman gave his comrade a friendly push.

'Keep going, son. Keep going.'

Eventually, they escaped the arc of the shellfire and immediately found the ground began to rise and sensed as much as they saw the presence of British troops around them. The major was met by another officer, obviously of senior rank by the deference with which he was greeted, but his badges were now completely covered in grime and smoke smudges. Hickman inched forward to overhear the conversation.

'What have you brought up?'

'A scratch lot, sir, I'm afraid. More or less a company, but from various regiments. We've even got a couple of stray Territorials.'

'Good God!' The colonel ran a weary hand across his brow. 'No question of a counter-attack now, I'm afraid. We've been completely disseminated. We must have lost a couple of thousand at least and we've had to leave two guns in the village and another four destroyed. Get your men spread out along the diggings here. The Hun is in great force up ahead and cock-a-hoop. I wouldn't be surprised if he didn't make a night attack. We must try and hold on if we can, and if not, we must retire down the ridge, but in good order, mind. We can't afford a rout.'

'Very good, sir. Captain Yates.'

'Sir.'

'Get the men up ahead into the makeshift trenches there. Spread along the line and reinforce it. No sleeping now. An attack is expected at any minute.'

Jim slipped back and found his section. As they all groped their way forward they suddenly realised that it was no longer dark. Ahead, it seemed that the whole of the ridge was aflame. The village of Geluveld was a fiery mass and the church spire looked like a torch, the flames licking round its tip. By its light, the straggling company found a thin line of Tommies spread along a trench which was hardly more than a scraping on the slope, with a low mound of earth thrown up ahead on the lip.

'Spread along here, chaps,' shouted Yates. 'Anyone found sleeping will be shot summarily.'

'What's "summarily"?' asked Bertie as he made room for himself between two riflemen of the Kings Royal Rifle Corps.

One turned a weary head. 'Don't think it matters, mate. We're all goin' to be dead by the mornin', anyway.'

''Ere, what's that?' Sergeant Jones had materialised behind them. He nodded up ahead. It was a strange sound, deep and rhythmical, but growing louder as they listened.

'The buggers are singin',' swore the sergeant. 'Would you believe it. They're singin' an' comin' on now.' He raised his voice. 'Fix your bayonets, but 'old your fire till the captain gives the order.' His voice dropped. 'No need to worry, lads. When they come over that ridge we shall see 'em beautifully against the light of the flames.' Then a note of derision and almost of glee came into his voice. 'We'll teach the buggers to sing, oh yes we will.'

Jim turned to look at the sergeant. He was on one knee in the half-trench and his right hand was stroking, almost caressing the stock of his rifle. Hickman noticed that the wound in his right leg had opened up again and his puttees were soaked in fresh blood. But it was his face that drew the attention. In the flicking light of the flames, it was alive with animation. His great moustache had been sucked down so that it had almost disappeared under his lower lip and his eyes were fierce and staring. He worked the bolt on his rifle to slip a round up the breech and half stood to catch a glimpse of the approaching enemy.

Then the bullet took him soundlessly in the breast, whirling him round so that his hands flew up, sending his rifle flying in an arc to the rear. He fell and lay still.

'Sarge!' Jim ran to him but the veteran's eyes were open and staring. He was quite dead. A shot rang out from the British lines.

Hickman whirled round involuntarily. 'Hold your fire!' he screamed, and ran back to his position, shouldering a rifleman aside to take his place next to Bertie. 'Sergeant Jones is dead,' he muttered.

Bertie's eyes widened and he tucked a stray lock of red hair back under his cap. 'Holy Jesus,' he whispered. 'If they can kill him they can kill us all.'

'Here they come,' cried the rifleman next to him.

The singing was loud now and the choir emerged over the brow of the ridge to reveal itself as a black mass against the flames, approaching ponderously but steadily, now down the slope. The flames at their rear reflected in golden flashes from the long sword bayonets that were levelled at the waiting British. It was a frightening sight and Jim Hickman felt his stomach churn. There were so *many* of them...

Captain Yates's voice rose loud and clear above the singing. 'Let them come,' he shouted. 'Hold your fire until I give the order.'

'Bloody hell,' Bertie murmured, squinting as he lined up his fore- and backsights. 'They've got lovely voices, so they have. Good baritones. Seems a pity to kill them, Jimmy, don't you think?'

Hickman licked his lips. 'No I don't, for God's sake, Bertie...'

'You know,' continued the little man, conversationally, 'I haven't had a proper wash for four days now. I don't know what me mother, bless her sainted soul, would say–'

The captain's voice interrupted in a high, barrack-square scream. 'At the enemy in front, rapid fire. FIRE!'

The fragile little line suddenly sprang to life and the fire was, indeed, rapid, the rifles barking as quickly as tired hands could work the breech bolts. The sound of the individual rifles discharging merged into a continuous crackle and it was as if the line was manned by machine-gunners, so quick was the firing. Framed in silhouette by the flames behind them and at a range now of less than a hundred yards, the infantry approaching in a close-order mass presented an unmissable quarry. The front line fell as one man, presenting the second line as a substitute target, like pop-up ducks at a fairground rifle stall, and it too disintegrated under the heavy fire. Several brave men knelt and presented their long rifles in an attempt to return the fire but they were soon despatched and what had seemed to be an irresistible phalanx broke up into individual units turning and scurrying back up the slope.

Hickman lowered his rifle in relief but then shied aside as a bullet buried itself into the earth by his thigh. It had come *from behind him.*

He turned and caught a glimpse of a group of shadowy, grey-clad figures advancing towards them up the slope.

'Enemy behind us,' he shouted. 'My section follow me.'

He scrambled to his feet, levelled his rifle and fired. Then, without pausing to reload, he presented his bayonet and screamed, 'Charge!'

He had no idea if he was alone as he bounded down the slope but he was aware that rifles were being discharged at him, for he saw their flashes and felt a tug as a bullet passed through the flapping corner of his jacket. Then he was among a group of Prussians, judging by their shining helmets, parrying their bayonet thrusts and thrusting in return, turning and stabbing, feinting and swinging his rifle butt.

But he was not alone. Bertie was at his side, ducking and weaving like a bantamweight boxer, swinging his bayonet-tipped rifle from side to side as though it was a Celtic claymore. Then they were joined by the five other men of the section and, suddenly, the Germans had faded away as though they had not existed – except that three of them lay on the ground, bunched over in pain, foetus-like, as blood oozed through their thick greatcoats.

'Well done, Hickman.' Captain Yates was at his side, his revolver hanging from its lanyard and his face glistening in the light from the flames still shooting up on the ridge. 'Now, we must find out if there are any more of them that have got round us.' He turned to the panting men of Jim's section. 'Spread out in a line, behind me. Go on. Fan out further than that. Right, keep your bayonets fixed and follow me slowly. Make sure that there aren't any Huns hiding.

'You,' he gestured with his revolver to Bertie, 'double back and tell the major what has happened and warn him that we might be surrounded.'

Together the little band walked down the slope, their heads down, dreading the sound of a rifle crack from ahead, behind or either side of them. They were completely exposed, well lit by the blazing village and with no cover. But they met no one, except a platoon of Service Corps clerks, forced off the Menin Road by the shell-fire and struggling up to lend support to the defenders below the ridge ahead.

Eventually, Yates held up his hand. 'Must have been a stray group who slipped through between us and the Bedfords on the right,' he confided to Jim. 'I'll report it to the major. Thank you for your quick thinking, Hickman. I shall commend you for it.' He turned to the others and waved his revolver. 'Back to the line.'

He led them back up the slope. The Germans

had retreated back over the ridge but, ominously, enemy light artillery was beginning to find their range. 'Dig in, as best you can,' the captain shouted, turning his head along the line, 'and get your heads down. They won't be able to get their heavy stuff on us because we're too near their line. But they will probably attack again at first light. NCOs, give me ammunition reports.'

For the first time, Jim realised that there was blood on his bayonet, but he had no recollection of having bayoneted any of the Prussians, only of frantically defending himself.

'Oh aye, Corp,' confided one of his section, a tall cavalry trooper. 'I got one,' he grinned. 'First time I've ever used a bayonet. More used to a sabre. But you got one and Paddy here,' he nodded to Bertie, 'got the other. Proper little terrier he was.'

Hickman nodded, gave a half-shy grin at Bertie, and then collected his section's ammunition reports. They were still well supplied, having come up to the line carrying their ammunition reserves. He reported as much to Captain Yates and also gave him the news of the death of Sergeant Jones.

'Damn.' The captain shook his head. 'He was the best sergeant in the company. Thank you. I'll send up a detail to bury him. It will have to be here, I'm afraid. Can't afford to carry him back.'

'Can I ask you something, sir?'

'Ask away but be quick. There's much to do before sunrise.'

Jim paused and shifted from one leg to the

other. Would he sound impertinent? 'It's the line, sir.'

'What about it? Come on, man. I haven't got all day.'

'Well, I don't see how we can hold it, either under heavy shelling or a few more attacks like the last. There's no time to dig in properly and we're more or less left lying out in the open. Even if they don't attack we'll be blown to pieces by a decent barrage. It's pretty obvious that there aren't any reinforcements to be had and well...' He tailed off, daunted by the look of impatience in Yates's haggard face. 'Sorry if I've spoken out of turn.'

Yates sighed. 'You're a Terrier, aren't you?'

'Yessir.'

'I know you've done well in the few days that you've been out. But I don't think that an eighteen-year-old amateur soldier should question the wisdom of experienced senior officers. If the colonel says we hold the line here, we bloody well do so. Is that understood?'

'Yessir.'

But Yates had a frown on his face as he watched him go.

As a miserable dawn broke, the enemy did not attack. It was clear that the frontal onslaught – was there no other way that the Germans fought, wondered Hickman? – had proved to be immensely expensive and, it seemed, they had other objectives and perhaps other problems on their minds, for both to the defenders' right and up above, in the village itself, came the sound of heavy gunfire. Whatever the reason, the makeshift company in the scraped-out half-trench below the ridge was left unmolested, except for sniper fire.

The opportunity was taken to issue the basic rations that had been able to survive the hazardous journey up the Menin Road – bully beef, bread, jam and hot tea – and then the company was set to digging again. It was not easy, for, as Hickman had pointed out, there was little cover from well-aimed fire from the ridge above them. It was difficult to dig when crouching or kneeling and two men were hit shortly after sunrise as a result of shots from one particular sniper, well sited at the top of the slope.

Yates called from along the line. 'Anybody here earned a marksman's badge during training?'

Jim looked about him. No one raised his hand. The Regulars, of course, all espoused a mantra of not volunteering for anything. But Bertie raised his hand and, reluctantly, Hickman followed suit.

'Ah, the terrible Terriers.' Yates, crouching, made his way towards him. 'Right, Corporal, I've got a job for you.'

Jim sniffed. 'Private Murphy here, sir, is a much better shot than me.'

'Really? Very well. Murphy will do.'

Bertie looked concerned. 'Well, sorr. I'm very happy to be of use to you, indeed I am. But I'm not particularly happy to be shootin' people, y'see. Our priest always told me...'

Captain Yates sighed and his face, still youthful with his moustache well trimmed despite the ravages of the last week, assumed the countenance of a man of fifty. He lifted his eyes to the heavens. 'Oh, I'm so sorry, Private Murphy, that you're not particularly happy about killing people. But I really must remind you,' and his sarcastic tone lapsed into a snarl, 'that you're in the fucking army now and that you are being paid, lad, *to* kill people. And if you don't obey orders, then I personally will shoot *you*. Is that understood?'

Bertie gave an accommodating smile. 'Ah well, sorr, put like that it would be difficult to refuse. Now, then, how can I oblige you?'

'How kind of you to agree to help. Now, keep your head low but look with me through this small gap in the mound. That's it. Now look up to the right along the ridge. See anything?'

'Ah, nothin' much, sorr. There's a low wall, but nothin' much.'

'Right. Come away, or you'll get a bullet between those blue eyes and what would I tell the priest then?' Yates pulled Murphy down.

'When you look again – and no, don't do it now – when you look again, you'll see a small hole in that wall to the right. There is a German sniper operating behind that wall and he is firing through that hole. He's already killed two of our men. It is a terribly small target at this range but if you could put a bullet through that hole, you will almost certainly get him, because he is peering through it all the time. And, my lad, if you can pot him, there's an extra allowance of rum in it for you.'

Bertie's face broke into a beam. 'Well, that's

66

very nice of you, sorr, but I never drink when I'm workin', see.'

Yates caught Jim's eye and then looked around at the grinning faces witnessing the conversation. The captain put a hand to his face to hide his own smile. He nodded sympathetically. 'Very wise of you, I am sure, if ... ahem ... a little unusual. Right. Now be very careful because he is watching us all the time. Try to take him, not from over the top, because you would be dead by the time you propped up your rifle, but from this little gap in the earth that's been shovelled up here. And don't thrust your rifle through it. Just rest the tip and sight from back here. The man's a killer. He's probably got telescopic sights but we lack them, I'm afraid. Do you think you can get him without them?'

Bertie took a look. 'Ooh, bless you sorr, I wouldn't know how to use them things. But yes, I can see him now, I think. Let's have a go.'

The little man knelt and slowly inserted the tip of his rifle into the gap and slipped back a little himself to thrust the butt into his shoulder. A silence seemed to settle on the battlefield and as Jim turned his head he realised that all those in the line and in the immediate vicinity had been listening to the exchange and were now virtually holding their breath.

Then, in a moment of ridiculous anticlimax, Bertie withdrew his rifle, adjusted his backsight to lift the range, licked his thumb, rubbed it on the muzzle and slowly slid the gun back again into the cleft. Yates removed his cap, raised his field glasses to his eyes and carefully directed

67

them over the parapet.

The crack as Bertie fired seemed to echo back from the ridge.

'You've got him,' yelled Yates. 'You've got the bastard. His rifle's gone clattering through the hole in the wall.' He slid back and seized Murphy's hand and pumped it. A cheer went up along the line.

'Ah.' Bertie looked far from elated. 'It's not a nice way to kill a feller in cold blood like that. God rest his soul and may He forgive me.'

'You should be a sniper, Murphy,' said Yates, replacing his cap. 'That was a fantastic shot at such a range with an ordinary rifle and no special lens. You're truly a marksman, lad.'

'Well, sorr, I don't know about that. But, on reflection, now that I'm not exactly working, so to speak, I think I might accept your offer of a little rum. Just a touch, now. Not much.'

Yates nodded. 'I'll see to it.' He exchanged grins with Jim and made his way back along the line.

The old sweats along the line were looking at Bertie now with new respect. 'Well done, Bertie,' said Jim. 'They'll probably make you a general now.'

The Irishman shook his head and his face was serious. 'You know, Jimmy, it wasn't a good thing to do, killin' someone in cold blood like that. It's different to when they come chargin' at you. It's fair enough then. But I'm not at all sure I approve of this war, after all. All this shellin' an' killin'. I don't see how the good Lord can give it his blessing, so I don't.'

Hickman gave him a playful push. 'You're talking nonsense, mate. Your priest didn't disapprove when you joined up, now, did he? I seem to remember that he told you that you would be doing the work of the Lord, now didn't he?'

'So he did. So he did. But he ain't here now, is he? If he was, seeing what we've seen in not much more than a week out here, I think he'd change his mind, honest I do.'

'Well, we're in it now. And you're the finest marksman in the whole of the BEF so you'd better shut up and get on with it.'

'Very good, Lance Corporal, sorr.'

Although the firing up beyond and to the right of the ridge continued throughout the day, the company was allowed to get on with its digging without too much interference from the enemy. Obviously, the battle was continuing elsewhere. And this was confirmed when, in the mid afternoon, Jim noticed that heads were turning along the line of the trench – now much more substantial – as news of mouth was being passed along.

Eventually, it reached him. 'The village up top has been retaken by the bloody Worcesters,' said the man to his right. 'They've broken through up on the top from the left. Looks as though we shall be movin' on soon.'

And so it proved. Within the half-hour, orders were given to load their equipment and move out. In open order, with bayonets fixed, they left the comparative security of their trench and moved up the slope towards where the blackened remains of Geluveld were smoking and serrating the skyline. Hickman realised that defending a position was one thing and attacking, over open ground, was very much another. It was the first time that he and Berrie had advanced in daylight and, walking steadily up the slope, they both felt unprotected and virtually naked. Jim remembered how easy it had been to mow down the Germans when they left their positions and came out into the open. At least now he and his comrades were spread out in open order, but even so, they would offer inviting targets to machine guns set up behind the wall.

Yet their advance was unhindered and not a shot was fired as they breasted the ridge. A disconcerting sight met their eyes. Hardly a building, it seemed, had been left standing in the village, and streets forming the crossroads were marked now only by rubble and blackened timbers. Corpses of soldiers, British and German, lay unburied where they had fallen, some of them scorched by the flames.

The little major bustled over. 'Take cover where you can and rest,' he called to the men. 'Captain Yates, take Lieutenant Baxter and a platoon and reconnoitre to the left and see if you can link up with the Worcesters. The colonel is establishing battalion headquarters in what's left of that school over there. Report back there.'

Yates beckoned to a young subaltern, a sergeant, another corporal and to Jim, and a makeshift platoon of some twenty-five men began cautiously to patrol down what seemed to be left of the main street.

They had been walking for perhaps ten minutes when a sudden rattle of machine-gun fire and then another broke out ahead of them and they all went to ground instinctively. A mortar banged and a fountain of earth and rubble sprang up to their right. Then another mortar shell exploded to their left, with the same result. A sharp crack of musketry sounded ahead and bullets began to strike the road and masonry around them, ricocheting away in a succession of pings and whines.

'Into that ditch on the right,' shouted Yates. They followed him and tumbled into a rubble-fringed irrigation ditch, but not before two of their number fell on the roadway and a third crumbled just as he reached the dubious safety of the ditch.

'Where the hell are they?' asked Yates of Baxter.

'Can't see 'em for the life of me.'

'In the churchyard, to the right,' called Hickman. 'Look, the place is crawling with them.' He pointed.

Grey-coated figures could now be seen flitting between the gravestones and the fallen masonry. As they watched, two men spreadeagled themselves on either side of a third man, who squatted and began assembling something.

'Can you see 'em, Bertie?' called Jim. 'He's setting up a machine gun just between those tombstones. It's a long shot. Can you get him? You'll have to be quick.'

Murphy nodded but did not reply. Instead, he adjusted his rear sight, licked his thumb and rubbed it on the end of his rifle, levelled it and

71

fired. The German machine-gunner rolled over.

'Good shot, Murphy,' called out Yates. 'Glad you've swallowed your principles.'

'Ah, it's different if I'm shit scared, sorr.'

'We can't stay here.' Yates was addressing his lieutenant.

'Withdraw, of course?'

'Good God, no. We've got to hold them up long enough to give the colonel time to set up a decent defensive position. We've got to spread out on the right here where there's cover and stop them coming down the road. Hickman.'

'Sir.'

'Get back to the colonel – he's in that old school back where we crested the ridge. Tell him that, by the look of it, a battalion of the enemy is on its way towards him and that we will do our best to hold them up before retreating. Tell him that there's no sign of the Worcesters. There must have been a massive counter-attack on the village. Go now and don't get shot, man!'

'Very good, sir.'

'I'll come with you,' hissed Bertie.

'Blimey, no. You can't do that. That would be desertion in the face of the enemy. You stay here and shoot all the buggers and I'll be back in a minute.'

'Ah, good luck, Jimmy boy.'

Jim swallowed. This would be the first time they had been parted since joining up. 'Keep your head down, Bertie.' Then he slung his rifle behind his shoulder, scrambled out of the ditch and jumped into what remained of a cottage garden, as bullets spattered against the rubble around him. He ran, head down, sprinting from splintered tree to tree, between scattered piles of stone and brick. Once he twisted his ankle in a pothole and was stung as he lay by a sharp flint, cut out by a rifle shot. Cursing, he scrambled to his feet and ran on, zigzagging as he reached more open ground, until the firing died away behind him.

He had little breath left as he found the colonel, attempting to study a map of Geluveld spread over a child's desk. He reported his news.

'How long have we got, Corporal?'

'No time at all, sir. The captain is very outnumbered by the look of it.' His heart was in his mouth as he thought of Bertie.

'Which way will they come?'

'Straight down this road, I should think. But there are probably enough of them to try and take you from the east, here as well,' he pointed, 'to get behind you.'

The colonel gave him an appraising look. 'Very well.' He turned his head and shouted. 'Major Chatwynd, here quickly. You, Corporal, get into the defences here.'

'No thank you, sir. I've got to get back.' With that, he turned and doubled away. Leaving the CO with his mouth hanging open.

Instead of following the route he had taken to the church, however, Hickman turned to his right and began trotting – he had insufficient breath left to run – through the ruins of the village. If he could approach the Germans from their flank, he reasoned, he could perhaps put up enough firing to make them think that they were being attacked from that direction, giving Yates and his men time to withdraw. Perhaps! If only he had that Lewis machine gun that he had practised with back on the Plain...

Gunfire to his left showed him that Yates's platoon, or what was left of it, was still in action. Treading stealthily now, Jim advanced towards the firing, taking advantage of houses that had only been partially destroyed by the shelling and treading fastidiously between the fallen bodies that he began to encounter. If it really was a German battalion, then they would have fanned out to enfilade Yates and his small party, so he should see them soon.

And he did. Six Germans in their flat, soft caps were doubling across his front, looking to their right and not towards him. He licked his lips. He would have to fire quickly, as though he was not alone. He knelt behind a partly destroyed out-house wall, settled his rifle on the top, took careful aim and fired. And then again and again until he had released six shots. He hit four of the men, the other two falling to the ground and turning to face him. He doubled away, out of their sight, and re-emerged further to their left, when he released two more shots, wounding one of the outstretched Germans, who released a loud cry.

But there was no time for self-congratulation, for a succession of bullets now crashed into the wall from a party of grey-clad men, bayonets drawn, who emerged from the ruined houses. Damn! Which way to run? He must out-think them. Make them think they were being surrounded. He ran further to his right and then doubled back to bring him, he hoped, further behind the Germans' left flank.

Now he could see a group of some twenty of the enemy cautiously edging their way through the ruins. He inserted another clip into his magazine – thank God he was not still armed with the old single-shot Lee-Metford! – took aim and let loose a succession of six shots quickly, working the bolt so that his thumb ached. He was not too particular about aiming carefully, for speed was preferable to accuracy, but even so, he brought down a further three men before he doubled back on himself.

This time, however, he was seen and a fusillade of shots followed him. Running like a hare, he turned and ran back into the heart of the village, back towards what he hoped would be the rear of Yates's position, if he had been able to fall back in good order. He easily outdistanced whatever pursuit had been mounted, turned and was relieved to hear gunfire coming from ahead of him, this time. Then he caught a glimpse of a khaki-clad jacket and shouted: 'It's Hickman. I'm behind you.'

A familiar voice responded. 'God bless you, Jimmy. Come on in with your head down, for they seem to be all around us, lad.'

Within a moment, having shaken Bertie's hand, he was reporting to Yates, whose left arm was bleeding and the hand tucked into his open jacket.

'Well done, Hickman, but I didn't expect you to come back, for God's sake. You say they are on the right of us now?'

'Yes sir. I think you'd better make a run for it.'

'No. Must retreat in good order, or they'll mow us down as we go.' The captain smiled ruefully. 'We've lost about half of our men, including Lieutenant Baxter and Sergeant Wilkins and the other corporal. I don't want to lose the rest. Now, you're my second in command. You take seven men, including your sharpshooter friend, and fall back about a hundred and fifty yards. I will cover you with what is left. Then we will fall back through you as you fire over our heads to cover our retreat. Then you must retreat similarly as we cover you. Got it? An orderly retreat, eh?'

'Of course, sir. But you're wounded. Why don't you go first?'

'No, it's only a scratch. Get your men and off you go. No time to waste.'

Jim nodded and scampered among the men touching every other one on the shoulder as they fired from a variety of types of cover. Then, as the captain and the rest set up covering fire, they all ran back, stumbling in the broken ground until Hickman judged they had gone far enough. He detailed Bertie to take up position on the extreme right of their position to warn of any outflanking movement and spread his men as widely as possible behind whatever cover they could find. Then he shouted back to Yates: 'Ready, sir.'

So began their retreat under fire. They could not possibly have regained the British lines if the colonel had not sent a skirmishing party out into the village to meet them, for they were vastly outnumbered and also enfiladed from either flank. As it was, they lost three more men but the covering fire of the rescue party was strong enough for them to limp back under its protection to where a rough-and-ready line had been erected in a curve projecting along the top of the ridge. There they found sanctuary.

'Thank you, Hickman,' said Yates. 'You saved what was left of us. Now get down into the line. I think it's going to be a rough evening.'

The Germans were upon them within ten minutes, firing from mortars, heavy machine guns and rifles as they spread out amongst the ruins. It became clear that the colonel's command was heavily outnumbered and, indeed, outgunned, for it lacked mortars and machine guns. Yet the marksmanship of the British was exemplary, for virtually all of them were Regulars and even the clerks and the cooks, who made up the numbers, had been well trained. As a result, the Germans were held at bay, although the casualties along the top of the ridge were growing.

Jim and Bertie were firing from the reverse side of the wall that had harboured the sniper. His body was still lying near the hole in the brickwork and Bertie's marksmanship was confirmed by the neat black hole that showed now in his forehead.

'Ugh.' Bertie wrinkled his nose. 'I'll move along a bit, if you don't mind.'

Jim wiped his brow. 'We can't hold out here much longer, I would have thought.' He looked behind him. From the ridge the slope fell away into a flat plain on which Ypres could be seen in

77

the distance, with the spire of the cathedral and the distinctive tower of the old Cloth Hall still standing tall. The plain was still dotted with red-tiled farmhouses but the woods that marked it in clusters were becoming ravaged by shellfire and craters had formed in clusters across all the fields. Despite the barrage to which it had been subjected, what remained of the Menin Road could be seen, dipping down to the plain and running as straight as a die to the west. The makeshift trench line that they had scraped out a couple of hundred yards below them stood out for its freshly turned soil rampart but, seen from the top of the ridge, it seemed to offer little cover.

'It would be stupid to fall back down to there,' muttered Hickman.

His faith in the judgement of senior officers was already becoming strained, for it seemed that both sides seemed to retain a blind faith in frontal attack against well-armed troops dug in. 'I just hope someone's forming a proper plan for retreat. We can't hang on here and that's not a proper line.'

Bertie wrinkled his nose. 'Why don't you leave it to the generals to worry about that?' he asked. 'Personally, I'm just going to concentrate very strongly on staying alive for a bit, without worryin' about grand strategy an' all.'

Over the next few hours, the position at the top of the ridge descended into a kind of stalemate, with both sides reluctant to make a frontal attack. But the superiority in numbers and firepower of the Germans began to tell and casualties began to mount among the British. Dusk, then, was welcomed by the defenders lining the ridge and as soon as darkness fell completely, whispered orders were passed down the line to retreat in sequence down the slope.

Jim Hickman gave up a silent prayer as they passed the rough trenches they had dug and continued to march down towards the plain, not wheeling to the right, to his relief, to resume their previously vulnerable positions at Nun's Wood, but continuing until the ground was level beneath their feet. Eventually, they were halted at newly preserved defensive positions at what he guessed would be roughly halfway between the ridge and Ypres. Here the trenches were comparatively sophisticated, deep enough to offer some protection from shellfire and were shielded, to some extent, by two lines of wire.

'Thank God for that,' said Jim. 'Someone's been thinking for once.'

'And have you heard the rumour?' asked Bertie.

'What's that?'

'The King of the Belgians, no less, has used his brain and has ordered that the slush gates, or whatever you call 'em...'

'Sluice gates?'

'That's just what I said. Anyway, the things have been opened on the canals to the north of Wipers, lettin' in all the North Sea, would you believe it. They say that the water is about half a mile wide and has stopped the Germans advancing and has made the town safe from that side. It's too deep and wide to cross, so the Belgian troops facin' them have been able to come across to help us out in the middle, so to speak.'

Hickman frowned. 'Sounds good. But it will also free lots of the Boche to move over here against us.'

'Ah, Jim lad. You're right. I never thought of that. You just can't win in this bloody war, now can you?'

Hot meals miraculously appeared via the shortened supply line and the refugees from the ridge were fed. Guards were posted and they were allowed to sleep until stand-to at dawn. No further attack was mounted by the Germans, however. It was as though the enemy were content to have forced back the British line and were themselves taking respite from the bitter fighting that had marked the last few days.

A veneer of civilisation in the form of regular meals, only intermittent shelling and the occasional bursts of machine-gun fire now returned to the two comrades as they settled into line duty in the trenches, standing to at dawn, taking their turns as lookouts on the fire step and, once, joining a young subaltern in an uneventful night patrol in no man's land. They both undertook the duty of writing home.

'Are you writing to Polly, then, Jim?' asked Bertie.

'Yes. Would you like me to send her your love?'

'No, thank you very much. I'm doing that myself, because I'm writing to her too.'

A slightly uneasy silence fell on the two and they returned to their letters. It was broken, inevitably, by Bertie: 'It's a bit funny, this, when you think of it, isn't it?'

'Funny? What do you mean, funny?'

'Well...' The little Irishman wriggled his bottom on the firing step. 'I mean, it's funny. Both of us together like this and loving the same girl and not ... well ... not bein' jealous and such. Not mindin', I mean.'

Jim sucked his pencil. 'I suppose it is, when you think of it.'

'I mean... Would you be glad if I was killed, see? And cleared the way for you an' Polly and so on.'

'No. Of course not.'

'Neither would I – if you was killed, that is. Funny, though, isn't it?'

'Yes. I suppose it is.'

The two letters were given to the mail clerk at exactly the same time but neither knew the contents of the other's. But Jim did ask Bertie a personal question that had been on his mind for some time.

'You was only four when you left Ireland to come to Brum, weren't you?'

'Yes.'

'Why then do you speak with as broad an Irish accent as I've ever heard? Growing up in Brum – you'd think you'd talk like me.'

Bertie scratched his head. 'I suppose it's me dad. Livin' with him, I mean. And goin' to the School of the Holy Mother. They're all Catholics there, like me, of course, and though some of them are not Irish, most of them are. So it's stuck with me.' His eyes twinkled. 'Personally, I think it's what gives me me roguish charm. It's why Polly loves me much more than she loves you...'

Jim gave him a playful punch in the chest.

'Hickman.' Captain Yates came down the trench, his arm in a sling. 'You and Hawkeye here, get your stuff together. You're going back down the line. You've been posted to a new Territorial battalion that has just arrived – part of the Warwicks. Sergeant Flanagan here has come to collect you and two others.'

The captain smiled at them both, a smile that seemed to take years off his age and make him look like the captain of the school cricket team, congratulating them for taking wickets. He held out his left hand. 'I shall miss both of you,' he said. 'You are both fine soldiers, if...' he grinned at Bertie '... a little eccentric. I have commended you for your action back up on the ridge, Hickman. Whether anything will come of it, I don't know. But good luck to you both. Now, grab your things and off you go.'

They both shook hands with the young man and ducked away to find their meagre belongings. Then they joined the sergeant, who was waiting for them at the junction with the communications trench. He was a tall man, muscular and heavily jowled, wearing a Connaught Rangers cap badge and a forbidding scowl.

Bertie gave him a welcoming grin. 'Sorry to have kept you waitin', Sarge,' he said.

For a moment, there was silence. Then Flanagan took two paces forward so that Bertie was forced to step back, so that he was pressed against the wall of the trench. The sergeant pushed his jaw forward and down so that his face was about an inch away from that of the little Irishman.

'You say "sergeant" when you speak to me,' he hissed. '"Sergeant". D'yer hear, you little papist cunt?' His accent, thick and guttural, was heavy with Northern Irish prejudice and his spittle hit Bertie in the eye, so that he blinked. 'Now *I'm* a regular soldier, not a part-time little fucker like the pair of you. You've been here just a few days. I've been whetting me bayonet in the service of the King for the last fifteen years. God knows why I've been put in with a bunch of Territorials but I can only think it is to smarten you up. So you'd better learn quickly that I don't approve of undue familiarity with officers, like you two have just displayed, and you will learn to address NCOs correctly and...' he looked down with disgust at Bertie's tangled puttees and mud-spattered tunic '...you will smarten up, cunt, or I'll have you on fatigues day and night for weeks on end, so that you'll wish that you'd never been born.'

'Sergeant.' Hickman took a step forward.

Flanagan whirled round. 'Don't you dare interrupt me, Corporal. I don't know how you got that stripe in just a few days wankin' about in the trenches here, but I'll have it off your arm in two seconds if you try to stand up to me, lad. Now. Follow me and don't hang about. If you lose me, I will have you put on a charge of desertion – and that means a bullet in the early morning.'

He turned on his heel and marched away, so

quickly that Jim and Bertie had difficulty in keeping him in sight at first in the crowded communication trench. Not once did he look behind him to see if the two were close behind.

'Blimey,' whispered Bertie. 'I think we could be in trouble with this bloke.'

'Don't worry. I'll handle him. You'll see.'

Bertie shot an anxious glance at his friend. 'I'm not so sure, Jimmy. I'm not so sure.'

CHAPTER THREE

Mrs Victoria Johnson heard the letter box click and hurried over to pick up the two letters that fell on the doormat inside 64, Turners Lane. She smiled with relief when she saw the handwritten envelopes and called up the dark narrow stairway to her daughter: 'Polly, two letters from Belgium. They've gotta be from the lads.'

'Oh thanks, Mum.' Polly took the stairs three at a time, sliding her hands down the rails on either wall, and swept up the letters. She turned and galloped back up the stairs, disregarding her mother's cry, 'You'll be late if you start reading 'em now.'

She shut the door of her bedroom and sat on the edge of her bed, face flushed. To read them now, or save them for later...? Read them now, of course, then she could return to them at her leisure as the day wore on. So she tore open both envelopes, without withdrawing their contents, tossed them both over her shoulder so that they fell onto the bed behind her and then groped blindly to pick up whichever one came to hand first. That way, she would show no favour to one of her boys before the other.

It was from Bertie and she grinned at the typically unscholastic, pencilled scrawl. It began by saying, without punctuation, that he loved her more than anything else in the world and that he and Jimmy had already been in action and that Jim had gained a lance corporal stripe. 'He is a good soldier Polly so he is better than me.' He had not washed properly for over a week and had a large hole in his sock. Would she tell his father that he would write to him later and would she then read that letter to him because, as she knew, the old man couldn't do the writing and reading stuff? And he loved her more than anything else in the world.

She put down the single sheet of paper and wiped away a tear.

Then, a smile replacing the tear, she opened Jim's letter. It was written, also in pencil – did they not have any pen and ink in France? – in his equally typical, forward-slanting hand. It began by recording chronologically their crossing of the Channel (the first sight of the sea for both of them), the journey to the front in open rail trucks, the march in darkness to the front and then a brief sentence outlining what action had followed. But, although he covered both sides of two sheets of paper, compared to Bertie's one, there were no details – and no mention of the award of his lance corporal's stripe, although he included a reference to Bertie shining as a marksman. They were, he said, looking after each other and were hoping soon for a period of rest away from the front line. Polly sighed as she looked in vain for some sign of affection. The letter, however, concluded only with 'your affectionate friend, J. Hickman.'

She carefully replaced both letters in their envelopes, held them both to her lips, put them in her handbag and stood to complete her toilet. Looking at herself in the mirror on the marble-topped washstand, she mouthed a prayer to God, asking Him to look after her boys. For a moment, she regarded herself critically. The face was long – too long and the chin perhaps a bit too square. But the cheekbones were satisfyingly high and the eyes shone this morning, now that she had heard from them. She pulled a green woollen dress over her head – the colour was supposed to match her eyes but it was too dark, she knew that now – shook her hair free and brushed it quickly. She applied a little face powder and rouge (no lipstick; at eighteen she felt still a bit too young for that and, anyway, she disliked its artificiality), grabbed her bag with its precious cargo and launched herself down the stairs, two at a time.

'For goodness' sake, girl,' chided her mother. 'Sit down properly and eat your bacon sandwich.'

'No time, Mum. Can you wrap it up for me and I'll eat it on the tram?'

Mrs Johnson sighed. 'That's no way to have your food. Give me a minute, then, and drink your tea. What did your letters say? Are they all right?'

Polly nodded, picked up a cup and took a sip. 'Yes. Jim's got a lance corporal's stripe already and Bertie's shot a sniper, whatever that is.'

'Golly! Ah well, everyone says they'll be home by Christmas.'

'No, Mum. For goodness' sake, it's November now and it looks as though we've lost two battles already.' Polly read the *Birmingham Mail* closely and she knew that the BEF and the French had been in severe fighting. It was clear that the Germans were not going to be the pushover that 'everyone' had claimed. 'It's not going to be as easy as that,' she said, struggling into her coat. 'Can't stop.' She grabbed the sandwich in its waxed-paper covering. 'Thanks. See you tonight.'

Once on the tram, she wolfed down the sandwich, pulled her coat around her against the cold of the morning and read both letters again, snuggling around them as though they themselves would keep her warm. Then she tucked them away carefully and looked unseeingly out of the window, her mind once again addressing the question that consumed most of her waking moments: which one?

Immediately, Bertie's face appeared before her, his red hair tumbling over his forehead, his round face grinning and those ridiculously blue eyes looking into hers with a love that was unquestioning and promising her a warmth that she could feel even now, on this cold November morning. Bertie was no sleeping volcano. On the contrary, he erupted every time the two were alone – which was rare, in that the three of them had been inseparable until, that is, the Kaiser had marched into Belgium. The little Irishman made no secret of his love. He proposed a future with him that waved aside the unimportant matter that he had no proper job nor qualifications that might bring security or prosperity. Of course, he had not proposed marriage. He simply insisted that they would marry when she was ready to have him and, in the meantime, the trio would continue to live in warm proximity and he would press his lips to hers and fondle her enticing breasts whenever they were alone. Ah, Bertie... She smiled and brushed away the tear that came whenever she thought of him, warm, passionate and vulnerable out there, in the trenches. She just hoped that Jim would be able to look after him...

Jim, 'her affectionate friend'! Jim: tall, quiet, capable, deep. The only time he had kissed her was on the platform at New Street Station when she had waved them goodbye. Then, when Bertie had pushed her lips apart and thrust his tongue through to mingle fiercely with hers, Jim had kissed her hard but chastely on the lips and held her tightly, but briefly. How strange that the fates had thrust the three of them together, living cheek by jowl through childhood. Jim, so very different from Bertie, and yet just as attractive in his own way. He would enfold her in his competence and equally deep love. Oh, she knew that he loved her, even though he never said so. Women knew these things. She swayed as the tram traversed a line crossing on its way up

Newtown Row. When was it that she realised that her feelings about them had changed from that of admiring chum to something more warm and deeply unsettling? And why had they both emerged *equally* as potential lovers *at the same time?* She sighed. It would have been so much easier, so much more *convenient,* had one or the other surged ahead in attraction. But no. They marched together in early manhood, as in child-hood and teens, as her boon companions; in-separable, the only men she could ever contem-plate giving herself to – the only men she fiercely *wished* to give herself to. But damn and blast it, she couldn't have them both! Which one, for God's sake?

Then her heart lurched as she realised once again that perhaps God would take that decision for her; that a German bullet or shell would kill either one of them or even, horror of horror, kill them both. She bit her lip. She had two much older brothers serving somewhere in France, yet the thought of losing them brought nothing like the agony of being parted from Jim and Bertie. For a moment she felt guilty about that. Then she turned and looked at the shopfronts rattling by and shook her head at her reflection in the tram window. She could not feel ashamed at facing up to her preference. She loved the two of them with a passion that could not be sup-pressed.

Polly had left school at thirteen – the same infants and junior school where she had played tomboyishly with her two boys – and she had been an undistinguished scholar. Yet she was no fool. Possessing a strong imagination, she had consumed all the news about Germany's strong naval and military build-up with a growing dread. It would lead to war, she could see that plainly. And the assassination of that remote archduke at Sarajevo was merely the accidental spark that fired the conflagration. It would be war and her two boys would fight in it.

She had not for one moment subscribed to the popular myth that it would be a short-lived affair, over in a few short months. The build-up of forces in Germany, France, Russia, Austria and, to a lesser extent, in Britain, must surely lead to a more titanic struggle, lasting for two years, at least. Please God her two boys would come through it safely, leaving her with this sweetly agonising decision to take when she was older and, of course, wiser.

Polly reported for duty at the Beehive, the old-fashioned drapers in the heart of Birmingham where she worked, only two minutes late. Not enough to earn the disapproval of Mr Bulstrode, the stout and stern general manager. She knew that she had a credit balance with him, for she was good at her job – better, in fact, much better than the stately spinsters whom the world had passed by and who made up the rest of the staff serving in the shop. For Polly not only knew all the merchandise – prices, quality, quantity – intimately, without having to consult the cards, but also had a fashion sense that could advise the customer at the other side of the counter about which cloth and colour would be right for her and the drive to sell it to her with charm. Ah yes, Polly knew that she would be allowed the odd indulgence, for she was irreplaceable.

Yet, after five years of loyal service in the Beehive, Polly was becoming restless.

The war was going to continue, she knew that. The men were going to the front now in increasing numbers. Kitchener's giant, moustached face loomed at her from hundreds of posters, urging young men to answer the call of King and country. There was, as yet, no balancing call to women, for they could not fight. But perhaps that would come, in some way or another. She fretted through that day as she sold cotton reels, strings of bright ribbons and packages of knitting wools. This was all so unimportant, so *peripheral*. Her boys were doing their bit. Why shouldn't she?

As five-thirty came and she headed home, she remained two stops on the tram beyond her normal destination and alighted near Kymestons, the gloomy factory in Witton where she knew that munitions were made. At the weekend she had walked by and seen a notice, advertising the need for workers. She had paid no particular attention to it and therefore had no idea if it was only men they needed. Surely it would be, for women were never used for this kind of work. But perhaps the call to men to join Kitchener's Army had had the effect of reversing that policy? She therefore felt a thrill of expectation as she hurried through the drizzle to the work gates.

The notice remained. It made a direct call to patriotism:

DO YOUR BIT TO SUPPORT THE LADS AT THE FRONT!
MEN – AND WOMEN – NEEDED FOR IMPORTANT WAR WORK.
LONG HOURS BUT GOOD PAY.

APPLY WITHIN AND DO YOUR BIT TO DEFEAT KAISER BILL!

Polly tingled. War work! What did Kymestons make? She had no idea, but Jim had written about being subjected to German shelling. How appropriate if this company made shells – shells that would help to counter the German bombardment and make Jim and Bertie safer. She could do nothing more appropriate to help them. It wouldn't matter that she would get her hands dirty and work longer hours. She was tired of being ladylike in a fusty old shop, dealing with matrons who didn't know a mauve from a magenta. This would be striking out for a new kind of independence; something that would match the sacrifices that Jim and Bertie were making out there, in the Flemish muck and fire.

She made a resolution and immediately spun on her heel and walked back to Turners Lane with a new sense of purpose. There was no chance of gaining time off from the Beehive to apply for the job, so tomorrow she would just have to be ill. And become a war worker!

She decided that she would tell her parents nothing of this, for they still cherished the thought that by working in a respectable draper's shop Polly had attained complete fulfilment. So she left at the usual time the next morning but dressed with rather more care. She explained to her mother that the fact that she wore her best hat – a black straw boater trimmed with red roses made of gauze – was 'just for a change' and pulled on her best white gloves from her bag once out of the house. As an afterthought, she had put a copy of her birth certificate in her bag.

It was easy walking distance to Kymestons and, on arrival, she stood outside the grimy building for a moment. Her eye followed the high grey-brick walls that fronted directly onto the street and seemed to march for miles. There was no break in them, apart from the open iron gates where she stood, and the place looked more like a prison than a workplace. She licked her lips and felt immediately that her sweet little straw boater was out of place. Then she settled her shoulders. To hell with it! They would have to take her as they found her: determined.

A commissionaire wearing what surely must have been Zulu war medal ribbons directed her to an office entrance and Polly found herself speaking through a hole in a glass partition to a severe woman wearing spectacles.

'You are applying for work?' the woman asked, eyeing the hat with disapproval.

'Yes, please. I want to do war work.'

'We do not take young ladies under the age of eighteen.'

'I am eighteen. I have my birth certificate here.' (What a stroke of luck that she had the foresight to bring it with her!)

'Very well. Please wait on that bench over there.'

It was all of ten minutes before a door opened and a large, bluff man in a khaki-coloured duster coat bustled through. 'Yes, good morning, Miss ... er...?'

'Johnson. Polly Johnson.'

'You are looking for work, Miss Johnson?'

'Yes. But only war work,' she added hurriedly.

The man chuckled. 'That's the only work we do 'ere, miss. Come along, then. Just follow me.'

They went through a door, down a corridor and then through another door into another universe. Polly's jaw dropped. The room was vast – it was called a 'shop' she was to learn later – and seemed to stretch for hundreds of feet. It was also high, at least fifty feet, she guessed, and lined with cranes at one end that towered to the ceiling and fringed one wall. For as far as the eye could see stood ammunition shells of various sizes, perched tightly together vertically, some moving very slowly on conveyor belts and being tended by men and women wearing identical brown-coloured duster coats. She noticed that all the women had their hair tied up in turban-like scarves. It was noisy but not intrusively so and the atmosphere was one of cheerful concentration. It was the smell, however, that hit Polly. It was clinical and difficult to define. Chemical, certainly, and rather acidic.

'War work, all right, luv,' said the man. 'Shells for our troops out in France.'

Polly licked her lips and wished she hadn't worn her hat. 'Will some of them go to Belgium

94

– to Flanders?' she enquired hesitantly.

'Oh yes, lass. They'll go there all right.' He gave her a quizzical glance. 'Got a special interest in Flanders, then, have we?'

'Well yes. I have two friends fighting out there.'

'Good for you. Well rest assured, luv, we 'ere at Kymestons are doin' our very best to supply them. Now, come on through to the office.'

They went into a glass-panelled room, looking out over the vast factory floor, and Polly was offered a dusty seat in a chair facing a desk overflowing with charts and papers. The man sat facing her and cleared away some of the papers and put his elbows on the surface.

He had kindly eyes, and a nose and a complexion that had clearly benefited from good ale. He smiled at her. 'Now,' he said. 'My name's Miller and I'm the manager for this section here. It is true that we are looking to take on additional labour and, given the fact that so many young men are – quite rightly – volunteering for the forces, we have decided that we will take on women to do work that previously lads had done.

'But I must say that you do look a bit young, lass, and I ... er ... can't 'elp wondering whether this kind of work wouldn't be a bit, well, hard for you. You are over eighteen, are you?'

Polly immediately reached up, removed the long pin that secured her hat to her piled-up hair and put the boater on her lap. A strand of soft brown hair escaped and fell down to her shoulders. She gave Mr Miller her best smile.

'Oh yes. I have my birth certificate here if you

would like to see it.'

Miller held out his hand. 'I believe you, lass, but better see it, I suppose. It's required by this new Ministry of Munitions, you see.'

He studied it perfunctorily and handed it back. 'That's fine. I would like to take you on, but...' His voice tailed away as he took in her small hands and trim ankles. 'The truth is I really don't think that what I could offer you would suit a nice young lady like you.'

Polly widened her eyes. 'Oh, but Mr Miller! I do want so much to do war work. I am a good worker and can bring a good reference from my present job, I know I could. It is true that I have only worked in a draper's shop but I am strong and very willing.'

Miller gave a wan smile. 'I don't suppose for a moment that you can drive a motor car, can you? No. Silly to ask. Course you can't.'

'No, but I can ride a bike.'

He was silent for a moment. Then: 'Do you have a head for heights?'

'Er ... well, yes. I've climbed the Lickey Hills.'

His smile widened. 'Look Miss ... er ... Johnson. Let me tell you what we do here. In this particular part of Kymestons we fill ammunition shells, of all shapes and sizes. That means we put in the timing devices but also the explosives that make 'em go off. We stuff 'em with a chemical called amatol. Yellow stuff. We've got quite a few girls doing this and we're probably going to have to recruit more as the lads go away to the front. It's not very pleasant because it's long hours and smelly work. After a time the chemical gives the girls' faces and teeth a sort of yellowish tinge, like. They get called "canaries" as a result.' He gave an apologetic shrug.

'Trouble is that I couldn't offer you a job doing that because we've no vacancies at the moment. In fact, the only vacancy just now wouldn't suit you at all...'

'How do you know? What is it?'

He smiled. 'It's sitting in a little glass box near the ceiling of the assembly shop and driving one of the overhead cranes that lifts the completed shells in pallets and swings 'em from the line to the despatch area.'

Polly's face dropped. 'What, sitting up at the top there?'

'Yes. We've got one lass doing it already, but it's really a man's job.'

Polly jumped to her feet. 'No. No. Mr Miller, if you've got one girl doing it, then I can do it too. I'm good with my hands and ... er ... what d'you call it? Coordination. That's it. And I don't mind heights. Please, Mr Miller. Let me give it a try, at least.' She gave a self-deprecatory cough. 'I do so want to do work that will help the lads out there.'

Miller regarded her with a half smile, then slowly nodded his head. 'All right, lass. I admire your spirit. We'll give you a trial of a month. When can you start?'

'I have to give a week's notice.'

'Right. Now you should know about the conditions. First of all, what are you earning now?'

'Eighteen shillings a week.'

'Well, we can start you at twenty-two bob. But

it's long hours. We are working eight-hour shifts at the moment, but the demand from the front has meant that we have to change to twelve hours, starting in a week's time. That will be twelve hours Monday to Saturday, then, on Saturday, changing to eighteen hours. That means going on duty at six o'clock Saturday evening and working to midday Sunday, when the opposite shift would take over and work through until Monday at six a.m. when we will resume twelve-hour shifts. Bit confusing, I'm afraid, and it cuts down on the dancing, too, love. Can you do it?'

'Of course I can.'

'Right. Well I am prepared to give it a try if you are. To get your notice through you'd better start a week on Monday. Sharp at eight o'clock. Come on. I'll show you the work.'

She followed him out, back once more into the huge shell assembly workshop. Miller pointed upwards to the side of the shop and towards the far end of it, where long crane booms swung out, their long chains dangling down like fishing lines, huge steel hooks at their ends. Distant figures were threading the hooks through strong nets on which the shell pallets rested. Then the pallets were hoisted, swung delicately from left to right and deposited somewhere out of Polly's sight.

'There you go,' said Miller. 'It's responsible work because you need to know exactly what you're doing. Dropping a pallet could be hugely dangerous.'

Polly realised that her mouth was gaping open.

'Golly. Would they explode?'

Miller chortled. 'No. The fuses are not fitted here. But if they fell on someone he'd have a nasty headache.' He pointed to the side. 'You would have to climb that ladder to get to your cabin. It's about forty feet or so up. Think you could do that?'

She forced a grin. 'Oh yes. Of course.'

'Just one suggestion, lass.'

'Yes, Mr Miller?'

With a half-embarrassed smile, he gestured towards her long skirt. 'It's better not to be wearing a skirt when you climb that ladder, if you know what I mean. There are plenty of blokes on the shop floor.'

She blushed and nodded.

'We can provide overalls but it would be best, if you've got trousers, to bring them to wear underneath. All right?'

'Of course. Thank you, Mr Miller.'

'Good. See you a week on Monday. Unless you change your mind, that is.'

Polly shook her head firmly. 'Oh no. No question of that. I will be the best crane driver you have, Mr Miller. I'll show you.'

He smiled, gravely shook her hand and waved her goodbye.

Outside in the street, a mizzly rain was falling again. She took a deep breath, pinned on her hat and then leant against the wall for a moment, impervious to the wetness. An overhead crane driver! It would mean entering a completely different world. No more genteel discussions with elderly ladies about types of knitting wool and colours. She would sit high above the world, in charge of her own piece of complicated machinery that could cause great harm if she got something wrong. She would pull and push levers and lift shells and then swing them away and gently – *so gently,* she supposed – deposit them down. Important work. Work that could help her boys in Flanders. War work!

Polly gulped and began walking towards the tram stop. There would be problems at home, she knew that. But she had always been able to get what she wanted from her gentle, hard-working father. And Mother could be overcome, if she was allowed to get used to the idea. Trousers! She must buy a pair. But most of all, she must write to Jim and Bertie and tell them. War work! The very sound of it made her feel closer to them.

CHAPTER FOUR

Polly's letters were given to the boys as they reached the little town of Poperinghe, some six miles behind Ypres, directly to the west. As a rail terminal it was the main supply point for men, supplies and ammunition to 'the Salient' as the Ypres battlefield was being called, but, now, in late 1914, it was also becoming essential as a convenient place of rest and recreation for troops down from the miseries of front line duty. The town was just in reach of the heaviest of the long-range German batteries on the ridges overlooking the Ypres basin, but, so far, it had escaped heavy bombardment.

Jim and Bertie tucked their letters into their jackets and marched to the rows of tents that marked their camp on the outskirts of 'Pop'.

'I'm not openin' mine till I've had me bath,' said Bertie. Neither of them had bathed properly since they had entered the line and the grime of trench warfare had imprinted itself on their faces and bodies. Worse were the vermin that infested their clothing.

'Good idea,' agreed Jim. 'Sort of "be clean for her", eh?'

Bertie nodded. 'I'd like first, though, to get rid of these little fellers.' He offered up his shirt where lice could be seen happily at home in the seams of the fabric. He ran his thumb along the main seam. 'The little varmints have moved in like lodgers, so they have. Look, I can't budge 'em and that bloody powder they gave us in the trenches doesn't seem to do any good at all.'

'No, but there's supposed to be fumigating machines at the baths, I've heard. So we can clean up completely there.'

'I don't know which is best, to kill the old ones or the young ones. If you kill the old ones, the young ones might die of grief, but the young ones are easier to kill and you can get the old ones when they go to the funeral.'

'Hmm. I'd rather rely on the fumigating thing.'

'Right. Let's go and get clean.'

Rain had set in on the Salient long ago and mud was just starting to be as much of an enemy as the Germans. The plain itself was low-lying, not far from the sea and soggy, even before rain fell. The farmers had cut in ditches to carry the water away but the shelling had opened them up so that they were as one with the sodden landscape, from which individual fields and woods had now virtually disappeared. The soldiers manning the trenches to which the British had retreated after repulsing narrowly the heavy German attacks of October were now cold, wet and lousy. It was a foretaste of what was to come.

The boys soaked themselves in the canvas baths, pitched under canvas and fed by large cauldrons set over field stoves. The water was hardly hot enough but it was luxury to soak and soap themselves all over. Their clothes were fumigated and then cleaned while they bathed. They picked them up, brushed their hair and, off duty, decided to walk into town, keeping their precious letters until they could find a corner of a congenial bar.

The streets of Pop were narrow and crowded but, fortunately, there was no shortage of *estaminets* ready and happy to take their money. The Café des Allies beckoned and they entered. It was smoke-filled and crowded with British Tommies (a corporal had told them not go to 'La Poupée', which was reserved for officers only) but they found a tiny round table, covered with dozens of wine-stain roundels.

'You want plonk?' demanded a stoutly bosomed waitress.

The two looked at each other. This was the

first time that they had come down from the line and their first experience of a French *estaminet*. 'What's plonk?' asked Jim.

The waitress sighed. 'It ees *vin blanc*. White wine. You Tommees call eet plonk. You want it? Ees one franc for a bottle. You want?'

'Er … yes. I suppose so.' Jim gave her a coin and she immediately seemed to magic from nowhere a bottle containing a yellowish liquid and two tiny glasses. She poured it and bustled away.

'Well, old lad.' Jim raised his glass. 'Here's to Polly.'

'Ah yes. Here's to Polly, bless her.'

They emptied their glasses in one gulp. Bertie wiped his mouth with the back of his hand. 'Not much to it, is there? I'd rather have a pint of Ansells.'

Jim replenished their glasses. 'Doesn't seem to taste of much, does it?' He looked around. Everyone seemed to be drinking exactly the same wine, from bottles carrying no labels. 'Everyone else is downing the stuff so I suppose it must be all right. Perhaps it's what you might call an acquired taste.'

Suddenly a piano accordion struck up. It was a lilting waltz and a little wizened man playing it and wearing a beret began to sing:

Après la guerre fini,
Soldat anglais parti,
Mademoiselle in the family way,
Après la guerre fini.

Bertie leant forward. 'What's he singing?'

'I think he's being rude about British soldiers. But everyone's laughing, so I suppose it's all right. Shall we read our letters?'

Immediately, they both settled back in their chairs, slightly turning away from each other, and began reading.

'Blimey!' Jim looked up in consternation. 'She's going to work in a factory. Driving a bloody overhead crane.'

'Ah.' Bertie screwed up his face in annoyance, his slowness in reading exposed. 'I haven't got that far. Hang on.' Then, 'Strewth! She's going to be slinging shells all over the place. Sounds dangerous. A lovely little slip of a lass like that can't be doing that stuff, can she? It don't seem right, does it, Jimmy boy?'

Jim sighed. 'These are strange times, Bertie. Six months ago, who'd have thought that we would be standing in mud, trying to kill people? Put like that, I don't suppose it's so strange. She's a plucky, marvellous girl, though, ain't she?'

Bertie's eyes lit up. 'Ah, so she is, Jim. So she is.' He looked down at his letter then up again at his friend. 'Does she ... er ... say she loves you, then, Jimmy?'

Hickman looked embarrassed. 'Bloody hell, no mate. She's, well, she's not that sort of girl. She's not sloppy and all that.' He paused uncertainly. 'Why, does she say that about you, then?'

It was Bertie's turn to show discomfort. 'Well no. Not in so many words, anyway. But you sort of know, don't you? I do, anyway.'

Jim did not reply but, frowning, filled their glasses again and fixed his eye on the accordion player. The two sat in awkward silence for a moment and then, in unison, as though pulled by a marionette's strings, they both slowly folded their letters, put them away in their tunics and lifted their glasses.

Inevitably, it was Bertie who broke the silence. 'You know, Jimmy, this life in the trenches, when it's a bit quiet like, with no chargin' about with bayonets and all that stuff, wouldn't be so bad if it wasn't for old Black Jack.'

Hickman slowly nodded. They had learnt that Sergeant Flanagan, seconded from a regular regiment – in his case the Connaught Rangers – with other regular NCOs to give 'backbone' to this territorial battalion on active service, had earned the nickname by his fierce demeanour in and out of action. It had quickly become clear that he was a bully with a sadistic bent, but also that he had taken a particular dislike to Bertie.

'He certainly doesn't seem to like Catholics,' mused Jim, sipping his wine.

'Ah sure, sure. And that's the funny thing, so it is. Y'see, the Rangers are from the west of Ireland and they're a Catholic lot themselves. What, then, is bloody old Black Jack, a Protestant heathen through and through, just like you, doin' serving in a Catholic regiment, eh?'

Jim shrugged. 'He's also a professional soldier, through and through, and the Rangers, so I'm told, are one of the finest regiments in the British army. I suppose he just happened to be from one of the few Protestant families in Galway, or somewhere like that, and he joined up to follow the flag in a good regiment. Now he's no longer serving with Catholics, perhaps he's enjoying the chance of showing his prejudice.'

'Hmm. Well, I wish the bastard would stop showing it to me.'

It was true that Flanagan seemed to take a delight in persecuting Bertie. As their platoon sergeant, he would single out the little Irishman for fatigues and special duties whenever he could. It was difficult, in the dirt and general discomfort of the trenches, for Flanagan to take advantage of Murphy's natural dishevelment for his persecution, but he pounced on him whenever he could. Bertie seemed to have spent more time as latrine orderly for the platoon than standing on the trench firing step. Jim had tried whenever possible to come between the two and, indeed, the sergeant seemed to be wary of the lance corporal – perhaps not least because the young Lieutenant Smith-Forbes, their platoon commander, fresh from public school and exactly the same age as Jim, had taken to the tall, quiet, obviously efficient soldier. But Flanagan chose his moments carefully and Hickman could not always protect his friend.

Jim took another sip of his wine. They were learning now to treat the pale yellow liquid with some respect and Bertie was already beginning to grin vacantly at everyone within sight. 'Trouble is,' he said, 'he's obviously a bloody good soldier. Have you seen the ribbons he wears?'

Bertie nodded.

'Well, he's got campaign medals from the Boer

106

War, I can see that. But he's got some other sort of medal which I can't recognise. It must be for bravery. Well, what the hell. Perhaps a sniper will get him.'

The smile left Bertie's face. 'No hope. They only get the lovely fellers.'

They were interrupted by the bosomy waitress. 'You boys like a little ooh la la, next door?' she enquired, as though she was asking if they needed another bottle.

Bertie looked up at her amiably. 'Thish ooh la la's loverly, me darlin'. Why should we go nesht door for another one?'

The woman lifted her eyes to the ceiling. 'Ooh la la ees not a drink, Tommy.' She eyed Jim's stripe and turned to him. 'You want, or not?'

'No thanks, missus. But we could drink another bottle, please.'

Seeing his soft brown eyes and broad shoulders, she gave him a smile and shrugged. *'Eh bien,'* she said and turned away.

'What was she on about, then, Jimmy boy?'

'I think she was offering us a woman. There must be a brothel next door.'

Bertie blinked his blue eyes. 'Ooh, I wouldn't do that, Jimmy. Would you? It wouldn't be right by Polly, now, would it?'

'No, it wouldn't. Now don't get too pissed, Bertie lad, 'cos the redcaps are patrolling the town and Black Jack would just love to have you up before the colonel. Let's see if we can buy a baggage, or whatever it is they call their bloody great sandwiches, to go with this next bottle. It will soak up the booze – and we deserve a drink or two tonight.' He raised his glass. 'Here's to the lovely little crane driver back home.'

Bertie's grin lit up his round and now very red face. He raised his glass in reply. 'Here's to the sweetest li'll crane driver thad ever lived.'

A *baguette au fromage* helped to reduce the effect of the alcohol and they eventually left the estaminet in reasonably good order, Jim keeping a wary eye open for the red-capped military policemen who regularly patrolled the little town.

Their period of rest out of the line lasted for just three days, after which they marched back up to Ypres, the town still bustling with civilians and comparatively unaffected by the shelling which was slowly reducing the plain before it to a morass. There, they waited for night to fall and then joined the dreary and dangerous convoys struggling to the east in the dark, through the mud, to the long, curving and now less fragile line occupied by the Allied troops.

It was rumoured that the BEF had sustained more than 55,000 men killed, missing or wounded in the first battle of Ypres and the French between 50,000 and 85,000. German losses were said to have been even heavier. It was clear that the weeks of the late autumn had to be a period of recuperation for Allies and Germans alike. There had been no real attack launched by either side since early November, although the German shelling of the front trenches and supply lines across the plain had increased and night parties still made sorties across no man's land.

For Jim and Bertie, now manning the line some two miles to the south-east of Ypres, near Hill 60 (in fact, merely a flattish hillock only sixty metres high but looming over that ravaged plain like a wart on a whore's cheek), the days passed in discomfort and boredom, broken only by the irregular arrivals of mortar bombs and heavier shells. The routine of trench life consisted of standing to at dawn, dodging the explosions, burying the dead, keeping look out during the day, repairing the trenches against the unremitting onslaught of rain and bombardment, cooking over open braziers, digging out the square, slime-filled latrine pits (Bertie's speciality), and crouching to find sleep in primitive dugouts at night, unless on patrol duty in no man's land.

The latter provided Sergeant Flanagan with an opportunity to reveal that his persecution of Bertie was something more serious than merely an idle diversion. He was selected by Black Jack to join the six-man party that was to raid the German trench opposite, in the hope of capturing a prisoner to give information about the identity of the regiment manning it. Lieutenant Smith-Forbes was to lead the party and immediately Jim volunteered to join it.

'No,' grunted Flanagan. 'Too many.'

'Oh, I don't know, Flanagan,' said the subaltern. 'Seven's not too many and I'd be glad to have a junior NCO along, just in case... ' he coughed, 'something happens to you, you know.'

Flanagan scowled but said nothing more. So Hickman joined the party, who assembled in the firing trench that night just after midnight. They wore no caps, nor greatcoats or capes, and carried only hand grenades, bayonets and revolvers. With faces blacked, they looked like a cross between pirates and burglars. They sat on the fire step as Smith-Forbes briefed them. It was clear that he was nervous, for he kept clearing his throat and licking his lips, his eyes glowing out from his face, like those of a piccaninny.

'Right chaps. The enemy lines are about a hundred and eighty to two hundred yards to our front. It sounds as though they have a wiring party out, which is bad news but good news also. It's ... er ... bad because we don't want to blunder into them, and good because they'll be out there, on the edge of the German trench making a bit of a noise, so that should cover us a bit.'

He coughed. 'Our job is to get quietly across no man's land to a stretch of their trench, cut the wire sufficiently for us to get under it, slip into the trench, take our prisoner and get back again. We don't want to make a fuss or start another war. Just get in, grab our bloke and out again. Now I've been chosen to lead this handsome band,' he gave a nervous chuckle, 'because I speak some German. So I shall say to the lookout in German that we are a wiring party coming back.

'Now we shall want someone to go just ahead of me to lie on his belly and cut the wire–'

'That can be Private Murphy,' interjected Flanagan quickly. 'He's the smallest.' Bertie shot a frightened glance across to Hickman.

The lieutenant nodded. 'Very well. I shall be

right behind you, Murphy, and Sergeant Flanagan will be behind me. Corporal Hickman, you will bring up the rear. We crouch at first, on leaving our lines, then go onto our bellies as we approach their lines. When a star shell goes up, we flop and freeze. The weapons we carry are for threatening our prisoner.' He gave his artificial laugh. 'Let's hope we can get one who is happy to get out of the war. To repeat, then, no shooting unless I begin it. Understood?'

'Yessir,' they chorused.

'Right, then.' He coughed. 'Over we go. No talking or unnecessary noise. Follow me and good luck.'

Jim gripped Bertie's arm and gave it what he hoped was a reassuring squeeze, as Flanagan roughly pushed the little Irishman up ahead of him. The raiders flattened themselves to crawl under the wire, the lowest strand of which Hickman held up for them and then, at the crouch, began to make their way between the shell holes towards the enemy line. The distinctive smell of no man's land – sweet decay and foul earth – assailed Jim's nostrils and made his stomach heave. The enemy line was too far away to discern in the darkness but then was lit by a star shell that rose into the sky and popped, shedding its strange, ghostly glare across the battered land. Lying flat, Hickman could just see a line of wire, with, to the left, what appeared to be a group of figures on his side of the German parapet, lying flat also to avoid being exposed by the flare.

Immediately, Smith-Forbes made a gesture

with his hand, indicating that they must crawl to the right and set off again. After about ten minutes, the lieutenant dropped onto his stomach and indicated for Bertie to move ahead of him. Flanagan immediately gave the little Irishman a shove, which caused him to drop his large wire cutters, so hitting a shell fragment and causing a large clunk to sound out across that frightful terrain.

The lieutenant turned his head in anger and they all lay inert, as if frozen, expecting a searchlight to probe the shell holes and reveal them. But everything stayed quiet and, with another push from Flanagan, Bertie crawled past Smith-Forbes, his elbows and knees propelling his plump body forward at a remarkably fast pace.

At the rear, Jim, his heart in his mouth, watched him go and filed away a solemn vow that retribution would reach Flanagan if anything happened to Bertram Murphy. But the little man got clear and, in single file, the party followed him, each man placing hand, elbow and knee forward with great care. The ground, with its many shell craters, made for hard going but it also gave them good cover and the mud and gentle rain muffled the noise they made. To their left they could hear the tap of barbed-wire stakes being driven into the soggy soil, although they could see none of the working party.

Eventually, after what seemed an eternity to Jim, he saw Bertie raise a hand, look nervously behind him and then, on a nod from the lieutenant, inch forward, wire cutters in hand. The

German wire was only some ten feet away. It was in three lines – far deeper, noted Jim, than the English wire – and four strands high. He watched as Bertie slowly wriggled forward, then turned onto his back and reached up to cut the first strand, and then the second above it. 'Don't go any higher, mate,' breathed Jim to himself and, as if hearing the advice, the little Irishman turned onto his stomach, wriggled forward and began cutting the second line. Within three minutes a passage had been cut through the barrier and Bertie lay breathing heavily on the ground, his cheek pressed into the mud, completely exhausted.

With great caution, Smith-Forbes edged forward, waving for the others to follow. Each man crawled past Bertie and, as Flanagan did so, Jim saw the sergeant press the little Irishman's face heavily into the mud and grit. As he grew abreast of Bertie, Jim paused.

'You all right, Bertie?' he whispered.

The Irishman lifted his blackened face, tried to grin and nodded.

Together, the two followed the others until they saw the lieutenant disappear over the parapet of the trench, followed by the sergeant. They heard a voice from within the trench begin to ask: *'Was is–?'*

Smith-Forbes cut in quickly and they heard him answer, *'Keine Angst! Wir sind nur die Stacheldrahtsmannschaft auf der Rückkehr.'*

Then, as they neared the parapet, they heard a scuffle and, peering into the trench, saw the lieutenant holding a revolver to the cheek of a wide-eyed German soldier, whose rifle and bayonet had been laid on the fire step beside an untended trench periscope. In his hand was a half-eaten sandwich. The sergeant was waving the other members of the raiding party to either side, to stand guard at the traverses, while he, revolver in hand, stood to the entrance of a deep dugout.

Jim waved Bertie back to the wire and, leaning down from the parapet of the trench, held out one hand to the German and motioned him to climb up, while covering him with his revolver. Meeting the eyes of the soldier, he put his hand to his lips to invoke silence, and gestured upwards with the handgun. Immediately, the man stuffed his sandwich into his mouth and climbed up the trench wall ladder, with an alacrity that made Jim feel that they had, indeed, found a German who was quite happy to leave his war behind him.

At the top, the sentry was unceremoniously bundled forward to where Bertie was holding the broken strands apart. To their right, they could now distinctly hear the low voices of the German work party, although the night was too dark for them to be revealed. Seeing that the lieutenant was now behind the prisoner, Jim wriggled underneath the wire and beckoned with his revolver for the German to follow him. Eventually, all of the party was through, leaving Bertie, who had held the wire open for them all, as the last man, keeping the strands apart for Flanagan, the last to leave the trench.

Looking back anxiously, Jim saw the sergeant turn as Bertie left the wire to follow him. Then he saw Flanagan suddenly thrust the little Irishman back onto the wire, so that his tunic caught in the barbs and he was spreadeagled against it. As Bertie desperately tried to untangle himself, the sergeant grinned, put his head down and began crawling after the main party.

Hickman cast caution away and ran back to where Bertie was struggling in the wire coils. He pulled out his knife, ground to razor sharpness for the raid, and cut away the fabric that had caught on the barbs and pushed his friend down. A fraction of a second later, a star shell lazily burst into life above them, revealing the moon-like contours of no man's land – seemingly empty, for its occupants had all flung themselves down flat into the mud.

'Thank the Holy Mother for you, Jim lad,' breathed Bertie. 'I would have been crucified out there on the wire, in the light, so I would. Did you see that bastard do that to me?'

'Oh I did, Bertie. Yes I did. The man's not just a bully, he's a bloody murderer, that's what he is. I'm going to have a word with him.' Then, as the star light faded: 'Come on. Let's get out of here.'

Just before they reached the halfway mark, Jim rose and, at the crouch, half ran, half stumbled to reach Flanagan, who brought up the rear of the party. As the sergeant rose to the crouch, Hickman reached forward and caught his ankle, so that Flanagan fell flat.

Immediately, Jim was lying at his side, his revolver pressed hard into the Irishman's ear.

'Now listen, Sergeant Flanagan,' he whispered. 'I saw what you did to Murphy back there. You are a fucking would-be murderer, that's what you are.' Flanagan began to try to rise, but Hickman pushed his head down into the mud and pressed the muzzle of the revolver harder into his ear. 'No. Stay still. Otherwise there will be a terrible accident and this gun will go off. It's easily done and no one will know what happened. So listen to me and listen carefully. If you lay another finger on Murphy, or continue to make his life hell, I shall see that you get an accidental bullet in the back. There are two of us and only one of you, so if you do the same to me or to Murphy, then the other one will get you. Understand?'

Flanagan half lifted his head. 'Fuck you, Hickman,' he growled. 'You're a kid and I'm a man. I'll see you off any time. So don't threaten me. Just watch yourself.'

Jim withdrew the pistol. 'All right. Now we understand each other. Get moving, Sergeant.'

Hickman held back a little so that Bertie could catch him up. 'Jimmy, don't do anything stupid, lad,' the little man whispered. 'He's evil. What did you say to him?'

Jim grinned. 'Oh, I just had a quiet word, asking him to be reasonable. I think he understood.'

The party regained the British line without incident and were welcomed warmly by the company commander, who shook the hands of Smith-Forbes and Sergeant Flanagan. The German was ushered away, his face white but his eyes bright. The rest of the party settled down on the fire step to drink hot tea and smoke their cigarettes. Flanagan walked away without looking at either

116

Jim or Bertie.

The members of the raiding party were allowed to avoid stand-to at dawn the next morning and sleep as best they could in their scooped dugouts in the side of the trench. Hickman, however, was shaken awake by the duty corporal. 'The colonel wants to see you right away,' he said. 'Blimey, lad, what have you been up to?'

Jim gulped. Had Flanagan levelled a charge against him? What to say? Would Smith-Forbes stand by him? The sergeant, he knew, was rated highly in the battalion, as a seasoned veteran, a good soldier, hard but fair. Would his word stand against a junior NCO?

Battalion HQ was way down the line in a dugout and Hickman reported at the top. There was no sign of Flanagan, either in the trench or in the smoky room below the steps. The adjutant and the colonel were both working at a crowded desk and a signal corporal sat at a tiny trestle table, on which sat a telephone with a cranked handle.

The colonel, a large, burly man with tired eyes and a clipped pepper-and-salt moustache, looked up as he entered. Immediately, he rose, as did the adjutant and they both held out their hands.

'Congratulations, Hickman,' said the colonel. 'Fine work.'

'Er ... what?' began Jim.

'First class, corporal,' tuned in the adjutant, wringing his hand.

'I'm sorry, sir. I don't quite understand.'

'We have just heard,' said the colonel, 'that the award to you of the DCM – the Distinguished

Conduct Medal – has been confirmed by Army HQ. This is for your work in your early days here at Nonne Boschen, you'd probably know it as Nun's Wood. I gather you virtually single-handedly repulsed an attack on the rear of the line and then helped to bring back a patrol under heavy enemy fire. Splendid work.'

'Good lord!' Hickman's mouth fell open. 'I didn't do much, sir. And I was bloody scared most of the time.'

The colonel laughed. 'Aren't we all, lad. Aren't we all. Look, I am particularly delighted that this award has come to a Terrier, eh George?' He looked across at his adjutant.

'I should say so, sir.'

'Yes. It will show we old soldiers that you young volunteers can behave just as commendably as a Regular. And I'm finding out that that needs to be said sometimes. Now, lad, you know that this award is only one down the scale in merit to the Victoria Cross?'

'Well no, sir. I didn't.'

'Well it is. You will receive it formally when the general next visits this part of the line. But I felt you should have the news now. Very well, you can return to your post.'

'Thank you, sir.'

'Ah, one more thing. I understand that you did a good job of work with that raiding party last night. That little bird you brought back with you has sung very sweetly and told us a lot that we needed to know. Splendid work by everyone on that party. That Sergeant Flanagan is a splendid chap, eh George?'

'One of the best men we have, sir.'

'Yes well, Hickman. Congratulations again. Now off you go.'

Jim saluted and climbed the rough wooden steps, his head in a whirl. The DCM! And Flanagan regarded as 'a splendid chap'. One almost seemed to cancel the other out. Strange things seemed to be happening to him in this awful place. Oh, how he wished he could be alone with Polly just now, to run his fingers through her hair and hold her close...

His musings were interrupted by a familiar voice. 'Corporal Hickman.' The name was uttered with a rising inflexion on the last syllable, as though it was a command. Sergeant Flanagan was standing with his back to the traverse.

'Sergeant.' Jim walked to the man and stood facing him.

'I've just heard your news, sonny. Now...' Flanagan leant forward and pointed to a small red and blue ribbon amongst the row on his chest. 'Do you know what this is?'

'No, Sergeant.'

'Well, I'll tell you. This ribbon signifies that I am a holder of the Distinguished Conduct Medal, as soon you will be. So don't you go giving yourself any airs and graces, lad. *I* got this under shot and shell at the Battle of Colenso, not in some little night-time caper against second-rate troops. This medal was deserved, unlike yours. So don't you dare think that you are as good as me.' He leant forward so that his face was within a few inches of Jim's, who could smell the rum on his breath. 'Because you are not and never will be.'

He withdrew his face. 'That will be all. Carry on, Corporal.'

'Thank you, Sergeant.' Jim strode away, but allowed himself a smile as he turned the traverse. To hell with Sergeant Flanagan!

The news of his decoration seemed to reach home almost as quickly as it trickled along his own trench, for he received warm letters from his mother *and,* of course, from Polly. For once, it was good to receive a letter from her that was not accompanied by one to Bertie, although he took care to keep the receipt of it quiet. He didn't wish to gloat. She told him that the *Birmingham Gazette* had carried a picture of him and the *Mail* had done a little feature. It seemed that he was the first of the Terriers to be decorated. But she didn't say that she loved him, nor did he expect her to. He just, however, hoped that she might have hinted at something like that, some word or two, anything... Later, he received his decoration from the hand of General Haig himself, commander of the 1st Corps, at a parade in Poperinghe.

That night he and Bertie got gloriously drunk at the Café des Allies, drinking red wine this time. They found it much more satisfying. They still, however, eschewed the idea of 'going next door'. As a safeguard against the redcaps, Jim pinned the medal on his tunic for the unsteady walk home and, although they were stopped twice, they were allowed to proceed with congratulations and a request to 'keep it down, lads'. It seemed that even the military police had hearts. Sometimes.

The first Christmas of the war came and went quietly for them, billeted as they were behind the lines. They heard rumours of the fraternisation on Christmas Day, when Germans and British stood in no man's land, exchanged souvenirs and even played football, but they saw little evidence of fraternal feeling when they returned to the shelling and constant sniping of the line a few days later.

After their brief conversation on the morning after the night raid, there had been no further confrontation between Hickman and Sergeant Flanagan, although Bertie still seemed to suffer more than his fair share of latrine duty. Short of complaining to their platoon officer, which was unthinkable, there was nothing that Jim could do about it and Bertie endured it stoically enough, excusing his many absences by saying that he was just 'goin' down to the Mountains of Mourne again, see.'

Hickman could still see no real reason for the sergeant's persecution of Bertie. The Protestant-Catholic divide was the obvious explanation, but there were other Catholics in the company and they were not singled out for bullying. Perhaps it was Bertie's perennial cheerfulness that irked. Yet, as the incident on the German wire had proved, it was more than bullying. Bertie's entanglement would have been illuminated by the star shell and his body would have been riddled with bullets within seconds, if Jim had not cut him free just in time. It was, in fact, an evil and malevolent act. Thinking about it, a little shudder of fear ran through Jim. He had to admit that, despite his angry confrontation with the man in no man's land, he was more than a little afraid of Black Jack Flanagan. Physically, there was not much to choose between them. Jim was marginally taller and as broad, but the sergeant was older, experienced and weathered by a dozen or more violent encounters on battlefield and in barrack room. Regular soldiers like him had served all over the Empire: India, South Africa, probably Burma. His skin was like leather and his attitude equally hard. He was, undoubtedly, a man to be feared and watched carefully.

Both Jim and Bertie were longing for their first period of home leave, but spells of relief behind the lines, days occupied with training, were all that came their way. Reinforcements were now beginning to pour into the Salient, not only from the first trickle of Kitchener's 'first hundred thousand' of volunteer recruits, but also from the Empire. Turbanned Indians arrived to take their turn in the line and show that, despite suffering from the cold more severely than British troops, they were their equal in courage and soldierly skills. Then came the South Africans and, in more strength, the Canadians. The children of the Empire, it seemed, had responded enthusiastically to the call of the Mother Country.

As winter progressed towards spring in rain, sleet and snow, it became clear that both sides were building up for a big spring offensive. It was incomprehensible that these vastly swollen armies should continue sitting in their trenches, facing each other across a few hundred yards of battered earth, without one or the other crouching back on its haunches, like a challenged stag, and then springing forward.

Hickman confessed his fears to Bertie one evening as they stood together on the fire step. 'We've been lucky, old lad,' he said, 'that we have not yet really been asked to do what the Germans did when we first landed. That is, charge across this bloody mud in the face of rifle and machine-gun fire. I'd rather they did it again before we try. It would be bloody suicide.'

His wish was granted, but in a strange manner and with horrific results.

The regiment were stationed in the second line of trenches as support troops some fifty yards behind the front, in late April 1915, when the German attack came. Rumours were rife that, the day before, the Germans had used a new chemical weapon against the French on the north-east of the line and that the Algerian troops had fled and the day had only been saved by the late intervention of the Canadians. As a result, flannel body belts – usually used by being wrapped around the midriff in tropical conditions to soak up excessive perspiration – were issued. Rum jars filled with water were placed at intervals along the trench and orders were given that, if gas was used, the belts were to be quickly soaked in water and tied around nose and mouth.

'Wish they'd kept the rum in the jars,' muttered Bertie.

Jim sniffed. 'It seems barmy to try and use gas. The Germans would need a reasonably strong wind to blow it across to us, I would say, and nothing's moving today. And what would they do if they let the stuff out and then the wind changed to blow it back to them? Bloody dangerous stuff for anybody to use, if you ask me.'

What did ensue, however, was a particularly heavy bombardment, concentrated, it seemed, on the reserve trenches rather than the front line. Usually, a barrage would be adjusted to creep up to the main line, but this one seemed to grow with intensity and remained crashing into the Territorials, shredding a wood behind them and causing the troops to cower in the trenches. It was unusually accurate and the trench walls, so carefully shored up with sandbags, were collapsing all around, burying men and equipment and sending up spouts of soil and timber cladding.

Jim and Bertie crouched down together, the latter telling his rosary under his breath and Jim swearing softly and consistently, both of them trembling. Then, suddenly, the shelling stopped as soon as it had begun and a shriek came up from the end of the communications trench that led to the front line: 'GAS!'

'Put on your belts,' shouted Jim. He pushed Bertie towards the nearest rum jar and pulled the little man's belt from his haversack, dipped it into the water and threw it at him. He did the same with his own, covering his mouth and nose and tying it behind his neck, urging his section to do the same. Then he saw the gas.

It looked like thin grey smoke and it was creeping slowly – quite slowly, for there was only the faintest of breezes to carry it – down the communication trench from the front line and over the top of the line towards the support trench. It advanced at the speed of a man sauntering, it hung closely to the ground, it rose to a height of about eight or nine feet and there was no way around it. It was unearthly and malevolent, something that no bullet or bayonet could repel.

Slightly in front of it men came rushing down the communications trench. Under the cloth belt, Hickman's jaw dropped as he saw them. They were shrieking with strange, hoarse voices, tearing at their throats, their eyes wide and staring. Some fell and were immediately trampled on by those behind, uncaring in their haste to get away from the grey cloud and the searing pain that it brought. Reaching the support trench they carried on running and screaming through what was left of the trench, out into the shattered wood behind and the shell-torn open country beyond that.

The first touch of the gas caught Jim. Despite the cloth protection, he inhaled the first whiff. Immediately, he choked and coughed, attempting to spit as his lungs burned as if he had sucked in naked flame. Unprotected, the eyes felt as though needles were being inserted. He dropped to his knees and buried his face in the mud floor of the trench to escape the vapour but – as he came to realise later – this was the worst thing he could have done because the gas was heavier than air and at its thickest at its base.

Somehow, he grabbed Bertie with one hand,

his rifle and bayonet with the other and rushed up the communication trench towards the front line, desperate to run through the cloud. He was vaguely aware that he was treading on living, squirming bodies and that others behind him were doing the same but, pulling the Irishman with him, he ploughed his way through to where the gas had left behind only thin billows, nestling at the bottom of the trench.

He expected to find the trench occupied by Germans and was prepared to find a less excruciating death at the end of a bayonet. But the only occupants of the trench were its former defenders. They had all been sheltering from the bombardment, caught by the chlorine before they could fit the crude protection of the flannel belts. They lay everywhere, black in the face, tunics and shirt fronts torn open in their last desperate attempts to rid themselves of that vapour that still surrounded them at the bottom of the trench. Some were still alive and one soldier, who had had his right hand torn away by a shell blast, was mutely rubbing his throat with the stump, covering his face and tunic with blood. As a horrified Hickman watched, he shuddered, twitched for the last time and lay still. One or two others were writhing in agony, a black liquid bubbling up from their lungs until they literally drowned.

Jim tried to shout, 'man the parapet,' but no words could come from his burning throat. So he waved to the men who had followed him down the communication trench and stepped up to the firing step. He expected to see a mass of grey-coated Germans advancing but no one was moving in no man's land. His eyes streaming and half blind, he fired his rifle to show the enemy that the trench was not deserted. Bertie did the same and the others followed suit, producing a pathetic half-volley. It was clear, however, that the Germans were lying low, allowing their new chemical weapon plenty of time to do its terrible work.

Jim felt a hand on his shoulder and turned to gaze into the streaming eyes of Lieutenant Smith-Forbes. The young subaltern tried to speak but could only cough. He nodded his approval and moved along the line, slipping and sliding on the bodies lining the ground and slapping the bottoms of the men lining the parapet, in support of their initiative, before joining them on the step.

Then, at last, the one element that could save them crept towards them: a stronger, healing, cool wind. It immediately swept away the remnants of the gas and enabled troops from further back in support to join them in the front line.

The Germans eventually came marching across no man's land, but it was as if they were either ashamed of themselves for introducing such a foul new weapon and breaking every code of warfare, or they feared that they too could be caught by their own gas, for they came slowly and hesitantly and their attack was easily broken up.

The crude protection of the flannel belt, soaked in water, had worked up to a point and it certainly saved the lives of the infantrymen in the reserve trench. The heavy vapour caught in the fibres of the sodden cloth, just long enough to stop most of it being swallowed and produce the consequent chemical reaction in the lungs that killed by drowning. As it was, Jim, Bertie and their comrades were sent down the line for treatment in the advanced dressing stations by hard-working – and disgusted – medics who were able to prevent further damage.

Even so, the effects of the gas lingered – bequeathing a cough and difficulties in swallowing – and, with other casualties, the two men were taken down the line, through Ypres to Poperinghe, for a brief period of recuperation. Both of them had been aware that earlier in the winter the Germans had begun to shell Ypres with their big guns, but the change in the town since they had last passed through it shocked them. With its tall spires, narrow streets and crowded buildings, some of them dating from medieval times, it had presented an easy target, of course, to the long-range artillery, and by the end of April very little of the town remained undamaged. All of the civilian population had long since fled and, as they rumbled through the debris-strewn streets by night in their Red Cross wagon, there was no one to be seen except red-caps directing the traffic and squads of morose Tommies marching up to the front. The town was no longer a centre of a community, part of a civilised social pattern. It had been reduced to a ravaged staging post for troops moving to and from battle. It was a reminder, if they needed one, that total war had come to Belgium.

Later, lying in their tents, recovering outside 'Pop', a Bertie whose face was no longer rosy red confessed to his friend that the conflict was disgusting him.

'What exactly are we doin' it for, Jimmy, lad? Why are we here, involved in all this killin', this mass extermination? I can't see God or Jesus himself approving of sending that horrible stuff across to kill poor young chaps in such a terrible way.'

Jim shook his head. 'I don't know, son. I just don't know. I can only say that we didn't start this bloody thing. We didn't invade anybody, if you recall. We just came over because that prick of a Kaiser decided that he would march through Belgium – which hadn't done him any harm – to attack the French. Belgium was too small to stand up to him on its own, so we came to help. And I think that was right.'

Bertie blinked his watery eyes. 'I'm gettin' a bit confused about what is right and what isn't. I just think that we can't go on like this. It's makin' animals of us all. Perhaps if we stopped tryin' to kill them, then they'd stop trying to kill us.'

Jim shook his head. 'No. Then they'd think they'd won and they could do anything they liked as a result.' He leant across his mattress. 'Do you really think that people who are bastards enough to launch that gas stuff across at us would just quietly fold up and go home if we pushed off? No, mate. They'd march on even faster. Think about it.'

Bertie lay with his eyes closed for a moment.

129

Then, 'It's not right, though, Jimmy. It's just not right.'

Two days later, Hickman received the news that he was getting a second stripe, making him a full corporal, and that he was being granted two weeks' home leave. Home to see Polly! His heart lifted. Then it fell again. There was no leave for Bertie, who would have to wait his turn, which meant that he would lack protection against Black Jack Flanagan. Jim thought long about what he could do about this and then shrugged. After all, Bertie was a man – undoubtedly the finest shot in the battalion, as he had proved on many occasions – and he would have to stand on his own two feet sooner or later. Now was the time. And he was going home – home to see Polly...!

Typically, Bertie was not jealous. 'Goin' home, are yer? Goin' home with two stripes *and* a medal. Och, all of the girls in the whole of Birmingham will be after yer. None of them will be able to resist yer. Particularly one.' He gave a sad smile. 'Now, Jimmy, you be sure to give her my love and tell her that I think about her all the time, even if I'm not much good at the writing game. Now will you do that for me, lad?'

'Course I will, Bertie. I'll give her a kiss for you as well.'

'Ah no, son. I think that would be takin' things too far. Leave the kissin' to me when I get back there – if I ever do, that is.'

'Oh, you'll get leave all right. Now, just keep out of Flanagan's way while I'm away. Don't catch his eye or anything like that. And, if he really goes too far, then have a word with the lieutenant. But leave that to the last resort.'

'Oh, I will, I will, Jimmy. Now you go and have a good leave and leave this piddling little war to me.'

CHAPTER FIVE

Polly Johnson had been driving her crane daily for six months when she received Jim's letter telling her that he was coming home on leave. She had grown to love her crane as much as ... no, not as much as, but, she conceded, almost as much as the two men fighting out there on the Salient. She wrote separate letters to each of them twice a week, on Tuesdays and Fridays, giving them virtually a diary of her life in the munitions factory, high above the assembly shop. They did not – they *could not*, of course – reply to her with that regularity but she did not mind. What was important was that they should know that she remained theirs and that they were always in her mind and heart.

She tried to describe to them the thrill she got every morning when she docked her ticket in the clocking-in machine, exchanged cheery greetings with the fellows and girls on the shop floor and the other crane drivers and then, with a wiggle of her bottom that she could not suppress, climbed the thirty-five rungs on her ladder and entered her tiny domain. It was completely enclosed in glass and she could hardly move inside it, for the cabin was small and cluttered with levers. But she had a thrilling view over that vast shed, where the shells, ranging from eight inches to twelve in circumference – the latter reaching up to her waist at floor level – stood vertically, like grossly fat stalks in a cornfield, stretching, it seemed, almost as far as the eye could see. The girls on the amatol line, the 'canaries', now wore surgical masks but, underneath them, their cheeks and teeth were still coloured. Polly was glad that she was up near the roof, where the shells appeared to have a strange, smooth beauty, not down there, where the chemical was a reminder of the role to be played by the things. Her crane was definitely *hers* now. She knew its little idiosyncrasies and had learnt to master them. Now it did exactly what she demanded: sliding along smoothly on its high track, moving its long arm over the stubbly shell field below, graciously bending it down to hook up with the net and then slowly, cautiously swinging its deadly cargo over to the despatch bay. So powerful, so satisfying!

She did not write of the only intrusive element in her life at the factory. George Wagstaffe was her foreman. He was a good-looking man in his early thirties with wavy black hair that he treated with pomade so that it shone. He protested – too often and too loudly – that he wished he was at the front but that his was a reserved occupation and his employers refused to spare him. When Polly had joined, it had been Wagstaffe, of course, who had squeezed into the tiny cabin and showed her the controls, pressing his leg against hers and leaning across her breasts to operate the levers. He was a married man with two children, but he made no secret of his admiration of her. So far, she had resisted all his offers of 'a quick little drink after work, just to relax', but she had to admit that she was beginning to find him attractive in an animalistic kind of way. For all kinds of reasons, then, she was glad that Jim was coming home on leave. His presence would put things into context.

Polly managed to switch her shift so that she could be at New Street Station on the evening that Jim arrived from London. She had retrieved the black straw hat with the roses for the occasion (such a pleasure to do up her hair properly after wearing that scarf for so long!) and wore her best and brightest summer dress, although it was still spring. She had no illusions about the life that her two boys were leading out in Flanders. Their letters were not particularly descriptive but she read the newspapers and she knew about the constant bombardments, the gas and, increasingly now, the mud. For Jim, she wanted to appear fresh and young. And, she had to confess to herself, she was stirred by the prospect of seeing him again.

She was alone to meet him at the station because he had discouraged his mother and father from coming, saying that he was unsure of the train he would catch from Euston and that he would see them at home. Polly was glad about that, for she wanted him all to herself for the meeting. Even so, she was apprehensive when, in a cloud of steam, the locomotive emerged from the long tunnel that led into the station.

About half of the arrivals were servicemen, carrying kitbags on their shoulders, and at first she could not see Jim. Then, he loomed out of the steam, looking about him anxiously, and she ran to him, her long skirt swishing in the dust of the platform, and sprang into his arms. He held her for a moment, then gently pushed her away so that he could look at her.

Inspecting him in response, she realised that he had changed. He seemed thinner and somehow taller than she remembered and she had to stand on tiptoe to kiss him. It was his eyes, however, that disconcerted her. They were set more deeply in his face, now, and the sockets were dark. It gave his face a superficially melancholy look and, she acknowledged to herself, made him seem more handsome than before. She kissed him again, chastely, and held her hand to his face. He had shaved badly and he coughed as she touched him.

'Oh, my dear. You look tired.'

The cough came again. 'Yes. Sorry. It's been a bit of a bad time recently. We're all right, though. Just a touch of a cough from the gas, you see.'

She smiled. How typical that he should say 'we'. 'How is Bertie?' she asked.

'Same as ever. Well, not quite the same. I think he's getting a bit low, because of the conditions out there. But he's all right really. He sends his love and hopes to get leave soon. Perhaps in about a couple of months or so, if he doesn't punch the sergeant major.'

'Good. Your mum and dad are fine and are waiting for you back home, of course. But...' she cast down her eyes, 'I wondered if perhaps you might like to have a cup of tea or something before we go home?'

His brown eyes sparkled for a moment, just as they used to. 'No,' he said, and her face fell immediately and then lifted again as he went on: 'No. I've got a better idea. I've developed a bit of a taste for wine. The French stuff. There's a Yates's Wine Lodge nearby, isn't there? Let's go there, shall we?'

She nodded enthusiastically and he shouldered his kitbag and they walked through the throng out of the station. He did not seek her hand but eventually she took his arm and he didn't seem to mind.

Outside they stopped in front of a large poster. 'Good God,' he said. 'What's this?'

The headline shouted 'RED CROSS OR IRON CROSS?' Underneath, the poster depicted a wounded British soldier lying with a supplicatory hand stretched out to a German nurse who tantalisingly poured water onto the ground in front of him. In the background two fat German officers watched and laughed. The copy ran: 'Wounded and a prisoner, our soldier cries for water. The German "sister" pours it on the ground before his eyes. There is no woman in Britain who would do it. There is no woman in Britain who will forget it!'

Jim took in the contents slowly and then said

softly, 'That's rubbish.'

'What?'

He turned to her. 'I've not been captured, of course, but I know blokes whose brothers were wounded and taken. They've written home to say how well they were looked after. We look after their wounded, too. This stuff is rubbish.' He went on, suddenly animated. 'You know, Pol, the Germans are good soldiers, very brave, but really just like us. They're miserable and scared to death, just like us.' Then he frowned. 'Except those bastards ... ah, sorry. The blokes who invented the gas and sent it over to us. They were a disgrace. A disgrace...' His voice tailed away. 'Sorry.'

Polly slowly nodded and pressed his arm tightly against her. 'Don't say sorry. You've got nothing to say sorry about. Come on. Let us have that glass of wine. And I will pay with my filthy earnings from the war. Come on, love. Don't worry.'

They found a corner and were served glasses of a red wine that Jim had never heard of. 'We get it cheaper over there,' he said sheepishly. 'Sorry.'

'Stop saying sorry. It doesn't matter. I can afford it now.' He had not sought her hand but left his lying on the table. She reached across and enfolded it in both of hers. 'Tell me about Bertie.'

He grinned. 'I think he's getting a bit fed up with the war and, like me, he got a whiff of the gas, but he's all right really. Very popular with the blokes.' He looked away shyly for a moment.

'I said he'd sent his love. Well, he didn't.' Polly's eyebrows rose. 'No, he didn't. Instead he asked me to tell you that he loves you more than ever. He gets a bit emotional, you know.' He returned his gaze to her.

Polly thought that his brown eyes were the most beautiful she had ever seen in a man. She looked away and then up at him through her eyelashes. 'You never get like that, do you? You never say things like that.'

Jim blushed. 'Well, no. I'm, er, not quite... I get sort of, you know...' He fixed his eyes fiercely on a port wine advertisement on the wall behind her head. 'I get sort of embarrassed with that sort of stuff. Not like Bertie.' Then he gripped her hand. 'But I love your letters. Thank you for sending them.'

They sipped their wine in silence and Polly wondered anew about what on earth she could do with these two men. Looking at Jim now, the long, haggard face, the fine eyes set in those dark pits, she felt a stirring within her, an arousal that was new, in its way. She had always loved him, as she loved Bertie, but this was different, more carnal, and it was her turn to feel embarrassment.

She leant over and touched the ribbon on his chest. 'Jim, you did so well to win your medal. We were all so proud of you – the whole street. Even Mr Jones, whose apples you used to pinch, said that you were always a fine lad, really.'

Jim grinned. 'Good old Jonesey. I really didn't do much to get the gong. Nothing out of the ordinary, really. No more than Bertie. But he's

137

so small they didn't notice him. Come on. Let's have another. My shout this time.'

In all, they drank four glasses of wine each and Polly felt distinctly cheerful and very, very affectionate as they walked arm in arm to catch their tram in Corporation Street. She snuggled up to him on the hard wooden bench.

'How long have you got, Jim?' she asked.

'Fourteen days, but I've lost a day and half of that already, in the travelling.'

She made a sudden decision. 'Look. Now don't be shocked, but I have an idea.' She giggled at the audacity of it. 'I'm working long twelve-hour shifts at the moment, so we can't see much of each other.'

Jim's face fell.

'No. That's all right. You must spend time with your dear old mum and dad anyway – and I expect you want to call in at the jewellery works, eh?'

He nodded glumly.

'But, look.' Her voice dropped. 'I've got some holiday owed to me. If they will let me off for three days or so in your second week – and I'll create a hell of a row if they don't – why don't we go away together? Somewhere not far. Say Malvern or the Welsh hills. I've never been. What do you say, Corporal?'

Consternation sent his eyebrows shooting up. 'What? Just the two of us? Away?'

She dug him in the ribs. 'Absolutely right. Sort of ... er ... get to know each other, sort of thing. What do you say?'

'But what will your mum and dad say – and

what will mine?'

She sighed. 'Well, now, Jim. You're supposed to be a brave man. You've got a medal to prove it. I should think you could handle that, couldn't you?'

'You mean, just the two of us together?'

'Golly, Jim. You're quick. Yes. Just the two of us. Away. Together.'

A slow smile began to spread across his features. 'Pol, you're a card and no mistake.' He spoke slowly now. 'That ... would ... be ... lovely.'

She snuggled up even more closely. 'Now, we'll have to plan it properly. We will say to our folks that it's just a break for you, away from the front. Nothing improper about it. Separate rooms and all that. I'll find somewhere nice for us to stay. I think Malvern would be good. It sounds nice and respectable and it would be lovely to walk on the hills there. Always wanted to go.'

Polly detected a sudden tension within him.

'Ah yes, of course,' he said. 'Separate bedrooms. Yes, of course.'

She sighed again. 'Jim, my love,' she said softly. 'We would *say* that but we wouldn't bloody well do it. We would have one bedroom, see?' And she looked up at him through her eyelashes again.

Slowly his face relaxed. 'Yes, of course. Of course. I always knew that's what you meant. Yes, right. Of course.'

The plan did not go through without some opposition. Wagstaffe immediately said that it would be impossible for her to have time off so soon. So she went to see Mr Miller, who smiled.

'We can manage without you for three days, love,' he said. 'Go and see your chap.'

Her mother and father were undoubtedly shocked at the proposition. But she played the card that Jim, blasted for nine months by shot and shell, needed recuperation in the green countryside and that she was going to look after him. There would be nothing improper. He was, after all, Jim. If it had been another man, a *new* man, of course she would not have been able to get away with it. But Jim was her childhood friend. Her *friend*. A hero. He needed – he *deserved* – her help. So she was allowed to go.

Exactly a week after first proposing the trip, they booked into a little boarding house, high on the Malvern hills, with a view from the bedroom to the west that seemed to take in all of Wales. Without mentioning the matter to Jim, Polly had bought a cheap 'gold' wedding ring from Woolworths and, with a red face, Jim booked them in as Mr and Mrs Hickman. If their widowed landlady had doubts – they were, after all, ridiculously young – the medal ribbon on Hickman's uniform quelled them.

In the bedroom, with its large, brass bedstead and giant, old-fashioned wardrobe, they awkwardly unpacked their respective cases and Jim hung away his uniform. Then, suddenly, he swung round and took her in his arms and kissed her.

'About time,' said Polly.

He hung his head. 'Yes, well, you know ... I always...' His voice died away. Then he looked up at her. 'Polly, have you ever ... you know...?'

140

She gave a histrionic scowl. 'Certainly not. What sort of girl do you think I am? More to the point, have *you*? Out there with all those French women, to be had, if what I hear in the factory is right, for about five francs a go? Well, James, have you?'

'Of course not. Neither has Bertie.'

She winced. 'Jim. Bertie has nothing to do with it for the next three days. Right?' Her voice softened. 'It's just you and me, isn't it?' She kissed him gently. 'While we are on the subject, my love, did you bring any thingumajigs?'

He nodded glumly. 'Don't know how to use the bloody things, though.'

'Well, we will just have to learn, my hero, won't we?'

They both laughed and he put his long arms around her and swirled her around the room until they both fell on the bed, laughing.

They walked to the local pub that evening, a picture postcard inn with thatched roof and, although it was spring and comparatively warm, a blazing log fire. They drank the only bottle of wine the landlord had – 'Don't get much call for it round here, son'– and ate ham and eggs and fried potatoes. Then, hand in hand, they walked back to their cottage.

That night they made love. It didn't begin well, in that Jim put on the condom before he was erect, so that the thing trailed like an old sock, reducing them both to helpless laughter. Then, inexpertly but tenderly and with increasing passion, they 'got to know each other', as Polly put it, and they lay in each other's arms until first light, when they made love again. 'It's called "standing to" in the army,' explained Jim and they laughed again. Old army habits died hard and Jim rose early and took some fresh air. Polly stayed in bed a little longer and, not for the first time, thought of Bertie...

The next two days were idyllic. They walked the hills of Malvern, those strange, green humps that stood up so unexpectedly from the plains of Worcestershire. They picnicked where Elgar had bicycled and they breathed in good air, so different from that of both Birmingham and the Ypres Salient. They made love in the afternoons on the grassy slopes and at night between the clean white sheets of the cottage. They exhausted the sparse supply of contraceptives that Jim had purchased but the nearest chemist was miles away and they didn't care. It was a time of pure escapism for them both.

For Jim Hickman it was not reality. Reality was the trenches, discomfort, danger and death. The real life was the latrine trench, lice in his shirt seams, the dread of the trench mortar and the enemy: the Germans and Sergeant Black Jack Flanagan. A bountiful Providence – not the malicious being that orchestrated the hell of the Salient – had granted him these few days of paradise. They were certainly not real. Malvern was a magical land where his love was consummated every day and he could breathe deeply and freely. He didn't understand it but nor did he want to examine it too closely in case it just disappeared. Malvern was Polly.

Polly Johnson shared much of this feeling of

magical escape. Once, as a little girl, her parents had taken her on a week's summer holiday to Abersoch in North Wales, where she had played on the sands and paddled in the sea. But otherwise, she had never left Birmingham, except for the occasional excursion to the brown, trodden paths of the old landmark Barr Beacon, which could be glimpsed from Whitehead Road, round the corner from their house. Malvern, then, was a rural surprise, with views that contained not one factory nor tall chimney stack and where the air on the top of the hills stimulated her whole being. As did Jim. Jim! She had become a woman with him and her fulfilment made her body tingle. And yet. And yet... By giving herself to him, had she made a commitment that could not be escaped? Did she *want* to escape?

By the third day, when they silently packed their bags, thanked their landlady and made their way to the little country station, Polly realised that her impulsive decision to emancipate them both had not broken the bonds that tied her, not only to Jim but to Bertie also. Jim, Bertie and Polly. They were still together. She loved Jim and their few days *à deux* had strengthened her love. But not, she realised, half sadly, to the exclusion of Bertie. He remained as much a part of her as did Jim, her first lover. How, oh how, was she going to resolve this dilemma? And had their idyll changed Jim, who had always seemed so happily acquiescent in the triangular relationship?

The answer came when they arrived back in Birmingham, the day before Jim was due to return to the trenches.

He suggested that, before going home, they should take a glass of wine – their other new passion – in Yates's Wine Lodge. They found the table they had first occupied on his arrival and, after the first sip of wine, Jim fumbled in his pocket.

'I've got something for you,' he said. He produced a scrap of tissue paper, inside of which was a small lump of plasticine. Embedded in the clay sat a small diamond. It sparkled and dazzled in the dim light.

'You mentioned that I should go to my old workplace.' He spoke shyly again, as though they had never been intimate. 'Well, I did. I went last week. But not to see my old mates, but to buy this.' He carefully lifted it from its bed and picked away fragments of the clay with his thumb. 'It's not mounted, of course, Pol, but I can do that on my next leave.' He spoke hurriedly now, as though anxious to make a sale. 'I'll find a good gold ring and you can choose a mounting for it: platinum, plain gold or whatever. I can do it for you. Look.' He held it up and rotated it. 'See how it reflects the light.' He handed it to her.

Polly realised that her jaw had sagged. She gulped and took the stone and put it into the palm of her hand, where it sat, like a reproach. 'Oh Jim. I don't know what to say. It's lovely. It's … it's…' She sought for words, something, anything that would buy her time to think. 'It must have cost a fortune. How could you afford this on army pay?'

He gave a slightly embarrassed grin. 'Oh, I've got savings. And I got it at trade price, of course.' He hurried on quickly. 'It'll look better when it's mounted and on the ring, of course.' He paused and the shyness came back. 'When it's finished, it'll be an engagement ring, Pol.'

She looked at him, still thinking quickly, still at this last minute trying to make up her mind. But she could not resist one last, gentle push. 'So, Jim...?'

He looked over her shoulder again. 'Er ... um ... well ... Pol...' Then it came out in a gush. 'Pol, I love you and I want us to get married. Particularly after these last few days. It was, well, all so lovely. I know you're fond of Bertie, Pol, but I would make you happy. Honest I would. When the war's over I would have a good job and, and...' He tailed away. 'I thought you'd say yes, Pol. Particularly, after ... you know.'

She felt the tears rush to her eyes. She seized his hand. 'Oh, I do love you, Jim. And what happened during the last three days was wonderful but it made no difference. I always loved you. But...' She paused and saw the look of desperation come into his eyes as she hesitated, and she tightened her grip on his hand. 'I don't think I want to get married yet. We are both only nineteen and this blasted war is making such a change to all our lives.' She picked up the diamond and put it to her lips. 'This is lovely and I love you ever so much, Jim, I really do. You know I have never been with another man...'

Jim looked up quickly. 'Bertie?' he asked.

Polly sighed. 'No. Not even Bertie. You are the first. But, Jim, I have to be honest. I am in a mess. You see, I love you both, you and Bertie. I really do. I wish there was a way in which we could all live together. I know that that's impossible, so I think time is the answer. I really don't want pressure being put on me.'

They sat in silence and the chatter in the crowded bar somehow seemed to lessen, as though the other customers were looking on, listening in sympathy. Slowly, Jim reached out and took back the diamond. 'I didn't want to put pressure on you, Pol,' he said. But his voice was dull and his eyes heavy.

'Oh, Jim.' Now the tears began to trickle down her cheeks. 'I gave myself to you – I suggested we should go away – because I wanted to show you that I loved you ... that ... that there was love for you in the middle of this terrible war. Now I have hurt you. I don't want you to be hurt.'

A new certainty came to her. 'Look. Will you let me keep the diamond? You will not make it up into a ring and I will not wear it, nor show it to anyone. So we will not be officially engaged.' Her voiced faltered for a moment. 'If ... if you do meet someone ... someone else ... then of course you must have it back. But I shall treasure it and, when things have sorted themselves out, I will tell you and then,' she gave his hand another squeeze, 'I will be the happiest girl in the whole world.'

He gave a wry grin. 'And what about Bertie?'

She held his gaze. 'I cannot promise you that I will stop loving Bertie but I can tell you that I

146

know I will always love you. Time, Jim. Give us all time, my love. Won't you?'

He looked at her steadily, noting the way a long lock of hair had escaped from its pins under her workaday hat and was straggling in a soft wave to her shoulders; the way her green eyes were wide and pleading and the freckles on her high cheekbones were gleaming under the tears. He remembered the hair curling across her white shoulders as she lay back on the pillow. He gulped.

'Of course I will.' He carefully placed the diamond in its waxen cushion, wrapped the tissue paper around it and slipped a rubber band three times around the little package. Then he handed it to her. 'Take care of it, Pol,' he smiled. 'It was bloody expensive. All of half a crown.'

Then he grew serious. 'If something happens to me, then take it to the works and get it made up how you want it – brooch, pendant, ring, whatever, and wear it, please. I shall leave some money there so it won't cost you anything. They will understand.'

Too full of tears to speak, Polly nodded and placed the package carefully in her handbag.

Long before Polly had left for work the next morning, Jim Hickman had left the house next door and, that evening, he was back with his battalion in France.

That same day, in May 1915, a minister in the House of Commons answered a question from a pacifist member by denying that any sentence of death had been carried out in France on any member of His Majesty's forces. He was lying,

147

for records later revealed that, up until that time in 1915, twenty men had been shot at Le Havre rest camp for cowardice or desertion.

CHAPTER SIX

Jim returned to find his battalion in the middle of the line – a new line that had been established after fierce fighting in what had become the Second Battle of Ypres. The Germans had attacked with forty-two battalions, forcing the Allies to retreat, trench by trench, step by step, until the line now bulged scarcely two miles east of Ypres at its furthest point from the ruined town. In the first five weeks after that first gas attack, 60,000 men had been killed, wounded or were missing. Now, there was to be no more retreating.

The spring rains had replaced the cold and storms of winter and the whole of the Salient was now a complete quagmire. Nothing was left of the tilled fields, farmhouses and woods. Looking at it now, standing to in the early dawn, Hickman felt that Malvern must have been a dream. Reality had returned in all its sodden misery. Now, in the pocket that formed the Salient, the gravelly topsoil that used to filter away the moisture for the farmers had long since gone, leaving only a few inches of clay. The guns had turned the area into a swamp as well as a killing ground.

The fighting had been fierce during Hickman's absence, as a very depressed Bertie related. 'Ah, Jimmy,' he frowned and shook his head, 'the killin' was awful. There was us goin' at them over the top hell for leather and then comin' back with our noses all blooded and then them, comin' at us and us fightin' an' retreatin', fightin' an' retreatin'. Like some bloody – and I do mean bloody – gavotte, son. So it was. But enough of that. How was the lovely girl? I haven't had a letter for two weeks now, y'know.'

Jim immediately felt guilty. 'Ah well,' he muttered, 'she's working so hard at this crane driving business. She does twelve-hour shifts, you know.'

'Ridiculous. Our lass should be in a flower shop or something. She shouldn't be driving cranes up there, above all them shells. They should leave that to the wankers who haven't been called up. What's it they call it? "Reserved occupation", or somethin'. Ridiculous. Bloody ridiculous.'

'Has the shelling been bad?'

Bertie's blue eyes clouded. 'It's never stopped, Jimmy lad. It just keeps on going. You know, old Jerry is throwin' everythin' at us now– Ah...' The whistle of an approaching shell made them both duck. It exploded behind the line with a V-shaped eruption of mud. 'It's like that all the time now. The Germans now shell at night. If a working party just chinks a shovel on somethin', then down comes a barrage. And we're out most nights, repairing the wire an' the sandbags.'

149

'What about old Black Jack? Has he been bothering you?'

'Ah, that's the good news. The bugger has been transferred. I don't know where to and I don't want to know. Perhaps he'll come back but I hope not. I've got enough trouble with the bloody Germans. Now, come on. Tell me about Polly. How does she look? What did you do? Did she kiss you?'

As the wet dawn came up and they sat on the fire step, rifles and bayonets in hand, for the duration of the stand-to, Hickman dissembled as best he could. Looking at the intensity with which Bertie soaked up everything he told him about Polly, he felt ashamed of himself. He had stolen – was stealing – his best friend's girl. He realised that the relationship was no longer what it had been, open and shared. Now, although Bertie did not know it, it was bitter rivalry, although he must never reveal that he and Polly had made love. Jim blew out his cheeks. What a bloody pickle!

The intensity of the Second Battle of Ypres seemed to have run its course, at least for the moment, and the Salient settled down into the most depressing stalemate. The Germans still held the ridges that commanded the Ypres bowl and their guns ranged everywhere. Until the enemy could be removed from the ridges below the village of Passchendaele, the Allies could not advance. Nor, however, could they retreat, for there was nowhere for them to go. Rumour had it that the British command had even now set in hand an ambitious plan to blow up part of the ridges by tunnelling underneath them, using Welsh miners who were paid six shillings a day (Tommies earned a shilling a day). For the front-line troops, however, the misery continued.

It was not just the huge, long-range shells that intimidated and killed. These were called 'Jack Johnsons', after the crushing knockout punch of the American Negro who was reigning heavy-weight champion of the world. They were fright-ful but were mainly used for shelling behind the front line, reducing Ypres to a ruin where hardly one brick now stood upon another. Yet the sup-porting cast of shells and projectiles employed by the German artillery had a variety only matched by the names given them by the British troops: minnies (the *minenwerfers* or trench mor-tars), flying pigs, coal-boxes, flying torpedoes, flying fishes and the pip-squeaks.

Each had its distinctive sound. The rifle gren-ades, on the end of sticks and fired high, mortar-like, from conventional rifles, made a popping noise. The 4.2-inch shells made a sucking sound in mid flight; the big stuff emitted a 'phew-ew-em' sound, rising to a crescendo and passing over with a roar that sounded like an express train entering a station. Many of these projectiles were filled with shrapnel, jagged pieces of steel that could cut a man in half. Jim hated the coal-boxes most of all, for they could be seen wobbling and turning high in the sky before descending. Judging where they would land became a life-and-death game, ending in a rush round the traverses that buttressed the trenches at intervals, providing a zigzag that gave some protection. So strongly had the bombardments come to epitomise trench life that no one spoke any more about 'the end of the war', instead they said 'when the guns stop'. Death was 'when Jesus called you'.

Usually, a shell could be heard approaching and it would be possible to take some sort of cover, if it was only possible to crouch with the hands spread over the face, but it was different with rifle shots, particularly those fired by snipers. Jim and Bertie learnt that if you heard the shot, the bullet had passed by, so that it was pointless to duck. Rifle bullets in the open hissed into mud without much noise, but in the trench they cracked sharply as they passed overhead. If they struck the barbed wire in front of the parapet, however, they would 'ping' as they went in a head-over-heel motion, careering back high over the support trenches harmlessly.

Night became a period of great activity, when phantom figures would climb out of the trenches into no man's land to repair the damage done to the walls and parapets by the shelling, but also to bring in the dead that remained after the last attack. After a few days corpses swelled up and stank. Those that could not be retrieved from the German wire expanded until the walls of their stomachs collapsed, either naturally or from being punctured by a bullet. Disgusting smells would then float across. The colour of the dead faces lying in the mud changed from white to yellow-grey, to red, to purple, to green, to black to slimy. As the summer wore on, figures seemed to petrify in no man's land and would remain in a ghastly tableau, depicting what they were doing at the moment of death: stretcher-bearers bending over corpses that were once wounded men; wire cutters stretching their bony arms upwards; and officers stretched flat except for one arm upright, beckoning their men forwards.

In the absence of daylight attacks across open ground, patrolling no man's land during the hours of darkness became a strange macho substitute for both sides. The concept was to prevent a sudden night attack but patrols rarely confronted each other, passing like ghosts in the night, dropping flat but noting the other's presence. Exchanging fire in the dark, open land would have been fruitless, bringing down a barrage and prompting raking machine-gun fire.

The dangerous drudgery of life in the line was now compounded by a rise in the water level, meaning that the bottom of the trench could be as much as a foot deep and bringing on a condition known as 'trench foot', whereby the feet became swollen and black. It was not, however, considered to be serious and a reason for leaving the line. Bertie, in particular, suffered from it, but was told to stamp his feet and soldier on. He sniffed: 'The next time I stamp me foot it'll fall off – and I won't notice, so I won't.'

Rats were now their constant companions. Encouraged by the decomposing bodies in no man's land, they invaded the trenches and the dugouts, eating not just scraps of food but also webbing, knapsacks, socks and mud-plastered puttees. Killing them became a personal crusade for Bertie and he devoted considerable ingenuity to the task. He sprinkled creosote on the walls and floor of the little dugout he and Jim shared with other members of the section, but the smell was so overpowering that the cure was voted worse than the plague. He experimented with placing cordite at the entrance to the rat holes in the walls of the trench and dugout, lighting it and then smashing the beasts as they ran out. More bizarrely, he tried sticking a piece of bread on the end of his bayonet, fixing the bayonet to his rifle and leaving it, fully loaded, on the floor of the dugout. Then, when the rat pounced, he would fire the rifle, sending the beast to perdition. This was quickly condemned as being dangerous, so he resorted to old-fashioned methods, such as storming around the dugout, smashing away with an entrenching tool.

Jim took delight in describing Bertie's personal war against the vermin in his letters to Polly after his return. It was a way of avoiding the embarrassing question of his deep, burning love for her. Neither he nor Bertie, of course, exchanged Polly's letters between them, nor did they reveal what they wrote to her. For her part, Polly had quickly resumed writing her twice-a-week missives, giving news of the home front, of how women were now giving white feathers to young men in civilian clothes – some of whom turned out to be soldiers home on leave. In her letters to Jim, she made no mention of Malvern, nor even of his leave. Perhaps she felt that the boys shared her letters.

On his return to the front, Jim had experienced no change in his feelings towards Bertie. In his darkest moments, soon after Polly had declined his offer of marriage – for that's what it was – he felt that he really ought to hate his friend, the rival in his affections for the woman he loved. But it was impossible to feel that way about the little Irishman, the boy with whom he had grown up and shared everything, even the girl next door. They were friends – and now fellow sufferers in degrading and dangerous conditions. It would be a step towards barbarism to turn on his cheerful, vulnerable mate. Things were bad enough in Flanders without that.

That warmth was tested, however, when, shortly after Jim's return, Bertie announced that he had, at last, been granted leave. It was his turn for fourteen days of escape back to Blighty and he was taking it in a week's time.

'You know what I'm goin' to do, Jim lad?'

'No, Bertie. Turn out for Aston Villa? Punch Lord Kitchener?'

'Don't be daft. Better than that. There's a wonderful show running in London, *The Maid of the Mountains*. It's on at Daly's Theatre. I'm going to get Polly down to London to meet me and take her to it. She'll love it. There's a great song in it, you know. It goes,

"At seventeen, he falls in love quite madly,

With eyes of tender blue..."

Do yer know it, now?'

'Er ... I don't think I do.'

'Ah, everyone's singing it. An' it's my story, see, Jim lad. My story. I fell in love with Pol –

155

well, it was a bit before I was seventeen, actually, and her eyes are green, rather than blue – but I still feel it's our song. See?'

'Hmm.' Jim felt as though his heart had dropped six inches. 'Will you ... er ... be staying in London overnight, then?'

Bertie flashed gleaming white teeth out of the dirtiest face in Flanders. 'Oh, I'll say we will. I'll find a nice little place. Just for one night, y'see. Then back up to Brum.'

'But she might not be able to get the time off, and anyway, what about her parents?' Jim felt an utter hypocrite as he said the words, but he had to go on. 'She's only nineteen, you know. You're an old mate, of course, but even so... '

Bertie's eyes twinkled. 'Oh, we'll manage that. You'll see.'

On the eve of his departure, Bertie waved a telegram. 'She's done it! She's arranged it for the weekend. This Saturday, she'll meet me off the train in London. She's even bought the tickets. What a girl, eh?'

Jim clenched his teeth but forced a smile. He held out his hand. 'Go and have a great time, lad. And give her my love.'

That Saturday night he volunteered to take charge of the work party that crept out after dark to effect essential repairs to the trench. As they toiled in the mud, uncoiling wire that insisted on springing back as soon as it was released, cutting fingers as it resisted all attempts to wind it round the posts, he forced his mind not to think about what might be happening in London, in some small hotel there, near the theatre. He told himself that he didn't care but he swore at the clumsiness of the men and kept them out, sandbagging and wiring, until nearly dawn.

While Bertie was away, new gas masks were issued. The original flannel belts had been replaced by a gauze pad fitted with chemically treated cotton waste, for tying across the mouth and nose. But they had proved ineffective against renewed gas attacks and they were replaced by a 'smoke helmet', a greasy grey-felt bag with a talc window and no mouthpiece. These were cumbersome, no more sophisticated and lasted only a few weeks before the new issue of what everyone immediately called the 'google-eyed-booger with the tit', with air breathed in through the nose from within the tight-fitting rubber mask and exhaled from a special valve within the teeth. Jim heard that gas was still being used by the Germans in other sections but thankfully he saw no evidence of it in his part of the Salient. The war was horrible enough there, without the return of that particularly ghastly form of warfare.

He forced himself to write to Polly while Bertie was away. His letters had always been stoically cheerful but this time he allowed a touch of melancholy and frustration to creep into the lines. Indeed, it was a fair reflection of conditions in the trenches. The dangers of replacing troops in the front line had now grown. The marches in the darkness to and from Ypres had now become frightful stumblings as everyone tried to avoid slipping off the slimy duckboards that picked out a kind of pathway between the shell holes. With distant star shells providing the only illumination

– even a glowing cigarette end could bring down a barrage – it was almost impossible to keep a footing. Yet to tread off the boards could end in a desperate slide down into the slime of a shell crater. Men were now drowning in these holes, for the mud in the depths was glutinous and seemingly bottomless. The whole of the Salient was a bog. As a result, troops were forced to serve longer in the line without relief – two, three, and sometimes four weeks without a break. And this meant going without a wash or proper food for that time.

Normally, Jim tried not to sound despondent in his letters but the thought of Bertie and Polly at the theatre – and then *in bed together!* – was too much. He made no reference at all to Bertie's visit but simply painted her a picture of what life was like in the trenches: the shelling, the sniping, the mud, the lice, the rats, the chloride of lime in the water that made it taste of paraffin. He threw it all in onto the pages, posted the letter quickly and regretted it immediately.

Bertie returned, a mixture of elation and sadness, and Jim resisted any temptation to question him about his leave. Strangely, Bertie, who was usually so eager to talk, spoke little of it. Jim tortured himself as a result: was the little man cock-a-hoop at his sexual conquest of Polly and didn't wish to crow with his best friend, or had he failed and was he being morose as a result? Polly did not write to Jim until two weeks after Bertie's return, although Bertie received a letter. Then, she was solicitous of their life in the trenches as described in his letter, but made no reference to Bertie, except to say 'how nice' it had been to see him. Didn't the woman know the agony he was going through? Then Jim shook his head. This was getting ridiculous. He resolved to put Polly out of his mind as much as possible and concentrate on staying alive – and looking after Bertie.

Their life on this part of the front was being made particularly unpleasant by a nest of machine guns that the Germans had mounted at the edge of what had once been a wood and which was now protected against the British shelling by a sophisticated emplacement, apparently constructed of concrete. The guns had fixed sights along the duckboard tracks leading to the British trenches and the faintest sound at night produced a hail of bullets, even though the Germans could not see their targets. A flash of a helmet above the parapet during daylight hours similarly prompted a burst of accurate firing. British snipers had tried and failed at distance to put a bullet through the slits through which the guns were fired.

'The colonel won't stand for this,' confided Jim to Bertie. 'I feel a night raid coming on.'

And so it proved. Twenty men were detailed from their company to take part, including Jim and Bertie – Jim because he was now a respected, experienced NCO and Bertie because he had earned a reputation as a crack shot, although, as he was careful to point out to Jim, that wouldn't be of much use in the dark on a raid where the main weapons to be used were hand grenades.

Once again the raiding party was to be led by Smith-Forbes, now a captain with an MC after his name, and a new sergeant, George Fellowes, a man who had earned popularity with the men already for being firm but fair. Another corporal had been added to the party.

The party gathered together shortly before midnight on a moonless night, stripped down, as before, to sweaters, steel helmets and revolvers, but this time each man carried six grenades in special pouches.

'Bloody hell,' whispered Bertie, 'I know I shall crawl all over mine and pull the pins out. I just know it. This is going to be the noisiest raid ever, son.'

'Clip 'em round the back, like this.' Jim showed him how.

The captain began his briefing. They were to crawl under the wire, cut the German wire and get into their trench. While six men bombed their way along the trench, the other fourteen would attack the machine-gun emplacement behind the line and put it out of action with their bombs. Because of the size of the party, a diversion would be created about two hundred and fifty yards to the left of them by the mounting of a dummy attack on the German trenches, presaged by a minor bombardment.

'The German star shells will go up over that way,' said Smith-Forbes, 'not over us. The Hun will probably send troops along the line to what they think of as the point of attack and, with any luck, we should be able to slip in while all the fuss is going on to our left.'

'And pigs will surely fly,' murmured Bertie.

'Once we are in the trench,' continued the captain, 'Sergeant Fellowes will take his party – he will nominate you – bombing up the trench to the left to clear it, Corporal Jenkins will do the same to the right with his men, and I, with Corporal Hickman and the rest, will go on and attack the machine-gun nest. The idea, chaps, will be to put the guns and the gunners out of action by throwing grenades through the slits. Then we will get away as fast as we can. Right. Any questions?'

'Yessir.' Hickman was amazed at the sanguinity of it all. 'Are you saying that we charge directly into fire from three machine guns?'

'It's not as bad as it sounds, Corporal. As we near, you will see that the gun encasements are about twenty feet or so behind the trenches and – and this is the point – they are on the edge of the old wood and about fifteen foot or so *above* the trench. Because they are firing through slits in the concrete, they can't depress the guns downwards to fire at us up close without moving 'em. And we shall be on them before they can do that. All right?'

'Yes, thank you, sir.' Jim exchanged glances with Bertie. It all sounded far too easy.

'Ah well,' whispered Bertie. 'We've all got to die sometime.' But his face was white under its dirt.

Suddenly the night was broken by the crash of guns behind their lines as the bombardment began. At the same time, machine guns from the British line opened up far to their left. The

161

immediate response was a couple of German star shells that climbed lazily into the sky, again to their left.

The glow lit up the tight anxious faces of the raiding party for a moment. 'I thought there was supposed to be no bloody light on this side,' murmured Bertie.

The noise of the gunfire was deafening and Smith-Forbes had to shout now. 'Right, lads. I will lead, Sergeant Fellowes and his section will follow, then Corporal Jenkins and his lot, then Corporal Hickman and his men at the rear. At the German wire, Fellowes and Jenkins will cut it and toss in grenades to kill the sentries. I will hold the wire up and they will lead their parties in and clear the trench and hold it. Then the rest of us will go in quickly and attack the guns. After that, it's every man for himself. Above all, we must be quick. Speed is the essence of this raid. We must clear the trench and put the guns out before the German support troops come up. It's all got to be done in about five minutes. All right? Good. Ah, one last important point. The password for tonight when you approach our trench on return is "Newmarket". Got it? Very well. Follow me and good luck.'

In sequence, the party climbed up the trench ladder and they all squirmed under the wire and began the crawl across no man's land. The noise continued on their left and was now joined by the chattering of enemy machine guns in reply, who were obviously expecting a night attack in some force. The guns that were the raiders' target, however, remained silent.

At the rear, Jim Hickman crawled after Bertie, close behind his friend's muddy heels and his face a few inches above the mud. As ever, the smell of decayed, mulched bodies turned his stomach but he was more concerned, as he watched the little man's grenades bounce up and down on his buttocks, that one would be dislodged and lose its pin. Ahead, he could dimly make out the captain's helmet disappear and then appear again as he negotiated the shell craters, for it was no longer possible to crawl across no man's land in a steady line. He realised that, as Bertie had pointed out, the enemy star shells that still climbed into the sky were near enough to cast some light over their section of the field and he prayed that the enemy sentries in the trench they were approaching were keeping their heads down.

As they neared the wire, he could see the machine-gun emplacements clearly enough. It was true that the barrels of the guns were not poking through their firing slits, but their muzzles were protruding *and they were slowly rotating from left to right!* He licked his dry lips. The gunners were, then, very much alert. Could they see the raiding party now and were they cleverly holding their fire until it would be impossible to miss? He shook his head and crawled on, noting that the British mini barrage was now fading away. Damn!

Now he could see the captain holding up the parted strands of wire and the shapes of Sergeant Fellowes and his men beginning to crawl through and, overtaking Bertie, he joined the others lying flat, waiting for the lead bombers to do their work. That would be the crucial point. If the machine-gunners could depress sufficiently to aim at the wire virtually under their noses, then those at the rear of the raiding party were as good as dead. Could he reach the emplacement with a thrown grenade from here? Might it deter the gunners? Unlikely. It was too far. He brushed the sweat away from his eyes, gritted his teeth and waited.

Expected as it was, the sudden explosions from the trench made him jump. He crawled to the wire and held up the cut edge, opposite the captain, to allow the other bombers to move through now, crawling as quickly as they could. He turned to his rear. 'Crawl up, for God's sake, Bertie,' he called. 'The guns could reach you there.'

Almost as he spoke, the chatter of the machine guns began, now frighteningly near, and he saw a row of holes appear in the mud as if by magic just behind Bertie's boots. With his free hand, he unclipped a grenade, pulled out the detonating pin with his teeth, waited for three seconds, then hurled it overhand in the general direction of the gun emplacement. Without looking to observe the effect, he waved through the captain and followed him, scurrying desperately as the machine-gun bullets hissed over his head, praying that Bertie was under the arc of their fire.

He levered himself over the trench parapet and tumbled onto the body of a German sentry. Two more lay groaning against the trench wall. Acrid smoke was issuing from the entrance to a dugout and a Tommy waved him away as he threw another grenade down the steps. To the left and right, the raiders were hunched by the traverses as, on the other side, their grenades suddenly exploded. Then, more grenades in hand, they scurried round the barriers to continue their attacks along the enemy trench.

'The ladder, quick, help me.' The cry came from Smith-Forbes, who was attempting to wrest the trench ladder away from the British side of the trench to prop it onto the other side. He rushed to help and found, to his relief, Bertie at his side. The three of them pushed the heavy steps to the opposite wall and followed the captain up the slippery rungs.

Six men in all emerged from the trench and looked up at the gun emplacement. It took the form of a wall of concrete that, as far as Hickman could see, had three sides, the front facing the British line immediately opposite and the other two, at angles of forty-five degrees, commanding the approaches obliquely. It was, in effect, a pillbox, for a concrete roof had been thrown across to give protection from artillery fire. Each wall contained a narrow slit through which projected the muzzle of a machine gun, spitting flame.

It was true, however, that their fire could not be depressed sufficiently to be directed at attackers up the slight slope that led to the fortress, for, although the guns blazed away, they were hitting only the already inert bodies of four of the attackers, sprawled on the far side of the German wire, too late to crawl through the gap before the guns got them.

'Where are the–' Smith-Forbes's question was stillborn as a bullet took him in the chest and he whirled round and fell onto his back, his arms spread wide.

'Rifles,' shouted Hickman. 'Through the slits. Spread out.'

He threw a grenade at the gun nearest him, as much to create a diversion as in hope of harming the gunners. It bounced off the concrete wall, fell to the earth and exploded with a satisfactory shower of mud and stones. Head down, Jim sprinted up the slope and slid to a halt at the base of the wall. As he fumbled for a grenade, he saw three of his party stagger and fall as the rifles picked them off. Bertie, however, arrived breathlessly at his side. He could hear the gun crews shouting inside the pill box.

'You take the slit on your left,' he said. 'I'll do this one. Move NOW!'

He plucked out the ring pin, waited three seconds then stood and deposited the grenade through the slit, as though he was posting a letter. He heard it explode inside the pillbox before crouching and running to the right, where he heard Bertie's grenade explode. With only three Mills bombs left he decided that he must save them for the escape, for surely no one could be alive within the emplacement. Bertie scurried back to him and they sat for a moment, their backs to the wall and their breasts heaving, looking down at the trench.

Rifle shots rang out from right and left within the trench but no further grenade explosions.

166

'We didn't bring rifles,' gasped Jim. 'Our lot must be wiped out. Where the hell, though, is the last man who came up with us?'

Bertie pointed. The last man lay to their left, only six feet or so from the redoubt, his head shattered by a bullet. 'It looks like we're the only two left, Jim. How the hell are we going to get out of here?'

'There's only one way. The way we came in. Come on, before the whole bloody German army comes back into the trench.'

They ran helter-skelter the short distance to the German trench, on the lip of which Hickman held up a hand and crouched. 'A grenade to the left and one to the right, just in case,' he gasped. 'NOW!'

They pulled out the pins and lobbed the bombs into the trench, lying flat, their hands over their ears, then, when the debris had fallen, they peered over the parapet. The trench was a scene of devastation. One wall had completely collapsed and bodies lay everywhere, British and German entwined in the final moments of death. It seemed that the remnants of the raiding party had been caught and mown down as they attempted to climb the trench wall on their return.

Jim pushed Bertie down. 'Get out of here,' he ordered, indicating where the trench wall had collapsed, near where the wire had been cut. 'Climb up there. Get as far out as you can and then dive into the nearest shell hole when all hell breaks loose. I'll try and give you cover.'

'What are you going to do?'

'Get going. Out as far as you can before the

lights go up. Go on!' And he gave him a push.

Bertie scrambled up the collapsed sandbags and rocks and squirmed under the wire. Slipping and sliding among the debris and bodies on the trench floor, Jim ran to the first buttress, where he lobbed a grenade over. Turning before it had exploded, he made his way to the other traverse, his revolver in hand. As the grenade exploded behind him, he was in time to see a bayonet-tipped rifle tentatively poked round the buttress. He dropped onto one knee and fired as the rifle's owner came into sight. The man dropped immediately, his shoulder shattered. Hickman pulled out the pin on his last grenade and threw it over the top of the traverse. Only when it had exploded did he scramble back to the collapsed trench wall and haul himself up and under the wire. He had just plunged head first down into a shell crater, using his hands as a brake to prevent him sliding into the slime at the bottom, before a star shell broke above his head, a searchlight suddenly began probing no man's land and a machine gun began stuttering and raking the top of the German trench.

'Thank the blessed Mother that you made it,' said Bertie, from the opposite lip of the crater.

'Stupid bugger. You should have been halfway across no man's land by now.'

'I was just coming back to give you a hand up the wall when you started to blow everything up. In truth, Jimmy, all this killin' is shakin' me, so it is.'

'Well let's hope Fritz doesn't send a party out

168

to get us. But perhaps we haven't been seen. There was so much going on that I think most of them would have had their heads down.' He gave a sad grin. 'That was the intention, anyway.'

'Ah, Jim. You did well.'

'Well let's hope they believe they killed us all. They damned nearly did.'

They fell silent for a moment. Then Bertie said quietly, 'They was a fine lot of men, that came out with us. Particularly the officer. A good feller.'

'That's true.' They crouched in silence for a little longer. Then, 'Bertie.'

'Yes, Corporal, sir.'

'Do you remember the code word for getting through our wire?'

'Yes, course I do. It's Aintree.'

'Ah, thanks very much. Now I remember it. It's Newmarket. Fine lot of help you are.'

'Ah well, I'm the only Irishman in the whole of Birmingham who never went racing. And anyway, I can't do everything.'

By dint of waiting until the firing had ceased and the searchlight had switched off its probing beam, they finally made their way back to the British lines. It took them some time, for dawn was beginning to send pink exploratory fingers out over the horizon to the east as they reached the wire. A sergeant major gave them both steaming cups of tea, which they held in trembling hands.

'Did any of the others get back, sir?' asked Jim. The warrant officer shook his head and

169

gnawed at his moustache. 'Not on this bit of the line, son. I'm surprised anyone made it. You put up quite a show over there and those machine guns certainly haven't fired since you called on 'em. It looked as if the whole of their line was aflame. Well done, my lad. You'd better go and make your report to the colonel. But finish your tea first.'

Minutes later they stood before the CO in his crowded dugout. He indicated a trestle bed and they both sat down as Hickman made his report.

'You are the only survivors of the raiding party?'

'Afraid so, sir. The captain and about half of our men got caught as we ran up to the guns. They couldn't get the machine guns low enough to fire but they had rifles. Then the others caught it after they had bombed up the trench. They must have run out of grenades and the Jerries counter-attacked as they were trying to climb up the trench wall. They were all killed.'

The colonel ran his fingers across his eyes. 'Good men, all good,' he muttered, his head down.

The adjutant, his hair tousled by sleep, interjected, 'Have you two had any tea or anything?'

'Yes, thank you, sir. When we got back to the line.'

The colonel lifted his head. 'Do you think you put the guns out of action?'

'Oh yes. We put two grenades through the slits and it was only a confined space. Everyone inside would have been killed and the guns would certainly have been destroyed. The sergeant

170

major down the line confirmed that they hadn't fired since and they won't now. I can tell you that, sir.'

The CO stood up and held out his hand. 'Well done, the pair of you. Go and get some breakfast. You might have difficulty in getting sleep, I'm afraid, because there is bound to be a bit of retaliation from our neighbours, so it will be noisy. But congratulations. I'll see you get sent down the line as soon as I can arrange it.'

Bertie summoned up his brightest beam. 'Ah, that would be nice, Colonel, so it would. Thank you very much.'

The colonel was prophetic about the noise. A barrage was immediately summoned and it continued for most of the day. Shortly after dusk a night attack was tried by the Germans but the colonel had ensured that the battalion had stood to through the night and the attack was rebuffed with no casualties on the British line, although the shelling had killed six men during the daylight hours.

Bertie and Jim were summoned to see the colonel the next morning.

'Normally,' he said, 'I would have recommended both of you for a decoration. Unfortunately,' and he gave a wry smile, 'army regulations in their stupidity tell me that I can only do so on the recommendation of an officer who witnessed the act of bravery. As you know, Captain Smith-Forbes perished, so I am afraid I cannot make the recommendation. The least I can do, however, is to promote you. You, Corporal, will be made up to sergeant with immediate effect and, similarly, you, Murphy, will become a lance corporal. It's not sufficient, I fear, but it's the best I can do. Congratulations again.'

They shook his hand again and wearily – for they had had no sleep for the second night in succession – they made their way back to their section in the line and sat exhausted on the firing step.

Bertie took off his steel helmet and ran his fingers through his hair. 'To tell you the truth, Jim lad,' he said, 'Stripe or no stripe, I am not sure that I can take much more of this.'

Jim looked at him sharply. 'Now, come on, Bertie. It's the same for all of us. We didn't start this bloody war but we've got to see it through. Jerry must be suffering just as much as we are.'

'Yes, but I don't see how the blessed Lord can allow all this misery to go on.' The blue eyes were now beginning to fill with tears. 'All this killin' and stuff, yer know. I was always taught "thou shalt not kill", and here I am killin' all the bloody time. Now I've been made a lance corporal because I am getting good at it. It's not as though it's doing any good. We kill them but they still keep coming at us. It's all so pathetic and so–'

He was interrupted by a mighty roar from a familiar voice. 'And what do you two think you're doing, lounging about as though you're sittin' out at the bloody 'unt ball, eh?'

'Oh bloody hell,' said Bertie. 'Sergeant Flanagan!'

'Oh no.' He strode towards Bertie and held up

172

his sleeve so that the badge on it brushed his nostrils. 'Address me properly, you papist arsehole. "Sergeant Major" to you, sonny. Company sergeant major. I've been sent back to look after you – and by God I'm going to see to it, I can tell you. Get up on the fire step. You're on lookout duty.'

Hickman took a step forward. 'We've been out on patrol the night before last, Sergeant Major,' he said, 'and up standing to last night. We're due some shut-eye. We're dead beat.'

A look of exaggerated sympathy crossed the leathery features. 'Ah, diddums. Did the nasty Germans keep you awake, then? Oh dear. Oh dear.' Then the bellow: 'Get up on that fire step and keep him company, Hickman.' He put his moustache close to Jim's ear and breathed into it. 'I haven't forgotten you, sunshine. I'm going to make your life hell. See if I don't.'

CHAPTER SEVEN

Wagstaffe, his hair shining as brightly as his shoes, approached Polly as she reported for work. She was not feeling well and the last thing she wanted was to have to fend off the foreman's advances that morning.

'Hello, sweetheart,' he said, attempting to put his arm about her.

'Piss off.' Polly did as good an impression of a flounce as she could muster that day and thrust him aside to put her card into the clocking machine.

'Now, just you listen, Miss Polly Johnson.' Wagstaffe looked around to ensure that no one was within hearing distance and dropped his voice slightly. 'I'm not the sort of bloke you think I am, but I can make things very difficult for you if you continue to be rude to me, you know. I am your foreman, after all.'

Polly sighed. 'Then just get on with your job and let me get on with mine. There's a war on, you know.'

She attempted to push past him but he put his arm out and leant against the wall to deny her. 'Oh come on, Polly.' He smoothed his clipped black moustache. 'I'm not so bad when you get to know me. Why don't you and me have a little chat together over a gin and it tonight, eh? Just an hour and no monkey business. We all deserve a break in this bloomin' war, I reckon. What do you say?'

'I say, Mr Wagstaffe, that you've got a wife and two kids and I've got a boyfriend risking his life in mud in Flanders. So please stop bothering me or...'

Her voice tailed away and he sneered. 'Or what, Miss Nose-in-the-Air? I'm highly thought of here and you can't say anything that will threaten my job, I'll tell you. But, I warn you, miss, that you are very expendable in your job, oh yes, very expendable.'

Tears suddenly came to Polly's eyes. She thrust him aside roughly. 'Oh, get out of my way.'

Climbing the ladder to her cabin she felt dizzy

174

and had to stand still halfway up, clutching the handrail firmly until she regained her composure. She was still there thirty seconds later, waiting until her head cleared, when she heard a call from down below.

'Pol, don't move. I'm comin' up after you. Stay still.' A moment later she felt the firm hand of Connie Walters, her friend from the assembly line, pressing the middle of her back forward onto the ladder. 'Wait a minute or two,' said Connie. 'Then come back down the ladder. I'm just underneath you and I'll support you.'

'No, Con, I'm all right, really I am. Just a bit dizzy.'

'Do as you're told. Breathe deeply and then, when you're ready, follow me down slowly.'

She relented and began slowly to descend, feeling very self-conscious and aware that a hundred eyes were watching from down below – probably including those of Wagstaffe. On regaining the concrete floor, she realised that perspiration was beginning to form on her forehead. 'I think I need to have a pee, Con,' she said.

'Yes, luv. Come on. Lean on me.'

Together they made their way to the ladies' toilets, a harsh environment, kept starkly functional to deter the factory girls from lingering to have a cigarette within its unpainted concrete walls. She sat on the lavatory seat and put her head in her hands and accepted the cup of water handed to her by Connie, a large woman in her late twenties, with the pallor and yellow teeth of the 'canaries'.

Connie regarded her in silence for a few moments, then squatted down before her and asked gently, "Ow long since you had your last period, love?'

Suddenly, Polly's shoulders heaved and the tears ran down her cheeks. She grabbed a piece of toilet paper and tried to stem them but they continued. She shook her head. 'I don't know. I just don't know.'

'Think, dearie. You will know. Take your time.'

Polly blew her nose and thrust the hair away from her eyes. 'Well, I am late, I know.'

'Do you feel a bit sick?'

'Yes. Last few mornings.'

'Yes, then. There you are. You must be careful goin' up an' down that bloody ladder. You 'ad a bit of love, then, did yer?'

Mutely, Polly nodded.

'An' yer not married, are yer?'

'No.'

'Does 'e know about it?'

She shook her head, the tears still cascading down her cheeks.

'Are you goin' to tell 'im?'

'Oh, I ... I ... don't know.'

'Yes, well, luv, you'd better 'ave a think about it. I think you should tell yer mother, though...'

'Oh no!'

'Well, Pol, you're goin' to need a bit of 'elp and yer mother's the best person to give that. And you ought to make sure, with a doctor, although if you're *sure certain*, then you don't need to.' Connie creaked upwards. 'God, these knees of mine are givin' me gyp. I think it's the screws.

176

Me mother 'ad them so I suppose it runs in the family.' She ran a kindly hand through Polly's hair and pulled it back from her forehead. 'I shall 'ave to get back to the line or I'll lose me money. Why don't you go 'ome now, luv, and lie down for a bit and think it over? I'll tell old Waggy that you've got a touch of the flu and if 'e argues I'll twist 'is balls.' She gave a lewd grin. 'Mind you, 'e likes that.'

Polly summoned up a smile. 'Thanks, Connie. No. I'll be all right now, thanks ever so much. I'll just clean up a bit and get up in my cabin. I know I'll be all right now.'

'As you wish.' Connie turned at the door. 'Will you keep it, d'yer think?'

'Oh, I just... I don't know.'

'No. Silly of me to ask. Too early. Mind you...'

Her voice tailed away. Polly looked up quickly. 'Yes?'

'If yer do want to lose it, I know someone. 'Ad to use 'er meself seven years ago before I met Albert.' She wrinkled her nose. 'It's not nice but it works. And ... no one needs to know. I'll be around if you want me. Good luck, luv.'

Polly washed her face thoroughly, pushed up her hair and pulled her scarf tightly around it. Then she took a deep breath and walked across the floor to the ladder and mounted it quickly. Once in her familiar cabin, her glass fortress, she nodded down below to where one of the men was waiting, pushed forward a lever to glide the crane along on its track and thrust all thought of a child out of her mind – for just three minutes.

Then, as she manipulated the crane and its long arm through the morning, she kept returning to Connie's questions. It had pressed in on her yesterday that something was wrong. She was never late and her period arrived usually like some form of alarm clock. This was the second one she had missed. Now she knew. She was pregnant. There was no hiding it from herself now. She was certain and she didn't need a physician to confirm it. She was carrying a child. She put a trembling hand to her mouth and bit her fingers. But who was the father?

She had given way to Bertie that night in London as she knew she would. It would have seemed grotesquely unfair not to have done so, given the deep warmth that she felt for him and the fact that she and Jim had made love a disgracefully short time before. Her eyes moistened again at the thought. They both so *deserved* to be given real, warm love, after what they had been through and what they were returning to. In a way, it was the least she could do. Bertie being Bertie, of course, had made no provision for contraception and she had allowed herself to be swept along with his passion, so very different from Jim's shy diffidence. Oh, and of course, she had loved it! God, did this make her a whore? She shook her head firmly. No, of course not. She loved them both. In fact, the loss of her virginity had done nothing at all to solve her problem. Her two boys had made love in entirely different but equally satisfying ways and her love for them both *equally* had deepened. Was there anyone else in this blasted war, she wondered, who could possibly be in a situation so damnably intractable as this? Now predictably – as she had worried since Bertie's departure – she was going to have a child. But whose?

One thing was certain, of course: it would mean marrying the father. Well, yes. That would make her decision for her. That would stop this shilly-shallying. Oh God! That would make up her mind all right. But who *was* the father? She frowned. Weren't you always supposed to know anyway, instinctively? She touched her stomach. No. Nothing moved and the foetus failed to respond as she pictured first the brown eyes and broad shoulders of Jim Hickman, then thrust them aside and summoned up Bertie Murphy's wicked smile and ridiculously blue eyes. Nothing. But then, most women didn't go to bed with two different men within a month. Unless, that is, she was a whore...! Then the tears flew again and she had to stop the crane to blow her nose.

But did they have to know? Did *anyone* have to know? Connie had opened an escape hatch – one through which she had climbed herself seven years ago. The thought made it more acceptable. Abortion was dangerous, she knew that, but it would remove the devilish necessity of having to make up her mind between her two lovers. She could postpone that decision and let fate take its course.

The more she thought of it the more the prospect became attractive. With this war seeming to continue for ever, was it right anyway to bring a child into a world dominated by shellfire, gas and lengthening casualty lists? And what – God forbid – if anything should happen to both Jim and Bertie? She would be left in a world with the awful responsibility of bringing up a fatherless child. Then she felt ashamed of herself. How selfish! Is that all she could think about if her two dear boys were to die? She felt as if she was going mad. She must control herself. She swallowed and put the crane into gear once again. She would just let things take their course for a few days more. After all – perhaps she wasn't pregnant? The world was full of false alarms. Her Auntie Edie had had so many longed for and ultimately false pregnancies that when she finally produced a child her father had refused to believe it! She began to feel better.

As the next few days passed, it became increasingly clear that she was, in fact, carrying a child. There was hardly a bump at all at this stage – nothing to stir suspicion at home – but it was there, she knew. The morning sickness was more difficult to conceal. She found a formula that served well enough for the moment: eating very little breakfast to hold back the nausea, vomiting in the public lavatory at the bottom of Witton Road on the way to work and buying an apple at the grocers to eat later in her cabin. This was all very short-term, however, and she knew that she would have to make a decision.

She sought out Connie.

'Is this woman still ... er ... practising, Con? It was a long time ago.'

'Are you sure, luv, that you want to lose it? For

all we both know, you may not be able to have another one when yer want it most.'

'Yes, I'm sure. I've thought it through. I don't want to have a baby at this stage in my life and I don't want to tie the father down, either.' She stifled a sob. 'It seems wicked, I know, but it's best all round to get rid of it. Does she still do it?'

'Oh aye. She's still at it. I don't know what it costs these days but I can find out for you. She's only just off Victoria Road. Shall I ask her?'

Polly took a deep breath. 'Yes please.' She looked at her shoes. 'I'm afraid I've only got about two quid saved. Will it be more than that?'

'Shouldn't think so. P'raps thirty bob. I'll see. Would you like me to come with you?'

Polly gripped her arm. 'I appreciate the offer, Con, but no thanks. I'll see this through on my own.' She drew in her breath. 'Does ... does it knock you about much?'

'A bit. But you get over it. She can do it at weekends or in the evening after work. That's probably best, so that you can go home straight to bed. I'll let you know.'

Six days later, Polly found herself knocking on the door of a terraced house in a street leading off Victoria Road. She felt alone, physically and metaphorically, and bit her lip at the sight of three five- or six-year-olds, two grubby boys and a little girl, playing tops on the pavement nearby. It could have been her with Bertie and Jim, not so very long ago.

The door was opened by a pleasant-faced, middle-aged woman wearing a clean apron.

'Hello, dear,' she said. 'All alone?'

Polly nodded, unable to speak.

'Ah well, better that way sometimes. Come on in and sit yourself down. You can call me Mrs Smith.' The room opened directly off the door to the street and was simply furnished, although there was no hint of family about it; no toys, no books, no clothing hanging from the hooks on the door. 'Slip off your coat and sit down for a minute. Have you brought the ... you know ... the doings?'

Polly handed over an envelope containing the one pound fifteen shillings that had denuded her savings and perched on the corner of a brocaded settee.

'Shan't be a minute, dear. Just make yourself at home.'

Mrs Smith bustled away, presumably to put away the money. For a brief moment, Polly experienced a flash of terror. People died at the hands of abortionists, she knew, and it would be terrible to die in this place, a stranger's house. No one apart from Connie knew she was here and, given that this was Friday evening and her next shift started on Monday morning, her parents would soon be in a state if she did not appear this evening. They would not know where to look. It was unfair to put them through this... Her mind flashed on. Unfair! What about the father, then? She would die and Jim – or Bertie – would be bereft, there was no doubt about that, and neither would know that his child had been ... what? Murdered?

Her miserable reverie was halted by the entry

of Mrs Smith, humming a happy tune from *The Maid of the Mountains:*

'At seventeen, he falls in love quite madly,
With eyes of tender blue...'

Polly winced at the memory of Bertie, clutching her hand tightly and leaning his head on her shoulder as they sat in the stalls of Daly's Theatre while he, embarrassingly, sang along, echoing the words in his reedy tenor.

'Sorry to keep you, dear. Would you like to come through here to the back?'

The room was curtained tightly and a coal fire burned brightly although the day was not too cold. A single bed jutted out from the far wall with what looked like a rubber sheet covering it, tucked in at the sides under the thin mattress. The handles of a large tin bowl, or perhaps it was a footbath, protruded from underneath the bed. Apart from the rather smoky fire, the room smelt of something chemical, probably disinfectant. Polly felt her stomach contract.

'Not too cold for you, dear?'

'No, thank you.'

'Good. It's not been too cold for the time of the year, has it?'

Without waiting for an answer, the woman poured a colourless liquid into a glass and handed to Polly. 'This is just a drop of gin, dear, just to relax you a bit. Like a drop of gin, do you?'

Polly shook her head but took the glass anyway. What had to be had to be.

'Yes, that's the idea. Just knock it back, there's a good girl.' Mrs Smith watched while Polly drank the gin – it was neat, of course. 'Yes, that's the way.' A pause, then: 'First time is it?'

Grimacing at the taste of the gin, Polly nodded.

'Yes. Well, you're only young, lovey, so I'm sure it's for the best. How long has it been since you had your last ... you know?'

'I've missed two periods. I've never been late before. And I'm being regularly sick in the mornings, although there's not much of a bulge yet.' Polly looked closely at Mrs Smith's hands. They seemed clean enough.

'Yes. Best not to leave it any longer.' The woman pointed at a door. 'Now, if you go through there you'll find the lav. Even if you've been recently, do what you can 'cos it all helps, see. When you've finished, come back in and just slip your clothes off and I'll get a nice clean towel for you to lie on, 'cos this rubber might feel a bit cold to your bum. Put your clothes on that chair there. I'll be back in a minute.'

The toilet was outside, in a little yard. There was no toilet roll, only pages torn from the *Birmingham Mail*, through the corners of which a piece of wire had been pushed and then hung on a nail driven into the wall. Polly tore off a piece and wiped the lavatory seat but, even so, decided to sit on her hands. No pee came and, deciding not to use the newspaper, she adjusted her clothing and moved back into the room. There, she stripped off her clothes and, carefully folding them out of habit, laid them on the chair. Then she stood with her back to the fire, her hands modestly folded across her breasts, shivering.

Mrs Smith re-entered, carrying a cotton pad and a small bottle. She gestured to the bed. 'Just lie on that, dear, and take a sniff of this. It'll put you out and when you wake up it'll all be over.'

Polly climbed onto the bed and, despite the towel, the mattress felt cold and hard. She stared wide-eyed and trembling as Mrs Smith upended the bottle onto the pad and then approached her. The woman then paused, holding the pad well away from her.

'Don't be worried, love. I've done plenty of these, particularly since the war started. You won't feel a thing. Just a bit sick, like, afterwards. Now, put your head on the pillow and take a good sniff of this.'

Firmly – almost roughly, as though tired of Polly's despair – she put her left hand under Polly's head and, with her right, pressed the pad onto her nose and mouth. Polly wanted to cough but within seconds found herself slipping away into oblivion.

She regained consciousness what seemed like only seconds later and immediately felt the need to vomit. Looking desperately to both sides of the bed she saw a zinc bucket on the left and was sick into it. She lay for a moment, hanging over the side, before vomiting again, perspiration dripping down her nose into the bucket. Exhausted, she lay back, her eyes closed, and felt Mrs Smith pull a blanket over her and begin wiping her face with a damp cloth.

'All over now, dearie,' she heard. 'Not as easy as I would have liked but I've had worse. Still, it's all done now. I've got rid of everything.'

The nausea had receded somewhat, but Polly felt a hard, unrelenting pain in her stomach. She forced her eyes open. 'Was it a boy or a girl?'

The woman shook her head. 'Didn't notice. Never do. And it makes no difference now, dear, does it? Anyway, it's all gone. Got rid of it.'

Polly stifled a groan as she thought of her son or daughter being flushed down that cold lavatory in the yard. But Mrs Smith was continuing: 'You just take this aspirin now with a drink of this water and lie to get your breath back, so to speak.' Her tone became apologetic. 'Then I'm afraid I shall have to say toodle-oo to you because I've got another client at seven. Have you got far to go?'

'No. Walking distance.'

'Well, don't rush. Close your eyes and I'll wake you if you go to sleep.'

Polly did not go to sleep, in fact, and not just because she remained in pain. Her brain seethed in a tumble of contradictory thoughts. She felt relieved that something that she had been dreading was over – both the decision and the act. But she quickly became consumed with an intense feeling of guilt. She had just consigned her son or daughter to oblivion – but not merely *her* child but also Jim's or Bertie's. She put a hand to her hot forehead. Ah, she still did not know and now never would. What sort of woman was it that killed her unborn child without knowing who had fathered it? Why a whore, of course! She shuddered.

The walk home seemed to take for ever and

she had to pause to lean by the side of a privet hedge protecting a front garden and vomit once more. An elderly lady put a concerned hand on her shoulder: 'Are you all right, dear?' She gave a distant smile, nodded and trudged on.

'Goodness,' said her mother when she arrived home. 'Wherever have you been? You look as white as a sheet.'

'Just a bit of overtime, Mum. Sorry, I forgot to tell you. I think I'll go to bed now, if you don't mind. I'm feeling a bit under the weather. Don't worry. I'll be right as rain in the morning.'

Once between the sheets she was dimly aware of her mother fussing and leaving a cup of tea on the bedside table, then she slipped into a deep sleep. In it, she dreamt that she was lying between Jim and Bertie, while shells screamed overhead. She was comforting them in the middle of the barrage, turning to one, then to the other, kissing and fondling them, cooing that she loved them both, each the same. Then they were suddenly on top of her, both at the same time, and she woke in the darkness, perspiration pouring down her face.

The tea was cold but she drank it. Then, on a sudden thought, she slipped out of bed and knelt down, beside the chamber pot, and prayed to God to forgive her for what she had done and, despite her sins, to keep both of her boys – her lovers – safe until the end of the war.

CHAPTER EIGHT

The letters that Polly wrote to her boys the next evening arrived together, as they always did, to end a period of two weeks without hearing from her that was beginning to cause concern to Jim and Bertie. She explained to them that she had been 'just a bit under the weather', but was feeling fine again. She enclosed, as she invariably did now, packets of cigarettes for them both and a little parcel of the sweet biscuits that Bertie loved. However, she asked if they would mind if she only wrote once a week to them both, because work was becoming more demanding, with long shifts, and she was sure that her letters were becoming equally boring, because 'nothing happens to me, except work'. She had been to the moving pictures, though. And did they know that the funny little fellow with the bowler hat, Charlie Chaplin, was British? She had read that in the *Birmingham Mail,* so it must be true.

The autumn crept into Christmas, their second in Flanders, and then a winter when the wind blew over the battered plain of the Salient and everyone in the front line wondered when and where the Big Push would be. For Jim and Bertie, as for all their comrades facing the Germans in that series of watery ditches that formed the line in Flanders, the deadly monotony of trench warfare in that tight, sodden pocket before Ypres was stressful in the extreme.

By March of 1916, few remained of the original draft of Territorials and Reservists who had fought with the pair in the First Battle of Ypres in 1914. The deprivations from the first two battles, the constant bombardment, the sniping and the losses resulting from the patrols and raiding across no man's land had produced a steady reduction in the ranks manning the line. Although no major clashes had taken place since the summer of 1915 in the Salient, there was nothing tranquil about the line and no day passed without casualties, many of them fatal. Indeed, a wound so serious that it meant the recipient had to be sent down the line and on to England for treatment – a 'Blighty One' – was coveted. But those caused by the ever-present explosions of razor-sharp fragments of shrapnel were to be feared, for, apart from death, they could cause horrific injuries, including dis-figurement.

All officers and senior NCOs were alerted to distinguish between genuine wounds and those that were self-inflicted. Single bullet wounds in the hand and forearm were viewed with extreme scepticism, for where the land between the two front lines was narrow – two hundred yards or less – the Germans had been known to obligingly respond to a cry of 'Go on, Fritz, give us one' by putting a bullet into the hand or arm so invitingly held aloft.

The pressure, however, sometimes drove men to further extremes. A cry of 'Sergeant, come quick' sent Jim hurrying down the trench one morning in the dark hours before stand-to. There, sprawled on the slimy duckboards, lay the figure of a young infantryman. His head was hideously disfigured, for a bullet had entered the roof of his mouth and exited through the top of his skull. Strangely, however, his right boot and sock had been removed and placed on the fire step near him. Jim stood stock-still in wonder, before he realised that the boy had put the muzzle of his rifle in his mouth, curled his big toe around the trigger and pressed it down. It was to become a not unusual occurrence as the war wore on during 1916.

Jim, in fact, was now beginning to worry about Bertie. This was not the concern that he always felt about the little man – that he would be found dozing on duty, that he would be arraigned for being incorrectly dressed or that he had fallen foul of Sergeant Major Flanagan again. Indeed, the stripes earned by the pair had proved to be a deterrent of a kind to Black Jack, who found it difficult, for instance, to put a lance corporal on permanent latrine duty. And, when he put his mind to it, Bertie was a competent soldier, still one of the best marksmen in the battalion.

No, the characteristic that was starting to cause Jim anxiety was a kind of fey depression that was emerging in the behaviour of this most buoyant of men. Bertie was beginning to exhibit a fatalism about the war – that it was becoming crueller by the day, impossible to be resolved by any conventional means and that death was the only outcome for them all. It must be said that

190

this attitude seemed, superficially, to be not uncommon along the line. But the average Tommy used it as a form of defence, a faux fatalism that concealed a cheerful scepticism about the conflict and the way it was being conducted by the generals on both sides. 'Bugger them all and bugger us, too,' summed it up.

Yet Lance Corporal Bertram Murphy was serious and was beginning to read strange things into the daily happenings of life on the Salient. Jim, whose attitude towards religion was one of lazy scepticism and who had always regarded Bertie's devotion to the teachings of the Roman Catholic Church with respect and a touch of envy, had thought at first that his friend was beginning to lose his faith. The rosary, for instance, had not been produced during the shelling for some time, and Bertie's calling on the Holy Mother to give them succour during particularly bad moments had virtually ceased. Then the little man surprised his friend.

'You know, Jimmy boy,' he said one early morning when they were both standing guard, 'God *is* with us in this cruel, awful place.'

'Oh yes,' said Jim. 'Where's the old chap hiding then, Bertie?'

'Ah, son, you can't see him. Now I was thinkin' a while back that he didn't exist, you know, what with all this terrible killin' stuff and us bein' forced to live in holes in the ground with the rats. Then I got to thinkin' it through.'

'Oh good. Tell me, then.'

'That's just what I'm doing, is it not, if you'll let me.'

191

'For goodness' sake get on with it, then.'

'So I will. So I will. So I remembered, of course, that although everything in the long run is his will, it's us, here on earth, that fucks it all up, see? He doesn't control everything we do. He has to let us get on with it and that's what we're doing now, with this terrible war – buggering things up. And the good Lord can't – or won't – stop us; it's up to us to stop it. But he is still with us, here, in the middle of all this misery, and he shows to us that he is.'

'What! With all the shrapnel tearing off blokes' balls, arms and legs? How does he show it?'

'Just think, Jim. What happens when the Very lights, the star shells go up? Eh?'

'Well, we all freeze. Nothing happens. We stop what we're doing.'

'*Exactly.*' Bertie thumped the sandbags in delight. 'He stops the bloody fighting, just for a minute, but it's enough to show that he's with us. To remind us that he exists and that we ought to stop this rubbishin' war.'

Jim frowned. 'But they're star shells. We send 'em up, and so do the Germans, to illuminate people moving in no man's land and to prevent surprise attacks.'

'There you are.' Bertie thumped the sandbag again. 'That proves me point. You said it yourself – "to stop surprise attacks". We may send 'em up but the good Lord prompts us to, to stop the killin' just for a minute or two. He *stops the war,* son. You can call 'em Very lights or star shells. But I reckon they're starshine. That's what those lights are, starshine. *His* light, to remind us He's there. And I feel much better as a result.'

Jim gave him a long, penetrating look. 'Well, I think you're daft, Bertie, but if it makes you feel better to think that, then I'm happy too. Mind you, if we could put one up Black Jack Flanagan's arse, then I think we would both be delirious.'

'Aw, Jim lad, I'm being serious.'

'So am I and God would surely be happy too.'

'Are you never serious?'

'Sometimes. Like now. Stand down. It's the end of your guard.'

Jim knew that things were building up on the Western Front. He read the newspapers that his father sent him out from home and he talked with those officers, usually during the quieter watches of the night, who were happy to discuss the pattern of the war with young, intelligent NCOs. He understood the basic strategic position. Four hundred and seventy-five miles of trench line now stretched from the Belgian coast, sweeping across the face of France to the very foothills of Switzerland. Until the autumn of 1915, the French were grimly holding on to four hundred miles of its length, while the British Expeditionary Force faced the enemy along a mere seventy-five miles. The Brits had proved that they could fight, at Ypres, Mons and Loos. But more was needed. The attrition of trench warfare over such a long front was imposing immense burdens on the French, who were beginning to bleed away a generation of young men at Verdun, and the British now had to assume a bigger share of that burden; to take over a larger portion of the line. So it was to the Somme, in the heartlands of Northern France, that Britain's new army made its way.

Never before had Britain sent abroad so many men – a civilian army who had answered the call of Kitchener's powerful poster, even after the great man had met his death in the icy waters of the North Sea. Kitchener's New Army – no Reservists (except for officers, alas often elderly, brought out of retirement) or Territorials this time, but clerks from their desks, butchers from their blocks, barristers from high tables, miners from deep labyrinths, shepherds from the hills, artisans from their factories, weavers from their looms and teachers from their blackboards – took on the khaki and trained hard. Many formed into 'Pals Battalions', from the same district or even company, so that they all knew each other. They were inexperienced and, alas, only hurriedly, if enthusiastically, trained. But they were confident and proud, inspired by the deeds of the young men who had gone before, like Bertie Murphy and Jim Hickman, and they marched in masses into the Somme – often behind their own pipe bands that had never seen Scotland – and they took over the old French section of the line, where it had faced the Germans from Hébuterne to Thiepval, on the Ancre, from Thiepval to the banks of the River Somme itself. Reinforced by the veterans of the Gallipoli disaster who landed in the south of France and marched to the north to stiffen the new arrivals, these were the young soldiers who were to launch the 'Big Push' that was to be known as the Battle of the Somme.

It began on the morning of 24th June, 1916, with the longest and most extensive barrage of artillery fire that had been known in warfare up until that point. Some seventy miles to the north, across the Belgian border, Jim and Bertie, disgruntled that they had not been allowed home leave for more than a year and yearning to see Polly, were on rest and recuperation leave from the trenches at Poperinghe when the news filtered through that the Big Push had been unleashed – and, thanked God it had not sprung from the Salient.

In fairness, it had been clear for some time that the reinforcements that had been flooding across the Channel were not destined for the old mud and bloodbath before Ypres. The regiments that garrisoned the Salient rarely seemed to change; only their constituent parts were supplemented to stem the steady erosion caused by the dead and the wounded.

'It's because they trust us to know where the Jerries are, you see,' said Bertie. 'We're good at it. I wish we weren't.'

They were sitting together in a billet at the west of Pop. A sergeant's mess had been established there but Jim preferred to spend off-duty time, as ever, with his old friend. The first day of the attack on the Somme, three days ago, according to the British army newspaper the *Wipers Times* had met with great success, with breaks through the German lines at several places.

Hickman threw down the paper with disgust. 'I don't believe it,' he said. 'From what I can see, the Germans – who got there first, don't forget – have had plenty of time to establish themselves on high ground, a bit like here, and set up really good defensive positions. We've seen here how good they are with concrete and stuff. With the heaviest bombardment in the world, I still don't see us just breaking through 'em on the first day.'

'Hmm.' Bertie was distant, his eyes looking out of the dirty window, but unseeingly. He was clearly not interested in the Somme. 'Jim,' he said, 'it's amazin,' ain't it, that you an' me have survived this long amidst all this killin'?'

'What? Well, I suppose so. We've just been lucky, I suppose. Although we've been out here long enough now to know what to do. How to get by, so to speak.'

'Yes, but think of all the good lads that have gone. Many of 'em were the old Regulars who knew more about anythin' than we ever did. But they went down and here we still are.'

Jim sniffed. 'Yes, well, best not to think about it. Just keep your head down and get on with it.'

They were both silent for a while. Then: 'One of us is bound to get it soon,' said Bertie. 'I do hope it's me rather than you. You'll be better able to look after Polly, that's for sure.'

'Stop talking rot. Shall we go to the pub to-night? Have you got any money?'

Bertie fished in his pocket. 'Sergeant, darlin' boy, I'm rich. Look. About twenty francs. Mind you, I was richer yesterday. I sent twenty-five shillings from me pay back to me dad. He'll spend it on Guinness. Wish I could.'

'Ah, come on. The wine here is not bad. I've got ten francs left. Let's get plastered and you can thank God that we're not on the Somme. Shame they can't distil your starshine here. I suppose it would be like getting pissed on communion wine.'

'Don't be blasphemous, Jimmy. Someone might be listening.'

Poperinghe had changed to some extent, since their visit in 1914, but overall it had remained unaltered. It was right at the extreme range of the German big guns on the ridges and so escaped the kind of bombardment that had devastated Ypres itself. But the enemy occasionally indulged itself from a distance in firing gas shells at the town. As always, the efficacy of a gas attack depended upon the direction of the wind, and a recent innovation at Pop was the establishment of a noticeboard outside the town hall, which gave daily indications of the state of the wind vis-à-vis a gas attack in terms of 'Safe' or 'Dangerous'. Otherwise, the little town retained its gruesome charm as a kind of military tourist spot, near enough to the front line to make it convenient for short-term leave (and sudden recall when a large-scale attack seemed imminent) but also far enough away to give it relative safety. And its streets remained narrow, crowded and full of bars and brothels, offering British soldiers an opportunity to put behind the misery of the trenches for a short time and to spend their shilling-a-day pay. The noticeboard that day had signalled that the wind direction was safe, and so for Jim and Bertie that night the Café des Allies beckoned.

Halfway through the second bottle – their taste had changed; now they eschewed the 'plonk' and drank the *vin rouge* – it became clear that Bertie was restless. His mood was not helped by the news, passed through the crowded room by word of mouth from table to table, that, in fact, the first day on the Somme had proved to be disastrous.

'Fousands went darn,' said the cockney gunner on their left. 'Fousands. Bleedin' wire 'adn't bin cut and they was 'ung out to dry. A massacre, it was. Bleedin' massacre. Just 'eard from me bruvver. 'E was there.'

Bertie raised his eyes to heaven. 'Ah, you were right, then, Jim lad. Oh, this stupid, *stupid* war.' He ran his fingers through his tangled hair and his wide eyes ran round the room as though he was seeking some conclusion to it, some salvation. 'Tell you what. Let's pop into next door. See what it's like. I've never ... been with a lady like that. Have you?'

'No, but...'

'Aw, come on. We needn't do anything. Just have a look, eh?'

'All right, then. But I'm not leaving this bottle. Let's finish it first.'

A little too hurriedly, they emptied the bottle, paid their bill and left the café, then, rather shamefacedly, they climbed the steps underneath the red lamp to the left and knocked on the door. It was opened by a woman with dyed red hair, a face that might once have been pretty and a gigantic frontage that offered no distinction between bosom and stomach. Her perfume hit them like a blanket, as did the hot air from within.

She took in Jim's stripes and addressed him. ''Ello, General,' she said. 'Come een. You sit and wait. We very busy. But you don't wait long. Take a drink, eh?'

She pointed to a red velvet settee, on the end of which perched a young infantryman, his hand unashamedly on his crotch. Nearby, two Signallers sat in plush, rather broken-down armchairs, sharing what looked like a bottle of yellowish absinthe. The room was large but only dimly lit. Faux candelabra, converted to hissing but inadequate gaslight, hung from the ceiling. Alcoves lined the walls and curtains had been drawn across their entrances. Around the edges, however, glimpses could be caught of beds and booted feet on them jerking uncertainly. The place smelt of stale cigarette smoke and something else indefinably but definitely unpleasant.

As they stood uncertainly, one of the curtains was twitched back and a woman of uncertain age slipped through. Nonchalantly, she thrust a sagging breast back inside her slip with one hand and completed the pulling up of her drawers with the other. She looked round the room. 'Cigarette?' she requested, holding out her hand to the waiting clientele.

Jim and Bertie exchanged glances. 'Well, I don't think–' began Hickman. Then from one of the alcoves came a scream. Not one of delight, but of pain, and then the sound of a blow and another, followed by a crash as a woman was hurled against the wall. She pulled at the curtain, which came down, to reveal Sergeant Major Flanagan, his face puce with anger, kicking angrily at the naked body of a young girl as she coiled at his feet, half draped by the curtain.

'If I say suck it, you whore,' shouted Flanagan, 'suck it, blast you, and don't argue with me. I'll kick your face in.'

The Madam shouted something in French and ran to intervene, only to be sent to the floor by a savage punch from the Ulsterman.

Bertie immediately started forward, but was held back by Jim. 'Outside, quickly,' he said. 'Come with me.'

As they rushed to the door, they caught a glimpse of girls emerging from the other alcoves, some of them brandishing what appeared to be carving knives, before they had gained the street. 'To the left,' shouted Hickman to Bertie. 'I saw a redcap when we came in.'

The sound of the altercation had obviously already alerted the military policeman, for he was striding quickly towards them. 'Inside the brothel, next to the café,' said Jim, pointing. 'There's a drunken Irish warrant officer beating up the women and causing havoc. He's already nearly killed one of the girls. Watch yourself. The man's a bastard.'

'Right,' said the policeman. He broke into a run and blew the whistle that dangled from his lanyard to summon assistance.

'Let's get out of here, son,' said Jim. 'I think we might have nicely dropped Flanagan in it. What a pleasure!'

The news came next morning, quickly passed round the billets with joy, for Sergeant Major Flanagan was not a popular man. He had been arrested by the MPs, kept in the guardhouse overnight and was due to appear before the colonel that morning. He had, it appeared, broken the jaw of the girl and had resisted arrest. Rumour had it that the French local authorities had tried to press charges but the British military authorities were insistent on handling the matter themselves.

'Ah,' nodded Bertie. 'What d'you think he'll get? Shot at dawn, or something more severe?'

Jim gave a reluctant grin. 'He ought to spend time in jug. Trouble is,' he said, 'the man's a bloody good soldier and the regiment won't want to lose him. We've lost enough fighters already and they won't want him taken out of the line. Demotion to sergeant, I should think.'

So it proved. On his return to the regiment a week later, there was a faded patch on his forearm where his warrant officer's badge of rank had been and three stripes were back on his formidable biceps. He bore, however, a raw, red scar on his cheek.

'A carving knife, I should say,' murmured Bertie. 'I'll tell you what, though, Jimmy. I'm glad now that we didn't – you know. Looked horrible, didn't it?'

Hickman nodded. 'And it wouldn't have been right by Polly, now, would it?'

'Ah, now, you're surely right there, lad. You're surely right.'

Flanagan's bearing on his return was no

different. He still carried himself with a swagger and he met everyone's gaze with a belligerent stare, as though daring them to ask about his new, or rather his old, rank. He gave no indication that he knew that he had Hickman and Murphy to thank for his demotion and they were unsure about whether he had seen them leave the brothel. Certainly, Hickman had not been called to testify. It was clear that the evidence of the fracas that Flanagan had caused and his resistance to arrest was sufficient to condemn him. The cold antipathy with which he regarded the pair, however, remained unchanged, although was there just a hint of extra malevolence in his gaze when his eyes met theirs?

The battalion returned to the line and Jim and Bertie were relieved to find that Flanagan, who had been their company's sergeant major, had been transferred to another company, although, of course, he remained within their regiment. This meant that his path did not cross daily with the two comrades. The new CSM, Sergeant Major Blackshaw, was another Regular, a veteran who had been nearing retirement age when war was declared and, accordingly, was more indulgent than his predecessor, a man who knew how to survive and who was all for finding a way of having a quiet life in the trenches, if the Germans – and his officers – allowed him to.

The hope of a quiet life for them all, however, eventually disappeared when the news came through that the battalion was being posted.

Every heart sank when they heard of their destination: the Somme, where the dreadful battle still raged.

CHAPTER NINE

'Well, thank the Holy Mother there's no mud.' Bertie Murphy gestured up at the hot sun as they marched at ease across the plain of Picardy in that late summer of 1916.

Since their transfer from Ypres, just over three weeks before, their battalion seemed to have marched up and down behind the British line without purpose as the great battle had surged on across a wide front ahead of them. The British army had hurled itself in a non-stop assault at German bastions at obscure places whose names would go down in history as virtual cemeteries: Thiepval, Beaumont Hamel, High Wood, La Boisselle, Serre and Contalmaison. As part of a support battalion, Jim and Bertie had been bombed and shelled and spent days in a series of broken-down, vermin-ridden reserve trenches without relief but, in a strange twist in the fortunes of war, they had so far not faced the enemy directly. Now, that was to end. They were marching forward – to take their place in the front line to attack the citadel of the Germans' second line at Guillemont.

It was August and, indeed, there was no mud. They were moving towards the sound of the guns after a period of rest, but there was one other sound now that vied with the cannon: the buzzing of thousands of black bluebottle flies. They followed the marching men, hovering above them like a swollen storm cloud. Sated on the corpses up ahead, they now preyed on the perspiration of the reserves moving up to take their part in the new attack the next day.

Jim waved his hand to drive the pests away. 'Flowers are nice, though,' he called. They were marching through banks of camomile and poppies. For once, they were spared the constant company of ambulances and wagons taking bandage-swathed men back for treatment, and those wounded able to walk, trudging with expressionless faces and vacant eyes. Going their way, however, and vying with them for space on the broken road, was an endless stream of gun-limbers, ammunition wagons, store carts, despatch riders and the occasional staff car carrying red-tabbed staff officers, going like them up to the line for yet another great attack. Lining the road and patiently suffering the clouds of chalk, dust and grit thrown up by the passing cavalcade, stood lines of Pioneer troops and German prisoners of war, waiting for gaps to appear in the traffic to allow them to continue the endless task of repairing the track.

Jim, marching at the head of his company, turned and grinned at Bertie in the front rank. They both knew that, like the rest of their comrades in the battalion, they had been lucky not to have taken part in the carnage that had characterised the British attacks north of the

Somme so far. Kitchener's New Army, fresh, optimistic and eager to fight, had been broken in the last few weeks, beating itself impotently against the well-prepared German line. Some progress had been made, cracks had been desperately chipped out of that line, but usually only a few hundred yards had been gained and at the expense of thousands – many thousands – of lives. Now, reinforcements of more seasoned troops, transferred from other parts of the front, were being fed in to make another attempt at the great breakthrough that the high command felt was just at its fingertips, if only...

Jim's thumbs-up sign was returned by Bertie, but unsmilingly. They both knew what was to come tomorrow and there was no point in pretending. They had seen what had happened since 1st July when the long British bombardment had ended and Haig had hurled his unseasoned troops against unbroken wire and the well-positioned machine guns. The bodies that they had helped dig out of the abandoned trenches left behind by the laboured advance, and the sad columns of wounded men trailing back from the front, had borne witness to the failure of the British tactics. Now they themselves would be going over the top for the first time in a huge, structured attack against well-defended positions in a sad repetition of what had gone before. Could this attack succeed when the others had so spectacularly failed? Jim bit his lip, looked at the poppies and thought yet again of Polly. Would he see her again?

The camomiles, the poppies and the flies

stayed with them until they reached the beginning of the communications trench that led windingly to the front line. Here, amidst the din and destruction of the ever-present cannonade, they crouched and were given hot tea, knocking away the bluebottles that clung to the sticky edges of their tin mugs to make room for their lips. Then they filed in line to be given the extra equipment that they would carry to blast their way through the German defences.

It was a formidable load. They shed the packs containing their personal items, capes, greatcoats and blankets which they had been carrying, retained their rifle, bayonet, entrenching tool, water bottle and first-aid kit, and took on board two hundred rounds of ammunition, a sandbag to be stuffed into the right-hand pocket of their tunic, emergency rations and one smoke helmet to be carried on the back away from bullets. Designated men took bombs, wire-cutters and flares.

So loaded, they made their way to the new front line, so expensively bought by the weeks of fighting. They trudged over abandoned trenches, pounded by the artillery so that they were merely crumbled ditches now and only manned by the deformed dead, bloated by the sunshine. Unexploded shells, still visible in the churned-up earth, added extra danger to their journey as they plodded towards where the live shells were sending up cascades of debris up ahead. And the flies stayed with them.

The equipment carried by each man weighed upwards of sixty pounds. In addition, each man had attached to his back a shining diamond of tin that would glint in the sun the next morning as he made his way forward and so inform the aeroplanes of the Royal Flying Corps of the progress being made by the new attack.

Except that, when morning dawned, there was no sun. Just a heavy yellow mist that prevented aeroplanes from taking off and which mingled with the smoke of the bombardment and clung to the shivering troops as they waited by the scaling ladders for the whistles to blow.

'What the hell are we supposed to attack?' asked Bertie. 'I can't see a bloody thing.'

'It's a village called Guillemont,' said Jim, 'or what's left of it. It's been knocked about a bit but the Jerries still hold it and they're hanging on like grim death. It's a tough nut to crack but until we take it, I am told, the French on our right can't advance properly. So we've got to take it to allow them to move.' He gave a mirthless grin. 'I don't think you'll have much trouble finding it, son. Just walk towards the machine-gun flashes.' His voice dropped. 'I'll stay with you, Bertie, don't worry.'

The stench of no man's land – a foul mixture of swollen corpses, acrid shell smoke and stale tobacco that hung on the uniform of every British soldier – was in all their nostrils as they crouched on the fire step, waiting for the barrage to lift. The plan of attack was going to be exactly the same as that which had failed repeatedly over the last few weeks: a heavy bombardment that would destroy the German wire, then, at timed intervals, the barrage would lift and then move forward, over and beyond the enemy trenches to deter reinforcements, and the infantry would attack in extended order, three to four paces between each man, behind the barrage, the attack to be synchronised to the lifting of the barrage. So far, Jim knew that things rarely worked to plan. Either the barrage would lift too early to give the Germans time to debouch from their deep shelters and man their guns, or too late, so that it fell on the advancing troops. And always, always, the wire was not destroyed, only left with inviting gaps through which the advancing Tommies would funnel to be cut down by the machine guns trained on them.

Now, the mist was an additional factor. Would it help or hinder the attackers? Jim licked his lips and took a quick swig from the water bottle which contained the customary 'over the top' slug of rum. He gave Bertie's arm a reassuring squeeze.

Then whistles blew all along the line and, as the queues formed to mount the scaling ladders, the officers called, 'Advance to your front and follow your officers. Don't stop for the wounded. Stretcher-bearers will follow.'

Muttering an incoherent prayer that the British barrage would, indeed, lift forward, Jim followed Bertie's swinging buttocks up the scaling ladder and through the passage that had been made in the British wire. They were immediately in the thick of the mist, a yellow fog that clung and swirled around each man as he plodded forward, steel helmet tilted down to just above the eyes (that inch could make the difference between life and death in deflecting a bullet) and rifle and bayonet held across the chest.

Jim desperately tried to keep Bertie in sight as he trudged forward, but the little man had somehow disappeared in the mist. Hickman comforted himself with the thought that Bertie had always found walking in a straight line to be difficult and that he was bound to have strayed.

It was eerie, advancing in the mist, stumbling down and up shell holes and endeavouring to keep somehow marching towards an objective that could not be seen. The shelling, British or German, seemed to have stopped and a silence of a sort had descended. The fog seemed to have acted as a kind of blanket – not, alas, protecting them from enemy bullets, for men were now falling in response to the dull 'phut' as a bullet hit them. They themselves made no sound, simply pitching forward, their rifles going before them and their arms outstretched, as if they were performing in some ghostly mime play. The fire was not continuous and was obviously serendipitous, individual shooting into the mist.

Then the yellow cloud lifted. To the right, Jim could see the low line of rubble and masonry that was all that was left of the village of Guillemont. Hickman's company had, indeed, lost its formation and the men were straggling too far to the left, Bertie predictably, to Jim's relief, among them.

'To the right,' shouted a young subaltern, gesturing with his revolver. Immediately, a bullet caught him in the breast and he fell. Then the grey stones that housed the Germans became a line of flashes as the enemy, presented with an unmissable target, opened fire. Hickman put his head down and lumbered into an ungainly trot towards the line, waving to the others to follow him. All around him, however, men were falling and, when the clatter of machine guns joined in, he dived into a shell hole for cover.

The bullets thumped into the lip of the hole and hissed away over his head. Tentatively, he pushed his rifle over the edge and attempted to sight it, only for a bullet to clang tangentially onto his steel helmet, sending it lurching askew over his right ear. He slid back hurriedly down the soil to find that the crater now also housed four other members of his platoon.

'What can we do, Sarge?' asked a young private, his eyes wide with fear.

'Bugger all, for the moment, son.' Jim looked around. 'Anybody seen Corporal Murphy?'

'Aye. He's okay. I saw him dive into the next shell hole on the left.'

Hickman exhaled. 'Good. Now, is there a bomber here? Ah yes, Higgins, isn't it?'

A thickset man wearing a strange leather jerkin nodded. He indicated his special pockets, bulging with Mills bombs.

'Right. We can't get out of here yet, but we can't give up. As soon as the fire slackens, we'll crawl towards the German line. I'm told that there is a German trench about fifty yards in front of the village itself. I reckon that if we get near enough, we could bomb our way into that trench. If we can hold it, then that will give our second wave a chance.'

He grinned at the four of them, with a confidence he did not feel. Jim Hickman was now only twenty years old but he carried no illusions. He half expected when in the line that every day would be his last. Nevertheless, with nearly two years' experience of fighting at the front, he had acquired expertise at this dismal, desperately dangerous form of warfare. He reasoned that to survive in this hell you had to learn from every day you were allowed. Back in Flanders, therefore, he had taken selected groups of his platoon out on quiet nights, out over the trench top and through the wire to lie out in no man's land, for an hour or two, so that every man in his platoon would eventually get to master the fright induced by being unprotected by sandbags and trench walls and to lie perfectly still when the Very lights illuminated the barren landscapes. (To Jim, Bertie's 'starshine' was a source of danger, not evidence of the presence of the Almighty.) He taught them to crawl quietly, on all fours and on their bellies. The four now crouching in the shell hole with him had shared that experience back at Ypres. Jim hoped it would stand them in good stead now.

The machine-gun fire died away for a moment and Jim called out: 'Bertie. Are you there?'

The reply came back, 'So I am, Jimmy, Sergeant, sir. What a relief to hear your voice, dear lad. I thought you might be gone.'

'Not me. Are there others in that hole with you?'

'Indeed there are. Six of us. There's plenty of

room. It's a big hole.'

'Is there an officer with you or another NCO?'

'No. Only me. I am the general in command.'

Hickman grinned. 'Now, listen carefully, Corporal. We can't move out of here while this firing is going on. But they can't keep on all day. As soon as it slackens, we must advance. I will give the command. But there's to be no standing up, or they'll cut us down easily. Crawl from shell hole to shell hole. To the right, towards the rubble from which they're firing at us. Do you understand?'

'Bloody hell, Jimmy. Are we going to attack the whole bloody German army all by ourselves?'

'No, only the Fritzes in that ruined village. There's a trench full of 'em out in front of the ruins. When we're near enough we will bomb it and then rush in and take it. Don't move till I tell you, though.'

'You can rely on that. Oh yes.'

Jim turned to the bomber. 'How many bombs have you got in those pouches, Higgins?'

'Eight in all.'

'Good. Keep three for yourself, give me two and give one each to the others.' It wouldn't do to say so, but Hickman did not want all the precious bombs to stay with one man who might be cut down as soon as they moved. This way, they stood more chance of getting within bombing distance with the grenades in hand.

The intensity of the shelling had long died away and the comparative lull caused by the cessation of the machine-gun firing now ended with a burst of distant firing far to the right, beyond the village (was it the French, on the move at last?) and also to the left, where Jim presumed the British regiment there had belatedly launched an attack on the German line. It was the diversion he had been waiting for.

He turned to the four. 'Come on, lads. Out on top and spread out. Make for the nearest hole and drop in – but don't stay holed up.' Then, louder: 'Time to go, Corporal Murphy. Go NOW!'

They scrambled and clawed their way up in the sliding grit that formed the sides of the crater and crawled away, over the undulations of the ground. Turning his head, Hickman saw that Bertie was leading his men similarly out of his shell hole. A machine gun based in the rubble about two hundred and fifty yards to their right began to chatter and Higgins, who was on the flank of Jim's group, immediately fell. Hickman prostrated himself, heard the bullets hiss over his head, then ran forward and dragged the bomber down into the next shell hole. The remaining three of his men immediately flopped down beside him.

Higgins was moaning and blood was pouring from two black holes in his stomach. Jim relieved him of his three grenades, opened his jacket and shirt and sought the man's field dressing in his pocket. He tore off the waterproof covering and took out the gauze pad, with its ampoule attached. Pressing the ampoule, he saw iodine released over the pad. He applied it to the two wounds, which were close together, and bound it clumsily to the stomach with a length of bandage. Tenderly, he lifted up Higgins's head and poured a little water and rum from his own water bottle between his lips. The man looked up at him and tried to summon a grin. Then he closed his eyes and Jim laid him down.

He distributed the bombs to the other three, then crawled to the lip of the crater. There was no sign of Bertie but, to the left, a small party of khaki-clad figures was crawling its way between the shell holes towards the German lines, using the undulations of the ground as cover. He could not see who was leading it but called out: 'Bertie.'

'Next hole to you. Lost one man.' His voice was very close.

'Can you get a bead on that bastard with the machine gun, do you think? He's in the corner, where the bricks are piled on the right.'

'I'll try.'

'We will count to ten and then try and give you a bit of covering fire. Okay?'

'Start countin', Jimmy lad.'

Hickman gestured to the three men and began counting. 'One – up to the lip; two, three, four, five, six – present rifles to the right; seven, eight – aim; nine – FIRE!'

The four rifles spat and then fired again as they worked the bolts. A single shot rang out from their left and then they slid back down into their craters as a rattle of musketry responded from the German lines. But this time there was no clatter of machine-gun fire.

'I think I got the bugger,' cried Bertie.

'Good man. Great shooting. All right, let's hop out again before they get a replacement up.'

And so the two little groups flitted between the shell holes, getting ever nearer now to the forward German trench, whose protective line of coiled barbed wire seemed, for once, to have been flattened by the British guns. The occasional flash of a fired rifle from its parapet, however, showed that the trench was still manned.

It took them half an hour to crawl to within about thirty yards of the German trench. It would have been impossible to make this progress had the ground been flat or the visibility clear. The terrain, however, had been blasted consistently by the British guns and was studded with craters and splintered tree stumps. It also undulated extremely. The corpses that studded the field gave additional, if unpleasant, extra cover. In addition, a faint breeze that came from the south was bringing smoke from the French guns and this, mingling near to the ground with what was left of the morning mist, reduced visibility.

So it was that Hickman was able to gather his small force in a crater so close to the German trench that he could hear the voices of its defenders. Bertie had scrambled alongside his friend and brought what remained of his section with him. The little group that gathered at the bottom of the shell hole therefore numbered nine.

'It's not exactly an army, Jim lad, is it?' Bertie had somehow lost his steel helmet and his red hair, no longer curly, was plastered in mud so that individual strands stood up vertically. The puttees on his right calf had disappeared completely. But his eyes were bright.

Hickman put a finger to his mouth and replied in a whisper – if he could hear the Germans in the trench, then they could hear him. 'No, but I reckon we've got enough to bomb our way into that trench.' Jim nodded to his left. 'The attack's not over, anyway. I saw another group over there still trying to advance. I think we'll get into the trench all right. Keeping it is another matter. Do your lot have any Mills bombs?'

'No. No bomber left. He was cut down.'

'Pity. I hope we've got enough.' He waved to the others to gather round. 'Now, listen. I am sure that the Jerries in the trench have no idea that we are this near. So we will have the advantage of surprise when we attack. The four of us with bombs will get out and crawl just a bit nearer, because I want to be sure that we can reach their trench when we throw. The rest of you will stay here making no noise until you hear the grenades exploding. Then get up and charge hell for leather, bayonets first, as we shall do. Once in the trench, Corporal Murphy will lead his men to the right, clearing the trench, and I will take my lot to the left, doing the same. Here are two bombs for use by your men, Bertie – use them to toss over the traverses once in the trench. We will keep two back to do the same as we go to the left. Pick up any German stick bombs you can see. They could be vital when we have to defend the place. Right. Any questions?'

No one spoke.

'Right. Good luck. Bombers come with me. Quiet as mice, now.'

Stealthily, Hickman edged his way over the lip of the crater, worming his way on his stomach, carrying his two bombs in the smoke helmet on his back so as not to impede his progress, and carefully planting his rifle and bayonet before him as he went. He caught a glimpse of a German coal-scuttle helmet above the parapet and he froze, then, as it disappeared, he inched his way forward until he judged he was near enough. He examined the German parapet and then, to his right, he saw what he had feared. The machine gun that Bertie had temporarily put out of action by killing its gunner was *in situ* behind a pile of rubble, but its muzzle was now slowly moving from left to right, scanning no man's land. It would cut them down as soon as they stood.

He beckoned his men forward so that they lay in a line abreast, some twenty yards from what was left of the German wire. He spoke to them in the softest of whispers.

'There's a machine-gun post to the right. I will try and wriggle nearer and put it out of action with my bombs. If they get me first, throw your bombs at the gun and then charge the trench. The gun must be put out. We've got six bombs between us. You, Hitchcock and you Brown, keep your bombs for the traverses in the trench. The others throw theirs into the trench from here when I have put out that bloody gun. Right? Stay here until I've killed those gunners. Good luck.'

He made his way with immense care to the right, thanking God for the patches of yellow mist and smoke that clung to the contours of the earth. He paused, lay still and examined what he could see of the gun emplacement. It was roughly made, with a semicircle of bricks and other rubble formed around the gun, which fired from a V-shaped aperture left in the wall. He could see the shape of the helmet of the gunner – but how many men manned the German heavy machine guns? Probably three, like the British. Luckily, there was no cover to the emplacement, so that he would be able to lob his grenades over the top.

Jim ran his tongue over his dry lips. Everything depended upon two things: his throw being accurate (they had all been taught to throw with a stiff overarm action to avoid obstacles in the movement); and the bloody bomb going off as it should, five seconds after the extraction of the firing pin. He had heard so many stories of the Mills grenades not exploding at all or of a fault developing in the timing mechanism, so enabling an alert enemy to hurl them back at the thrower. Ah well...

Unprompted, his mind suddenly summoned up a picture of Polly hurling a cricket ball at Bertie batting in Aston Park, while he kept wicket. The boys howled at her that it was an illegal delivery because she bent her arm, but she insisted that it was the only way she could bowl, otherwise, she said, the ball would 'go all over the place'. He smiled to himself. Bugger the rules and the training, he would throw the bombs with a bent arm to ensure accuracy.

He took one last look at the gun, breathed in, lifted himself on his left elbow, pulled at the extractor pin ring and hurled the bomb over the low rubble wall. It exploded in a white sheet of flame behind the gunner – perhaps a little too far back. He adjusted his movement with the second bomb and threw it on a shorter traject- ory. This sent the gun hurling over the barrier and the gunner spreadeagled over the rubble.

'Yah,' he shouted, half in exhilaration, half in relief. Almost immediately he saw two more ex- plosions erupt over the parapet in the trench and he staggered to his feet, rifle in hand, and ran towards the trench, aware that he was over- taking the others in a ragged charge.

Just one shot was fired from the German lines as they trod down the battered wire and hurled themselves into the trench. The lookout was des- perately working the bolt of his rifle as Hickman's bayonet took him in the ribs. Two other soldiers lay crumpled on the broken duckboards at the bottom of the trench, showing where the gren- ades had exploded. Bertie was moving to the right and, meeting the traverse, pulled the pin on his grenade and waited for three precious seconds before lobbing it over the barrier and then bounding round the corner, bayonet presented. The rest of his party followed him and out of sight.

The rest of Hickman's party was similarly occupied to the left and Jim saw the grenade ex- plode beyond the traverse and he hurried to follow, then stopped. There was a dugout entrance in the section of the trench into which they had vaulted and he didn't want to be attacked from behind. He waited by its entrance, rifle at the ready, for a moment. Then he saw, slung from wooden battens buttressing the side of the trench (the German trenches were so much better constructed than the British), a sling containing stick bombs. He selected one, withdrew the firing pin, waited two seconds, then tossed it down the steep steps leading to the interior of the dugout. A muffled explosion followed. He did the same with a second bomb, then selected two more and followed his men round the buttress into the next section of the trench.

All three were facing four Germans, bayonet to bayonet, while two more defenders lay on the duckboards, killed by the grenade explosions. He put down his bombs and lifted his rifle, desperately trying to get a clear line of fire past the members of his platoon. But this was an anachronistic contest, a melee in a crowded space, steel clashing with steel, such as might have taken place when, bullets spent, infantryman might have confronted infantryman in the trenches before Sebastopol. It was all of thirty seconds before Hickman could get a bead on one of the protagonists, who then fell with a bullet in his chest. Standing back, he reworked the bolt and brought down the other three Germans.

As he did so, a greatly moustached officer, in shirtsleeves but with revolver in hand, emerged from a dugout, cried 'Mein Gott', fired twice at

Hickman, missed and was then brought down by a bayonet thrust to the stomach. Jim picked up one of his discarded bombs, pushed the officer down the steps of the dugout and hurled the bomb after him. The consequent explosion hurled the dead man halfway up the steps again.

Hickman stood, shaking for a moment, with perspiration dripping down his face. His men stood looking at him. 'Round the next traverse, Sarge?' one of them asked. Jim thought quickly; with only nine men, how much of the trench could he possibly hold? Very little more.

He shook his head. He gave the soldier the other stick bomb. 'Toss this over the traverse,' he said. 'Then pull whatever you can out of the dugout to barricade the corner. And we will need something overhead to prevent them bombing us over the top. Find what you can, now. Quickly.' He gestured to the third man. 'You, stand guard by the traverse in the meanwhile. Bayonet anyone who tries to get round.'

He held up his hand for a moment. The shaking had stopped. He had just personally killed nine men – plus goodness knows how many more down in the two dugouts – and he had now stopped shaking. Was he becoming a professional killer, a cold, steel-hearted slayer of men with not enough conscience left in him to summon up a shudder or two? God, what would Polly think of him? Then he heard two grenade explosions up the trench, the way he had come. He shook his head. This was no time for self-flagellation. Bertie could be in trouble.

He rushed round the traverse. The section of the trench by which they had entered it was empty, except for the bodies of its dead guardians. He ran to the next traverse and met one of Bertie's party rushing towards him.

'Sarge,' shouted the man. 'Corporal Murphy says 'e's cleared this section and the next one. 'E's got no more bombs left, but 'e's picked up some German ones. Do you want 'im to go on bombin' up the trench?'

'No. Stay here. I'll go and find the corporal.'

Hickman ran round the next traverse and found Bertie tying a tourniquet onto the leg of one of the men, above a wound that was bleeding copiously. He looked up at Jim and blew out his cheeks. 'He's copped it with a bullet from a bloke who's buggered off up the trench,' he said. 'I didn't think we should follow him. I think we've killed enough Fritzes for one day, Jimmy.'

He jerked his head over his shoulder and Jim saw several Germans lying still but disfigured by bomb blasts at short range. What was left of Bertie's party were standing guard at the furthest traverse.

Hickman shook his head. 'Quite right. We can't hold all the bloody trench if they counter-attack, as they surely will. We've probably bitten off more than we can chew already.' He looked at the wounded man. 'Can you walk a few yards?'

The man nodded, sweat pouring down his face. 'Hobble more likely, Sarge.'

'Good. Help him back to the section behind me, Bertie, and I'll bring your chaps. Three sections is as much as we can hold.'

Then Bertie pulled the arm of the stricken man round his shoulder and together they hobbled to the traverse. Jim beckoned to the men standing guard at the far barrier. He posted one man at the angle of the trench and then, as before, ordered the rest to blockade it, with whatever they could find from a dugout from the entrance of which smoke was still seeping. He was hurrying back when, from ahead, he heard the cry, 'Sergeant.'

Overtaking Bertie, he rushed to the furthest section they had taken, to where the men he had left barricading the traverse were standing. One of them gesticulated to the other side of the barrier. 'They say they're English over there,' he said. 'Could be Jerries, pretendin', like.'

'Who are you?' shouted Hickman.

'Lieutenant Hamilton, A Company, Third Warwicks. Who are you? Call your man off, he nearly shot me.'

Jim did not know a Lieutenant Hamilton, but then he did not know all the subalterns in A Company. 'Tell me the name of the CO.'

'Colonel Angus Bradbury.'

Hickman nodded and gestured to his man to remove the barricade and stand aside. 'Sorry, sir,' he called. 'Just had to be sure. We've only just taken this section of the trench.'

The broken bed and table, splintered by the explosions in the dugout, were pulled aside and a young officer stepped through, followed by a swarthy, moustached sergeant and a handful of men. They were all plastered with mud and grit from crawling across from shell hole to shell hole.

'I saw you put out that machine gun and go in, Sergeant,' said Hamilton. 'Bloody well done. What's your name?'

'Hickman sir. B Company. And this is Corporal Murphy. We've cleared three sections of the trench, sir. I thought we should barricade the traverses and try and hold it until the next wave of the attack comes across. We could give support from close up.'

'Hmmm. This is Sergeant Flanagan.'

'Yes. I know sir.'

Flanagan extended his grin. 'We're old friends, sir.'

'Ah good.' Hamilton ran his hand across his face. 'How many men have you got, Hickman?'

'Eight fit and one wounded.'

'Right. I've got ten. Eighteen to hold about three hundred yards of trench, with a low side facing the enemy. I doubt if we can do it.'

As if to emphasise his words a machine gun opened fire from the village and began traversing along the top of the trench, causing them to duck and take cover against the German side of the trench, as the bullets thudded into the sandbag line low on the other parapet.

'If they shell us we're done for.' Flanagan spoke between gritted teeth.

'Doubt if they'll be able to drop shells down on us accurately,' responded Hamilton, his brow furrowed. 'Too close to their own lines. But they are bound to counter-attack, probably along the trench, feeding in from their communication trench connecting to the village, as well as over the top. We're only about a hundred and fifty yards from the rubble. It will be damned difficult to hold them off.'

'What about the second wave of our attack?' asked Hickman.

Hamilton gave him a slow, ironical smile. 'These ten men are all that's left of my company, Hickman. About ninety men wiped out trying to reach that bloody village over open ground. It looks as though your company has been reduced similarly. God knows what happened to C Company. Maybe no survivors at all, except for what's lying out there in the shell craters. So, the whole battalion has been decimated. I don't think we can look forward to a second wave. In any case, it would have been on its way by now – and nothing has happened.'

The machine gun sprayed the top of the trench again.

'Get out of here, as fast as we can, is what I advise, sir,' said Flanagan.

'Not in daylight, sir,' said Hickman. 'We'd stand no chance.'

Flanagan's face was set in a fixed grin. 'Then we'll just be slaughtered here.'

Hamilton stood erect. 'One thing's for certain. We can't stand arguing the toss here. You say, Sergeant, that you have cleared three sections of the trench? Have you barricaded the ends?'

'Yes sir.'

'Good. Then by hook or by crook we hang on here until the light goes. Then we'll hop it, the way we came in, crawling on our bellies.

Hickman, take six men and man the far section. Flanagan do similarly with the section here and I will take the middle section. Get the men building up the parapet on the German side – use the bodies. There's no time to be squeamish. I expect that they will try and bomb us along the trench first. And, if that doesn't work, they'll come over the top, though that will expose them to fire from our trenches as well as this one. Try and get cover over the top of the trench to prevent bombs landing at either end. Off you go now.'

They exchanged nods and broke up. Jim called Bertie and tapped five others of his original party and they trotted to the far section. They found the men there had built up a convincing enough barricade to close up the gap around the traverse, but nothing over the top.

'Can't find anythin' that'll stop a bomb comin' over,' said an elderly soldier, a Reservist with experience from the Boer war.

'Right. Build some kind of cover around the corner to allow a man to lie there and pick off anyone who comes along the next section of the trench near enough to throw a bomb. You go first. We'll relieve you.'

Jim and Bertie exchanged glances.

'How's the chap with the wounded leg?' asked Hickman.

'It's nasty. I've tried to stop the bleedin', so I have. But I don't honestly think he'll last long. I think it's an artery.'

Hickman nodded. 'Well, in a way I hope he goes. I don't see how we can drag him across no man's land in the dark.'

'Ah, that'll be sad, so it will. Tell me, Jimmy lad…'

'Yes?'

'How many men would it be that we've killed in the last half hour, d'yer think?'

Jim put his hand on his friend's shoulder. 'Now, Bertie. It doesn't do to think about. It's horrible, I know, but this is war, matey. You know that.'

'Oh, I know that well enough, Jimmy lad. I know it all right. I only hope that God will forgive us, that's all.'

Hickman could only shrug his shoulders.

'Ah. There's another thing. D'yer know, I can't remember for the life of me the colour of Polly's eyes. I should know, o'course, but I just can't remember. It would be lovely to have something like that to think about, laddie, wouldn't it, among all this filth? Eh? But I can't bloody remember.'

'Green, Bertie. A wonderful, wonderful shade of green.'

They were interrupted by a rifle shot from around the traverse: 'They're comin', Sarge.' Then another report, followed by an explosion.

Hickman ran and put his head around the traverse. The Boer War veteran had built himself a refuge capped by a sheet of corrugated iron. He was lying spreadeagled under it, his rifle propped on a sandbag, its butt nestling in his cheek. At the far end of the trench the body of a German lay, with the signs of an explosion around him.

Without looking up, the veteran said, ''E tried

227

to get close enough to throw 'is bomb. But I got 'im. They can't reach us by getting along this trench. They'll 'ave to go over the top to us.'

'Good man.' Jim knelt and patted his calf. 'Stay there for half an hour and then you'll be relieved.'

'Very good, Sarge.'

It seemed as though the Germans in the ruins of the village had not quite known what to make of the part-invasion of their trench, for there was no immediate rush to retake it. Maybe the lone bomber had acted on his own initiative, for no other attacks followed – at least at first. The machine gun continued to play across the top of the far parapet, making it suicide to stand on the firing step or move too close to the British side of the wall. Nevertheless, it did not prevent the trench defenders from building up the parapet on the German side, using bodies and sandbags taken from the dugouts.

Then, however, the attacks began. They came along the trench from Hickman's sector. Just after the veteran had been relieved and his replacement was crawling into the tiny redoubt built on the other side of the zigzag, two men emerged from behind the far traverse and ran along the trench to get to within throwing range. They were about to hurl their bombs when Hickman, who had been standing guard as the replacement crept into position, brought them both down before they had had a chance to withdraw their timing pins. A third came from behind the traverse – clearly with trepidation – but a bullet sent him scurrying back.

No one else came forward. It was obviously suicide to attempt to round that traverse now. Shouts and rifle shots (but, significantly, no sounds of grenade explosions) came from down the line, in Flanagan's section.

Hickman ceded his post at the traverse once the replacement guard was in his place and met Hamilton, running along the trench.

'You all right here, Sergeant?'

'Yes, sir. I don't think they will try to bomb us along the trench now. At least not from this end. Has Flanagan held out?'

'Yes, but they got a couple of bombs over. One failed to explode but we lost one man. They will probably try to come at us over the top from the village now. Space the men out as best as you can. When the machine gun stops – that's when they will come. Good luck.'

'Same to you, sir.'

Hickman looked at his watch. Useless, clogged with mud. Then up at the sky. The sun was at about forty-five degrees towards the west. Perhaps – what, five o'clock? They would have to hold out for at least another three and a half hours before they could retreat after dark. And then they would have to leave smartly because the enemy would almost certainly try to swamp them as darkness fell. Space the men... He could not risk taking away the guard at the traverse buttress, for the smart thing to do would be to attack frontally and along the trench at the same time. Would the Germans be smart? Almost certainly. 'Never underestimate the enemy', that's what the books all said. Right. That left only five men, including himself and Bertie, to defend something like sixty yards of trench. Could they do it? They would have to.

He spaced the men out, Bertie next to him, of course, and he distributed sandbags for them to stand on so that the parapet could be reached, for there was no firing step on the reverse side of the trench. Then he checked everyone's ammunition. They had all set out with two hundred rounds per man. Luckily, it had been bayonet and bomb work for most of them so far and their pouches were comparatively full. Ah, the German bombs! He ran to where the bomb holsters were hanging. Three left. Good! He gave Bertie one and, reckoning that he was probably the best bomber among the five, kept two for himself. They could be useful if the enemy attacked in close order.

'As soon as the machine gun stops,' he shouted, 'man the top. That's when they'll come. When they do, it will be rapid fire, so put clips of ammo on the parapet where you can get them easily. Good luck, chaps.' He looked across at Bertie, whose face was drawn and wan and, on impulse, he leant across and shook his hand.

They did not have long to wait. Suddenly everything was quiet as the machine guns stopped clattering. Then they heard a whistle blow.

'Up on the top,' shouted Jim.

As he levelled his rifle he saw that the ruins ahead – so dangerously close – seemed to have come alive. Climbing over the rubble was a line of scuttle-helmeted infantry, their bayonets glinting in the early evening sunlight. Immediately, the thinly held trench burst into fire.

There were many attackers and few defenders, but the British were expert marksmen by now and the range was short. The grey-clad men advancing could not run, for the shell holes broke up the ground and, at that range, the defenders could not miss. They fell in crumpled heaps and Hickman could not help but feel sorry for them as the attack broke up and the remnants retreated.

Nevertheless, remembering the old sergeant in the First Battle of Ypres, he called out, 'Keep firing. It's not against the law to shoot the buggers in the back.' So the fusillade continued until the last German had found the shelter of the ruined village and the torn land in between was left bestrewn with the enemy dead.

'Will they try to outflank us, Jimmy, d'yer think?' called Bertie. Hickman looked to right and left. 'It would mean them coming out into no man's land if they did and the blokes in our lines could pick 'em off. But it's a thought. I'll keep an eye on the back. I only hope the Lieutenant or bloody Flanagan will do the same.'

They exchanged grins at the mention of Flanagan's name.

'D'yer think he knows we shopped him to the redcaps, now?'

'Probably. I think he saw us in that ... er ... bar. But to hell with that. It's getting out of here that's going to be the problem now, Bertie lad.'

'Aye.' The blue eyes regained their twinkle for a second. 'We could do with a bit of starshine now, Jimmy love.'

'Keep watch to the front. I'm going to see the lieutenant.'

Hamilton was kneeling over the original member of Hickman's party who had been wounded in the groin. He looked up at Jim's approach. 'He's gone, I'm afraid. Nothing really we could do. He was beyond just being patched up. Any casualties from that attack?'

'No, sir. Have you lost any – apart from this poor chap, that is?'

'No. But Flanagan's down to four in his section, including himself. One fellow caught it in the head. But Flanagan's a good soldier and can shoot for two. Better get back, Hickman – oh, one thing.'

'Sir?'

'I saw you put out that machine gun and lead the attack. I'm going to recommend you for the Victoria Cross when we get back.'

'Very kind of you, sir. But not necessary.'

'No. I'm lucky to have two good sergeants with me.' Hamilton pushed back a stray lock of blond hair that had escaped his steel helmet. 'It's my first action, this.' He smiled apologetically, looking, thought Hickman, about sixteen years of age. 'Only been out two weeks. Still ... good to be blooded early. What?'

'Oh yes, sir. You're doing bloody well, anyway.'

'Thank you. Good of you to say so. Better get back, Sergeant.'

The Germans came again an hour later, after they had launched a salvo or two of trench mortars at the defenders. Most of them fell short

232

or overshot, but one fell on Hickman's section, wounding one of his men in the shoulder, and another fell on Hamilton's section. Jim was administering first aid when Bertie's cry brought him to the parapet.

This attack was much more sophisticated. The enemy was now crawling across the open ground, making use of the shell holes – as the British had done – while covering fire was being put down from the rubble behind them.

'Wait until they get near and have to show themselves,' ordered Hickman. 'Then the Jerries in the village will have to stop shooting. Don't man the parapet until I tell you.'

Jim had found a trench periscope attached to the far side of the trench and had wrenched it from its mounting. Now he watched through it and observed the grey figures appearing and disappearing as they climbed in and out of the shell craters. To his left, the two other sections in the trench were somehow maintaining firing of a sort but could do little against the shooting from the rubble of the village. At last this fell away a little and he was able to shout, 'Up now. Rapid fire!'

He saw a group of about six Germans emerge from a shell hole dangerously close – some thirty yards away – and he launched himself upright, withdrew the pin from a stick bomb, waited two seconds and hurled it at them. It landed amongst them and exploded, sending two figures tossing into the air and others falling to the ground, their rifles spinning away. A similar group emerged through the dust and he hurled his second bomb at them, only to see it fall at their feet and lie, unexploded. Cursing, he returned to his rifle and worked the bolt rapidly, firing six shots at them at point-blank range. They fell just ten yards from the trench.

The fire from the rest of the defenders in Hickman's section was equally devastating and the attack at their front melted away. But had some of the attackers taken shelter in the pock-marked ground, merely waiting their chance to run forward once the British guard was lowered?

Hickman looked along his line. Every one of his men was still standing. 'Bertie,' he called. 'Keep watch to the front. They may be in the shell holes waiting nearby to rush us. I'm going to check with Hamilton. I will be less than three minutes. Scream if they attack.'

He doubled back to the traverse and rounded it to find only four men left in the section manning the parapet. In the centre of the trench a mortar had exploded. The main force of the explosion had been taken by one infantryman, whose remains were scattered against the trench wall. Nearby lay Lieutenant Hamilton, with much of his chest blown away.

'He's dead, Sarge,' called one of the men at the parapet. 'Didn't stand a chance.'

'Neither do we if they come again,' said the man on his left. 'I reckon we'd better give it up, like.'

'Say that again,' snorted Jim, 'and I'll put a bloody bullet through you myself. That's court martial talk. Look to your front. Corporal Murphy will take over here.'

He ran back and brought Bertie. 'That man there,' he said, pointing at the soldier, 'has talked of surrender. Shoot him if he says it again. I'm going to see Flanagan.'

He rounded the traverse, half dreading what he would see. But only the mortar victim lay on the duckboards. Every other man was standing to, with Flanagan in the centre.

'Sergeant,' called Hickman. 'Can you come?'

Slowly, Flanagan stepped down from his sandbag and approached Jim. Rum was heavy on his breath. 'What's the trouble, sonny?' he drawled. 'Is it gettin' a bit too hot for you?'

'Balls, Flanagan. Listen. Lieutenant Hamilton is dead. That means that there are only fourteen of us to defend about two hundred yards of trench. If they rush us, we're done for. I suggest that we concentrate on just two sectors of the trench. That means you bring your men into the centre section, and move the barricade to this traverse here. We'll stand much more chance if we only have to defend about a hundred and thirty yards. What do you say?'

Flanagan took a draught from his water bottle and then spat. 'I say that's the obvious thing to do. But I'm fucked if I'm goin' to take orders from you, sunshine. You bring *your* men into the centre sector. I'm stayin' here.'

'Very well. But from now on, you're on your own, Flanagan.' He turned on his heel and doubled back to the centre section. He stood next to Bertie. 'Anything happening?'

'Not a thing. I think most of 'em have pissed off back to the home comforts of their billets in

235

that village place. If there are any in the shell craters, they're lyin' very low.'

'Good.' Jim gave the news of Hamilton's death and related the conversation with Flanagan. 'I don't trust the man and I've told him he's on his own. I'm going to barricade his traverse. That means that we will have eight men to defend our two sections. It's not impossible but it's going to be bloody hard. Keep a good watch through that periscope.'

Hickman was barricading the traverse when the Germans began to mortar bomb the trench again. There was little the defenders could do but huddle close to the side of the trench wall and pray that the mortar settings would be inaccurate. These weapons were notoriously difficult to aim in that the bombs were set to hurtle high into the air and fall down virtually vertically. So it proved as long as the bombardment lasted, for none of the men was hit.

Nevertheless, the nerves of the defenders were stretched to the limit as they crouched in the trench. The heat from the sun had long since dissipated as the shadows lengthened, and most of the men had eaten their hard tack rations and, although Hickman and Murphy warned against it, they had drained their water bottles too. There seemed no likelihood of another attack, so Jim set three of the men to dig a ditch on the English side of the trench, leading away out into no man's land. He explained his thinking to Bertie and the men.

'I reckon they will attack soon after darkness has set in. They'll wait a bit until they think we have dozed off, because they know we've had a bit of a hard day. But they will set up that bloody machine gun to traverse the back side of our trench just on the parapet, to stop us popping back over the top. Now, if we can dig a ditch, not a trench but something wide enough for one man to go out and under the traverse of that bloody gun, I reckon we can creep out and get away, if we take great care. Push the earth back down into the main trench, so the Hun won't see what we're up to. Right?'

'Genius,' said Bertie.

Two men set to, one shovelling, the other passing the soil back. It was difficult at first because they had to dig well within the sights of the machine gun, but the gun had stopped firing and it was not long before the ditch was deep enough for the diggers to move beyond its horizontal arc. Soon, as the sun began to set, the ditch had snaked out into no man's land.

'What about Flanagan?' asked Bertie.

'To hell with him. He's on his own.'

As Hickman had predicted, no further attack was mounted on the trench and, as the sun slipped below the horizon, Jim marshalled his men.

'Corporal Murphy will lead,' he said. 'The rest of you will follow in single file and I will bring up the rear.'

'Now, that bit's not a good idea–' began Bertie.

'That's how it's going to be. Now, Corporal, take a bearing now on our lines, so you know where you're going and I'll follow on.' He screwed his eyes to the west. 'Pretty dark now. Better get going, Bertie. Keep your arse down. You don't want to make a target for that machine gun.'

'Ah Jimmy, son, you shouldn't–'

'Start crawling, Corporal.'

It took at least twenty minutes for the snake to wind its way forward so that Hickman, after one last look through the periscope to the darkness of the German lines, could take his place at the rear. It was difficult to make progress, for each man had to place his rifle and bayonet on the soil in front of him and inch his way forward. Eventually, however, the man in front of Hickman had crawled his way onto flat earth and then slithered down into a shell hole.

As Jim began to follow, a voice rang out from the abandoned trench. 'Hickman, where the fuck are you, you bastard?'

Immediately, a searchlight sprang into life from the shattered village and a machine gun began raking the ground. A bullet caught Hickman in the calf and another in the foot as he hugged the ground. A fierce shaft of pain shot up Jim's leg and he cried out as he rolled over and down into the crater, clutching his leg.

Only one other man was in the shell hole. 'Have you been hit, Sarge?'

'Ah.' Hickman gritted his teeth. 'Where are the others?'

'They've gone on.'

'Right. Well, you get going as soon as that light goes out. They'll send up a star shell so be ready to freeze. Don't worry about me. I'll get back in my own time. Go on, lad. The light's out. I'll be all right.'

Reluctantly, the man nodded and cautiously began to climb up over the lip of the crater and was gone.

Biting his lip with the pain, Hickman tried to examine his wounds. One bullet seemed to have gone straight through the muscle of the calf, for he could feel two holes. The other had made a mess of his foot and he began the painful task of removing what was left of his boot. That done, he fumbled for his field dressing and swabbed both wounds with iodine and bandaged them as well as he could, stopping as he nearly swooned with the pain. He realised that there was no possibility of him crawling, let alone walking, back to the lines. He would have to drag himself back through the mud and debris.

Jim drained the last of the liquid in his water bottle and jettisoned it. He took off his pack and threw that away too. Rifle and bayonet? It was a court martial offence to throw away one's weapon, but to hell with that. There was no way he could move while dragging them along too. He took a deep breath and began the slow, agonising journey towards the British lines.

He had no idea how long it took him, for he paused often, not knowing whether he was fainting or just slipping momentarily into sleep. He only knew that, just when he felt he could pull himself no longer over that rough, pain-inducing earth, he heard a familiar voice: 'Jimmy, son. Is that you?'

He raised a weary hand and it was taken and

immediately grasped by Bertie. 'Holy Mother of God, I've bin crawlin' all over this fuckin' battleground lookin' for yer. Are you all right?'

'Never been better, considering I've got two bullet holes in me right leg. But I've never realised before, Bertie lad, what a wonderful voice you have.' Then he passed out.

CHAPTER TEN

Hickman regained consciousness as he was being handed down into the trench. He could hear Bertie saying something but he had no idea what it was, for he was adrift in a sea of pain which seared into intensity as he was jolted along the line and then lowered onto a stretcher. He was dimly aware that his injured leg was being strapped to the other when blessed unconsciousness took him again.

He came to amidst the noise of what he immediately recognised as an advanced dressing station. A doctor was speaking, in the tones of a man who had had little sleep and was harassed and clearly near the edge. 'For God's sake man, don't bring me any more like that,' he was saying. 'There's no hope for them so it's a waste of time and stretcher space to bring them back. Leave 'em out there to die. Bring me ones I can treat...'

Oh Lord, thought Jim. Which one am I?

He was answered when someone rapidly

untied the bandage binding one leg to the other. 'Oh good.' The doctor's face came into focus: moustached, perspiring and haggard. 'You're conscious. What was it?'

'A machine gun,' he croaked.

'Hmmm. Better that than a shell, anyway. Calf's all right. Gone clean through. Foot's a mess, though. Can't do anything with that. You'll have to go down the line. In much pain?'

'A fair bit, yes.'

'Right. I'll give you a jab. Hold still...'

He awoke again – he knew not how much later – to hear someone softly singing: 'At seventeen, he falls in love quite madly, with eyes of–'

'Bertie.'

'Aw, bless the Lord you've come round.' The red, round face came into view, bending over him. 'How're you feeling, old lad?'

'Could be worse. Where am I and what the hell are you doing here?'

'Well, now, that's a fine way to talk to a bloke what's brought you in from no man's land, I must say. Jimmy lad, you're well behind the line at a field hospital. What's left of the battalion – and that ain't much, old son – has been granted a few days' leave behind the lines and I managed to find you here. Can't stay long, so I'm glad you've come round, like.'

'Many of the lads have gone, then?'

'Oh aye, Jim.' The blue eyes had now lost all their sparkle. 'Most of the whole bloody battalion, including the colonel, the adjutant and virtually all of the officers. All attacking that bloody village, so it was. It was a massacre, son.

241

A bloody massacre.'

Hickman grimaced. 'Did Flanagan get back?'

Murphy's face reflected the grimace. 'Yes. The Devil favours his own, so he does. Unlike you, though, he didn't bring anyone back with him. An' he tried to cause trouble but didn't succeed.'

'What do you mean?'

'He reported you to the only one of our officers to survive, Captain Willerby of C Company. He said you had deserted the trench with what was left of your platoon an' left him stranded, so to speak.'

Hickman stirred. 'So I bloody well did. What happened?'

'I told the captain that Lieutenant Hamilton had told us to get out after dark and one of our blokes backed me up. Willerby wasn't much interested in Flanagan, anyway. Comin' back with none of his men an' all that. It left a nasty taste in everyone's mouth, so it did. But you brought your blokes back.'

'Ah.' Hickman looked down at the cage that formed a blanketed frame above his right foot. He nodded downward. 'What happened there? I've been under for what seems like days.'

The smile came back to Bertie's face. 'I gather that they've operated on yer foot. I don't know how successful it's been, Jim, but the good news is that it's a Blighty One.' He leant over the bedside, his face now beaming positively beatifically. 'You're goin' back home, lad. You'll be seein' Polly before long.'

Jim returned the grin. Then it faded from his

face. 'That means you will be left with Black Jack.'

'Well, yes and no. We are being posted to a new battalion that's being made up of bits and pieces from others that have been knocked about. He's in a different company still. Anyway, I'm a bit senior these days, a two-striper and all that, so he won't find it as easy to sit on me. What...?' He looked up as a nurse gestured to him. 'Ah. Time's up. You're supposed to be a bit delicate at the moment, 'cos you've lost a lot of blood. So I'm off.'

He sought Jim's hand and grasped it warmly. 'Don't worry about me. Go home to dear old Brum and Polly and enjoy yourself. Kiss her for me – though not too much.'

Jim returned the grip, as best he could. 'Thanks, Bertie, for bringing me in,' he said.

'Ah sure that was nothing, you'd virtually reached the line by then. God bless yer, dear lad.'

'Goodbye, Bertie. Stay clear of Flanagan – and the Jack Johnsons.'

Five days later, via Boulogne, Folkestone and Victoria Station, Hickman was in a hospital in Islington, North London, where a letter was awaiting him from Polly, obviously prompted by Bertie, for Jim had not written. It was full of concern about his wound, asking how long he would be confined there and telling him that if it was longer than a week she would get leave and journey down and see him. Would it mean, she asked a little wistfully, that he would be invalided out?

It was a question that had been hanging over

Jim since the operation had been carried out on his foot in Flanders. So hectic was the pace at the field hospital that there had been no time for a consultation with the surgeon. He had been given a blood transfusion, his foot and ankle had been encased in plaster and he had been shipped back to England within a matter of hours, so keen was the pressure on the staff there. It was, he reflected, like a production line serving the grim machinery of the ever-continuing Battle of the Somme.

In Islington, however, a charming lady doctor – he didn't know there were such exotic creatures – had removed the plaster, examined him carefully, had a new plaster dressing put in place and reassured him that the broken bones were beginning to knit together satisfactorily and that he should be walking again within two months.

'Does that mean I can get back to the front again?' he asked.

She looked at him quizzically. 'Most of the men in your situation aren't so anxious to get back,' she smiled. 'But yes. If that's what you want, I think we will be able to make that recommendation. You've got a fine constitution that has held you in good stead in losing all that blood. You must stay in bed here for a couple more days and then we'll show you how to walk on crutches. Then you can go home on convalescent leave. But don't overdo it.'

He grinned. Jim penned a letter to his parents, a longer one to Polly telling her not to waste precious leave in journeying to London for he would be home soon, and, finally, a note to Bertie, thanking him again for dragging him to the British line. He had been told that, left out in no man's land, he would have died from loss of blood if he had not received attention. The Irishman had undoubtedly saved his life.

Hickman could not help noticing that the England he had returned to had changed subtly, even in the year since his last leave. The ongoing fighting on the Somme was now creating the kind of horrendous casualties that no British army had ever faced before. And these grim lists were being printed in the newspapers daily, so that the frightful cost of Haig's policy of attrition was there for everyone to see. It was rumoured that the average life expectancy of an infantry officer in the front line was now about three months. Jingoism had disappeared from the home front in the late summer and early autumn of 1916 and a grim acceptance of suffering had taken its place – that and growing criticism of the conduct of the war.

The indolent Asquith had been replaced as prime minister by Lloyd George, his Minister for Munitions, and a coalition government had been formed. A new sense of dogged resolution seemed to be in the air; a realisation that the suffering that was now entering into almost every home was likely to continue for the unforeseeable future. Military conscription had now been introduced for men between eighteen and forty-one, unless they were widowed or ministers of religion, and married men had ceased to be exempt from May 1916.

On his gentle perambulations on crutches in Islington, however, Jim noticed that volunteers were still being sought for the armed forces. Following a recent air raid on London, one poster urged:

IT IS BETTER TO FACE THE BULLETS ON THE FRONT THAN BE KILLED AT HOME BY A BOMB. JOIN THE ARMY AT ONCE AND HELP TO STOP THE AIR RAIDS. GOD SAVE THE KING!

Polly was waiting for him on New Street Station when, eventually, he was released from hospital and sent on home leave. His heart leapt when he saw her, emerging like some mythical princess from the steam issuing from the locomotive. Her hair was bunched up underneath the little straw boater – although the summer had gone – which was tied by a scarf under her chin and she wore a long, full skirt and a tight-waisted jacket of blue that showed off her figure. She was already crying as she saw him, lumbering towards her on his crutches and in his hospital 'blues'.

She raced towards him and almost knocked him over with the force of her embrace, burying her face in his neck and then covering his mouth and cheek with kisses.

'Whoah,' he called. 'I'm supposed to be a frail, wounded soldier.'

'I know,' she said and kissed him again.

He pushed her away to study her for a moment. Her face seemed drawn, accentuating her high cheekbones, and the green eyes seemed now to be luminescent under the tears. To him, she seemed to be more beautiful than ever.

'Oh, Poll,' he breathed.

'Come on, hero.' She smiled at him through her tears. 'Let's go to Yates's and I'll buy you a drink. Here, I'll take that.' She leant down and, with an effort, picked up the heavy kitbag which had been on his shoulder when she'd leapt at him.

'No, no. You can't carry that.'

'Course I can. I'm a strong factory worker, keepin' the machinery going while you loaf at the front line. Come on.'

She set off, staggering a little under the weight of the bag and almost disappearing under its size. He could not catch her, though, to relieve her of her burden and she strode ahead while he hopped and skipped behind, shouting for her to stop. They attracted smiles from a dozen hitherto gloomy faces on the station platform.

In the wine lodge, they drew more sympathetic glances as Polly dumped the bag by a small table in the corner and imperiously beckoned the waiter. 'Something red and expensive,' she ordered.

Jim grinned. 'My God, Pol,' he said. 'You've become quite a big girl.'

For a moment, Polly's grin faded. 'Oh yes,' she muttered, turning her head for a moment and thinking of that back room off Victoria Road. 'While you've been away, my lovely boy, I've grown up a bit.' Then she smiled again. 'But now that you're back, I'm just a little girl again. Perhaps we can play marlies in the gutter when you're better.'

So they talked, bantered and chattered – of Bertie, of his wound, of the factory, of their parents, of the rationing now increasingly in force and, just a little, of the war. Jim realised that Polly was under no illusions about how bad it was at the front. The newspapers now were telling it as it was, so she was aware of the growing casualties and the futility of many of the attacks. Jim, however, steered the conversation away.

He cleared his throat. 'Still got my diamond, Pol?' he enquired lightly.

She blushed. 'Oh yes, love. I've still got it.'

'Haven't changed your, mind, then?' He tried to keep his tone conversational and cheerful.

She looked down at her lap and then, quickly, up at him. 'Can I keep it a bit longer?'

'Of course, Pol. You keep it as long as you like, as long as you don't give it back to me.'

'It's just that...' She looked around the room, as though for inspiration, then leant forward and took his hand. 'I love you, Jim. Please be sure of that. Let me be for a bit longer, eh?'

'I shall let you be until you're ready. Now,' he reached for his crutch, 'I think we should make for the tram. My folks will be beginning to worry. No.' He prevented her from taking the kitbag. 'That's too big for a little thing like you. I can manage it on my shoulder, though you'll have to take it off me to get on the tram. Come on, lass.'

Together, they walked through the crowded streets to the tram stop in Corporation Street, a wounded soldier and his girl, a not unfamiliar sight in wartime Birmingham. They parted with a light kiss in front of number 66, with the promise to meet later, for Mr and Mrs Hickman had invited her parents and Mr Murphy in for tea that evening to celebrate Jim's return.

The next evening, Hickman waited outside the works gate at Kymestons to meet Polly at the end of her shift. Because his foot was throbbing, he chose to wait by a brick buttress supporting the outside wall, where he could lean and relieve the ache. He was, then, half hidden as he eventually glimpsed Polly in the middle of a stream of workers. She was chatting happily to a tall, older woman when he saw a man hurry to catch her arm and say something to her. She shook her head and hurried on but he grabbed her arm again. This time, she shook her arm free and gave him a half push and ran after the woman. Then she saw Jim, turned and ran towards him, her face aglow.

She pecked his cheek and took his free arm, holding it tight.

'Who was that?' he asked, nodding his head.

'Oh, that's Connie, she works on the line. She's a good mate.'

'No. Not her. The bloke who grabbed your arm.'

Polly flushed. 'He's our foreman. He's nobody really. Just a bloody nuisance.'

'Oh.' Jim let a silence develop for a moment. 'Why is he a bloody nuisance?'

She shook her head impatiently. 'He keeps trying to get me to go out for a drink with him after work. I suppose he fancies me. He's married with two kids and–'

'Why isn't he in the army, then?'

'It's supposed to be a reserved occupation.' Polly sniffed. 'But I, or Connie for that matter, could do the job just as well. He ought to be at the front.'

'I'll break his bloody neck.'

She tightened her grip on his arm. 'No you won't, love. He's harmless, really, and I wouldn't dream of going out with him. I don't fancy him for a minute. I like my men to be either six foot two inches tall or very short with red hair.' She giggled. 'And that's enough for me, thank you very much.'

He smiled but looked back over his shoulder to see the man with the slicked-back hair turn up a side street and he made a mental note.

The days were cold now and Hickman ached to make love to Polly. She was affectionate as they did the normal things that courting couples did – go to the moving pictures, once to Aston Hippodrome at the bottom of Potters Hill to see Eugene Stratton and even taking a tram to the Lickey Hills, as his walking improved – but she was careful to restrain him as they kissed and cuddled at the evening's end. He wondered about Wagstaffe. Could there be something there? Then he dismissed the idea. Polly was not that sort of girl. Nevertheless, he decided that, once his foot had recovered, he would have a quiet word with the man with the shiny, wavy hair.

This peacetime idyll was disturbed about ten

days after Jim's return when they both – Polly and Hickman – received a letter from Bertie. He had secured leave! If the Holy Mother spared him, he reported, he would be back in Turners Lane within the week. They were both to meet him at the station, for he would catch a train from London that would arrive in the evening. And would they tell his father because the old feller couldn't read, as they both well knew.

Jim felt his heart fall at the news. Then he felt ashamed. His best friend, the man who had saved his life, was coming home to join them for ten days – it should have been a cause for rejoicing. Now, he realised, he would have to share Polly. Well, he shrugged his shoulders, they always used to. They were inseparable. A trio linked by pure, unsullied love. No. He shook his head as he looked at the pencilled scrawl. There was no getting away from it. Things were, well, different now. He realised he was jealous. Ridiculously, stupidly jealous. Why had things changed? It was, he knew, the thought, the suspicion, that Bertie had made love to Polly that night in London. 'With eyes of tender blue' be buggered! That was why she was restrained with him now. She loved Bertie more. He felt a sadness consume him that was more acute than the pain from his wound. This, he realised, was going to be difficult to live with.

He put on a brave face with Polly who, of course, was consumed with delight that the three would be reunited for the first time since the war came to blight their existence. They must, she said, make arrangements: a party at her house with her and their parents, visits to the picture palace and the theatre for the three of them and she would try and get the holiday time that was due to her so that they could spend days together. Why, perhaps they could all go away together! For one terrible moment, Jim thought that she was going to propose a few days in Malvern – and perhaps she was, for she suddenly fell silent and nothing more was said about that.

They dutifully paraded on Platform No 1 and waited for the London train to emerge from the tunnel. Polly perhaps sensed Jim's ambivalence for, as they stood there, she suddenly reached up, kissed his ear and smiled up at him. Nothing was said. Was she trying to reassure him or was it the beginning of a long, rather sad farewell?

It was the old Bertie who half fell out of the train in his eagerness. His kitbag was undone at the top, of course, and what appeared to be a pair of long johns were beginning to trail from the opening. One of his boots was undone and he trod on the laces as he rushed towards them, falling onto the bag and then, getting up, and laughing, laughing.

They all embraced, with Bertie giving Polly the kind of kiss that Jim felt should be reserved for the bedroom. Then the talking began – or rather, Bertie began. His was stream-of-consciousness stuff: a non-stop recounting of the journey, the new battalion to which they both now belonged, how he missed them both, and wait until Polly saw the French perfume he had brought her, and how nothing had been seen of Black Jack Flanagan so perhaps the good Lord had taken him in His mercy ... and so on.

Polly interrupted him. 'Let's go and have a glass of wine at–' she began but Jim intervened. 'No,' he said hurriedly. Dammit, he was not going to share even that precious table in the corner – *their table* – with Bertie. 'I think Bertie could do with a pint of ale. I could certainly do with one. There's a good pub around the corner. Come on.'

He bent to pick up the kitbag but Bertie was quicker. 'Good idea, son,' he said, throwing the bag over his shoulder so that the long johns hung down his back from the bag like some strange pennant. 'How's the foot and the leg, then? Looks as though you're hoppin' about quite well. Did I tell you about old George Cooper in C Company...?'

That night there was a convivial party in Polly's house, to which other neighbours as well as the soldiers' relatives were invited. Mr Johnson, of course, had an upright piano in the parlour and Bertie insisted on singing 'At Seventeen' to Polly, whom he lifted onto the piano top. Jim observed that she had the grace to look embarrassed, for what Bertie lacked in musicality in his rendition, he made up for in passion, clutching her hand at the end with the words '...And he loves her as he's never loved before.' Dammit, the little man was becoming almost proprietorial about Polly, in front of everyone, too!

For Jim Hickman, the ten days of Bertie's leave seemed to drag slowly. Polly had been unable to get leave so the threesome were reunited only in the evenings, for she was on the day shift, and at one weekend, when they went rowing, as of old, in Handsworth Park and borrowed bicycles – by this time Jim had been able to substitute a stout walking stick for his crutches – and cycled up the dusty track to Barr Beacon, one of the original beacon signal points established across England to warn of the Spanish invasion. The old comradeship, however, seemed to have slipped away, to be replaced by a rather forced conviviality. At least, so it appeared to Jim – and, he sensed, also to Polly – although Bertie seemed sublimely happy in their company.

He and Bertie had taken to meeting Polly at the work gates every evening and twice he had noted that Wagstaffe – he had learnt his name from Polly – had walked to the gates with her, earnestly chatting (or was it beseeching?) before peeling away when he saw the two men in uniform. He began to hate the appearance of the man, with his gleaming shoes and shining hair. This was matched with a growing annoyance at Bertie's open flirting with Polly and his constant touching of her and snatched kisses. Hickman ached to be alone with Polly and was torn with a sense of disloyalty to his old friend. The result was that he became even more taciturn and monosyllabic in their company. He realised that this was doing nothing to help his relationship with Polly, who occasionally upbraided him with it: 'Come on, Jim, love. Give us a smile.'

On the last day of Bertie's leave, for which Polly had managed to wangle a day off, Jim deliberately arranged a hospital appointment, an examination he said had been set up weeks before and could not be changed, for it involved a complicated series of tests. In some sort of compensation for his behaviour, he argued with himself that it was only fair that the lovers should have the day to themselves. As a result, he brooded in the corridors of Birmingham's General Hospital, deliberately wasting time before and after his appointment with the military doctor. It was only Polly, therefore, that went with Bertie to the station.

Sitting on a wooden bench in the hospital, Jim's frustration grew until, at roughly the time that Polly would be kissing Bertie goodbye, he came to a decision. He limped out of the hospital, swinging his wounded leg with energetic conviction, and boarded the tram, getting off two stops later at Witton. He looked at his watch. Good, he had only about five minutes to wait. Taking up position behind the brick buttress near the Kymestons gate, he clenched and unclenched his fist as he reflected on his position. The girl he loved was undoubtedly in love with his best friend – whatever she said, that must be the truth, otherwise she would have accepted his proposal of marriage. This was not Bertie's fault, nor Polly's. It was just sad, bloody sad. No, worse than that...

His internal fulminations were interrupted by the appearance of Wagstaffe, walking in his smart shoes and suit, head in the air, amongst a crowd of girls. He let the man pass him, then fell in step behind him, hurrying to keep up with his dot-and-carry gait until the man turned into the quiet side street into which he had made his way the first time Hickman had seen him.

'Excuse me,' Jim called. Wagstaffe turned and a quick look of recognition flashed across his face.

'Sorry,' he said quickly. 'Can't stop.'

'Oh yes you can.' Balancing unsteadily, Jim reached out with the curved handle of his stick and caught it underneath Wagstaffe's chin and pulled him back as the man tried to walk away.

'I want a word with you.'

'Now, there's no need for violence,' said Wagstaffe. 'I've never laid a finger on Polly. And besides,' he gestured, 'you've got a bad foot.'

'Ah, you've noticed. Now I wonder how I got it?' A slow burn of rage began to rise within Hickman's brain. All the frustration of his love for Polly, his affection for Bertie and of the mess that it seemed his life was descending into came to a head within him. The man in front of him was not to blame but, by God, he was a mean, despicable object, the sort of man who was doing well in a safe job at home while good men were being killed!

He hooked his free hand under Wagstaffe's tie and pulled him close. 'I'll tell you how I got it, friend. I was shot twice by a German machine gun on a day on the Somme when thousands of good men died. They died while you were feathering your nest back here and trying to pull innocent young girls into bed, you fucking little

256

twit.' He released his hold, swung his fist back and hit the man on the cheekbone.

Wagstaffe immediately went down with a cry. In a fury, Hickman lifted his stick and beat the man about the head and shoulders, hitting him repeatedly as the foreman crouched, foetus-like, on the pavement screaming, his hands lifted in an attempt to protect himself.

How long the beating would have continued Jim had no idea, for he saw in the pathetic figure cowering at his feet the symbol of all his troubles. Then a firm hand seized his arm and a voice said, 'Now, that will do, Sergeant. The man's an Englishman, not a German.'

He turned, perspiring, to look into the eyes of a large, elderly policeman. 'What?' he said. 'What? Oh, yes. I'm sorry. Dammit ... lost control. Sorry. Sorry.'

The policeman said, not unkindly, 'Now just you stand against that privet hedge there, Sergeant, while I help this man up.' He turned to Wagstaffe, who remained crouched on the pavement. 'Are you hurt, sir? Can you stand? Yes, get up now, I'm sure you can. There will be no further violence.'

The foreman scrambled onto his hands and knees, his oiled hair hanging over his forehead, blood on his tie and shirt and his suit covered in dust. Then he stood, unsteadily. 'The man's a lunatic,' he gasped. 'Don't know the man from Adam but he suddenly starts hitting me. I think me collarbone's broken. Bloody lunatic.'

'I see, sir.' The constable looked at Hickman and back at Wagstaffe. 'I presume then, sir, that you will be proffering charges, in which case I must ask you both to come with me to the station.'

'What? Er ... no. Let it drop.'

'What about your collarbone, then, sir?'

'I think it's all right.' Then in a sudden burst of anger, 'But this bastard should be locked up.'

The policeman waited a moment. 'Well,' he said, 'this "bastard", as you call 'im, is wearing the ribbon of the Distinguished Conduct Medal, 'e's earned the rank of sergeant and 'e's obviously been wounded. If you wish to have him locked up you must proffer charges. Which is it to be?'

'Bah.' Wagstaffe snarled. 'Let it go. I've got to get home for me tea, anyway.' He brushed his suit with his hand, pulled a comb from his pocket and adjusted the waves in his hair, glared at them both and walked away.

'Now, Sergeant.' The policeman turned to Hickman. 'What was it all about?'

Jim found himself trembling. 'Sorry. I lost it, I'm afraid. Glad you came along, otherwise I might have killed him.'

'Exactly. So ... what was it about? You obviously knew 'im?'

'Yes, well sort of. He's my girlfriend's foreman at Kymestons. He's a married man in what they tell me is a reserved occupation, but he's been trying to get her into bed for over a year. She wants nothing to do with him, but he keeps bothering her. I was going to try and reason with him, but I saw red, I'm afraid. It won't happen again.'

'It had better not. He could 'ave brought a case of grievous bodily 'arm against you. You mustn't be violent, you know. I should think you see enough of that at the front. Now, from now on, Sergeant, avoid the man – and tell your girlfriend to do the same. All right? If he carries on, then perhaps the thing to do is to 'ave a word with the management at the works. Eh?'

'Yes, thanks. Thanks.'

'Good. Now here's your stick, son. Walk all right back 'ome?'

'Oh yes, thank you. I'm all right now.'

'Very well. Good day to you.'

'Goodbye, officer.'

Hickman found he was still trembling and his foot was throbbing from where he had twisted it in making the assault, but he hobbled away, engulfed in a sense of shame and embarrassment. Thank goodness no charges had been made! Whatever would Polly have said if it had got back to her? He shook his head as he limped back to Turners Lane. He had undoubtedly become a violent man, there was no escaping it. If the constable had not arrived he could well have killed Wagstaffe. And killing now came easily to him, he recognised; a resolution to escape difficult situations, whether they were in the trenches or back home in peaceful Birmingham. Aah, he looked up at the heavens, this dreadful war had so much to answer for!

Polly had been put on night-shift working immediately after Bertie's return and Jim did not see her for a couple of days, deliberately leaving her to herself as he wallowed in a mixture of shame and embarrassment. But he did not escape the aftermath of his attack on Wagstaffe.

'Did you do it?' she demanded the next afternoon, as they met to go to a Chaplin matinee at the Globe cinema.

'Er ... do what?'

'I think you know, Jim, don't you? Did you attack Wagstaffe and beat him up? Did you? He's come to work with his arm in a sling and a black eye. Everyone's talking about it.'

Hickman thought briefly about lying. With Wagstaffe's reputation, there could well be other jealous boyfriends. But there was no way he could dissemble in the face of the cool, inquisitorial glare from those green eyes.

'Yes, I did, Pol.' He looked at the pavement. 'Didn't mean to. Just meant to have a word with him and warn him off you, so to speak. But I lost it, I'm afraid. Sorry Pol. It's not like me.'

'Oh Jim. I do hate violence. You shouldn't have done it. The man is a prat but I can look after myself and you have no right to interfere.' She stood outside the cinema, her head back, her eyes blazing. 'Whatever made you do it?'

'I well ... er ... I meant to protect you, I suppose. But I lost my temper. The bloke said something about my foot and it set me off.'

'I don't *need* protection, Jim. If I do, I'll call the police, thank you very much.'

Hickman stood in awkward silence for a few seconds. 'Yes, well,' he muttered, 'I suppose I've been under a bit of stress. You know,' he added slowly, 'I don't like violence either, Pol. The real me, that is. But my life for the last two years has been a bit different, I suppose, and it's made me a bit different, too. But I'm sorry if it's upset you.'

Suddenly, she relented. She threw her arms around him and held him tight. 'Oh Jim, it's me who should say sorry. And I do, I do. Talking to you, of all people, like that.' She put her head back and looked up at him through the tears in her eyes. 'I feel like a spoilt little bitch with two chaps fighting over her.'

Relieved, Jim grinned back at her. 'As a matter of fact, he didn't fight back at all. If he had done, I would have fallen over bloody quickly. I can't fight on one leg, you know.'

'Oh Jim.' She nuzzled her nose under his chin. 'I'm sorry. I think we've all been under a bit of a strain, what with Bertie being here, and all. I suppose we are not three children any more, playing marlies and football together. We've all grown up and you, my love, most of all. Never mind.' She withdrew her arms and blew her nose. 'Come on, Sergeant, let's go and have a laugh with old Charlie.'

They did and, indeed, they did laugh. But things were never quite the same; never quite as open, quite so uninhibited. With Bertie back in France, Jim had resolved that he would ask Polly to find a way of coming away with him for at least one night, so that they could make love. Now, however, he dreaded her rejection and decided to let their relationship find its own level again. So, as his convalescence leave began to draw to a close, they resumed a relationship of gentle courtship, unconventional only in the erratic working hours kept by Polly. The affray with Wagstaffe was not mentioned, except once, when Polly grinned and said, 'That bloody man, by the way, has not said a word to me since you hit him. I think you've sent him back to his wife!'

Despite its wrench in the scuffle, Jim's foot continued to mend (the calf wound had healed completely much earlier) and he requested of his army doctor that he should be allowed to rejoin his regiment in France. The major shook his head. 'No,' he said. 'Much better that you spend a bit of time back here as an instructor. The army desperately needs experienced NCOs like you to teach the youngsters going over how to do it.'

Hickman's thoughts immediately fled to Bertie and he squirmed on his seat. 'With respect, sir, if I'm any good at all it's in doing, not teaching. I think I am needed over there much more than here. I'm not a good teacher and I would make a hopeless instructor. My battalion has been re-formed and made up of kids just over. They will need me, I know, to help the youngsters to fight. I can do that better by example. I'd be grateful, sir, if you would send me back. I want to be with my regiment.'

The major looked at him appraisingly and with a slight smile at a twenty year old speaking of 'youngsters'. 'Well, if you're that keen, lad, I will make that recommendation. Keep off the foot as much as you can until you're over there and, if there's a problem, use the ankle bandages the nurse will give you.' He stood up and extended his hand. 'Good luck, Hickman. May God go with you.'

Polly, of course, came with him to the station and there, as they stood waiting hand in hand on the platform, she referred only for the second time since his return to their relationship.

'Nothing's changed, Jim my love,' she said shyly. 'I still love you. But I want to wait – for all kinds of reasons. Do you understand?'

'No. But I will wait.'

Then the tears streamed down her face. 'Oh, Jim. Don't get killed. And give my love to Bertie.'

The words 'bugger Bertie' flashed through Jim's mind briefly and were instantly dismissed. He kissed her and wondered if it would be for the last time.

CHAPTER ELEVEN

Jim Hickman knew that he had to return to the front. He hated the thought of getting back to the ritual of the trenches, with its danger, discomfort and brutal discipline, but the strange life he had lived in Birmingham for the last few weeks had been artificial; he had been existing without purpose in a civilian world where he had felt out of place and virtually impotent. By assaulting a man, he had revealed a side of him that shocked, although he supposed it could be blamed on the savagery of the war. Otherwise, he had little to do but yearn for Polly and, he realised grudgingly, the company of Bertie. He had pleaded to be returned to his old regiment, now re-formed, and to its A Company, where Bertie served. Amazingly, in an army where such considerations were usually crushed in the unthinking bureaucratic grind, he found his wish granted.

The battalion was now well behind the line, still on the Somme but in an area where the intense fighting of the summer had died away, with both sides bleeding and desperate to re-group.

Corporal Bertram Murphy, of course, was delighted to see him and although the new CO, Lieutenant Colonel Wilberforce, a tall, seemingly nervous man, gave him only the briefest of acknowledgements when he reported, his company commander, Captain George Cavendish MC, was delighted to get such an experienced, although young, sergeant under his command. Predictably, the company sergeant major, the placid Sergeant Major Blackshaw, had survived the carnage of the mid-summer fighting and immediately marked Hickman down to relieve himself of much of the arduous duties in the company. Sergeant Flanagan, of course, was tucked away in B Company and was rarely to be seen.

'It's cushy here,' Bertie explained. 'We're mainly on supply duties and too far back to be bashed by the shelling all the time. How's Polly – oh, and how's your foot?'

Jim noticed that Bertie had lost some of the

bounce that had so characterised him when on leave. Now, he seemed thoughtful, almost introspective, although he remained one of the most untidy and scatterbrained NCOs in the battalion. After Jim had been back a few days, he also noted that Bertie seemed to have lost his reputation for marksmanship, of which before he had been very proud. Then, of course, he realised that there were hardly any veterans left who had shared their early days together, so few would know of how good a shot he was. And there were no opportunities behind the lines for him to display his skill, anyway.

The opening months of 1917 on the northern plains of France were cruel and wet, even for support battalions well behind the line who were housed in billets. For the British army in France it seemed almost as though the war had peaked in the great effort of the Somme. There was no actual hiatus, of course, for the fighting continued along the long line of the trenches and high overhead, where the Royal Flying Corps daily duelled with the German pilots. But the high tempo had died away. It had become clear that the great Somme offensive had really been a succession of battles fought over a wide front and it was rumoured that a hundred and fifty thousand British soldiers had died in them and that three hundred thousand or more had been maimed or wounded. It was whispered that the end of June alone had seen a count of one hundred and sixty-five thousand casualties – almost double the entire strength of the British Expeditionary Force which had set off to confront the Germans at Mons. Ground had been won but at such a high cost that it seemed unlikely that Britain could sustain such losses. From where would the next Big Push come? Would there be one? Had both sides, indeed, fought themselves to a standstill?

The soldiers of Jim and Bertie's new battalion were a mixed bag, made up of the survivors of other units decimated in the Somme battles and batches of new recruits recently arrived from home – the products of the new, compulsory conscription. The aggressive spirit that had so characterised the volunteers of 'Kitchener's Army', however, was missing from both the old hands and the new arrivals. The survivors carried their sad experiences with them and the new boys had read the long casualty lists in the newspapers. Both knew that this war now possessed no elements of romance or glamour; that the reality of it was bitter, savage fighting where death was sometimes the better option than dreadful mutilation and maiming.

The conscripts had received basic training in Britain, of course, but survival in the line carried an extra dimension. Despite his assertion to the doctor that he was no instructor, Hickman found himself in the role of teacher to most of the men in his platoon, once the battalion marched up to the front again. He was not proud of the violence that he knew he could call on quickly, or of the temper that he realized now lay just below the surface of his seemingly equable character. He was determined that, for Polly, he would survive this nightmare world in

266

which he had lived for so long and he realised that controlling his aggression and using it to be a good soldier was the route to follow. He accepted that he must pass on what he knew.

So, when in the line, he resumed his old practice of taking handfuls of men out into no man's land after dark, to lie beyond the wire and absorb the tensions and dangers of that frightening place. He passed on advice about taking great care in using the latrine trench in daylight, for snipers often trained their sights on such places. And he warned never to light three cigarettes from one match, because the ever-watchful sniper would be alerted by the first glow, would sight his rifle on the second and fire on the third. Smoking indeed produced its own dangers all along the line. The need 'for a draw and a spit' was so strong that members of nocturnal working parties had been known to light up when out in front of the wire. It was such stupidities that Hickman was at pains to stamp out.

Jim's feeling of friendship with Bertie was rekindled in these days and he felt ashamed of his old, incipient jealousy. So he took great care to write fully and cheerfully back to Polly, mentioning his friend whenever he could. Her letters and gifts to both of them continued to arrive regularly and she wrote warmly.

Nothing, however, seemed to revive the sparkle that used to make Bertie such a popular member of his platoon and company. It had been regained, of course, when he was on leave in Birmingham. But the drudgery and brutality of life in the line now seemed to have almost completely extinguished it. He regularly attended Mass when they were out of the line and he seemed to take comfort from the services. Yet the effect soon wore off. It seemed as if the killings that had been incurred in the attack on Guillemont, what he had seen and heard of other, similar offensives, and the continuing brutality of life in the line, had made a permanent impression on him.

For Jim, at least then, the news that the battalion was being posted was a relief. The move, the change, might shake the little Irishman out of his lethargy. That relief, however, was quickly removed when he heard that they were going back to Ypres – to the dreaded Salient. Was this going to be the next Big Push...?

The talk, then, as they went by train and marching, south and then north-east again over the Belgium border, was all about 'breaking out of the Salient'. For well over two years, the great armies had faced each other in Flanders and fought each other in successive battles that had produced stalemate, with each side aggressively on the defensive. The Allies were entrenched in a line that ran from the coast in the north, at Nieuwpoort, skirting the virtually impenetrable flooded swamplands north and south of Diksmuide, down to the bulge of the Salient before Ypres, the town itself now nothing more than a pile of bricks and stone, and then sweeping back below the high ground of the Messines Ridge to the Belgium-France border and the plains of Northern France. Everywhere, however, the

Germans commanded the high ground, particularly from the ridges overlooking the Salient. From these vantage points, they had won every round in the fight so far.

On the march back to Flanders, Jim used every opportunity to talk with his company commander, Captain Cavendish, a well-read, approachable young man, not much older than himself. It was Cavendish's theory that the spring of 1917 would see the Allies making a huge effort to break the stalemate on the Salient.

'It makes sense, Hickman,' he said. 'These bloody U-boats are causing hell with our shipping across the Atlantic and threatening to starve us out back home. They are creeping out from the Belgian coast, from the canals around Bruges and so on. We're not far away in the Salient. If we could only break through the German line along the ridges, out onto the plain behind, then swing left and down to the coast we could take those ports, liberate Belgium and win the naval war right under the noses of the navy.' He grinned. 'A double triumph, don't you think?'

'Hmm ... yes, sir. If it wasn't for the Germans in between, eh?'

'Ah, we've both seen enough to know that they're tough nuts, I grant you that. But we've sorted out the shell problems that blighted us in the early years, there's this new tank thing that's being spoken of highly and we're starting to get command of the skies. I reckon we could do it.'

'Well, I hope you're right, sir. I hope you're right.'

Hickman had his doubts. Everything he had seen so far had proved that the Germans were magnificent defensive engineers. He could not see them sitting on top of those hills for well over two years without reinforcing their line with steel and concrete constructions, the concept of which the British seemed to scorn. To 'dig in' so comprehensively would be to refute the Allied conceit of being an attacking force, mobile and always ready to advance. Jim sniffed at the thought. He could not see the merits of a waterlogged trench as an attacking springboard.

And they returned to the Salient to find that it was, indeed, waterlogged.

No roads existed to the east of the mounds of crushed stone that was all that was left of the once architecturally proud town of Ypres. The definition of a road everywhere now was a line of duckboards that wound between shell holes. Soil had disappeared to be replaced by mud. Back up to the line they went, cold and wet, back to trenches whose walls kept crumbling and whose bottoms were under water.

'This is bloody disgraceful,' said Jim, pulling up the collar of his cape. 'We should build proper trenches at the bottom of the Salient, back on the other side of the canal, fortify the rubble of Ypres, like the Boche did at Guillemont, retreat down the slope, and let the Germans beat their heads against us until we are ready to advance properly.'

'Ah yes, James.' Bertie nodded his head dolefully. 'But you're not a general are yer? At least, not yet.'

270

They were in a part of the line where the Germans were comparatively close, less than two hundred yards away. They could be heard digging and there was much activity at night, after dark, with patrols criss-crossing the holes and mud pits between the lines. The point of it was not for patrols to clash, but to forestall a sudden frontal attack in the dark and to bring back intelligence about the digging of mineshafts by either side.

Part of the defensive ploy by the British battalion was the digging of a sap, or narrow trench, at right angles to the line, out towards the German trenches. The purpose was to establish a listening post as near to the enemy as possible. Manning the post after its completion was a three-man job, but it was an extremely dangerous task, for the men were comparatively exposed out in no man's land, in a shallow trench and near the German line. The tension in what was little more than a muddy ditch was high and, as a result, the men nominated for the task were relieved at three-hourly intervals.

In the midst of this activity, the genial, laissez-faire Company Sergeant Major Blackshaw was killed, a sniper's bullet taking him neatly through the centre of his forehead, just underneath his steel helmet, as he was supervising, a little too obviously, the changing of the men in the sap.

'You'll get the job, surely now, Jimmy,' said Bertie. 'Jesus – a company sergeant major at the age of twenty. Now, there's a thing!'

But he did not. Given the high casualty rate in

the front line, promotion came quickly for good young soldiers. Hickman, however, was probably a shade too young for the job and the worst happened: Sergeant Flanagan was transferred back to his old company and promoted to company sergeant major to lend an experienced, steadying hand to the young company commander.

'Ah shit, Jimmy,' said Bertie, when the news came through. 'Why couldn't they have sent the sod to guard the King at Buckingham Palace?'

With him came Black Jack's bullying ways. He regularly patrolled through the night as well as the daylight hours to ensure that no one on the fire step closed his eyes, for even a second. Thanks to him, two men were court-martialled for the offence. He reduced the guard in the sap to two men, saying that there was insufficient room for three men to defend the post if it was attacked. So strong was Flanagan's personality that no one considered complaining to Captain Cavendish and, anyway, Flanagan was old-soldier enough to stay always just the right side of army regulations and within his authority.

Corporal Murphy knew that his turn for persecution would come and so it did, just a week after Flanagan's transfer.

'I'm to stand to, *all through the night, mark you,* in the sap tonight,' he confided to Hickman, his face white under the dirt. 'And I'm goin' to be on me own, so I am. Just me out there, within touchin' distance of the bleedin' enemy, all night long. It's murder, Jimmy, that's what it is. He wants me shot or plucked out of the bloody trench by a raidin' party.'

Hickman frowned. 'He can't do that, Bertie. What reason has he given?'

'He says that one man on his own will concentrate better at the listenin', see. And it would be too dangerous to relieve him in the hours of darkness.'

'That's bloody ridiculous. It's the best time to make a relief.'

'I know. He wants to see me dead, Jim. Just because I'm a Catholic.'

'I'll have a word with the captain.'

'Thanks, lad. But I don't think it will do any good. The company commander seems to think the sun shines out of Flanagan's arsehole.'

Bertie proved to be right. Cavendish listened, frowning, to Hickman's complaint but then shook his head. 'Flanagan is a hard man, Hickman,' he said, 'I know that. But he is very experienced and I want to give him his head in the company. It's no good having a dog and barking myself, you know. And I can't allow him to be undermined by an NCO. That will be all, Sergeant.'

'But, sir–'

'I said that will be all.'

As dusk fell over the smoking battleground, Bertie inched his way along the shallow sap carrying his rifle and bayonet and flattening himself against the side to allow the two men he was relieving to return to the main trench. He had hardly settled down, however, nervously peering over the top to the German wire, when

273

he heard a sound behind him and whirled round, his rifle at the ready.

'I thought I'd keep you company,' said Hick-man.

'Bloody hell, Jim. You scared the livin' Jesus out of me. But what are you doin' here?'

'I told you. I'm keeping you company. Here, I've got some grenades. Take these. We shall need 'em if we get visitors.'

'Aw, Jimmy lad. You're a real friend, so you are. But you'll cop it, if Flanagan finds out. He wants me quietly murdered and you're spoilin' his party.'

'Balls to that. I'll stay with you through the night and creep out just before your relief comes.'

A relieved grin stole over Murphy's face. 'Thanks, son. I have to tell yer that I was shittin' myself at the thought of staying out here all night on me own. Two's company, they say, don't they? We could almost play marlies, so we could, to relieve the monotony.'

Hickman returned the grin. 'I have a feeling that it's not going to be exactly boring out here.' He risked a peep over the top. 'Jerry knows we've dug this sap out and I've been expecting him to have a go at it one night since we finished the digging a couple of days ago. It could just be tonight.' He was silent for a moment. 'In fact, the more I think of it, I feel that Flanagan had the same thought. He's no fool. That's why he stuck you out here on your own tonight. He expects the sap to be raided.'

'Oh, bloody hell. Then I'm glad you're here,

son. He's an evil man, that Flanagan. So he is.'

'Okay. Settle down and be quiet. We've got to listen. I've bought a couple of flares to send up if we think they're out there coming at us.' He smiled wryly. 'Good old starshines. They just could save our bacon tonight.'

Bertie nodded eagerly. 'Aye. Send 'em up and the Lord will be with us.'

The dusk settled and the night began – a nervous, worrying period for the two men, crouched in discomfort at their listening post, in what was little more than a prong stretched out towards the enemy, and so near to him that it presented almost an invitation to slip out from his own lines and snip it off.

Hickman had already ascertained that no patrols were to be sent out that night from the British lines, so he knew that any noises he might hear would almost certainly come from the enemy. They decided, therefore, to take it in turns to doze, while the other kept watch.

It was just before 3 a.m. when Jim heard, out to the front, the scrape of a buckle against stone, followed by the distinctive slurp of a boot being freed from the embrace of mud. He nudged Bertie and the two now listened together, intently. There it was again. People were moving out there, quite near to the sap head.

Slowly, Hickman picked up the Very pistol, pointed it high and fired it. The cartridge hissed up high, vertically, and then exploded in a shower of blue light, showering stars – starshine undoubtedly – as it slowly sank. Both men looked over the top. At first, there was nothing to be seen but the moonscape of no man's land in blue relief: mud everywhere, puddles of water and blackened and stunted remains of trees. Then, concentrating, Hickman saw small mounds of grey mud, symmetrically lined up some forty yards away. They did not move, for they had frozen close to the ground, of course, as the Very light sizzled upwards, but he recognised them for what they were: the small battle packs strapped to the backs of a platoon of German soldiers.

'Bombs, Bertie,' he whispered and he seized two Mills grenades, pulled out their pins and threw them in quick succession at the prostrate attackers. Bertie followed suit and the four bombs exploded, almost as one, straddling the line of Germans. Immediately, a shrill command was given in German and half a dozen figures topped by distinctive coal-scuttle helmets rose from the mud and ran – or rather slipped and slithered in the mud – towards the sap head. At the same time, a machine gun stuttered into life from the British lines behind them, but its fire was random and its bullets hissed high over the heads of Hickman and Murphy as they stood erect to meet the charge.

Jim was aware of a second Very light climbing high from the British lines as he levelled his rifle and brought down the nearest of the attackers. Bertie did the same and both men hurriedly worked their rifle bolts to insert another round into their breeches and fired again. Two more Germans fell but the remaining two were nearly upon them, discharging their rifles from the hip as they ran.

Bertie exuded a cry as a bullet took him in the upper arm and he slipped to the ground, struggling in the mud to regain his footing. But Jim firmly put his boot on his comrade's spine and pressed him down again, then standing astride the little Irishman, he presented his rifle and bayonet at the two men virtually upon him. He locked his bayonet onto that of the leading German, swung it round and crashed the butt of his rifle into the man's face, sending him staggering back. As he did so, he heard a rifle shot close behind him and the second attacker was sent sprawling, a bullet in his chest. Another bullet – this time from no man's land – plumped into the sap wall at his side and Jim picked up a Mills bomb, withdrew the pin and hurled it in the general direction of the marksman.

He turned to see Sergeant Major Flanagan right behind him, working the bolt of his rifle. The warrant officer was alone but, disregarding him, Hickman bent down to see to Murphy. The Irishman was clutching his upper arm, from which blood was gushing freely. Jim used his bayonet to tear open the cloth above the wound and extracted his own field dressing and hastily applied it to Bertie's arm, tying it tightly to restrict the bleeding.

'Leave him alone, you stupid fool,' said Flanagan. 'There might be a second attack at any second.'

'Then you'll just have to deal with it, won't you?' He looked up at the sergeant major, who had rested his rifle on the parapet of the sap head. 'You bastard,' he said. 'You deliberately put Murphy out here on his own so that he would be killed. You're a murderer, Flanagan, that's what you are.'

The man turned his head for a moment and his teeth flashed in the semi-darkness. 'That would have served you both right for shopping me to the redcaps in Pop, wouldn't it? And you be careful how you address a superior officer, Sergeant, or you'll be put up against a wall and shot. I'll see to it. Anyway, you would both have been dead if I hadn't kept my eyes open and helped you out. You–'

He broke off as a lieutenant and three men scrambled up the sap to join them. 'Any casualties?' cried the officer. 'Ah. Corporal–'

'It's all right, sir,' gasped Bertie. 'It just hurts me when I laugh.' Then he fainted. He was carried back to the junction of the main trench where he was revived on the fire step with the aid of a little water and rum. One of the dead Germans was also brought back so that his regiment could be established. The man that Hickman had hit with his rifle butt had vanished; presumably he had crawled back to his own lines with whoever had survived the Mills bombs, for no further sign of life could be seen in front of the German wire. The lieutenant left his three men to man the sap – three men, Jim noted – and Hickman made his way along to the cramped dugout that was company HQ. He found Captain Cavendish awaiting him.

'With respect, sir,' said Jim, 'Corporal Murphy would be a dead man and we would have

278

had a bombing party creeping along the sap to attack our line if I had not supported Murphy out there. One man would have been overwhelmed.'

Cavendish had the grace to look uncomfortable. 'Quite so, Hickman,' he said. 'I thought about it after we spoke and that's why I ordered Flanagan to go up the sap to report on how Murphy was coping. I gather he arrived just in time.'

'Yes, sir. I have to say that sticking Murphy out there on his own, through the night, was an act of personal malevolence on the part of Sergeant Major Flanagan towards the corporal.'

The captain frowned and gestured for Hickman to sit on the camp bed. 'That's a very serious charge, Sergeant. Why on earth should Flanagan take so against Murphy, a Northern Irishman like himself, indeed?'

Jim shrugged. 'I have to say I don't really know. It is certainly to do with religion, in that Murphy is a Catholic and I presume that the sergeant major is a Protestant. There was also a bit of business...' he tailed off and squirmed in his seat '...back in Pop, when Flanagan was arrested by the military police for assaulting a prostitute. He thinks we put the redcaps on to him.'

'Hmm. And did you?'

'Yes, sir. If we hadn't he would have killed the girl.'

'Yes, I seem to remember something about that.' Cavendish stood, as did Hickman. 'Now look here, Hickman. If you want to make this a formal complaint, then it will have to go up to the colonel and possibly the brigadier. I am not sure you would want that, would you? Prejudice is awfully difficult to prove you know, and Flanagan is a first-rate soldier. It might well go against you.'

'Well, I–'

The captain broke in quickly. 'What I would propose is this. I can't have this sort of animosity going on in my company.' He ran a hand across his brow. 'I have enough problems as it is. So there will have to be a posting...'

'Don't break up Murphy and me, sir. We've been together since we were four years old and have served together throughout the war so far, on the Salient and on the Somme...'

'I am aware of that. I believe that Flanagan will have to go. Now listen,' he held up a hand as a grin spread across Jim's face, 'not a word of this conversation must stray from this dugout. Do you understand?'

'Of course, sir.'

'Very well. D Company have just lost their CSM. I will try and get Sergeant Major Flanagan transferred to that company and you, my lad, will become my sergeant major. A bit early for you, I fear, but I have observed your training of the men. You've obviously got pluck, and you have shown commendable ability and leadership – not least on this last night's miserable business – so I hope you won't let me down.'

'Of course not, sir. I'm very grateful.'

'Well, I haven't fixed it yet, but I think I can. I think the colonel and the adjutant will agree. No more arguing with Flanagan, now. Stay well clear of him. Now bugger off and get some sleep.'

'Very good, sir. Thank you.'

'Ah, one more thing. While you were in the sap, did you hear anything? Are they mining us, do you think?'

'I didn't hear a thing. So I should doubt it.'

'Good. Off you go.'

Once outside, Jim wanted to let out a yell of triumph but thought better of it. He hurried to tell Bertie the glad news but Murphy had been sent back to a field hospital. It seemed unlikely, he was told, that the Irishman would go back to England for treatment, because the German bullet had gone right through the upper arm, tearing a few ligaments. It would be treated in the hospital and then he would return to the regiment.

Jim's next thought was of Polly. Would she be impressed by his promotion to warrant officer? It was unusual for one so young to be so elevated, but she, of course, would be unaware of that. Would his success make her think more kindly of him as a husband? His brow wrinkled. Polly Johnson was an enigma. He had to recognise that. She said that she loved both of them equally, but how could that be? Perhaps – horrible thought – Bertie's wound would win him sympathy in her eyes; she was, after all, a most sentimental person. He shook his head. For all he knew, dear old Bertie had slipped her a diamond, too! – he also had contacts in the Hockley trade. He blew out his cheeks and settled down to write a letter to Polly, telling her of Bertie's wound but emphasising that they were both alive, well (comparatively, that is) and still smiling. As a PS he diffidently gave the news of his promotion.

Cavendish was as good as his word and Flanagan disappeared to D Company, without a further word with Hickman. Jim dutifully sewed on his new crown, just above the wrist, and assumed the duties of a warrant officer grade II. His was a popular promotion, for he knew, better than any newly arrived subaltern, the hell that was life in the trenches and he did all he could to alleviate the conditions: taking particular care that the men got their mail regularly, that the food came up to the lines even under bombardment and that petty stupidities of line discipline were eased away.

So the regiment took its turn at line duty and then rested back, usually at Pop, where the dangers of meeting Flanagan were increased, of course, because the battalion trained as one unit. If Black Jack noticed Jim's promotion he gave no sign. After four weeks of rest and recuperation – but no home leave – Bertie returned to his duties. Hickman tried not to recognise his satisfaction that Murphy had not earned a trip to Blighty and so had an opportunity to woo Polly, but, nevertheless, was delighted to have his old comrade back in the line with him.

The winter of 1917 gave way to a spring that seemed no drier, and rumours that 'a Big Push' was in the offing increased. It seemed clear that the high command was waiting merely for better weather before attempting to break out of the

Salient. Certainly, training back down out of the line became more intense and specific. Gone were the instructions about how to survive in the trenches. Now, the emphasis was on attack: how to advance in units of platoon rather than company; how to recognise objectives; how to relay messages back to battalion and then brigade headquarters about the specifics of land and targets taken; what to do about prisoners of war. Something, definitely, was in the air.

Whatever it was, however, was transferred to the line in France for a while and in the spring of 1917 the British attacked between Bapaume and Vimy Ridge in what became the Battle of Arras. The men waiting and training in the Salient watched the battle in the south but the Germans at Arras had retired to their Hindenburg Line, defending in depth with well-wired, concreted pillboxes. Once again the British attack faded away and Jim and Bertie realised that the next push must come in their area of battle, the long fought-over few square miles of mud and holes that formed the Ypres Salient.

Throughout that spring the preparations intensified. The battalions were now rotated strictly, with periods in the line punctuated with spells at the rear, where training was precise and sophisticated, compared with what had gone before. Previously, the company had been regarded as the principal unit of the army in attack. By now, however, the emphasis had shifted to the platoon. These units had now been reorganised, making each one self-contained, almost a miniature army of four sections: two

Lewis guns, a rifle grenadier section containing bombers, plus two sections of rifle and bayonet men. When advancing, the Lewis guns supplied covering fire, the rifle grenadiers acted as artillery and the riflemen made the assault.

It became clear as the spring of 1917 wore on that the new system was to be tested in full on the Salient. Yet the attack did not come.

'Why the hell don't they let us go?' asked Bertie, now in command of two Lewis guns. 'If they wait much longer, I shall be too bloody old to carry this gun, so I will.'

Then, as they were under training out of the line, one of the great secrets of the war was unveiled. Since early in 1916, miners had been active on both sides tunnelling towards each other's lines. This was known even to rankers like Jim and Bertie and, indeed, there had been a kind of subterranean warfare conducted under no man's land across the front, with mines being exploded pit-shaft to pit-shaft with sometimes horrific deaths resulting when men were buried alive. But these were comparatively minor affairs – a clash of specialists – resulting in few casualties. The scale of the excavations carried out by the British at the southern end of the Salient had remained unknown to the rank and file.

In fact, throughout that year and far into the winter and spring of 1917, special teams of miners had been digging twenty-one tunnels, sometimes to a depth of eighty feet, along more than three miles of the British front on its right flank, creeping out beneath the German emplacements on Messines Ridge. Huge mines had been laid at their ends and, at 3 a.m. on the morning of 7th June, they were all exploded at exactly the same time.

It was, said observers, 'as though the earth itself had risen up in anger' and, lying three miles behind the line, Jim and Bertie, whose battalion was part of General Gough's Fifth Army, had been woken in alarm at the sound of these massive explosions, far stronger and louder than anything produced by shellfire. For weeks they had watched as thousands of fresh troops of General Plumer's Second Army had marched through their lines and up to the front. Now these men – eighty thousand of them, supported by tanks – were launched at what was left of the enemy's lines in this hitherto impenetrable sector and reports flooded back of 'white-faced Germans', weaponless and with their clothing torn, surrendering to the advancing British.

The British surged forward and were only stopped when, further up the rise, they met with fierce resistance from a sophisticated German second line of defence, involving massive concrete and steel strongpoints, camouflaged so that they could not be detected from the air and surrounded by strategically sited foxholes holding machine guns and snipers. The attackers, tanks and men alike, were badly mauled and fell back.

Hickman's prediction about the German foresight in preparing defence in depth was proved true. Nevertheless, the Battle of Messines had undoubtedly been won and that ridge taken.

There was general rejoicing across the Salient. It was clear that the Great Offensive, breaking out along the whole of the line, would follow.

And yet again there was a delay. Company Sergeant Major Hickman, back in the rear, drilled and re-drilled his men, some of whom were recruits brought in to replace the inevitable casualties that resulted from life in the line. Meadows were marked out and taped to represent the areas of attack. The orders went out consistently: 'Advance with your company. Do not stop to help the wounded, the bearers will do that. Stick with your platoon. Stop and consolidate at your objective while the next wave passes through you to the next line of attack...' Incongruously, nightingales began to sing as they trudged back to their tents at the end of each day.

As though in retaliation to the Messines explosions, soon afterwards the Germans to the left of the front used their own new weapon, mustard gas. After release, it became a dark oily fluid which not only emitted deadly fumes but seeped into the earth and clung in the holes and at the bottoms of the shell craters. It often had a delayed-action effect, clinging to the uniforms of the poor devils who had sought shelter in the craters, and it even attacked the nurses, way behind the lines, who removed the gas-drenched uniforms of their burnt and blistered patients. They became dazed, with dreadful coughs and hair and skin that had been turned yellow. It was the latest horror in a conflict that was becoming more barbaric by the day.

Bertie heard of this and he fell silent and did not speak for two days, except to converse to do his duty. Then, in a quiet moment, he confided to Hickman that he could no longer see any point in the continuation of the war.

'Jimmy,' he said, resting his hand on his friend's shoulder, 'it's just pointless. We blow them up, buryin' alive hundreds of the poor bastards, and then, in retaliation, they shower us with this awful stuff, burnin' the poor lasses who are just helpin' the wounded in the hospitals. It's just ... what's the word? ... escalatin', that's it – it's just escalatin' all the time. Where's it goin' to end, matey? All of us poor devils standin' and lyin' in the mud tryin' to kill each other. It's barmy, Jim. That's what it is. Just plain barmy. It's against nature and not at all what the good Lord put us on earth to do.'

A silence fell between them. Jim swallowed. 'Well,' he said eventually, 'I suppose, Bertie, that those views are probably shared by all of us poor buggers in the front line – on both sides. But, son, we can't stop now. We've got to finish it off and push these bloody Germans back into their own country. Don't forget, we didn't invade Germany. It was them who invaded Belgium and France. Now they break all the rules with this new gas. They have to be stopped and that's all there is to it. We've just got to get on with it, lad.'

Bertie sniffed, but no more was said.

One of the inevitable consequences of Jim's promotion was that he and his old friend could not spend much time together, for the company sergeant major was the right-hand man of the company commander and was on call through day and night. Nevertheless, when at last the bombardment started, on 16th July, the two of them, having felt the earth shake underneath them in their camp behind the lines, walked towards the front up a slight promontory to gain a view of the giant cannonade. As they stood, the darkness was lit up ahead by an arc of flame that danced from one side of the Salient to the other. The slimy, pockmarked approach to the front was illuminated by the fire of three thousand heavy guns only a little ahead of them, which was supplemented by pinpoint flashes of light artillery in the distance, standing wheel to wheel just behind the line.

'Ah,' intoned Bertie, 'pity the poor buggers takin' all that.'

'Aye,' agreed Jim. 'On both sides.' He knew that the German guns would reciprocate.

The bombardment, of course, formed the overture to the great attack and it was said that the guns could be heard in London some one hundred and twenty miles away. At almost exactly that moment, heavy rains began.

The British command, it emerged, had waited until the French were in position to lend support for the attack and the delay meant that the fine spring weather had been allowed to slip away in inactivity. If the field of the Salient was bad before, the rains of late summer 1917 made it unbelievably worse. From what was left of the gates to Ypres, to the heights where stood the little village of Passchendaele, about five miles away, the shell craters stood lip to lip, separated only by the slimy bridges of mud that snaked around their edges. Worse, the bottoms of the craters were all now filled with liquid mud that promised a slow and frightful death. Even if the mud didn't suck a man down, many of the craters were impregnated with mustard gas that could still cause terrible burns if it touched flesh.

It would be sheer murder to send troops over that ground to attack established defensive positions but as General Haig, the British commander-in-chief, explained to the War Cabinet, if all else failed, the campaign could still be won by attrition. The side with fewest casualties would win. When the bombardment eventually finished, then, on 31st July, the attack began. The final objective would be the small village of Passchendaele that perched on top of the highest ridge. Here, Haig was assured, his troops would be 'as dry as a bone'. Yet the rain continued to pour onto the boot-sucking mud fields down below.

It was the beginning of four months of hell for Company Sergeant Major Jim Hickman, Corporal Bertie Murphy, and the rest of the British soldiers condemned to advance over them.

CHAPTER TWELVE

Jim and Bertie moved up with their battalion to join the attack four days after it opened. They moved, of course, at night to avoid attracting attention from the German artillery which, as ever, commanded the whole of the Salient and which throughout the British barrage had replied in kind, showing that, once again, the long, supposedly devastating, Allied shellfire had not put out the German guns.

It was, of course, dark – except for the Very lights up ahead and the flashes of the explosions – and raining. The movement up to what passed as the front line was almost as dangerous as attacking the German line. The threat here – apart from the speculative enemy shelling – was the mud. In fact, as Jim attempted to put one squelching boot after another, he realised that the terrain he was attempting to cross was not mud, it was a surface made up of liquid gunge, under which lay the thicker ooze that could hold a man and pull him down. The real danger here lurked in the bottom of the shell craters. A false step in the darkness could lead a heavily laden man to slip down the sloping sides into the glutinous bottom, from which it was extremely difficult and sometimes impossible to extricate him.

'For God's sake, Jimmy,' murmured Bertie,

'grab me if I go. With this gun, I'll never be able to stop meself sliding.'

The two-gun Lewis section was at the back of Bertie's platoon, which, in turn, brought up the rear of A Company. As company sergeant major, Hickman was last man, there to pick up stragglers and help maintain some form of uniform company advance. In fact, this worthy objective was impossible to attain. There was no track or road, only the slippery edges of the shell holes to negotiate and with only the man in front to show the way. As the troops groped their way forward, attempting to avoid the remains of pack mules and other corpses that emerged from the mud, they could hear a great sigh from the bottom of the craters as a bubble would burst and release the foul air expelled from some bloated human or animal remains caught in the depths. It was, mused Jim, like picking your way through Hades.

He attempted to establish some kind of discipline, with each man holding onto the shoulder of the man ahead, but this too was impossible to maintain as the soldiers slipped and sank in the slime. The marchers attempted to help each other as a leader would murmur to the man behind 'deep one here, keep to the right' and the warning would be passed on. Sometimes a man would go waist-deep and have to be hauled out. It was not a march, more a wade through and between a series of devilish obstructions, waiting to pluck men down. The Lewis gunners were at a particular disadvantage because they had to carry these four-and-a-half-feet-long, twenty-eight-pound machine guns as well as their own equipment. Hickman attempted to relieve Bertie's men of part of their burden at the rear by carrying some of the forty-seven-round magazines. As he staggered along, he prayed that, elsewhere in the darkness, they were not losing men to the mud because of their similar millstones.

The men were, indeed, heavily laden. Marching – or rather slipping and sliding – into battle, each man now carried eighty pounds of equipment: rifle and bayonet, haversack, gas mask, water bottle, bombs, ammunition and, down the back of every fourth man, the pickaxe or shovel that would send him ramrod straight into action, unable to crouch and dodge the enemy fire. The machine guns were additional burdens.

It was 3 a.m. by the time the last stragglers came in to find the tape at which they were to line up and dig in. They were all exhausted, but they were now close to the German line and in the morning they would attack it. Digging a trench of sorts was vital, for the enemy artillery was hurling shells at them consistently, if not exactly accurately. And, as Bertie observed, you couldn't attack another trench if you didn't have one to attack it from in the first place. That just wasn't like the army...

Once again the first assaults had not met with the predicted success. It had become apparent that the Germans regarded their front-line trenches as mere outpost positions. Their real defences lay further back, concealed by the folds in the ground between the ridges: pillboxes, heavily fortified; deep dugouts from which the men would emerge once the barrage had ceased; and the hidden machine guns.

Jim Hickman knew this and had no illusions. As the men of his company crouched in the ditch they had dug for themselves just before dawn – a ditch that had filled with water as soon as it was dug – he sloshed along the line, pouring extra slugs of rum into their water bottles. As he went he kept repeating the attack mantra: 'Open order, now, keep with your platoon, don't stop for the wounded, not even for your best mate. The stretcher-bearers will be right behind...'

Would he stop for Bertie? He knew he would. Please God – Bertie's good, merciful God – that the situation wouldn't arise.

Then, as a pewter-coloured dawn began to lighten the rain clouds, the whistles blew and Jim urged his men forward. He moved to where Bertie with his two men servicing his Lewis gun brought up the rear and he put his hand behind his comrade and pushed him and his heavy gun up the slight slope ahead. Their first objective was the German trench that could dimly be seen ahead, as a long grey line, some one hundred and fifty yards away.

Heads down, rifles and bayonets held across the body, the men advanced. It was not a cohesive movement, certainly not an attack, for they could hardly extract one mud-clogged boot after the other as the slime sucked at their feet and legs.

'Open order,' screamed Jim. But there was not, could not, be order of any kind as the men plodded on.

Then the machine guns began. The fire came from much further away, behind the German trench and up the slope. Perhaps because of this it was not as devastating as it should have been, given the slow progress of the troops. Even so, men began falling. Because of the weight on their backs, the stricken men fell forwards, face downwards into the mud, some of them sliding down the sides of the shell craters. Either way, the result was death, for it was as possible – no, as likely – to drown in a few inches of mud as in three feet of the stuff.

'Get on, Bertie, for God's sake,' yelled Jim. 'Get into that German trench. It looks as though it's unoccupied.'

In fact, it was not, although only lightly manned by the look of it. What was left of the company's advance guard had bombed their way into it and only a few, frightened men in grey were left, hands held aloft.

'Get your guns set up, Bertie, and direct your fire on their gunners.' This was easier said than done, for the reverse side of the German trench, their 'friendly' side, had no fire step and Bertie and his men had to pull out sandbags for them to stand on and then form some sort of protection on the trench top for their own guns before they could fire them.

Hickman looked behind him. The slope up which they had so laboriously climbed was littered with the men of A Company, a few of them trying to crawl forward but most of them ominously still, their faces in the mud. Up ahead, he could make out an indistinct line of grey-painted, concrete, round boxes sited along the top of the ridge. Some of them leant over crazily, steel bars projecting out from the concrete, having received a direct hit from the British guns. Most of them, however, were very much occupied and spitting fire from their gun slits. The first few yards beyond the German trench were lined with British dead, where the deadly fire had caught them.

Jim wiped the rain from his eyes and realised that Captain Cavendish was standing by his side.

'We've got to get on, dammit,' said Cavendish, gesturing to the men huddled in the trench.

'Madness, sir. We'll be mown down as soon as we climb out into the open. There's no way we could get over this open ground in this mud without being cut to ribbons. You'd lose the whole of your company.'

'Huh.' The captain gestured behind. 'Haven't got many left.'

'Can't you call down a barrage on those pillboxes?'

'All my signallers with their equipment have been killed.'

'Very well. We'll direct our Lewis-gun fire on their slits and see if we can crawl forward under their cover.'

'Yes. But I agree. Don't do anything foolish. We may be forced just to stay here and hold this trench. I've lost my subalterns already. I'll try and find the colonel. Carry on, Sarn't Major.'

As if on cue, Murphy's two Lewis guns chattered into life. They fired in short bursts and, through his field glasses, Jim could see fragments of concrete jumping away from the wall fringing the firing slits in the pillboxes. Immediately, the German fire slackened. It was good shooting at such a range and Hickman grinned. Bertie had regained his skill as a marksman.

He pulled out his whistle. 'Right,' he shouted. 'At the whistle, get over the top and let's put those bloody pillboxes out of action. Bombardiers at the front. Try and leave a field of fire for the Lewises. Right. Go!' And he blew his whistle and climbed up the trench ladder at the head of what was left of A Company.

Immediately, he was floundering in the mud. This was ground that had been pounded for weeks in the heaviest bombardment that the war had known and the heavy, consistent rain had made it a morass even worse than that lower down the slope between the old lines. Before he had taken three desperate, lunging strides, he was up to his thighs in mud and sinking. Bertie and his men were still firing their guns, but he knew they would have to change their drums soon and then the attackers would all be stuck, literally, facing the Germans in the open like sitting ducks.

He looked around and as far as he could see, men were thigh-deep in mud. Turning to go back would be suicide.

'Make for the nearest shell crater,' he screamed, 'and fire from the lips.' They had to maintain some form of aggression.

He turned towards a crater to his right and winced as he heard sharp plops as he struggled through the mud. All around him, bullets were hissing into the morass. It was like being trapped in a nightmare; he wanted to move faster but the mud held him back. And now the foot that had taken the German bullet all those months ago was hurting like hell, as he twisted and turned it to free it from the mud.

How he made those few yards to the shell hole without being hit he did not know and he offered up a brief prayer to Bertie and his fellow gunner whom he could hear were still directing their fire at the machine-gunners in the pill-boxes. He half rolled, half fell over the lip of the crater and clung on for dear life to stop himself falling into the yellow, stinking pool at the bottom.

A lance corporal and four men were already lying on the slope beneath the lip. They looked as though they had stepped out of a painting from Dante's inferno. Caked from head to foot in mud, their eyes white caverns in their dark faces, they looked like demons and regarded Hickman half in astonishment, half in fear.

'What the bloody hell are you doing, lying still like that?' he roared. 'Get your bloody rifles over the edge and return their fire.'

'Can't sir,' said the lance corporal. 'They're clogged with mud. Can't fire 'em.'

Jim blew out his cheeks. 'Then clean the fucking things. We're not going to stay here until the Jerries come walking over and pick us off. Go on. Clean 'em. Use your bloody handkerchiefs.'

Slowly, the men began to pick the mud off their bolts and firing mechanisms. Jim eased himself to the top of the crater. Bertie and his fellow gunner were still blazing away and the fire from the pillboxes had reduced noticeably. He eased his own rifle over the lip and sighted it at a slit from which came an occasional flash of fire. Then he stopped. Would his gun fire? He inspected it discreetly. Hmm. Would it...? He sighted again and – it fired. He turned to the others and grinned.

'Always look after your weapons, lads,' he said. And laughed to himself at the thought. He had become the very model of a modern sergeant major!

The little group stayed in the crater for about an hour. Then slowly, Hickman in the lead, they eased themselves over the rim and crawled upwards, dipping into the next shell hole as they attracted fire, then crawling on again until, reaching a patch of firmer ground, they stumbled forward at the crouch. On the way, Jim collected other remnants of the advance who had taken refuge in holes and craters, until he had about twenty men under his command, crammed together on the slopes of a large shell hole. For one blessed moment the rain stopped and a wan, watery sun began to appear.

'What are we going to do now then, sir?' asked a grey-haired corporal. 'Can't quite take on this German line on our own, eh?'

'No, Corporal. But we can give 'em a hell of a fright. How many bombs do we have?' He counted five Mills grenades. 'Good. That's enough to put out a couple of pillboxes. Right. Now, listen.' He wiped a grimy hand across his brow. 'We stay here until dark. Sorry, but it's going to be quite a wait – probably about four hours or so. We lay low so Jerry will think that we've either bought it or buggered off. Break out your field rations and let's share what rum and water we've got left...'

He left his sentence hanging for a moment. The corporal said: 'Er ... and then what, Sarn't Major?'

'We take on the whole bloody German line on our own. No. Only joking.' He grinned and indicated over his shoulder. 'We are going to put out those two pillboxes nearest to us. But first, you, Corporal,' he indicated the lance corporal whom he had found in the first crater, 'will wriggle back to our line. Find either Captain Cavendish or Corporal Murphy with the Lewis guns, and tell them that...' he wiped the mud from the face of his wristwatch '...at about eight pip emma tonight, just when it's getting dusk, the Lewises should open fire on the four pillboxes up ahead and keep it up for about five minutes. That should give us a chance, in the dusk and under cover of the firing, to crawl up to the things and post our letters through their boxes. Got it?'

The lance corporal gulped. 'Blimey. Very good, sir. Should I go now?'

'No, wait a bit. Break open your rations first. Set off in about two hours. It looks as though the attack has completely failed so the Jerries won't be keeping such a close watch. Any questions?'

The grey-haired corporal raised a hand.

'And when we've knocked out the pillboxes?'

Jim took a swig from his water bottle. He wrinkled his nose in disgust. Too much rum! He wiped his mouth. 'Then, Corporal, we make an orderly retreat back to our own lines, crawling on our bellies and sliding down shell craters on our arses for much of the way, I expect. Right, do your best to relax, lads.'

The taste of the rum inspired a sudden thought. 'Anybody know the date?'

The corporal responded. 'I think it's the fourth of August, Sarn't Major.'

Hickman put his head back, so that the edge of his steel helmet tilted upwards revealing his face. He was grinning. 'Well blimey! Do you know what, lads,' he said. 'Today's my birthday.'

'How old are yer, sir?' one of the younger men called.

He answered slowly, emphasising each word. 'I am exactly twenty-one bloody years old today.'

The corporal's disbelief echoed that of the rest of them. 'What? Only twenty-one...?' he said, his mouth open. His thoughts were unspoken but clear for all that. This tall, supremely confident warrant officer acted and looked – mud-covered and completely dishevelled as he was – like a veteran, as though he was at least in his mid thirties. Yet he was one of the youngest in the group.

Jim grinned and nodded. 'Yup. If I was at home now, I'd be given the key of the door.'

The thought removed the grin from his face. The key of the door! It would be a party – probably with his parents and those of Polly, with Bertie and *his* dad thrown in, too, of course. And most of all, with Polly. They would be crowded into the little front room and his dad would sing 'Lily of Laguna' and everybody would be a bit tipsy. And he would be with Polly... He gulped, then realised that they were all staring at him.

Then, slowly, the corporal raised a finger and, turning to the others, said, 'Right, lads. One, two, three...'

Hesitantly, at first, then more strongly, the words of 'Happy Birthday to You' rose from the shell hole. Jim put his finger to his lips and the volume dropped a little but the song was concluded, 'Happy birthday, Sergeant Major, happy birthday to you.'

Hickman realised that his nose was running. He sniffed. 'Very kind, lads. Thank you very much. But best keep our voices down.' He handed his water bottle to the corporal. 'Here, have a drink with me. There's too much rum in it for me, anyway. Pass it round. There's just about enough for everyone if you just take a sip.'

And so passed one of the strangest birthdays that Jim Hickman had ever experienced, tucked into a shell hole, just about fifty yards from a line of enemy strongholds that they proposed to attack in a do-or-die attempt to silence them.

'Well, anyway, sir,' said the corporal, 'you'll remember this birthday as long as you live...'

His voice tailed away, for the unspoken ending

to the sentence was in everyone's thoughts: '...which will probably not be very long.'

Jim ventured a look over the rim of the crater, anxious in case the singing had been heard. But he saw no movement to the front or between the pillboxes. More to the point, there was nothing from the other shell holes, either. They were, of course, out in no man's land on their own.

He looked at the elderly corporal who had conducted the singing. He was not from A Company but Jim had noticed him in the line, a quiet, efficient NCO, doing his work without fuss or bluster – a touch unusual in the brutal British army of 1917. He moved over to sit next to him.

'What's your name, Corporal?'

'Burgess, sir.'

'You can drop the "sir" till we get back to the line. First name?'

'Martin.' Jim noticed that he had crinkly laugh lines at the corner of his eyes.

'What did you do in Civvy Street, Martin?'

'I was a teacher, at King Edward's Grammar in Birmingham.'

'Oh yes? The one in Aston or the posh one?'

Burgess grinned. 'I'm afraid it was the posh one.'

'And what did you teach the posh kids?'

'Latin.' He laughed. 'Not a damned bit of use out here.'

Hickman nodded. 'Why didn't you go for a commission?'

'Well.' The man thought for a moment. 'For one thing, my age would have gone against me,

I felt – I'm forty, you see – and for another, I wasn't sure that I was cut out to be a soldier. Oh, I'm fit enough, though this mud and rain plays hell with my knees. Seeing so many of my sixth-formers going straight out to the front, I felt a bit of a fraud, so I volunteered into the ranks. I just wanted to do my bit.' He looked around ruefully. 'I think now, perhaps, that I may have overdone it a touch.'

Hickman laughed. Then, instinctively, he ducked his head as a shell hissed overhead and exploded some two hundred yards down the slope. 'Damn,' he said. 'They know we're here and they're going to try and blast us out. Heads down, everybody.'

So began twenty minutes of intensive shelling, a mixture of high explosives adding to the craters all around them. This form of bombardment was less than effective, however, for not one shell landed in their refuge and the danger of the near misses was virtually nullified by them landing in the soft mud. More of a threat were the shrapnel clusters that exploded above them and sent their jagged steel fragments raining down like deadly confetti.

Three of the men were hit, as they crouched face down on the slopes of the crater. Two were killed outright, the shafts penetrating their backs and necks, and the other sustained wounds to his legs, which rendered him unable to walk. The little party was now reduced to an effective force of only seventeen.

'Sorry, chaps,' said Hickman as the shelling eased and then finally ceased. 'We can't bury these lads, so we'll just have to leave them here. You two,' he gestured at two of the men, 'will stay with this wounded man and help him back to the line as soon as it gets dark. That leaves us with fifteen men to take possession of the whole German line.' He grinned. 'Can't think of a better army to do it with. Now, Corporal,' he gestured to the lance corporal, 'I think you'd better be on your way. Remember: covering fire from the Lewises on the pillboxes at about dusk. Good luck, lad. Take your time.'

The lance corporal clearly did not fancy his chances, for he gulped. But he gave a cheery nod and wormed his way out of sight over the edge of the crater.

Hickman cursed that the two dead men were both specialist bombardiers, for he would have needed them in the assault, but he pocketed their grenades and, like the rest, sat down to wait.

'Do you think that Jerry will send a party out to see if we're still here after the shelling?' asked Burgess.

'Good point. You'll be an officer yet. Thank you. Take first watch looking up to their line and then I'll relieve you. Don't show much of yourself.'

So the minutes ticked away until the grey clouds began to get darker and, inevitably, the rain came on again. Jim welcomed it for he hoped that, after the shelling and the failure of the British attack, the German sentries might be just a touch less on guard as the rain tumbled down. At least, those deadly machine-gunners out in their foxholes might be miserable and a touch careless, huddled and sheltering under their capes. He looked about him and then at his watch. Eight-twenty-five and visibility now considerably reduced. He would attack, he resolved, as soon as Bertie and his men began to shoot.

But they did not.

By eight-forty there was still no firing from down the slope, so Hickman decided they had to go before it became too dark to see what they were attacking. Accordingly, he slipped the bolt on his rifle, took out his three grenades and called to them all.

'It looks as though my message back to our line has not got through,' he said, 'so we shall have to attack without covering fire. Never mind, it should be sufficiently dark for us to get close enough before they see us. Listen, we can't hope to seriously damage the pillboxes just with Mills bombs, but, if we deposit one in each of the boxes that I intend to target, that should kill the crew inside. That leaves three grenades for the machine-gun posts dug in around the boxes. You and I,' he indicated one of the men, a large bombardier, 'will each take a pillbox with a grenade each; just one bomb, so we must make it count. Corporal Burgess, you will take the other bombs and the rest of the men and attack the machine-gun nests.' He distributed the grenades and then took a deep breath. 'Right, boys. Let's go. Good luck.'

He crawled to the lip of the crater and peered over. Everything up ahead seemed quiet and so, distressingly, did everything behind him along the old German line recaptured by the attack. Gritting his teeth he crawled over and began to make his way, as best he could, squirming through the mud between the shell holes. It was a depressing way to begin an attack, crawling in the mud and the rain, but at least he was distributing his weight more or less evenly over the mud and he did not sink down. He looked behind. The rest were following.

Suddenly a flare soared upwards from the German lines. 'Freeze,' he shouted and lay still.

The star shell hung and then slowly descended, lighting the dismal scene. But nothing ensued. Hickman breathed again. It was obviously just a precautionary measure by the Germans. He waved his arm and resumed his crawl, awkwardly holding his rifle to keep its firing mechanism out of the mud.

After a further ten minutes, he realised that he was only about thirty yards away from the nearest pillbox, which loomed ahead out of the dusk, a machine-gun barrel poking out of each of its slits. He examined it carefully; could he reproduce the successful tactic of the raid of 1915 – crawling below the lowest trajectory of the guns so that they could not fire down at him? Doubtful. He attempted to locate the machine guns that he knew had been dug in surrounding the stronghold, but he could see no sign of them in the gathering gloom. He crawled on.

Then another flare hissed upwards. Damn! This must mean that they had been seen. He eased his rifle into position and aimed at the nearest slit, just above the gun barrel poking out from it. Before he was able to squeeze the trigger, however, it blazed into life. Its flash, though, gave him a target and he fired. Immediately the gun ceased firing but only to be replaced by about six others, from the other pillboxes and from hitherto hidden pits arranged around them.

The flare died away in dozens of tiny star-shines but the guns continued to fire, the bullets thudding into the mud around Hickman and behind him. He attempted to rise to his knees to give himself a base from which to hurl his bomb but he slipped, lost his purchase in the mud and rolled down a crater, ending with his boots just inches above the gas-shrouded pool at the bottom. Behind, he heard cries as the bullets found their targets. He also heard a rattle of machine-gun fire from the British line, presumably in retaliation.

Jim lay winded and realised that tears were running down his cheeks; tears of what – frustration or sadness at the losses he knew the men he had led so foolhardedly must now be incurring? He didn't know. But he realised that his attack was over before it had begun. They could never hope to get near enough to this new kind of line without being cut down. Two explosions up ahead showed that two men, at least, had been able to release their grenades. And then there was silence.

Suddenly, there was a disturbance at the edge of the crater and he swung his rifle upwards, to catch a glimpse of grey hair under a steel helmet.

'You all right, sir?' called Burgess.

'Only wounded pride. What about the others?'

Burgess shook his head. 'Myself and another chap got close enough to hurl our grenades at the machine guns but they fell short. The other bloke was just ahead of me and he got riddled with bullets, but I sheltered behind him for a bit and stayed unhurt and then slid down here. I'm afraid all of the others were shot down as they tried to get on. Sorry, sir...' His voice tailed away.

'Don't call me "sir" out here. I've completely fucked it up. I'm not worthy of being called anything.' Hickman wiped his brow, spreading more mud across his face. 'I should never have tried to – what was it you called it? – take on the whole German line. Bloody barmy. Ah well.'

'Now, don't take it so hard. We had orders to attack and you did your best to carry them out.' Burgess's voice, its upper-class accent sounding somehow incongruous in the shell hole, took on a bitter tone. 'It's not your fault that our high command consists of idiots who have no idea of what they are ordering us to do. It might help if some of them came up to the line sometime to see for themselves. I consider it disgraceful.'

Hickman gave a wan smile. 'Spoken like a Latin master. Just as well I am stuck out here and no longer a sergeant major, otherwise I would have had to run you in for ... something or other. Ah shit, Martin. What a mess! All those good men gone. I just hope that the two chaps with the wounded bloke made it.'

'What do we do now, then?'

'We get back. I am determined that two of us, at least, get out of this. We wriggle back, Corporal. But let's wait a bit, until they settle down. Let them think they have killed us all.'

'Do you think they will send out a patrol to check?'

'I doubt it. A bit too dangerous, I would say, with the lines so close. It's pretty dark now. Let's give it just five minutes and then go. Ah, blast it. Do you remember the code word for the day? I don't want to be shot by our own blokes.'

'Yes. I should. It's Horace.'

'What? Ah, yes. Latin, of course. It's good to be stuck in the mud with a scholar.'

The crawl back was horrendous. Not so much for the danger, for both lines were now quiet, but for the obstacles – the once-human obstacles – that they had to avoid. It was impossible to be certain that any of the bodies that lay strewn across that fetid slope were still alive but certainly none was moving. Halfway along the journey, Jim came across the body of the lance corporal whom he had sent to ask Bertie to give cover to the attack. He was lying face down, his back riddled with bullets. He lay with many others.

There was no wire in front of the old German trench and the password saved them from nervous friendly fire. They slipped over the edge of the trench and lay gasping on the fire step, as much from relief as exhaustion.

The word went along the trench and Captain Cavendish squatted by their side. 'Bloody glad to see you back, Hickman, and you, too, Corporal. Any wounded men left out there, do you think?'

'I doubt it, sir. We crawled back over so many bodies. The attack was hopeless, you know.'

The young man coughed. 'Mustn't talk like that, Sarn't Major. Orders are orders.'

'How many men have we lost, then, sir?'

Cavendish's voice was weary. 'About sixty per cent of the battalion, I would say. Colonel's dead, so is the adjutant. I am the senior one left and in temporary command. A Company is in shreds – just about a dozen men left. One good bit of news for you, though, Hickman. The two chaps and the wounded man you sent back made it all right. They told me about your attack on the pillboxes. Sorry, we couldn't do much to help.'

Jim looked along the trench. 'Corporal Murphy. Is he all right?'

'Ah yes. He wanted to go out and look for you but I ordered him to stay here. We needed him and his Lewises in case of a counter-attack. Look here, Hickman. You'd oblige me if you could do a final count on the company. I just haven't had time. Can't let you sleep, I'm afraid, because we are to be relieved during the night. A new lot are coming up and...' his voice dropped in tone, as though in disbelief, 'they're going to renew the attack in the morning, God help them. There's food at company HQ – get what you can.'

With a nod, he was gone.

Jim found Bertie Murphy cleaning his Lewis

gun with a piece of oily rag, his movements slow and fumbling, his face melancholic in the darkness. It lit up, however, when he saw his old comrade.

'They wouldn't let me come and look for yer,' he said, grasping Hickman's hand. 'I really thought you'd gone to Jesus this time, son. I really did. Oh, Jim.' He shook his head. 'I don't know how long we'll be spared in this terrible business. When the firin' started, with you out there, I guessed you'd be tryin' to do something daft, so I blazed away as best I could to give you cover, but bullets don't do much against concrete, so they don't. But you're back, so thank the good Lord.'

'Bad pennies always turn up, Bertie. But we've lost more than half the battalion and what's left of us are going back down the line in an hour or so, when the relief comes. Then they're going to have another go in the morning.'

Bertie blew his nose in the oily rag and shook his head once again. 'Mad bastards. That's what they are. Mad bastards. It's just not doin' any good.' He waved his hand. 'All of this stuff. We're gettin' nowhere, but this stupid killin' goes on. Jesus must be weepin'.'

'Are you on guard?'

'I think all of us are. Nobody's told us to stand down.'

'Right. Well you stand down now. I'll go along the line and get a guard mounted. Try and get some sleep, old lad.'

The relieving battalion came in at about 3 a.m. and what was left of the battalion – some one hundred and fifty exhausted men and only three officers – slipped away down the slope, picking their way warily between the shell holes and the bodies of their dead comrades. Dawn was breaking when they eventually reached Ypres and began filing through the wreckage of the old town.

They lay in rest near Poperinghe, licking their wounds and taking in contingents of men from other battle-wrecked regiments and drafts of white-faced youngsters from back home. Black Jack Flanagan once again had survived the fighting, as had the battalion's regimental sergeant major, a fiercely moustached old Regular who had fought at Omdurman with Kitchener. This was a relief to Jim and Bertie, for Flanagan would surely have been next in line for promotion to that post if the old man had gone.

Two parcels were awaiting Jim. One from his mother, revealing the usual packets of Woodbines and a knitted woollen scarf, and the other from Polly, containing a pair of very fine leather gloves. Birthday cards came with both.

'Ah, damn me eyes, Jim, I forgot yer birthday,' cried Bertie. 'Sorry, lad. Now, tell me what the sweet lass says.'

'You've got your own bloody letter, Bertie. Don't pry. But look. These fit exactly right. What a great girl, eh?'

'She is that. So she is.'

'Hey. Listen to this.' He began to read from Polly's letter: 'You'll never believe this, Jim. Wagstaffe has volunteered and joined up! He's called himself an engineer and become what they call a Sapper, I think. So you won't see him in the Warwicks, which is a good thing. We don't know what's come over him, but he went off last Tuesday. Connie – you remember her – has become foreman...'

'Well, well,' mused Jim. 'The world's a changing all right.'

The changes continued all around them. Captain Cavendish was made adjutant and Hickman was in camp talking to him when their new commanding officer arrived. He trotted in riding a magnificent chestnut, his brown boots gleaming, and his groom riding behind on an equally resplendent polo pony, leading a donkey carrying the colonel's baggage.

The colonel vaulted to the ground, a stocky man of five foot four inches, with a red face and sporting a closely clipped, salt-and-pepper moustache. He immediately strode towards Cavendish and returned the salute of both men.

'Lieutenant Colonel Cox,' he said brusquely. 'Are you the adjutant?'

'Yes, sir. Cavendish. Welcome to the regiment, Colonel.'

'Thank you.' His eyes cold, he looked Cavendish up and down, completely ignoring Hickman, who remained at attention.

'Cavendish. Cavendish. You're not from the ... ah ... Devonshire family in the north, by any chance?'

Cavendish looked faintly embarrassed. 'Yes, sir. The ... er ... Duke is my uncle.'

Cox's frown immediately disappeared and what could only be interpreted as a faint smile came to his countenance. 'Really, well now. Splendid... Yes, splendid. Good to have you as adjutant.'

'Thank you, sir.' Cavendish hurriedly indicated Hickman. 'This is the company sergeant major of my old company – A Company. Sergeant Major Hickman.'

Jim, still at attention, inclined his head. 'Good morning, sir. Welcome to the regiment.'

Cox regarded him with faint distaste. 'Sergeant Major. Sergeant Major! How old are you, Hickman?'

'Twenty-one, sir. In fact it was my birth–'

'Ridiculous.' The colonel cut him short. 'A warrant officer at twenty-one. Far too young. How long have you served?'

'Since August 1914, sir. I joined up immediately war broke out.'

'What! You're not a Regular soldier?'

'Er no, sir. I joined as a Territorial.'

Cox swung on his heel and spoke to Cavendish. 'I might as well tell you now, Cavendish, that I do not approve of Territorials reaching that sort of rank. Just can't rely on them.'

'Sir, Hickman is one of our very best warrant officers. He won the Distinguished Conduct Medal as a corporal–'

'Humph! Ten a penny these days. Now, let's get on. There is much to do if I am to knock this battalion into shape. Have the men paraded for me to address them in an hour.' He looked at his watch. 'Let us say eleven-thirty?'

'With respect, sir, that might be a little difficult. Some of the men are off duty and are probably in the town...'

'Very well. Make it twelve noon. I want them all back by then. See to it. You,' he addressed Hickman, 'show my groom where he can stable the horses.'

Jim looked aghast at Cavendish.

'I'm afraid we don't have any stables here, Colonel,' said the Captain. 'We've only just come out of the line, you see. We are under canvas here. However,' he turned to Hickman, 'have a word with the RSM and see what he can suggest.'

'Very good, sir.' Jim gave them both his best salute and wheeled away, glad to escape.

Somehow, the battalion was assembled for twelve noon and stood at attention, with every eye fastened on the little man who stood before them, slapping his shiny boots with his riding crop.

'At ease, men.' His voice, now raised, was predictably squeaky. 'We are shortly going to go back up to the line and I want to make it quite clear to you what I expect of you all. I understand that you have had quite a mauling in your last attack. Well, these are no times to be feeling sorry for ourselves. General Haig's intention is to knock the Boche off their perches on those ridges and I intend to make sure that this battalion is right at the front when we do that.'

He strode up and down for a few seconds, as though allowing his words to sink in. Then he continued: 'We will not have long here before we move up, but we will make the most of every second we have here in ensuring that we are fully trained for the task ahead. There will be no – I repeat – no sloppiness; no undue familiarity between NCOs and men. The usual procedures for saluting will be strictly adhered to and, when out of the line, kit will be cleaned, boots polished and brasses buffed until they gleam. There will be no leave from the camp unless I am assured that the necessary standards have been achieved.

'This is my first time in the Salient but it can be no worse than Palestine, my previous posting. So you will find that I know the ropes. I will be hard but fair. I expect you all to do your best. Right, Adjutant. Dismiss the parade.'

The men broke up and Bertie found an excuse to find Hickman. 'Bloody hell, Jim,' he said, 'what was all that about?'

Hickman looked about him. 'I think it was about bullshit, that's what it was about. The man's a prat, that's what he is. When he found that Cavendish was a duke's nephew, he nearly pissed down his trousers. And if he thinks that two years on a fucking camel is preparation for this mudbath, then he's got another think coming.'

'Ah Jim, that's all we need. An eejit for a colonel.'

'Better break up or we'll be beheaded for talking to each other.'

So a period of hard, non-stop drilling ensued. They were all back on the barrack square: marching, turning, stamping, shouldering arms, moving to the right in threes, saluting, all leavened with only the occasional imparting of practical skills, such as finding natural ground cover, avoiding trench foot and recognising a sniper's lair.

Meanwhile, up beyond the ruined town, across the acres of mud, shell holes and un-buried corpses, the great battle continued – as did the rain. Haig pitched more and more troops into what was now being called 'Pass-chendaele' back home. It was the third and greatest Battle of Ypres, the fight by the Allies to reach the little village at the top of the series of low ridges that dominated the killing ground. Inch by inch, the Germans yielded terrain, sometimes taking it back again and then losing it once more. The conflict now raged beyond trenches and up among the rows of pillboxes and fortified positions that formed the second and far more formidable line of the Germans' positions. Into this maelstrom, Colonel Cox's re-formed battalion was thrown.

Once again, Jim and Bertie slogged with their comrades between the shell holes in the dark-ness, to take up their positions before dawn for yet another attack. A Company had another new commander, Captain George Simmons, a tall, thin, taciturn young man who had been at the front for two years. Like the rest of his men, he seemed resigned to whatever fate awaited them. Since his arrival two weeks before, Hickman had never seen a smile on his face.

As they trudged on they realised that the line was where a helmeted head stood out briefly here and there above the ground in the dim light. Machine-gunners with their heavy Vickers were now dotting the edges of the craters, partly shielded by sodden sandbags. Below the edge of the crater, near the gun, a hole had been dug in the side and covered by a groundsheet. This was where the gunners were trying to sleep.

This time, the dawn attack was no longer a case of 'over the top', for there was no trench top to surmount, only slurries of mud that had been piled up to give a fragment of protection in front of the tape along which they crouched. Jim had no idea of where they were in the line. It didn't seem to matter. The objective was always the same: to destroy the pillboxes up ahead and surge on up to the top.

Jim found Bertie trying to keep his Lewis gun dry under his cape. The little Irishman greeted his old friend with lacklustre eyes. 'We can't keep gettin' away with it, Jim,' he said. 'We've bin lucky so far but I can't help feelin' that we're runnin' out of time and luck now.'

Jim clapped him on his shoulder, sending a shower of rain over them both. 'Don't talk rubbish, Bertie. The Irish were born lucky, you know that. All we can do is keep our heads down and do our duty. I'll keep an eye out for you, lad, so don't worry. We'll both get back to kiss Polly, I promise.'

Murphy gave a woeful smile. 'Ah strewth, Jimmy, I do hope so. But if not, I hope it's me that gets it. You'd make a better fist of lookin' after the girl, so you would.'

'Balls.' Jim looked at his watch. 'One minute to go. Don't forget, Bertie. Set up that bloody gun of yours as soon as you can out in front to give us a bit of covering fire.'

'Very good, Sergeant Major.'

The whistle blew and the men slipped and slithered over the mud piles immediately in front of them and began to flounder up the slope to where grey boxes were spitting out flame. This time, however, the Germans were concentrating their shells on the advancing troops, rather than on the supporting lines behind. As before, it was the shrapnel that caused the most casualties, for these razor-sharp steel missiles were capable of causing the most horrific injuries.

A man immediately ahead of Hickman suddenly whirled around, his face a crimson mess where a piece of jagged steel had sliced away his jawbone and part of his nose. He slumped down, trying to speak but only gurgling blood. He held up a supplicatory hand but Jim put down his head and struggled by. All around men were falling. Turning his head, Hickman looked for Bertie but there was no sign of the little man, nor any chatter from his gun.

A growing rage at the futility of it all consumed him and he broke into a shambling, slipping run, disregarding the shouts, screams, explosions all around him. Nearing a pillbox that was spitting fire, he dropped to his knees and crawled under the fire until he sat, his breast heaving, immediately under the machine gun. He unclipped a grenade, pulled out the firing pin with his teeth, waited two seconds and then rose and slipped it through the gun slit, falling back as he heard the muffled explosion from within. Getting to his feet, he floundered to the back of the pillbox, kicked down the door and thrust his rifle and bayonet into the interior. Three men lay dead inside, the muzzles of their heavy machine guns tipped to the sky through the firing slits. Three others lay wounded on the concrete floor. Hickman shot them in turn and stumbled outside, spitting to rid his mouth of the foul taste of cordite.

A machine gun stuttered into life from behind a stunted tree ahead of him and brought down two Tommies to his right. Hickman dropped to the ground and fired two quick rounds in the general direction of the gun but the emplacement was well camouflaged and he saw little effect. Others were firing at the gun and he wriggled forward on his stomach until he was able to hurl his last bomb. It exploded just behind the stump of the tree and the gun fell silent.

He stumbled to his feet, sensing rather than seeing other troops at his side, and, meeting firmer ground, ran towards a pillbox set in a fold in the ground further back. He realised that it had been taken, for white-faced Germans, some seeming no older than seventeen, were being taken back, their hands held high, under the guard of a single soldier. Passing them, he reached the edge of what had been the wood. British troops were straggling, knee-deep in the mud, upwards beyond it. Despite the explosions from the shells and bursts of rifle and machine fire, a little knot of soldiers had gathered at the side of one of the holes. Reaching them, Hickman realised that they were trying to rescue one of their comrades who had slipped down to the bottom. A human chain, linked by extended rifles, stretched down the slope of the crater but it was impossible to reach the man, who was now up to his armpits and screaming. Reluctantly, the attempt had to be abandoned and the last man was pulled to the top.

'Shoot me, mates, for God's sake,' the sinking man was shouting. No one could do it.

'Get on,' shouted Hickman. 'Get on.'

Looking away, the men trudged on. The man was now up to his neck. Jim took quick aim and fired. A black hole appeared in his forehead and, mouth open, he sank beneath the mud. Kneeling down, Hickman was sick. Then, wiping his mouth, he staggered on.

Up ahead he could see a long line of what appeared to be practically undamaged concrete machine-gun posts with barbed wire entanglements in front some fifty yards deep. It was an impregnable position that seemed to have been completely untouched by the British bombardment, except for a few spaces in the wire that had been cut. Into those gaps the Tommies were funnelling and Jim saw dozens caught up in the wire, many dead but some of them still alive and twitching.

Men were now falling all around him and Jim saw a figure running back towards him. He recognised Captain Simmons, blood running down his arm from a tear in his uniform.

'It's useless, Sarn't Major,' he shouted. 'Get the men to fall back and dig in just at the edge of the old wood. We simply can't afford to lose any more men.'

'Very good, sir.' He turned and waved his arm. 'Back chaps. Back to the edge of the wood. Quick as you can now.'

Where was Bertie? He could see no sign of him. And then, from the edge of the wood, came the familiar sound of a couple of Lewis guns opening up, to give cover to the retreating men. He prayed it would be Bertie but could not be sure, for every platoon had set out with two machine-gunners, and the gunners themselves were indistinguishable in the rain.

There was precious little cover to be had from the few splintered tree trunks that still remained in the wood, but entrenching tools were produced and, somehow, Hickman oversaw the establishment of a line of sorts, linking the craters on the edge and piling up bodies to extend the height of the slipping, slopping mud walls of the so-called trench.

'Good man, Hickman.' The captain slumped down.

'Let's have a look at that arm, sir.'

Jim produced his pocketknife and cut away the sleeve of Simmons's uniform. It looked as though a bullet was still lodged against the bone of his arm and the captain was obviously in great pain. Hickman swabbed the wound with iodine and put a temporary dressing on it.

'Better get back down the line, sir,' he said.

Simmons shook his head. 'No. I'll stay here. There is bound to be a counter-attack and we must hold what we've got here. I think the rest of the battalion – what is left of it – is to the left of us and we've got the Suffolks to the right. So we've got a line and we've got to hold on here until reinforcements come up.' He nodded behind him. 'Our objective is that ridge there. The colonel should be able to call up a barrage on those emplacements and we can have another go with more chaps in the morning. But we must hold this line against the counter-attack. I suggest...' His voice tailed away and he slumped down, unconscious.

Hickman lifted his voice. 'Bearers. Any stretcher-bearers here?'

Two men appeared, wearing the distinctive red cross on white arm bands. 'Sir?'

'Can you take the captain down the line?'

'Sorry, sir. No chance at the moment. We've got six bad cases on stretchers back there and only the two of us. We've got to wait for more of our chaps to come back. It's taking six men to carry one man 'cos we're sinking up to our 'ips in the mud, see.'

'All right. But take him back to one of the captured pillboxes and give him an ampoule of morphia or something.'

'Very good, sir.'

Jim looked along the line to where the Lewis guns were still firing. It was important to see who was on either side, for it would be fatal to be outflanked if and when the counter-attack came. He splashed along to the left and met the mud-spattered figure of Sergeant Major Jack Flanagan.

'I never thought I'd be glad to see you, Flanagan,' said Jim.

'Ah, *real* soldiers don't run, sonny.'

'Have you got a line established along there?'

'Course we have. And you?'

'Yes. But I don't know who's on our right. I'm about to go and check. Who's in command?'

Flanagan flashed his teeth in that familiar grin. 'Why our brave colonel, of course. I think he's just sauntered in.'

'What about Cavendish?'

'Yes, he's made it. But none of my subalterns have.'

'My company commander is wounded and I haven't seen any officers since we attacked. Look, they're bound to counter-attack. I'll see who's on our right and I'll come back and let you know.'

'Very well. I'll be here.'

With a curt nod, Hickman made his way along the makeshift line, checking ammunition and preparing the men for the defence of the position. At the end, to his huge relief, he saw the diminutive figure of Bertie Murphy, crouched over his machine gun and seemingly asleep.

'Corporal!' barked Jim in mock barrack room tones. 'You're not asleep at your post, are you?'

A weary eyelid was raised and a slow smile spread over Bertie's face, smeared with mud and yellow cordite stains. 'God bless you, Jimmy lad,' he said. 'I thought again you'd gone this time, I really did.' And the two solemnly shook hands.

'Are you all right, Bertie?'

'As well as can be expected, as they say. I think I've killed more men today than yesterday so I've had a jolly day, so I have.'

'Look, Bertie, they're going to come at us

before it gets dark. Have you got plenty of ammunition?'

Murphy lifted a weary hand. 'Bless you, lad, me and Stanley here,' he jerked his head at his fellow gunner, 'have got about six drums left. So that's ... what? Somethin' like 280 rounds or so – I never could do sums, yer know, Jimmy.'

'Well, be sparing. Who's on the right of you?'

'I don't know, but they're ranged along behind tree stumps. I don't think they're Germans, 'cos they seem quite nice chaps.'

'Good. I'll go and see. Sleep, but make sure one of you is awake. We're going to need you.'

He climbed past the gun emplacement and met a young private of the Suffolks, nestling in the mud and cradling his rifle.

'Have you got an officer, son?'

'Yes, Sarn't Major. He's along there, I think.' He spoke in the soft burr of East Anglia.

Jim crept along and found a young subaltern, cool and seemingly confident, and established that the Suffolks had suffered similarly to the Warwicks but had entrenched, with orders to hang on at all costs. He retraced his steps and met an anxious Captain Cavendish, whom he assured that their right flank seemed covered.

'Have you seen the colonel?' asked Hickman.

Cavendish looked up sharply. 'That will be enough of that, Sarn't Major,' he said. 'The colonel is in the line and is ... er ... in command. You know the orders – we hold this line at all costs until reinforced.'

'Very good, sir.'

The counter-attack came, as expected, late in

325

the afternoon, after a dank day spent huddling in the drizzle. The Germans first laid down a barrage and then came squelching down the slope in a grey mass.

Although severely depleted, the British line belched fire and it was the Germans' turn to fall in swathes as the Lewis guns and rapid rifle fire raked across the black mud. With superb bravery, however, the men in grey came on, presenting their long bayonets and – without wire to protect them – it was touch and go for a time for the British, before the attack eventually faded away, almost on the edge of the wood. Hickman wiped his brow, his rifle hot to touch. Would the Huns come on again – perhaps with a night attack? But they did not.

However, reinforcements did arrive during the night and, with the dawn, a new barrage was laid down by the British gunners. It began by crashing all about the exhausted troops crouched at the edge of the wood and only after frenzied signals had been sent back and the line further depleted by friendly shells did it creep forward and begin to play on the German defences ahead.

After an hour it lifted, and once again the men of the Warwickshire Regiment trudged upwards into the mud and the fire of machine guns whose gunners re-emerged from their bunkers to cut the British down, like a scythe going through corn. Hickman had hardly cleared the makeshift parapet of the trench when a bullet took him in the shoulder, whirled him round and sent him tumbling back into the mud.

The force of the impact was what he felt first, then came the pain, as though his shoulder was on fire. He tried to lever himself back onto his feet, slipped back again and at least had the presence of mind to fall onto his back and so escape drowning in the mud. There he lay before blessed unconsciousness overcame him.

He came to, in great pain, and realised that he was being carried on a stretcher by four men who were ploughing through the mud, swearing and shouting as they did so. The jolting caused by their struggles sent shafts of agony searing through his body, but he gritted his teeth and hung onto the side of the stretcher with his good hand. Eventually, he lost consciousness again and regained it – he knew not how long afterwards – to find himself in a tent, lit by a hurricane lamp. Other men lay around him and he could hear moans.

He caught sight of an orderly whom he recognised. 'Where am I, Jones?'

'Field hospital, Sarn't Major. You're waiting your turn for surgery.'

'Ah. You're a bearer from A Company, Warwicks, aren't you?'

'Yessir. Well, I was. They've brought me back here to help out. The bloody battle is still going on. Hundreds of wounded are coming in. Sorry, gotta go.'

Jim held up a hand. 'Hang on. Corporal Murphy. Irishman. You know – is he all right?'

The orderly looked embarrassed for a moment. 'I don't really know, sir. I did hear that he'd deserted, pushed off, and they'd caught him and he's in jug. But I'm not really sure. Gotta go, sir.'

'Oh, my God.' Jim's head fell back onto the pillow.

CHAPTER THIRTEEN

The surgeon took a bullet from Hickman's shoulder and told him he was lucky. 'No fractures,' he said when he made his quick post-operative tour of the beds. 'The round missed the clavicle and the scapula and was lodged between the two. It tore tendons and messed up the joint. It will be painful and means you won't be able to use your left arm for a while. But,' he gave a wan smile, 'I'm sorry it's not a Blighty One. You will be able to rejoin your battalion in about three weeks and undertake light duties. In the meantime, you'll recuperate here in Pop. Questions? No? Good. Must get on.'

The questions that Jim wanted to ask were not of the shoulder but of Bertie. He had tried but failed to gain more than the disturbing fragment given to him by the orderly. The battle continued to rage and the hospital was like a conveyor belt, handling the constant stream of wounded that were fed to it. There was no time to indulge one man's search for his comrade.

Answers came, however, when Hickman vacated his bed in the hospital and was installed in a billet in Pop reserved for officers and warrant officers who were recuperating from their wounds before rejoining their regiments. Captain Cavendish paid him a hurried visit in between supervising another intake of recruits to fill the gaps sustained by the battalion, now recovering outside the town.

'Murphy?' said Cavendish, perched awkwardly on a camp stool. 'Yes, I knew you would ask.' The young man's face was now that of a middle-aged man, drawn and with deep-set eyes that had developed a permanent blink. 'Miserable business, I'm afraid, Hickman.'

'Yes, but tell me what happened.'

The captain drew deeply on his cigarette. 'Well, you will remember that we fought off the counter-attack and then we went over the top again at them. Like a bloody rally at tennis. We lost again and had to retreat, but we hung on to that rotten line on the edge of the wood for God knows how long, under heavy shell and gun fire all the time, before we were eventually relieved.'

He sent a blue wreath of smoke upwards and watched it climb towards the ceiling. The silence hung like heavy vapour in the small room before he resumed, 'Sometime during that period when we were clinging on to our position there, Murphy must have cracked. It appears that he just got up from his machine gun, left his rifle behind, and walked back towards Ypres.'

Hickman licked his lips. 'He was arrested?'

'Yes. It seems that CSM Flanagan had been sent back down the line to organise more stretcher-bearers and ammunition. He was on his way back up to the line, picking his way between the blasted shell holes, when he met

Murphy coming the other way, so to speak. He asked him what he was doing and the chap simply said that he had had enough and that the whole bloody war was stupid and he was getting out of it. Something like that, anyway. Flanagan arrested him then and there and made him retrace his steps back to where we were entrenched. He immediately came before the colonel and was put under guard.'

'Where is he now?'

'He is in detention, here in Pop.'

'What's going to happen?'

'Well, there's been no time to charge him formally, but there's no doubt that he will be court-martialled.'

'And if he's found guilty?'

Cavendish took another reflective drag on his cigarette. 'Well, Hickman, you know as well as I do what that means. He will be shot.' He wrinkled his nose in disgust. 'Disgraceful, I know, but at this stage of the war the high command is frightened to death that the "French disease" – you know there have been outbreaks of mutiny in the French army...'

Hickman nodded.

'They're worried that it might spread to us, given these bloody awful conditions in which we're fighting. So the penalty for desertion is rigid. *Pour encourager les autres,* you know.'

'No, I don't know. What does that mean?'

'To make an example, I suppose. To be a warning against others thinking of doing it.'

Jim groaned and put his head in his hand. Eventually he looked up. 'You know, sir, that

Murphy is a bloody good soldier. He's fought side by side with me in the regiment since the very beginning of this shambles. Our previous colonel told us both that he would have been decorated if circumstances had been different. He must be ill now. You said yourself that he had probably cracked. Surely the regiment can't let this happen to one of its own?'

Cavendish stirred uncomfortably on his stool. 'I know how you feel, but the colonel–'

Hickman interrupted him fiercely. 'Ah, that bloody idiot.'

Cavendish rose to his feet and stubbed out his cigarette. 'That's enough of that, Sarn't Major. You know I can't allow that sort of talk. And I must go now.'

Hickman rose to his feet. 'Can I see Murphy, sir? It would mean a lot to me and to him.'

'I think I can arrange that.' He forced a weak smile. 'It's the least I can do.' He extended his hand. 'Get well soon. We need you. I'll send you a message about Murphy. Goodbye.'

They shook hands and Jim sank back down onto his seat. His shoulder was throbbing and so was his head and the old wound in his foot. The worst had happened. He had foreseen that something like this – he did not know what, exactly, but something – would make Bertie crack. If only he had been there! He had always protected his volatile, lovable friend and now a single German bullet had put him out of action at the very moment when he was needed most. He lit a cigarette with a shaking hand. How could he tell Polly? And *what* could he tell Polly?

That the man she loved – well, of whom she was terribly fond – was going to be shot as a coward and a deserter? He groaned.

Two days later a message came from Cavendish to say that it would be possible for him to visit Bertie at 4 p.m. that day. He was being held at the military police guardhouse on the edge of Pop and the visit could last only twenty minutes.

He found the little man in solitary confinement, sitting in a small room lit by the light from one barred window. He was lying on his bunk reading a Bible, his rosary by his side.

'Ah, Jimmy!' Bertie rose to his feet and immediately embraced his friend. 'I heard that you'd been wounded – although at first I thought you'd gone. I was so worried about you. Here, sit on the bed. Sorry, lad, they don't give me a chair. How's your shoulder?'

Hickman regarded his comrade carefully. He had been given a brutal army haircut, so that he looked like a criminal, and his eyes were red-rimmed. It was clear that he had been crying, although he was attempting to smile now, and he seemed smaller, somehow.

'How are they treating you, Bertie boy?'

'Och, like a bleedin' criminal. But you'd expect that of the MPs now, wouldn't you? Have you heard from Polly? I haven't written, yer see...' His voice tailed away.

'Only one letter – just the normal one. She hadn't heard that I'd been wounded and, of course, knew nothing about ... about ... you. I haven't written back. I just didn't know what to say.'

Bertie hung his head for a moment and then looked up again with a forced smile. 'Ah well, that's understandable, I suppose. But it's good of you to come, Jimmy. I haven't had any other visitors at all, except for the adjutant, that is. Nice bloke. He came to check that I was bein' looked after and all that.'

'I think you'd better tell me what happened, Bertie. Then we'll see what we can do.'

'Yes, well, it was like this.' The little man shifted uncomfortably on his mattress. 'Is that arm givin' yer pain, now? It's a mighty fine sling you've got there–'

'For God's sake, Bertie, tell me what happened.'

'Ah well. When I heard that you'd been hit and been carried away I didn't know whether you was dead or what. I got to thinkin', yer see, an' prayin'. It was night-time an' a lot of starshinin' goin' on. I seemed to hear the Lord say, "Bertie, you've had enough of this stuff, lad. You've killed enough men when I specifically said thou shalt not kill. It's time to stop it."'

He looked up at his friend earnestly. 'Jimmy, it was all so senseless. We kill them and they kill us. All in the rain an' the mud and stuff. Nothin' was gettin' settled by all the killin'. Both sides just went on doin' it and good men were dyin' all the time and when they weren't dyin' they were gettin' awful wounds and livin' like rats in shit. And it was all for nothin'. Nothin' was being settled. An' I thought about that officer chap I'd read about in the papers. What's his name? Strange German-soundin' name, though

333

he was a captain in the British Army with an MC. What was it – Saxton, or somethin'...?'

'Sassoon.'

'That's the feller. Well, he just packed it in and wrote to *The Times* sayin' that the war was senseless and ought to be stopped. They didn't shoot him, yer know. They just put him in hospital for a time, or somethin' like that.'

Hickman sighed. 'Bertie, Sassoon was from a very rich family that was very well connected. He was also a bit of a hero because of his MC, and a poet. They couldn't possibly shoot him. Anyway, he has volunteered to go back to the front now.'

'Ah so he has, has he? Well.' Bertie fell silent and twisted the end of his tunic between his fingers. Then, his voice a little tremulous, he looked up at the ceiling and asked, 'Jimmy, will they shoot me, then, d'yer think?'

Jim bit his lip. 'I don't know, son. We've got to do all we can now to see that you get a good defence if they try you. Have you been charged yet? What did the colonel say?'

'Ah, that eejit. He said that I was a coward and a deserter and a disgrace to the regiment. Somethin' like that. Not very nice, he was. He said I'd be court-martialled, but he said nothin' about bein' shot, d'yer see.'

'Hmm.'

The door suddenly crashed open and a burly sergeant of military police shouted, 'Time's up, Sarn't Major.'

Jim rose and took his friend's hand in his. 'Goodbye, Bertie, I'll try and come and see you again soon, if they'll let me, and I'll go and see the colonel and plead with him. Perhaps we can get you sent to hospital. Do you want me to write to Polly?'

'Ah, would yer, Jimmy? Thanks. An' write to me dad, although remember the old feller can't read.' Tears were now running down Bertie's cheeks. 'Thanks for comin', son.'

The red-capped sergeant cleared his throat histrionically.

'Goodbye, Bertie.'

'Goodbye, Jimmy. May the Holy Mother watch over yer. I'll pray for yer.'

Hickman submitted a formal request to see Colonel Cox and four days after seeing Bertie he found himself saluting in front of the CO in the bell tent that was serving as battalion HQ.

Cox was working at a table, his adjutant, Cavendish, at his side. 'At ease,' he said, but did not offer a seat. 'It's ... er...' he peered at the paper in front of him '...Hickman, isn't it? What can I do for you? I can't spare you long. This is a busy time, we are due back in the line shortly.'

'Yes, sir. Thank you for seeing me, sir. It's about Corporal Murphy, sir.'

'What!' A look of distaste settled on Cox's face. 'That man. What about him?'

Jim gulped. This was not going to be easy. He looked for support at Cavendish but the captain was earnestly studying a file before him.

'Can I ask what you intend to do with Corporal Murphy, sir?'

Cox's already flushed face took on a deeper shade. 'What? What on earth is it to do with you what I do with him? Eh?'

'Sir, Corporal Murphy and I grew up together in Birmingham and we have served side by side, mostly in this battalion, since we came to the front soon after war was declared in 1914. Until recently, sir, he has been a fine soldier and a credit to the regiment–'

Cox's fist slammed onto the table. 'Well, he bloody well isn't now. He is a deserter and a coward and he will be court-martialled. If he is found guilty – and if I have any influence in the matter that will certainly be the outcome – he will be shot at dawn. We cannot allow this sort of thing to happen without imposing the severest punishment.'

Hickman felt his temper rising and he fought to control it. 'With respect, sir, I believe Murphy to be ill now after suffering many months under bombardment in the line. Until this incident, he performed his duties admirably and–'

Once again he was interrupted. 'That is not the view of CSM Flanagan. It was he who made the arrest when he found Murphy wandering back behind the line, having abandoned his weapons in the face of the enemy. Flanagan, a veteran warrant officer and Regular soldier, informed me that the man was an idler and deceitful and what's more–'

'That is not true, sir. I knew Murphy far better than Flanagan and–'

'How dare you interrupt me.' Cox was on his feet now. 'Murphy is probably an Irish subversive and I shall see that he is tried as soon as that can be arranged. That will be all, Sarn't Major.'

'Perhaps Captain Cavendish could–'

'I said that will be all, Hickman. Get out before I lose my temper.'

Jim saluted, cast a contemptuous glance towards Cavendish, made a smart about-turn and marched away, his face glowing with suppressed fury.

Back in his billet, he put his head in his hand. Bertie was right, of course. The war was a mess. No side was winning. Both seemed to be led by unthinking dinosaurs who had lost all regard for human life and whose only idea of waging battle was to fire more shells and throw more men into their path. And he, himself, was being corrupted. He had shot defenceless wounded men and put a drowning man out of his agony without a second thought. He groaned at the memory. He was no better than the rest: a thoughtless killing machine. That's what this war had made of him. Could Polly possibly marry a man like that when she knew what he had become?

The thought of Polly brought him back to Bertie. Cox was determined to have him shot, that much was clear. And Cavendish was not strong enough even to attempt to dissuade him. There was one last source of help, however. He decided to seek out Company Sergeant Major Jack Flanagan.

He found him, in his element, bawling out recruits on the temporary parade ground to the east of Pop. He waited until the parade was dismissed and then approached Flanagan.

The Irishman's face lit up at the sight of Hickman. 'Ah,' he grinned, nodding at the sling.

'Caught our finger in a rifle bolt, did we?'

Jim forced a smile. 'Something like that. Got a minute, Flanagan?'

'No. Not really. I'm fighting a fucking war. What do you want?'

'It's about Murphy.'

The wolfish grin lit up Flanagan's face. 'What about him?'

'If he's court-martialled, he'll almost certainly be found guilty and almost certainly be shot.'

'That's right.'

'Look. You know he's no coward nor no deserter. He just broke under the shelling. He's really a very sensitive bloke. He's not a deserter, he's just ill. He ought to be in hospital. Look, Jack, you could save him. You arrested him.'

'Oh yes. And what do you want me to do, then?'

'Go and see the colonel. Say that you've thought it over and talked about Murphy to his mates in the platoon and company and feel that perhaps you were mistaken. Say that everyone says he's a good soldier and that he was ill when you found him. He was wandering without knowing where he was. Say anything, but save him from that firing squad. Probably only you can do that.'

'I see. Pleading with me, are you? I rather like that. Well, I've got just two words for you, sonny. Fuck off.'

'Look. This bloke's life is at stake—'

'And I don't care a toss, mate. You and him put the redcaps onto me, so this lily-livered, Papish cunt is going to get just what he deserved.' He turned on his heel and marched away.

Hickman ran after him, caught him by the elbow and spun him round. The two faced each other, their faces a few inches apart. They were big men – each a little over six feet tall and broad-shouldered, although Flanagan was the more solidly built of the two – and for a moment they stood head-to-head, unflinchingly. Jim realised that, close up, the Irishman's face was pock-marked and his complexion swarthy, as though permanently tanned by his years of service abroad.

Hickman spoke slowly and with emphasis. 'I want you to know that, if Murphy is shot, I shall hold you to account. If he dies, you will, too. I promise – before God, I promise you that.'

For a brief moment, a cloud seemed to pass over Flanagan's face. Then it disappeared and the black eyes flashed and his moustache lifted in a sneer. 'And you think that worries me?' he said, with a vehemence that left a trace of spittle on Hickman's cheek. The Irishman prodded a finger into Jim's chest to emphasise his words. 'Listen, sonny. I've tackled blokes better'n you all over the fucking world. Most of 'em didn't get up and I survived it all, even the inquiry afterwards. So you don't frighten me. Stay out of my way, if you know what's good for you.'

He remained for a moment to let his words sink in. Then, with a smart parade ground about-turn, he marched away, his head up and his back ramrod straight.

Jim watched him go and bit his lip. The last

hope gone. Or had it? He stood for a moment, deep in thought. Bertie would have one last chance, of course, in the court martial itself. The man charged always had his rights and perhaps a spirited defence could swing the court. After all, Bertie had a clean record and he was a non-commissioned officer with three years of service behind him. But who could help? Certainly not the adjutant. Captain Cavendish, the Duke's nephew, had proved to be a broken reed. Perhaps Simmons, the company commander? He had heard that he was convalescing from his wound similarly somewhere outside Pop. And he knew Bertie.

He found the captain, with his arm similarly slung in white, in a billet to the west of the town. They sat together outside, in a rare break from the rain, and shared a cigarette and a cup of tea. He found Simmons withdrawn but not averse to helping.

'Well, Hickman,' he said. 'I have no time for cowards. If desertion goes unpunished it can spread like wildfire. But I always thought Murphy wasn't the type, so maybe he has a chance. Look, I'm no expert on military law but I did a brief course once at Aldershot on courts martial. The procedure, as I remember, is fairly straightforward.'

Jim leant forward. 'Yes, what happens? It could help me to know.'

'Well, for a start, no one on the panel, or whatever you call the presiding officers – there's usually a major or a lieutenant colonel as president, with two other more junior officers – can have served in command of the accused. So,' he looked away with just a touch of embarrassment, 'there is no danger of Colonel Cox presiding.'

'Good.'

'Then the drill is that an officer will prosecute and another will defend as "prisoner's friend", although he's not always appointed.'

'Are these professional army lawyers, sir?'

'Oh no. Ordinary serving officers. That's why I went on the course, although I never served on a CM.' He paused, frowned and looked up at the sky. 'Bugger it. I think it's going to rain again. Anyway... I'm not too sure that the prisoner gets a defending officer if he pleads guilty. But he can call witnesses, both to the circumstances of his ... er ... desertion and to his character. As can, of course, the prosecutor. And the accused can make a plea in mitigation.'

Hickman bit his lip. 'Is the sentence for desertion in the face of the enemy always ... er ... death?'

'Oh yes, particularly if the accused had jettisoned his weapon or weapons, as, from what you tell me, Murphy had done, yes?'

'Afraid so, sir.'

'Yes, well it would have to be a bloody good defence to get him off that one, I'd say.' He flicked away the ash from his cigarette. 'But, of course, the cases of chaps on a capital charge always go right up to the top for confirmation. So Field Marshal Haig would have to approve the sentence, don't you know. He might take a lenient view. But, on the other hand, with the

French desertions and so on...'

He left the sentence unfinished and then continued. 'One thing you must remember, Sarn't Major, is the old Duke of Wellington.'

Jim lifted an eyebrow. 'What on earth has he to do with it all?'

'Well, if I recall rightly, the Grand Old Duke laid down the foundations for the present procedure, which has hardly changed at all since we shot men at dawn with muskets for running away from the bloody French. He wrote something like: "It should always be borne in mind that courts martial are there as a deterrent. That is their prime function." So you see, leniency is not something that the army encourages in these cases, even without the example of our dear French comrades-in-arms deserting to the right of our front. Damned miserable business all round, if you ask me. How's your arm by the way?'

'What? Oh. It's mending quickly, sir. I should be back soon.'

'Yes.' Simmons raised two languid fingers to his lips and drew on his cigarette. 'Sooner we all get back to be bloody well killed, the better, I suppose. Anything more I can help you with?'

'Yes. Just one thing. Would you be prepared to be a character witness for Murphy?'

'What? Say he was a good feller and all that?'

'Well, yes, sir. Speaking as his company commander, at least say he was a good soldier who, up until his desertion, carried out his duties well.'

Simmons sniffed. 'Well, don't know the feller

that well, to be honest, because I haven't been in command of the company for that long. But yes, I'll stand up for him if I'm needed.'

'Oh, I think you will be. That's good of you, sir. Thank you.'

Back in his billet, Jim faced up to the unsavoury task of writing to Polly to tell her about Bertie's arrest. He thought it best to be optimistic about the chances of reaching a not-guilty verdict, pointing out Bertie's good record and promotion to corporal. He advised her against unnecessarily worrying Bertie's father at this stage. After posting the letter he sought permission from the adjutant to see Bertie again. This was granted and, two days later, he greeted his old friend once again in that dark room.

This time, it was clear that the little Irishman was ill. He was lying on his mattress with his face to the wall as Jim entered, but he immediately rose and tried to shake his friend's hand, but his own was shaking so much that he found it difficult to exert any pressure.

'For God's sake, sit down, Bertie,' said Hickman. 'Have you seen a doctor?'

'Ah yes, son. He said there was nothing wrong with me that he could detect.'

'Bloody idiot. I think you've got this thing they call "shell shock".'

Murphy ran his hand across his forehead. 'Well, I don't know what it is, Jimmy, but I know one thing: I can't go back into them trenches, lad. I just can't do it. What's more, I'm sure that the good Lord doesn't want me to. This war is evil, Jimmy, and me goin' back will help to keep

343

it goin', so it will. So I'm not doin' it.'

Hickman put his head into his hand for a moment, then lifted it. 'For God's sake, Bertie,' he said, 'don't say that or they will bloody well shoot you out of hand. Your only hope is to say you were confused by the shelling, that you're feeling better now and say that you're ready to go back into the line. Will you do that?'

Slowly, Bertie shook his head. Then he reached across and clutched his friend's arm. 'I can't do that, son. I've had enough. I'm not goin' to go on killin' people any more. It's just not right.'

'But you know you face the death penalty?'

Bertie gave a sad smile. 'But it's a death penalty either way, dear old lad. Either they shoot me or the bloody Germans do, 'cos I know I'm not fated to last much longer under them guns.'

Hickman sighed. 'Have you seen the adjutant again?'

'Oh yes. He came in yesterday and told me me rights at this court martial thing. Can't remember what they were exactly but he told me that I could question the witnesses if I wanted to and that I could enter somethin' called "mitigation", in writin', that is.'

'Have you been appointed someone to act in your defence, a prisoner's friend?'

'Dunno. Not heard about that.'

'Ah!' Jim shook his head. 'I'm sure you have the right to be defended by an officer.'

'Och, I don't want no officer bloke defendin' me, Jimmy. Somebody who doesn't know me from Adam.'

'But you must have. How are you going to plead?'

'What d'yer mean?'

'Guilty or not guilty of the charge of deserting in the face of the enemy?'

'Oh, I dunno. Guilty, I suppose, 'cos it's true.'

'No. Don't do that, that will mean automatic execution. You must plead not guilty and let your prisoner's friend speak for you.'

Bertie was silent for a moment. 'Only if you'll speak for me, Jimmy. You've always been a good speaker, you've always looked after me and you're me friend. You do it, lad. Say whatever you think necessary. But, matey, I'm not doin' any more fightin' and shootin' people.'

'Oh hell! I think they only allow commissioned officers to be prisoner's friend. But I'll see what the adjutant says. God knows, he owes us a favour.'

The door flung open. Jim spoke over his shoulder. 'Yes, Sergeant. Coming now.' Then to Bertie: 'Has a date been fixed for the court martial?'

'Oh yes. It's the day after tomorrer.'

'What! You should have told me. There's no bloody time to prepare anything. They're rushing this through, Bertie. We've got to fight.'

The red-capped sergeant gave his theatrical cough.

'Yes, virtually finished.' Jim took Bertie's hand. 'I'll see if they'll let me represent you, though, God knows, I'm no lawyer. Keep your chin up, lad.'

'Have you heard from Polly, now?'

'No. But I've written. You should get a letter.

'Bye, Bertie.'

Impelled with the need for haste now, Hickman applied for permission to see the adjutant again and he found him in his tent, packing his papers preparatory to the battalion moving up the line again. 'What is it, Hickman?' he asked, a touch of asperity in his tone. 'It's not about Murphy again, is it?'

'Yes, sir.'

'Oh Lord. Look. Everything possible has been done for him but he doesn't seem to want help. There's nothing more I can do.'

'Has a prisoner's friend been appointed for him?'

'What?' For a moment the captain looked uneasy. 'Oh, I don't think that's necessary in this case.'

'Why not, sir?'

'What? Well, it's really an open-and-shut case. An automatic plea of not guilty will be entered for him but he won't stand much chance. I'm afraid that's the end of it.'

'No. He's going to plead not guilty himself and I wish to speak for him in court to conduct his defence as prisoner's friend.'

'Good Lord. Oh, I don't think that's on. If he has one, it must be an officer – at least,' he faltered for a moment, 'I have always understood that was the case.'

Hickman took a deep breath. 'Look here, sir. This battle has been going on for months and every fit man is needed in the line, particularly officers.' He lifted up his injured arm. 'I am wounded and the doctors tell me that it is going

346

to be at least another three weeks before I can rejoin the battalion. So I can be spared and save someone else coming out of the line to do the job. I understand that it is every accused man's right to be represented and I know Murphy well and have studied the procedure. I intend to call Captain Simmons to give character evidence. He has agreed to do so. Will you please inform the authorities accordingly?'

He stood very erect and directed a level gaze at the adjutant. 'Well, I ... I don't think the colonel would approve.'

'The matter is not in his jurisdiction now, sir. If Murphy's right to a defence is denied then I shall have no alternative but to take up the matter with brigade HQ and, if necessary, with the commander-in-chief himself.'

'You are making yourself bloody awkward, Hickman.'

'I don't wish to do that, sir, but this is a matter of some principle. A man's life is at stake.' He leant forward slightly. 'Captain Cavendish. You were our company commander. Murphy was one of your men. It is not much to ask, surely?'

Cavendish sighed. 'Very well. As I am adjutant of Murphy's battalion I can go directly to the president of the court martial. You should hear from me by tomorrow.'

He was as good as his word and Hickman received a hastily scribbled note from Cavendish, instructing Jim to report to the president of the court, Lt Col George Williams of the South Staffordshire Regiment, at the opening of the Field General Court Martial in a French

347

magistrate's court in Poperinghe at 8 a.m. on the following morning.

Jim spent a sleepless night, for he had not had time to seek further advice on his duties nor to do anything other than sketch a brief plan in his head for Bertie's defence. It was important, however, to speak to his charge before the proceedings began, so he made his way to the prisoner's gloomy billet a little after 7 a.m. and waved the note from Cavendish under the military police sergeant's nose, exclaiming, 'Prisoner's friend. I wish to speak to my client before the proceedings begin.'

'What?' The sergeant was clearly taken aback. 'Well, Sargn't Major, I think that's a bit irregular.'

'No it isn't. I can do it, if you like, while we march him over to the courtroom.'

'All right, sir. 'E's 'ad 'is breakfast and 'e's ready to go.'

They found a bewildered Murphy trying to do up his buttons with a trembling hand. Hickman helped him and, bending, completed the winding of his dirty puttees. The Irishman looked on, his mouth open. 'Are you goin' to speak for me, Jimmy?'

'I am indeed. Now, listen. You are going to plead not guilty – I shall do that for you, on the grounds of your ... er ... diminished responsibility after being in the trenches for so long without a break.'

'My what?'

'I shall say that you were ill. Now, you don't have to say anything unless you are directly

348

asked. I will do the talking for you–'

The red-capped sergeant intervened, 'Gotta go now, sir. You can talk in the wagon.'

They travelled together to the courthouse, with the sergeant and two military policemen, sitting incongruously in a covered cart drawn by a very old horse. During the short journey, Jim made Bertie recite again the circumstances under which the Irishman was arrested by Flanagan and went over with him what he understood about the procedure of the court martial. The little man, however, began shaking again and it was clear that he had very little interest in such detail. 'You do it for me, Jimmy,' he kept saying.

In the courtroom, four men were sitting at a table in the well of the court. Jim studied their names on the charge sheet. Flanking the president, Colonel Williams, were a Captain Jones, of the Norfolk Regiment, a Captain Beverley, of the Somerset Light Infantry, and a Lieutenant Barnes, of the Seventh Lancers. As Bertie was marched in to sit with the two MPs at a small desk, they passed, waiting in a corridor outside, Captain Simmons and CSM Flanagan, whose jaw dropped for a moment when he saw Hickman accompanying the prisoner.

Jim was immediately beckoned to the table by Colonel Williams, who addressed him in low tones, as though he was anxious to keep their conversation confidential. The colonel was balding, with a drawn face and very pale-blue eyes. His words emerged from behind a large, walrus moustache.

'Now look here,' he looked down at the scrap

of paper before him, 'Hickman. It seems to me to be highly irregular that a warrant officer should take the role of prisoner's friend and, indeed, this seemed to be such an open-and-shut case that I didn't feel that it warranted us appointing one in any case. But we couldn't get hold of anyone in the Attorney General's department to advise us and I am prepared to let you take on this role rather than delay the case.'

'Thank you, sir. I appreciate you doing so.'

'Ah yes. Well. I do so on the understanding that you won't hold up this business. We are in the middle of a bloody great battle in a bloody great war, don't you know, and we are all needed by our regiments. We don't want to waste good fighting time.'

Hickman drew in his breath but forced a distant smile. His time would come. 'Very good, sir.'

The court was called to order and the charge read out: Murphy had deserted his post in the face of the enemy, leaving behind his weapons, and been found well behind the front line, making for the rear. Bertie stood, his red hair tousled, his eyes sunken, and was told that, as this was a capital charge, an automatic plea of not guilty would be entered.

Williams nodded his head in the direction of Lieutenant Reginald Prentice, of the Oxford and Bucks Light Infantry, the young subaltern who had been appointed to prosecute the case. 'Evidence,' he growled.

Prentice, slim and elegantly moustached but

looking distinctly nervous, stood and gestured to the piece of paper in his hand. 'I have here, sir,' he said, 'the deposition of Company Sergeant Major Flanagan, DCM, of the accused's battalion, the 1st Royal Warwicks, who arrested Corporal Murphy, which I shall read to the court. CSM Flanagan is waiting outside, sir, in case you wish to question him on the evidence.'

'Not necessary,' said Williams. 'Just read the evidence.'

Prentice read out the statement. It was short and to the point. Flanagan was returning to the line, under shellfire, when he met Murphy walking between the craters back down towards Ypres. He had no weapons and said that he had had enough of the fighting and was 'getting out of it'. Flanagan immediately arrested him and brought him back up to the line where he was paraded before the Lieutenant Colonel Cox and put into detention to await trail. The defendant offered no other explanation for his actions.

'Thank you,' said Williams. 'I understand that there is a statement from the defendant's CO?'

'Yes sir. This is from Lieutenant Colonel Cox, Commanding Officer of the 1st Battalion Royal Warwickshire Regiment, that is, of course, the ... er ... defendant's battalion...'

'Yes, yes, we know that. Let's have it.'

'Sorry, sir. Yes. The colonel writes,' Prentice cleared his throat and read, '"Corporal Murphy is not a Regular soldier but a Territorial. He has served in this battalion for some eighteen months. I do not regard him as a good soldier in that he has shown lassitude in the line in recent months. It is clear to me, from my discussion of this case with CSM Flanagan, an experienced and long-serving Regular soldier, that Murphy deserted his post when the battalion needed him in his capacity as a Lewis gunner. Therefore I recommend that the court takes a most severe view of his case."'

Williams put down his pen and grunted. Then he looked along the line of his colleagues on left and right. 'Pretty conclusive, I would say, gentlemen.' He received three nods of agreement. He looked up at Hickman. 'Right. Let's get on with it. Let's have the accused's statement.'

Jim felt a surge of anger flood through him. He took a deep breath and stood. 'Not quite, sir.'

'What?'

'If you are allowing the colonel's statement to stand, then I would wish the court to call him so that I may cross-examine him.'

Williams's brows rose and his chin dropped below the extravagant moustache. Along the line, mouths gaped open and the Somerset Light Infantry captain said, 'Oh I say...'

'You wish to do what?'

'I wish the colonel's statement to be struck from the record. If, however, you wish it to stand, sir, then, on behalf of the defendant, I must cross-examine him, which would mean deferring the trial until Colonel Cox can attend.'

'On what grounds?' The question came from the most junior of the panel, the young cavalry lieutenant, a fresh-faced man who looked as though he had just left the sixth form of a major public school.

'In that, sir, the evidence submitted contains one and possibly more inaccuracies.'

'Now look here.' Colonel Williams's face had taken on a deep glow. 'You cannot question the word of your commanding officer.'

'With respect, sir, I can. I am here as prisoner's friend and in that capacity I have the right to question evidence that is inaccurate. I must do my duty. Anyone in the Attorney General's department will confirm this, sir.' Jim had not the faintest idea of whether or not the Attorney General's staff would confirm what he had said, for he had had no time to test the ground. But he had nothing to lose. He gambled that Williams would not defer the case to check.

The young lieutenant leant forward to Williams. 'If I may, sir?' he enquired, indicating Hickman.

'Carry on,' growled Williams.

'Very well, Sarn't Major. In what way is the evidence of the accused's commanding officer inaccurate?'

'On one, and possibly two counts, sir. Firstly, Corporal Murphy has not served in the battalion for eighteen months. He has done so for just under two and a half years, as his record will confirm. Before that, he served as a Territorial – as did I – in the line in Flanders and France from September 1914, having enlisted on the outbreak of war in August of that year. Secondly, the colonel cannot say that he has observed Murphy's attitude in the line over the last few months, so I must question the colonel's competence to judge Murphy–'

'You bloody well can't do that!' Williams rose and he emphasised his words by slamming the table.

Hickman remained cool, but he was thinking on his feet now. 'With respect, sir, I can. On a matter of fact. Colonel Cox only took command of the battalion just under a month ago so his remark that he had observed Murphy's attitude over the last few months is inaccurate. It would be difficult, if not impossible, for a commanding officer to form a judgement of a junior NCO – one amongst some seven hundred soldiers – in less than a month unless that NCO had either distinguished himself in some way or shown himself to be incompetent or cowardly. Speaking now as Murphy's company sergeant major, I can swear that he did not step out of line in that time in either way. I believe that the court should not condemn a man on a capital charge for showing lassitude in the line. We were all tired in that battle. I intend to call our company commander as a character witness for Corporal Murphy and he can confirm this.'

The young lieutenant intervened again. His voice was cool. 'Then why should his commanding officer give such a derogatory report on him?'

Hickman thought quickly. 'Well, sir, if I am allowed to call Colonel Cox–'

'Which you are not!' Williams's voice was high-pitched.

'But if I was,' Jim kept his own voice steady, 'then perhaps we could discover this. My own

354

guess is that he has taken the word of Company Sergeant Major Flanagan, who arrested Murphy and who I intend to show has a grudge against the accused.'

Hickman shot a quick glance at Bertie, who was still standing and, open-mouthed, was following the exchanges avidly.

Williams was seated now but his face was still livid. 'Well,' he said, 'I am not having this—'

He was interrupted by the captain on his right, clearly the oldest of the three junior officers, judging by the flakes of grey in his hair, who leant across and spoke to the president in a low voice. Low enough for his words not to be heard by Hickman. The two spoke together in low tones for a few moments. Then, Williams, with a face like thunder, sat back.

'Well,' he said, 'we have to take a decision, either to call Colonel Cox, who I understand is at this moment leading his battalion into the line,' he emphasised the words heavily, 'and so hold up this prosecution, or to reject the evidence of the colonel as being unsubstantiated, which means that it will not feature in the report of the court martial. Of the two, I suggest we follow the latter course as being the most expedient, although I personally hate to reject the words of a senior officer. Do you agree?' He looked along the line of his colleagues, who all nodded in agreement.

'Very well.' He nodded to Hickman. 'We will continue with this court martial, but I must warn you, Sergeant Major, that I will not allow you to disparage a senior officer in my court. I am warning you as to your conduct. Is that understood?'

'Of course, sir. But I must point out that, like you, I am only doing my duty.'

'Hrumph. Let's get on with it, then.' He looked at Prentice, who had been following the exchanges with some bewilderment. 'Anything more from the prosecution?'

'Er... No sir.'

'Very well.' Williams looked grudgingly at Hickman. 'You want to call CSM Flanagan?'

'Yes, sir.'

'Call him, then. But I warn you, Hickman, you must not attack the sergeant major. He is a distinguished soldier who has been awarded the Distinguished Conduct Medal.'

'So have I, sir.' He nodded quickly to the sergeant of military police to avoid a further explosion and Flanagan appeared, looked askance at Hickman and stamped to attention in front of the panel, giving his name, rank and number.

Jim held up Flanagan's evidence. 'What state was Corporal Murphy in when you arrested him?'

The Irishman regarded Hickman through narrowed eyes. 'What's it got to do with you?' he snarled.

The young lieutenant intervened quickly. 'CSM Hickman is acting as prisoner's friend, for the defence,' he said. 'You must answer his questions.'

'Sir.' Flanagan turned to Hickman grudgingly. 'He was in a mess. No weapons – although he was wearing his steel helmet, oh yes, he was fit

356

enough to remember that because there was a bit of shelling going on, although he'd remembered to leave his rifle behind. He was rude. He said that he wasn't going back up to the line for anyone and that he'd had enough.'

'He was perspiring and shaking, wasn't he? Not knowing where he was going?'

The lieutenant leant forward again to address the colonel. 'Excuse me interrupting again, sir, but I was studying law at Cambridge to become a barrister before I joined up, so, with your permission, I would like to warn the prisoner's friend...'

'Oh, do warn away. Glad of your experience.'

'Thank you, sir. Now, Mr Hickman, you may of course question the witness, but you must not lead him. You must not ask leading questions, so putting your opinion to him. Rephrase your question.'

Damn! Jim cursed inwardly. That's all he needed – a lawyer on the judging panel. But he nodded deferentially. 'My apologies, sir.' He turned back to Flanagan, who was now grinning. 'You said that Corporal Murphy was a mess? What did you mean?'

'His tunic was undone but I don't remember him sweating or anything. But he knew where he was going all right. He was going away from the enemy, that's where he was going. I've seen enough cowards in my time to recognise one.'

Hickman swallowed. He must try a different tack and play his last card – if he was allowed. 'Now, Sergeant Major. You know Corporal Murphy quite well, I understand?'

'You know I do. I was his company sergeant major before you – his pal – took over.'

'I took over, did I not, because you were demoted to sergeant and transferred to another company?'

Williams banged the table. 'Now stop right there, Hickman,' he shouted. 'I warned you that you must not denigrate the witness. He is not on trial. Murphy is. Stop that line of questioning.'

'But, sir–'

'No. Flanagan arrested this man walking away from the line while his regiment was engaged with the enemy. The accused said he would not return to the line. Are you disputing those facts?'

'No, sir.'

'Then, Sergeant Major, you may return to your unit.'

'Sir.' Flanagan stamped an about-turn, leered at Hickman and marched out of the court. Jim looked in appeal at the young lieutenant but he was doodling with his pencil on the pad before him.

'Get on with it, then, Hickman.'

'I wish to call Captain Simmons, the officer commanding A Company in the 1st Battalion of the Warwickshire Regiment.'

Simmons, now with his arm unslung, answered Hickman's questions languidly. Yes, Murphy had been a competent soldier, as far as he could say, but then he didn't know the man well, having only been brought into the battalion a month ago, with Colonel Cox. No, he did not seem unduly slow or tired in the line. Most of them were. Nor had he shown any signs of subversion. Jim realised that, by attacking Cox's ability to know Bertie because of the colonel's brief time in command, he was also, for the same reason, undermining Simmons as a definitive witness of good character. With a sigh, he let Simmons go.

'I trust there are no more witnesses, Hickman?' Colonel Williams's voice was now overlaid with sarcasm. 'No? Good. Do you or the accused wish to make a *final'* – he emphasised the word heavily – 'statement in his defence?'

'Yes, sir. I will speak on behalf of the prisoner.' Jim took a deep breath and looked hard at the board. Only Williams was looking at him. The other three officers were doodling on their pads, their heads down, seemingly disinterested.

He began: 'Bertram Murphy has served continually – except for short periods of well-earned leave – in Flanders and on the Somme for three years now. He was not called up but joined the army of his own accord because he wished to serve and fight the Germans.

'He was gainfully employed in Birmingham, in the company where I worked, and he was of good character in that he was never in any way in trouble with the police. He was promoted in the field after a sharp engagement in the second battle of Ypres and, until he was apprehended behind the lines, he served well as a front-line soldier, as I can testify as his company sergeant major.

'However,' Hickman gulped here, for he seemed to be making no impression on the board, 'he had been in the line under constant shell, rifle and machine-gun fire for nearly three weeks without relief. It is my belief that his mind cracked at that point under the strain...'

The lieutenant looked up. 'Has a doctor reported this?'

'Er ... no, sir. I understand he was examined but no conventional illness was discovered. But I believe that it is very difficult to establish shell shock without considerable–'

'Ah, shell shock!' Williams's voice was full of derision. 'We've all got that.'

Hickman continued, stoically. 'I believe that this man is ill, sir. He is no coward, as I can testify, having gone over the top with him many times. As a soldier of a civilised country, he should be sent to hospital for examination and treatment, not to a firing squad.'

The young lieutenant raised his pencil. 'Yes, but is Murphy happy to return to the line, then?'

Blast! The question he dreaded. 'I believe that Corporal Murphy is not capable of answering that question properly, sir.'

Williams sprang into the opening. 'Well, I believe it is our duty to ask him that question ourselves.' He directed a withering glare at Bertie. 'Corporal Murphy.'

'Yes, sir,' answered Bertie dreamily.

'Will you go back into the line?'

Bertie shook his head. 'Ah no, sir. I believe that it is wrong for us to go on fightin' and killin' without gettin' any result. The good Lord does not want us to do that. I know.'

Williams nodded slowly and turned his head triumphantly to his fellow judges. 'Well,' he said.

'I think we have our answer, gentlemen.' Then to Hickman. 'Do you have anything further to say of *relevance* in mitigation?'

Jim shook his head. 'No, sir. Except that he's a good man, a sick man, who should not be shot out of hand.'

'Humph. There is no question of anything being out of hand in this matter, I will have you know. That is what this court is about.' He turned back to his colleagues. 'Now, gentlemen. Is there any need for us to retire?'

The four of them leant together and conferred in low tones for some minutes. Then Williams nodded in satisfaction and then sat back and addressed Bertie: 'Corporal Murphy. You have been found guilty of desertion in the face of the enemy, with no mitigating circumstances. You are therefore sentenced to death by firing squad at a place to be arranged. A report of this court martial will be submitted to the Judge Advocate General's department and, for approval of the sentence, to the brigadier commanding this brigade and thence to the Commander-in-Chief, Field Marshal Haig. That will be all. Take him away.'

CHAPTER FOURTEEN

Hickman watched in despair as Bertie was led away by the MPs. He turned to catch the eye of any member of the board, but they all disappeared through a back door and he and Prentice, the prosecuting officer, were left standing together.

The lieutenant offered his hand. 'I'm terribly sorry, Sarn't Major,' he said. 'I think you put up a magnificent show in here and you are quite right. The man should be sent to hospital, not back to jail.'

Hickman felt his temper rise. 'That's all bloody well. But they're going to shoot the poor little fucker. And you helped to do it. Upper-class shits. All of you.' He realised that tears were running down his cheeks.

Prentice bowed his head for a moment, then he lifted it. 'This is a terrible war, Hickman,' he said. 'Good men are being killed all the time. You have my condolences.' Then he turned and walked away.

On a sudden impulse, Jim turned and ran to the door through which the officers had disappeared. He was just in time to see the young cavalry lieutenant mounting a smart grey.

'Excuse me, sir.' He put up a hand to the rein.

The young man looked down on him with a cool gaze. 'There's nothing more to be done about this, you know,' he said.

'Look,' Jim's grip tightened on the rein. 'You are an intelligent and well-educated man. You're going to be a lawyer, if you get through this. You must know that what happened in there was a travesty. It was ... it was ... unjust. That's what it was. Unjust.'

'No it wasn't, and say "sir" when you speak to me.'

'Why wasn't it unjust, for God's sake?'

'Because the man was caught fleeing from the front line without his weapons. If he had admitted that he was confused and immediately said that he would return to the line, I for one would have opted for a reduction to the ranks and three months hard labour. But, as it was...' He shrugged his shoulders.

Hickman looked up at the face above him. The young man's cheeks were pink and his brow unlined. His eyes were steady and they revealed that he was very, very sure of himself.

'Have you ever been in the line?'

The man jerked his horse's head round sharply, taking the rein away from Jim's hand. 'How dare you speak to me like that,' he said. 'If you continue in that fashion, I will have you on a charge, DCM or no bloody DCM. Now get out of my way.'

He dug in his heels and cantered away. Hickman watched him go with hate in his heart. Then he turned and walked towards where Bertie was being held. There was no avoiding it, he had to go and see him.

This time the sergeant MP gave him a nod and, speaking strictly to attention said, 'Bloody well done, Sarn't Major, back there. The little bugger doesn't deserve that sentence. Do you want to see him?'

'Yes, please.'

'Stay as long as you like.'

It was clear that, once again, Bertie had been crying, but he rose with alacrity and embraced Jim. 'Thank you very much, Jimmy, for tryin' so hard for me. The best lawyer in the land – and I include Ireland – couldn't have done better, for sure.'

Hickman sank onto the bottom of the bed. 'Sorry, Bertie, I think I buggered it up by taking on that shit of a colonel. I got up his arse and he was determined to sink you. I don't know whether there's a chance of a formal appeal but I'll have a go.'

'Och, no son. I've had enough, one way or another. I'm happy to go and see what Jesus has got to say to me. A bit of perpetual starshine would be nice. Oh, I could see they'd made up their minds to shoot me. It's just...' His voice tailed away.

'What?'

'Well,' he sniffed and took out a filthy hand-kerchief and wiped his cheeks and eyes, 'it's just me dad and Polly. I'd hate them to think of me as a coward.'

Jim seized his hand. 'There's no question of that, lad. I promise. I will explain everything to Polly. I've already written to prepare her a bit and I will write and explain everything properly as soon as I get a chance. As for your dad. Well – he can't read, can he?'

364

'Not a bloody word.'

'Right, then ... er ... when the time comes, I will get a nice company letter done by the clerk saying what a bloody fine soldier you'd been and ... er ... you know.'

'Now that would be nice of yer, Jimmy. Yes. I must write to Polly meself, of course, now I know what's going to happen.'

'There's still a chance, Bertie. The brigadier and the big man himself, Haig, has got to approve it. They could well look at your record and say "this bloke's been a marvellous lad and there's no way we're going to shoot him".'

Bertie forced a smile. 'I don't think so, Jimmy. I really don't. Apart from anything else, them fellers don't like the Irish after what happened in Dublin last year. They think we're all goin' to talk the blokes in the front line to give it up. And, if I got back, I'd probably have a go at it, I would so. No. Let it be.'

They were silent for a while. 'Yer know,' Bertie continued, 'gettin' shot like this is very clean, ain't it? I mean it's a good, clean way to go. None of this horrible shrapnel stuff cuttin' you up in little pieces. I wouldn't want me good looks spoilt now, would I?'

Then it was his turn to lean across and take his friend's hand. 'The other good thing is that it leaves the field clear for you with Polly.' He held up a hand as Jim opened his mouth to remonstrate. 'No, no. It's better all round. You'd make a much better husband than me and we couldn't go on embarrassin' the dear thing any longer with the two of us mopin' after her and she having to make up her mind now, could we? I'll be writin' to her to tell her that.'

Jim shook his head but couldn't speak.

'Now, how's your shoulder?'

'Oh, I should have this dressing and sling off within a few days. I kept it on deliberately in the hope of getting a bit of sympathy from the board today. Waste of bloody time.' He grinned. 'Should have known better.'

They chatted for a time in a desultory fashion, then Jim got up to go. 'Is there anything you need?'

'Ah well, I'd love a run down the bars of Pop with you one last time before I go, but I doubt if they'd allow that, would they now?'

They embraced once more and Jim left, his eyes moist. He returned to his billet and sat on his bed, staring at the wall unseeingly. There could be no hope for Bertie, he knew that. The French mutinies, Bertie's Irishness, the need in the middle of this most horrible of battles to 'encourage the others', all militated against the verdict being overturned further up the chain. He also knew that there could be no formal legal appeal, the adjutant had told him that. What a travesty! What a bloody travesty!

He lay back on the bed and closed his eyes and tried to think. A letter, perhaps to his MP back home? He couldn't even remember his name, but he could get it. Or – what was the name of that journalist bloke who edited *John Bull*, the weekly magazine? He was also an MP. He was supposed to be the soldier's friend. Bottomley, that was it. He pulled a sheet of paper towards himself and began writing. He described the court martial and the prejudice of the chairman of the board and of Flanagan. Ah yes, Flanagan! There would be a score to pay there later!

He finished the letter, addressed it to 'Mr Bottomley, Editor of John Bull Magazine, Fleet Street, London, England', and posted it. One last hope! Was there anything more he could do? A personal appeal to the commander-in-chief, Field Marshal Haig, was probably hopeless. What could a humble warrant officer grade II say to a field marshal that could possibly have any effect? But it might be worth trying. He sat at the table again with pen and paper and made his appeal, on the grounds that Bertie had a good record and was undoubtedly ill. He had no idea where Haig was based but addressed the letter to him at 'British Army Headquarters, France' and hoped for the best. He sat back – that was the best he could do. Bertie was now in the hands of his God. The thought made him kneel and offer up a prayer, clumsily pleading for whoever was up there to intervene for his old friend. Then he slumped back onto the bed. He felt useless. What was he now? No longer a skilled craftsman who could set a diamond proudly onto a gold or platinum base, but a crude killer of men. That's what he was good at now. Better get back to it and get on with it. It didn't matter now if he was next in line for a shell or a bullet.

The next morning, Hickman went to see the army doctor who had been treating his shoulder and requested that he be signed off and allowed to return to the line. The man examined him thoroughly and then reluctantly agreed. He was to report back to his battalion in three days' time.

The following morning, however, an official army letter arrived. It told him that he had been posted to a battalion of the Suffolks that had limped out of the line after a thorough mauling up on the ridges and was now, in the well-practised manner, having its holes plugged with new recruits and men, like Hickman, who had recovered from wounds. Jim smiled at it. It was perfectly clear. Williams had reported back to Colonel Cox and the latter had acted quickly to get rid of him. A bad influence! Shovel him off to another regiment, but keep him in the dreaded Salient until that final bullet or shell found him. The smile hardened. Well, he didn't fucking well care! But he had to see Bertie again before the end. He had two days more before he was due to report.

The next day another letter arrived, the envelope this time carrying his address in Polly's much loved, precise handwriting.

It was clear that she was distraught. What, she demanded, had happened? Bertie could not possibly be a deserter or a coward, nobody could possibly convict anyone with his engaging personality – his innocent blue eyes and curly red hair. He was only a child, for goodness' sake. What was Jim doing to help? Could she have the details? Was it true that soldiers who deserted while on active service could be shot? She had tried to gain permission to travel to Flanders but had been told that the region was closed to anyone outside the serving forces. What could she do? What about writing to her MP, would that help? She had written to Bertie at his old battalion address. Would that get through to him? She would not mention anything to Bertie's father at the moment... And so it went on.

Jim's heart sank. It was clear that she loved Bertie dearly, much more than she loved him. Then he felt ashamed at the thought – a narrow, self-centred thought. She wanted to *do something*. Perhaps the plea to the local MP would help. So, wearily, he picked up his pen again. This time he explained to her all that had happened at the court martial and all that he had tried to do. Yes, he wrote, an appeal to her local MP might be of use. But there was little time. The army acted quickly on these things.

He sealed it sadly. Perhaps this was the end of whatever she had felt for him – perhaps, in her heart, she was blaming him, for she knew he had always felt paternal about Bertie and attempted to shield him from the miseries of life. He sighed. Then he remembered that he had forgotten to tell her about his wound. That would explain why he was not there to look after Bertie. He opened the letter again and added a PS – a seeming afterthought of no real importance and clearly not seeking sympathy.

The following morning, the last day of his sick leave, he walked to see Bertie again, confident that his new friend the redcap sergeant would allow him to visit. The sergeant was there but

Bertie was not.

''E's gone to a place with one o' them unpronounceable names, sir,' he said. 'I know it because ... well ... others 'ave gone there. It's called Oostbeke – dunno where it is, though. Somewhere back in Belgium, I think.' He felt in his breast pocket. ''Ere's the address. I thought you'd be over so I wrote it down.'

Hickman frowned and accepted the paper. 'Why would they send him there?'

The sergeant looked embarrassed. He lowered his voice. 'I think it's where they send 'em off – you know, early in the mornin' like.'

'Oh God!' The army was rushing it through, sweeping the execution away so that no further trouble, no possible last-minute embarrassment, could be caused. He thanked the sergeant and strode away. The thought of not seeing Bertie again, of not being able to comfort him, of giving him some hope – Haig, Bottomley, the local MP – before the end, was intolerable.

His new battalion was resting at Pop, so he found his new adjutant and requested two days' further leave so that he could visit Bertie.

'Sorry, Sarn't Major,' said the officer, a tough-faced veteran with the ribbon of the Military Cross pinned to his tunic, 'we're going up the line again the day after tomorrow and we need you pretty desperately. In your company, we've got four sergeants and they're all under twenty-one. Can't spare you, I'm afraid. You've got to knock these lads into shape. I shall expect you at eight ack emma in the morning.'

And so Jim Hickman went into battle once again but this time without his old comrade, except for the memory of his tear-stained face which sat atop the battle pack on his back as heavy as three extra entrenching tools. He scribbled a note to Bertie – the last one? – telling him about the appeal to Bottomley, Haig and the local MP and that Polly and he were thinking of him and urging him to keep up his spirits. He would write again from the line as soon as they had moved in.

It was now mid October and the seemingly constant summer rain had been replaced by early autumnal storms. But the British had fought tenaciously up the series of ridges to the point where they were just below their precious target: the iconic village of Passchendaele, which had given its name to the battle that had raged since 31st July. Jim was now fighting like a machine: snarling at his men when they were slow to move, demanding constant watchfulness and combativeness and prowling the succession of craters that made up the line like some black-faced creature from Hades, calling for 'one last push' as though he was Haig himself.

The truth was that now Hickman did not care if he was wounded or killed. He led every attack across the morass personally, perfecting a technique of firing his rifle – he was entitled to a revolver now, but he scorned it – from the hip accurately as he squelched, often thigh-deep, from one shell hole to another. Although men fell all around him, miraculously he survived.

Always, he looked around him with cold eyes

for Company Sergeant Major Jack Flanagan but he found no trace of him. The 1st Warwicks were obviously in some other part of the line. It was of no consequence, he could afford to wait.

However, the letter he was awaiting, from Bertie, came at last. It had been held up with the rest of the mail because the battalion was engaged in non-stop fighting. It was scrawled in pencil and told him that the execution date had been fixed and that it was to be at 5.45 in the morning. 'I shall never get up in time!' wailed Bertie. He would not tell Jim the date for he did not want him to be distracted on that day. He had had a 'wonderful letter from the lass', which gave him strength. He was reconciled to death and was looking forward to 'a lovely bit of starshine'. He loved Jim and continued to pray for his safety and long life after the war.

He ended it, 'with so much love from your old friend, comrade and champion marlie player...'

Hickman read it crouched against the side of a crater, just below the final ridge that was Passchendaele. Tears poured down his cheeks and his shoulders heaved but no one noticed because it was, of course, pouring with rain and, once again, they were being shelled.

Jim's company was among the Canadians who, on 10th November, finally entered the battered ruins of the village. It had taken 156 days, from that great explosion at Messines, to reach this objective, with the Germans fighting heroically all the way. The Third Battle of Ypres, as it came to be called, had cost thousands of lives – post-war estimates put them at up to three hundred thousand. The truth was that it was impossible to count all the dead for so many of them had literally disappeared into the mud. Certainly, as Hickman looked around him on that November morning, he hardly recognised anyone left of the company with whom he had left Pop six weeks or so ago.

They were relieved, at last, and trudged back down again through the black, stinking cemetery that the Salient had become. Waiting for him at the relief camp were four letters. The first was a cryptic note from an ADC to Field Marshal Haig, rebuking him for bothering the commander-in-chief at a critical moment in the war on a matter which had already been dealt with 'satisfactorily'. The second was from Horatio Bottomley MP, sympathising with him over the fate of Corporal Murphy but saying that he could not possibly intercede on individual cases. However, CSM Hickman would be glad to hear that he, Bottomley, had every intention of calling in the House of Commons for an official commission into the workings of courts martial once the war was over.

The third, at last, was from Polly, from whom he had not heard since her letter of despair. He opened it with trembling figures, for he was sure that her silence meant that she had not forgiven him for not protecting Bertie. It was a poignant, if short, missive. She apologised for not having written for so long and hoped – oh, how she hoped! – that he was alive and well. She had felt just too upset to write to anyone. Of course, the MP had declined to help because he, too, could not interfere in individual cases. Now, however, she had become reconciled to Bertie's fate (he had written her a heart-rending letter just before the end) and she was writing now to say that she in no way blamed Jim for their friend's death and that she loved him desperately and prayed for him every day.

Jim kissed the letter and folded it carefully and put it into his wallet. Then, puzzled, for he did not recognise the handwriting, he opened the fourth letter. It was from a Sergeant Martin Burgess, of his old company in the 1st Bn Warwicks – ah, yes. The schoolmaster! He had obviously been promoted.

Burgess began by sympathising with Hickman for Bertie's death, for he knew – as did everyone in the company – how close they had been. He, Burgess, had been wounded and on recovering miles behind the lines at a place called Oostbeke, had been ordered – with other recovering men – to form part of the twelve-man squad to end the life of a condemned deserter. To his shock he had found that the man to be executed was Corporal Murphy. He had tried to fall out of the detail on compassionate grounds but was refused. So he had been there when Bertie had died.

Jim took a deep breath and looked away from the letter for a moment. Then he regained his composure and returned to it. Burgess was writing, he emphasised, to reassure Hickman that his old friend had died 'splendidly – head up and refusing the blindfold'. He had even been singing when the bullets struck home: 'some-

374

thing about falling in love at seventeen with eyes of tender blue...'

Shoulders heaving, Jim crumpled the letter and put it in his pocket.

CHAPTER FIFTEEN

At the camp, Hickman was awarded fourteen days' leave. He could have used it for a return home, but, on reflection, he decided against crossing the Channel. Firstly, he felt apprehensive about meeting Polly just yet. He yearned to see her (lusted?) but, although he knew it was irrational, he knew he could not face her yet. Bertie's death was too close and the wound was still open. It was a risk not returning when he had the chance, for, despite her assurances, there might be other men back home who had come into her life or might still do so. After all, it had been almost a year since they had last met. Yet he knew he must take the risk. Let things settle, he reflected.

The other, more compelling reason, was that he had things to do in Belgium.

He had always worried about how the news would reach Bertie's father. Polly, he knew, did most of his reading for him. It was likely, then, that when the formal letter informing Mr Murphy of his son's death had reached him, she would have intercepted it. What would she have done? She had made no mention of it in her letters since. There might still be time to retrieve the situation. He made his way, therefore, to the tent that was battalion headquarters and, casually walking by, established that its only occupant was a clerk, pecking away at a noisy typewriter. Good. The colonel and the adjutant were away.

By this time, Hickman had established a reputation in the battalion as a fearsome fighter and a man not to be trifled with, despite his age. The clerk looked up, then, a touch apprehensively. 'Mornin', Sarn't Major.'

'Morning, Jones.' Jim gave him a warm smile. 'Are you in the market for earning ten francs on that bloody machine?'

'Wouldn't mind, sir. Wouldn't mind at all. Is it legal?'

'Perfectly legal. Bit of private business that's all. Bending the rules slightly but you will stay out of it. Look. I would like you to type this letter. Don't use battalion notepaper – even if you've got it, which I doubt. No. Just type on plain stuff, typin' the battalion name on the top. I've scribbled out what I want you to say.' He pointed. 'Put 1st Battalion, Royal Warwickshire Regiment on the top, with "somewhere in Flanders" as the address. Date it a month ago. It's to go to Mr P. Murphy, number 62, Turners Lane, Aston, Birmingham 6. Here, I've written it out but I'll read it to you in case you can't read my writing.'

Jim took a quick look to make sure that no one was approaching the tent and read:

Dear Mr Murphy,
906372 Corporal Bertram Murphy, Royal Warwick-
shire Regt.

I am writing to inform you of the death of your son,
the above, in action against the enemy on the Ypres
Salient. He was killed while advancing in the face of
fierce enemy fire and met his death instantly. He will
have known no pain.

In sending you my condolences, I would like to tell
you that your son died a hero's death, facing the
enemy and showing no sign of fear. He was a splen-
did soldier and will be missed by all his comrades in
A Company.

You have my deepest sympathy.
Yours sincerely,
J. Smith, Captain, company commander.

'I'll sign it. Do the envelope and I'll find the stamp.'

Jones's jaw dropped. 'Ooh, Sarn't Major,' he said, 'I'm not sure I should do this. It's impersonatin' an officer, ain't it?'

'No, it's not, because Captain Smith doesn't exist. Look, Jones, this bloke was my mate. They shot him a month ago for desertion. He was not a coward, he was just ill. I don't want his father – who can't read or write – to know about the way he died and I am gambling that I can get this letter to be read to him by a neighbour before the real one gets there. But for God's sake don't tell the colonel or the adjutant or we shall all be in the shit. Can you do it today?'

A smile crept over the clerk's face. 'Yes, sir.

Colonel and adjutant won't be back until late this afternoon.'

'Good lad. Here's the ten francs. You might have saved an old man's tears. I'll be back at three. Get typing.'

Hickman then walked to the railway station and bought himself a ticket to Oostbeke and scribbled a letter of explanation to Polly to cover the fake letter about Bertie's death. He just hoped that she had intercepted anything that had come earlier and could make the substitution. It was worth a try. Later that day he picked up Jones's effort, impeccably typed, and slipped it into the letter to Polly and posted it.

The journey to Oostbeke did not take long – nowhere did in Belgium – and he found it to be a small village, near divisional headquarters, with a large military police presence. Could it be the centre for executions? He thrust the thought aside. For God's sake there couldn't be *that* many surely? There did seem, however, to be an army padre in residence, who turned out to be Roman Catholic.

A small man with a gentle manner, he had officiated at Bertie's death, giving him the last rites and praying with him right to the end.

'He was your friend, Sergeant Major?' he enquired.

'My dearest friend. He should not have been shot. He was not a deserter or a coward, he was ill. But the army felt it had to kill him.'

The priest gave a sigh. 'Ah yes, my son. I can see you are angry. But so many men meet their maker unjustly in this war. At least Corporal

Murphy met his with equanimity, with great faith and fortitude.'

Hickman resisted the urge to shout 'Balls!' and asked, 'Can you show me where he is buried?'

'Yes. I'm afraid it's not consecrated ground. But it's a charming little glade just outside the village. We use it for ... er ... this sort of thing. I can take you there now.'

It was, indeed, a quiet spot, which, in summer, must have been gently shaded and green. Now, it merely looked sombre. Seven or eight mounds of earth, topped with plain wooden crosses, were tucked away in one corner. The priest took Jim to one with freshly turned soil.

'This is your friend,' he said. 'I'll leave you alone for I'm sure you'll want to pray quietly. You can find me back in the office if you want me.'

'Thank you, Father.'

But Jim did not pray. He stood looking down for more than a minute, then scuffed the earth with his boot. 'We'll soon have you out of here, son,' he said.

Back in the village, he found that there were two churches, both Catholic, of course. The first was red-bricked, huge and gloomy and it gave out an image of respectability and religious rectitude. He walked on until, at the far end of the little community, he found a smaller church, built of stone and looking as though it had been aged when the Conqueror sailed for Hastings. It had a tranquil churchyard fringed with yew trees and containing many headstones. The heavy wooden door to the church yielded to the latch and Jim entered. It was, predictably, dark but, even on this autumn day, quite warm and welcoming. It was also empty.

Outside, a noticeboard gave the name of the priest as Georges Picard but no address for him. And would he speak English? Hickman accosted a passing woman and, pointing to the notice, asked, questioningly, *'Le père. Monsieur Picard?'*

Puzzled, she nodded in acquiescence, then, realising the point of the question, indicated a house that stood by the churchyard. Luckily, Father Picard *was* at home and, even more fortunately, he spoke English.

'Come in.' He waved Hickman towards an overstuffed armchair, selected a much more austere seat for himself and leant forward. 'How can I help you?' The priest had a long, thin face with jowls that reminded Jim of a worried hound, but his eyes – as blue as Bertie's – were kind.

Hickman had long since decided that he would not dissemble but rather tell the story of Bertie in some detail and then make his request as a logical sequence at the end. He did so now: 'You see, Father, he has been buried, without a headstone, in unconsecrated ground in a wood not far from here.' He slapped a finger into the palm of his hand to emphasise his last points. 'He was, first of all, not a coward or a deserter, merely a sick man. Secondly, he was a good Catholic – the army priest will verify that – and it is not right that he is buried in unconsecrated ground.'

The priest's lugubrious face broke into a

smile. 'And thirdly, he was your friend. Yes?'

'We grew up together and this would never have happened had I been with him when he cracked. But I was wounded and out of the line and was not there to help him.'

'Hmmm. And what do you want of me, my son?'

'Father, I would like to ... er ... dig up my friend and have him buried in your lovely churchyard here, with a proper headstone erected above his grave. And I would like you to conduct a proper Catholic burial service for him. I will pay all costs. I have money. I have been saving from my army pay. Here.' He took out his wallet and put one hundred and twenty francs on the table. 'I hope this will pay for moving my friend and his reburial. I will send more money to you for the headstone. Please, Father, say that you will help me, because I know that the army authorities will not do so and I would wish it to be done quickly before my leave expires.'

Father Picard was silent for a moment, his hands folded on his lap, and Jim's heart fell. He realised that what he was asking was difficult. It would demand the priest's intrusion into the affairs of the British army, which at this place, was virtually an occupying force.

'I think,' mused the priest, 'that this ... er ... removal would have to be done at night, so that we do not upset my colleagues in your army.' He gave a sudden, disarming grin. 'We would be grave robbers in the dark, eh?'

Hickman grinned back, in huge relief. 'Yes, but Bertie would see the joke,' he said. 'Father, would your local gravediggers do this, do you think? I would be with them, of course.'

Picard picked up the money. He selected a few of the notes. 'For twenty francs – not all this money, my son – they would do anything.' He slapped his knees and roared with laughter. Jim offered up a silent prayer that he had found probably the only grave-robbing priest in the whole of France – and one with a sense of humour!

He offered the remaining notes back to Hickman. 'You keep this for the moment – no, I take another ten for the offertory box – and, when the stone is cut and erected you will send what is necessary to me to pay the mason. We have a good man in the village but you must tell me what it is you want to put on the ... er ... tablet, eh?'

Jim fumbled in his pocket. 'I have it here,' he said, 'laid out as I would like it. Here.' He handed it to the priest, who read it out aloud:
'In Loving Memory of a Brave British Soldier
Bertram Murphy
1896–1917
Still Alive in Our Hearts'
'*Ah oui,*' muttered Picard. 'Very fine.'

Hickman picked up the remaining notes and handed them back to the priest. 'But you must keep these for the stone,' he said. 'I am due to return to the front soon. I have been lucky for three years but this luck is due to run out and I could be killed. You must have this to pay the mason. Will you need more, do you think?'

'I think not. But I tell you if it is necessary.'

'When can we do the ... dirty deed?'

The priest roared with laughter again. 'Ah, it should be when the moon is – what do you say in English? – riding high in a black sky. No, no. We must joke no more. This is not something funny we do. The good Lord would approve, I know. You do this in his name, my son, I know that. Now, I think, perhaps tonight. Where do you sleep?'

'Nowhere at the moment.'

'There is a good auberge at the end of the lane that goes by the side of the church here. Go there and say I sent you. They will probably double the price then,' the great roar of laughter came again, 'but they will find you a bed. I will send you a message when I have talked to my gravediggers.' Then he slapped his knee. 'Ah, I am a poor host. I did not offer an Englishman tea.'

Hickman rose. 'No thank you, Father,' he said. 'I have already taken too much of your time. I cannot say how much I am grateful to you–'

The priest interrupted. 'Too early for thanks yet. We may end in jail first.' And he laughed again.

Jim found the inn, a tiny building with an old sign showing a keg of ale hanging outside its entrance. The bed was found and he ordered ham and bread and a flagon of light Belgian beer and thanked his lucky stars again that he had found Father Picard, surely the only priest who would contemplate opening up a grave in the middle of the night and dodging the British military police in moving the body elsewhere. Yes. How Bertie would have chuckled – and Polly, for that matter!

The message came at six o'clock. Jim was to rendezvous at the church at 8 p.m. Moving a body after midnight, obviously, was rather too much of a risk for the priest. And so it proved.

'We cannot move at night,' he explained when they met, 'because it is – what you say? – the criminals' hour. But at eight or nine, we could be moving chairs for the church meeting tomorrow. I do not mind if we lie. God will understand we do it for one of his good servants. Here, the men have already dug a grave. I show you.'

They picked their way through the dark churchyard to a corner, near where a lilac tree would bloom in spring. The diggers had dug out a deep grave, piling the earth to the side. It was an ideal spot for a man deserted by the army for which he had fought. Hickman was satisfied.

As the church clock struck eight, half a dozen old chairs were loaded onto a cart pulled by a sad old horse and covered in tarpaulin. Then they set out for the glade, the two diggers in their corduroys, woollen jackets and berets riding on the cart, the priest and Jim walking by its side. Picard wore his wide-brimmed clerical hat and a black raincoat over his cassock and Hickman his uniform greatcoat and army cap. He had brought mufti with him but had decided against wearing it. If they met the military police, his warrant officer's crown could be useful.

The night, indeed, was dark, if not stormy, and black clouds raced across the sky. It was, Jim reflected, the right sort of conditions for exhuming a body on one side of a village and reinterring it on the other. A shiver ran through him.

But it would be worse on the return journey, he knew. No one spoke until they entered the glade.

'There,' Jim pointed. He wrested the wooden cross from the ground. 'Sorry Bertie,' he breathed. 'Soon have you moved and settled, old lad.'

Working by a guttering lantern, the diggers shovelled away the earth while the priest and Hickman kept watch. Shadows swept across the toiling figures from the single candle and the moon kept slipping in and out of the clouds, sending its silvery light to add to the bizarre nature of the tableau in the clearing. Jim kept looking over his shoulder, half expecting to see a short, ever-willing figure in unkempt uniform and with dishevelled hair stumping up to say, 'Here lads, I'll give you a hand.'

It did not take long for the diggers to uncover the coffin, for it lay under the ground only four feet or so. And a coffin it was, much to the relief of Hickman, who was half expecting his old comrade to be buried in a winding sheet. As it was uncovered, the priest stopped the workmen and he knelt, saying a brief prayer, as they all removed their hats. Then the work began of lifting the coffin out of its slot – not easily, for the coffin was a cheap affair, without handles, and Jim worried for a moment that it might break open.

But, with a heave, it was extricated and put, with surprising tenderness, onto the cart and covered with the tarpaulin. Then the earth was shovelled back into the opening and stamped down. Jim carefully tucked the wooden cross under the canvas and they began the journey back, this time all four riding on the cart, sitting on the coffin – Hickman's idea, in case they were stopped. Bertie wouldn't mind, he explained to the priest, who translated so that they all smiled.

They were indeed intercepted. A corporal and private of the military police stepped out of the shadows as they neared a crossroads.

'Evenin', Padre,' said the corporal. 'Where are you all off to at this time of the night?'

Hickman put on his cap and stepped down from the cart. 'Sergeant Major Hickman, of the 2nd Battalion Suffolks,' he said crisply. 'Nothing to worry about, Corporal. I'm here on a few days' leave.' He produced his leave warrant and offered it. 'Father Picard here is an old friend and I'm staying at the pub round the corner from his church. I'm just giving them a hand in moving some gear for a church meeting tomorrow. We're miles from the line. Is there a problem?'

The corporal, who with the other policeman had stiffened to attention, shook his head. 'No, Sarn't Major. But, as this is where divisional headquarters is based we have to be careful, you know. Come on, we'll escort you to the church.'

'Good lad,' said Hickman and smiled inwardly.

And so with an escort of military policemen, Bertie Murphy undertook the journey to his last resting place. Jim Hickman thought it most appropriate and only wished that the Colonels

Cox and Williams could have been present to witness the procession. The redcaps offered to help unload the cart but the priest and Hickman declined their offer with profuse thanks and the two men marched slowly away into the blackness.

The coffin was hurriedly taken down and then, with each of the men at the four corners, it was carried carefully to the open grave under the lilac tree. Here, they all knelt as the priest produced a small black book of prayer and conducted a service of sorts in either Latin or French – Jim had no idea which – and then they stood as the earth was shovelled back onto the coffin as Picard intoned a blessing or final benediction. As they stood silently at the end, Jim broke away and rescued the wooden cross. He rammed it into the ground at Bertie's head. It would have to do until his fine headstone was erected.

Before he left for his train the next morning, Father Picard introduced Jim to the young widow of the churchwarden who had died the year before at Verdun. She had taken over her husband's responsibilities and Hickman pressed forty francs into her hand on her promise to take a special interest in looking after Bertie's grave.

The priest insisted on accompanying him to the railway station and there they shook hands, with Jim promising to despatch more money, as necessary, for the payment of the stonemason and the maintenance of the grave. Then, with a heart lighter than it had been for weeks, he went back to the war.

Back at the camp, Hickman wrote a long letter to Polly, explaining all that he had done. He lied in saying that it had been impossible to get home leave but promised that he would return to her as soon as he was able. He had, he wrote firmly, every intention of surviving the war, now surely moving towards its end, and returning to marry her.

The Third and greatest Battle of Ypres officially ended on 10th November 1917, with the Allies atop the ridges at Passchendaele, at the end of one of the most costly campaigns in history. Since 1914 the defence of Ypres had cost the British and its Allies 430,000 troops, killed, wounded and missing. The Allies at last looked over the green fields of Belgium beyond the mud of the Salient and opportunity was taken to transfer five divisions to the Italian front and send several more to take part in the Battle of Cambrai. Jim Hickman travelled up with his regiment to take post just east of Passchendaele at the furthest point reached by the British in the Salient and stayed there throughout the bitterly cold early months of 1918, still engaged in fighting with a stubborn enemy, but he and no one else doubting that it would take only the smallest of Big Pushes to send the Germans in final and full retreat, particularly now that America had entered the war and the first of the doughboys – raw, inexperienced but keen and confident – had begun to land.

It was, however, the Germans who had one last great, heroic offensive left in them. Reinforced by troops sent to the Western Front after their defeat of Imperial Russia, they launched a fierce attack in the spring of 1918 along the whole of the front – and particularly against the denuded British atop the Salient ridges. Summoning up the last of its strength and fighting with an energy and bravery prompted by 'the last chance' calls of its high command, the Germans rolled back the British line down from Passchendaele, forcing them to give up within a few weeks the soggy muddy acres they had sacrificed so much to gain over the previous three and a half years.

A 'strategic withdrawal' the British called it, but it was more a fierce rearguard action fought down the slope, each standpoint being overwhelmed by the vastly increased German forces, until the Salient was reduced to a tight little circle before Ypres, smaller than it had ever been – roughly, in fact, the perimeter Jim had proposed to Bertie so many lives ago. Here, the British stood fast.

Jim Hickman fought stoically, step by step in the retreat, knowing now, it seemed to him, every shell crater, bloated corpse and protruding skeleton in that abominable battlefield. The impetuosity that had characterised his behaviour in combat immediately after Bertie's death had now subsided into a determination to do his duty but to survive, using all the experience he had gathered in constant fighting on the Western Front over the last three and a half years.

At one point on the retreat, near Frezenberg,

he and his company fought with their bayonets to provide rearguard cover for the weary troops retreating behind them. Despite heavy losses, they held up the enemy for two hours or more and their leadership in that encounter earned Hickman's young company commander an MC and Jim himself the Military Medal (crosses were only awarded to officers) to add to his Distinguished Conduct Medal.

It was, then, a still young but now distinguished and experienced Jim Hickman who formed part of the defences at the bottom of the Salient, his battalion crammed together with others in the tight little ring around Ypres, as the spring began to give way to the summer of 1918.

It was not, however, a completely defensive ring. Reinforcements, even at this late stage in the war, continued to arrive to repair the gaps in the British regiments and 'offensive patrols' were launched to test the enemy's strength after all the desperate fighting of the last few weeks. Could the Germans have expended all of their reserves?

It was on one of these that Hickman had his last brush with death.

Shortly before dawn, he and his company commander led a force of two platoons out on a raid to newly established German positions in Chateau Wood, astride what remained of the Menin Road. They were providing left-flank support for an attack in company strength by troops on their right – Hickman had no idea of the regiment manning the line at that point.

It was a repeat in miniature of many such

attacks on a grander scale, except that there was no British artillery barrage to warn the enemy and it was thought that the Germans had had no time to erect wire defences in any depth at the wood. The idea was to hit the enemy positions a little before daylight, cause havoc, capture prisoners and then retire.

But, as had happened so often in the past, it did not work out that way. Hickman with his platoons crept forward in the darkness with bayonets fixed, dimly aware of the other British troops on their right. They had crossed little more than a hundred yards of the two hundred that separated them from the enemy, however, when star shells went up and machine guns starting raking their lines from well-prepared positions in the wood.

'Charge!' shouted Hickman's company commander before he was cut into two by a burst of machine-gun fire.

'Keep going,' yelled Jim, but once again it was the mud that was the Germans' main ally. The harsh winter had done nothing to repair the heavy swamp that the Salient had become. It was impossible for men to break into a run when up to their knees in glutinous slime and they went down in dozens before the fire of the machine guns.

Jim saw the men in front and either side of him fall and felt the kiss of the bullets as they plucked at the sleeve and bottom edge of his tunic. He slipped in the mud and half fell, half rolled into a shell crater, desperate for cover. In the semi-darkness, he was conscious that the hole had one other occupant, a shadowy figure in British uniform.

He heard the click of a rifle bolt being slid into place and he frowned as the gun was presented to him.

'Hey,' he shouted. 'I'm British.'

'I know you are,' hissed back Company Sergeant Major Jack Flanagan, 'and I'm goin' to kill you, you bastard.' Hickman sensed rather than saw the grimy finger tighten on the trigger. The hammer clicked onto an empty chamber. Flanagan had exhausted all of his ammunition in the attack.

'Fuck it,' screamed the Irishman and he threw himself across the sloping sides of the crater, his bayonet poised for a fatal thrust.

But the mud of the slope was no place to mount an attack of that sort and his feet floundered and slipped in the slime until he was below Hickman, as he scrabbled to gain a foothold and stop his descent. But down he went, the mud on his boots now built up to a wedge of some four or five inches under the soles as he struggled in vain to stop himself slipping into the faintly steaming, yellowish liquid that awaited him at the bottom. The more he struggled, however, the further he descended, until his feet slipped under the surface of the liquid slime.

Flanagan held up his rifle in supplication. 'For God's sake help me,' he cried. 'I'm going under.'

Hickman, his eyes wide in horror, inched down towards the bottom and held out his own bayonet-tipped rifle. 'Throw away your rifle,' he shouted, 'hold onto the end of mine.'

Flanagan did so and reached up until his fingertips clutched the end of the bayonet. Then he screamed as the remnants of the mustard gas lingering on the surface of the liquid below bit into his flesh. At the same time, his fingers slipped away from the tip of Hickman's bayonet, leaving a trail of blood on the blade and he sank down, hip-deep, then chest-deep, until the dreadful mire at the bottom of the crater had reached to just under his chin. There he stayed for a while, thrashing his arms about in an attempt to keep afloat, but his heavy boots were now down at the bottom and whatever it was that was down there gathered him to it until, his mouth open in terror, he slowly disappeared below the surface.

Jim watched in horror as a few bubbles reached the surface and then the pool regained its baleful tranquillity as though nothing had happened. He rested his cheek on his arm and found himself shaking. Then he carefully retrieved his rifle and bayonet and rested for a moment on the slope in an attempt to regain his equanimity before he began slowly – very slowly – to inch his way up to the lip of the crater. There he lay, his head just below the edge, gasping in great gulps of comparatively fresh air.

The encounter with Flanagan had been so sudden, so unexpected, and it had all happened so quickly that it seemed almost like a fragment of a nightmare. He looked below him at the evil water below. Nothing stirred. He could not have imagined it, for there was the Irishman's rifle lying just above the level of the liquid. He shuddered and closed his eyes.

He did not know how long he lay there, but it had begun raining again and the clouds above had become lighter, much lighter, when he heard a voice say, 'Are you wounded, Sarn't Major?'

He looked up into the eyes of Sergeant Martin Burgess, hardly recognisable, so covered in mud was his face.

'Hello, schoolmaster,' gasped Hickman. 'I never did thank you for your letter. Congratulations on your promotion.'

'Bugger that,' said Burgess. 'You're shaking. Are you wounded?'

'No, Sergeant. I've just had a shock, that's all. Can we get back to the line, do you think?'

'Yes, I believe so. It's a case of crawling, though. It's virtually light.'

'Let's crawl, then, as we did once before. Get crawling, I'll follow.'

They reached the lines, freezing when the machine guns opened up again, but making it in company with the few other survivors of the unsuccessful sortie. The men on Hickman's right in the attack, of course, were from the 1st Warwicks. Jim had no idea how many men had been lost from his old company there, but the two platoons which he had helped to lead suffered badly, losing more than a hundred men, it was estimated.

Thanking Burgess and saying goodbye, Hickman decided he had to report the loss of Flanagan. He did so curtly: 'He fell into the crater,' he said, 'and slid down to the bottom. He may have been wounded. I did all I could to save him but

394

he drowned down there.'

Burgess nodded and tightened his grip on Jim's hand. 'I'll tell the colonel,' he said. 'All I can say is good riddance.'

'Have you still got Cox?'

Burgess grinned, a flash of white brightening his dark face. 'Good Lord, no. He was sacked three months ago. He broke down in the line.'

'Good riddance a second time.'

'Absolutely.'

'Good luck, Jim.'

'Good luck to you, and thanks again, Martin.'

Hickman couldn't sleep that night. He felt no sense of triumph, relief or satisfaction in Flanagan's death. Just disgust in the manner of it, the horror of it. So many men had gone that way; men much more deserving than Flanagan. Then, just before he slipped into blessed sleep, a smattering of relief began to sneak into his consciousness. He had been saved from the task of killing the man, of meeting his pledge. He knew that, if he had seen the Irishman first in the shell hole, his reaction would have been to shoot the bastard – and yet, would he have had the nerve to kill a man in cold blood, a fellow British soldier, however evil the man? Probably not. Then he turned over. It didn't matter now.

CHAPTER SIXTEEN

The Germans had, indeed, overreached themselves. Riots in the Fatherland, caused by the growing food shortage resulting from the British naval blockade, and the huge losses of life throughout the war and particularly in the last great offensive, caused a widespread collapse across the whole front. The end was as sudden as the spring attacking surge had been. An armistice was signed in November 1918 and the most devastating war the world had ever seen was over at last.

Jim Hickman returned home at the end of November, granted leave before his final demobilisation. He and Polly, of course, had exchanged letters several times after Bertie's death but there had been a certain formality, even stiffness, in their correspondence that had never been there before. As Jim stood in the crowded corridor of the train, therefore, as it trundled through the long tunnel before Birmingham's New Street Station, he was apprehensive. Polly had promised to meet him, of course, but would she have bad news for him? That epistolary awkwardness must have been caused by eruption of other men in her life, surely, since they had last met eighteen months ago?

As he stepped down onto the platform, kitbag on shoulder, he saw her suddenly materialise from the steam escaping from the locomotive, as she had done before. She wore a dark woollen coat but had retained her summer straw hat, held on top of her bunched hair by a silk scarf tied under her chin. As she saw him, she began to run and then stopped uncertainly.

He threw down his kitbag and held out his arms. This time without hesitation she ran into them, throwing her arms around his neck and sobbing. He lifted her off her feet and gently swung her around before putting her down and, for a time, they stood there, her face buried in his shoulder as her own shoulders heaved.

Eventually, he eased her away and, putting his finger under her chin kissed away her tears. 'The war's over, my love,' he murmured.

Sniffing, she nodded and then dabbed her face with her handkerchief and said, 'I thought it would never end.'

They stood looking, shyly, at each other. Jim saw again the high cheekbones, striking green eyes and firm lips that he had conjured up so many times in France and Belgium. There were lines now, however, faint but clear, at the corners of her eyes and perhaps her figure was a little fuller. 'You haven't changed a bit,' he said. 'Even more beautiful, perhaps, but not much.'

She grinned. 'You have, my love. You're older.' She traced the lines on his face. 'And you're thinner. But I think it makes you look more handsome.'

'Blimey. It must be dark in here. Let's go. The Wine Lodge?'

She nodded and he shouldered his kitbag and

they walked away arm in arm through the crowds to their old rendezvous. The place had been redecorated and the bunting that had been put up to celebrate the Armistice remained, but their corner table had gone. They found another one and Jim ordered a bottle of St Emilion 1912. His newfound assurance about wine was slightly punctured when told that they had no such wine in stock, so he settled for a St Estèphe 1913. They sat in silence for a moment, regarding each other over the rim of their glasses.

Then Polly fumbled in her handbag and brought out a small object wrapped in tissue paper. She unwrapped it and produced the diamond. She looked down at it and said, without raising her eyes, 'Jim, I love you ever so much and, if you still want me, I would like you to mount this into a ring for me.' Then she started to sob again.

He reached across and gave her his large white handkerchief. Then he took the diamond and held it up to the light. 'Not bad for five bob,' he said, grinning. 'Consider it made, Mrs Hickman.'

She looked across at him through her tears. 'Oh, Jim,' she said, 'it's been such a terrible time, what with Bertie and all. I didn't know what to say to you really in my letters. I had a feeling that you had grown away from me – and that you'd found a pretty little French girl.'

'Oh, I did. So you'll find me much more experienced the next time.' He paused. 'I never stopped loving you, Polly Johnson, you and your green eyes, but I have to say I was worried a bit about Bertie...'

'Yes.' Polly dried her eyes and returned the handkerchief. 'I was confused, Jim. Terribly confused.'

'I know, because I loved the little bugger too. But you never did tell me: my fake letter to his dad about his death. Did it arrive before the official one?'

'Sorry, I should have told you, but I was so upset about Bertie I didn't even want to write about him. Yes, I had stopped the official bloody thing. So heartless! So hurtful! I burnt it. I just didn't know what to say to old Poppa Murphy and I was working around to seeing if I could fake my own letter, when your wonderful piece of work arrived.'

Jim tried to smile, but it was difficult. 'How did the old chap take it?'

'He was terribly upset, of course, 'cos Bertie was his only child, as you know. But he had the letter framed.' She leant across. 'Jim, as I wrote and told you, I was so pleased and proud with what you did with Bertie at the end. Perhaps we can go and see the grave one day?'

'Of course.'

'And as regards Poppa Murphy, the poor old chap died just two weeks ago. We had his funeral a week ago. I'm sorry you missed it.'

'Ah. I'm sorry.'

'He had nothing more to live for. I think he just faded away.'

'Good way to go.'

An apprehensive look crept over Polly's face and she took a deep draught of wine, as though for courage. 'Jim, there's something else.'

Hickman frowned. 'Yes?'

She fumbled in her handbag again and took out something else wrapped in tissue paper. Another diamond emerged, also unmounted and slightly smaller than the first.

Polly cleared her throat. 'It's from Bertie,' she said. 'He gave it to me that ... er ... weekend when we saw *The Maid of the Mountains*. I gave him the same answer I gave to you – that I wanted to wait.'

A slow smile crept across Hickman's face. 'The cunning little bugger,' he said. 'I had a feeling he might be up to something like that.' He frowned and gave Polly a stern gaze. 'Blimey, Pol. An outsider might think that you were waiting to marry the last man standing.'

The green eyes blazed for a second. 'Oh, Jim. That's a terrible thing to say. You don't mean it, do you?'

He reached across and took her hand again. 'You don't listen. I said an outsider might think it. I never did. But I must say the dear lad did make it easy for us in the end.'

She nodded. 'Yes. He wrote me a wonderful letter on the eve of his ... you know. I will show it to you some day.'

'Yes, do. Not now.'

Polly put Bertie's diamond in his hand and spoke hesitantly. 'Jim, don't misunderstand this. But do you think ... would you consider ... putting this with your own diamond when you make the ring? Would you be upset?'

He held the diamond to the light, as he had

done his own. 'Bloody thing's only worth half a crown,' he said. And then, as her eyes widened in dismay, he grinned. 'Only joking. I always suspected he would do this so I am long prepared for it. It would be wonderful to have the two together. I promise I'll make you a ring that we'll be proud of – all three of us. Oh God, Pol, don't start crying again.'

'I can't help it. You're such a lovely man.'

They were silent for a while again as they eased into the relief and joy they had found again in each other. They let the glow of the wine seep into them – a new experience, because Polly only drank on 'special occasions' and then never as good a vintage as this, and Jim because he was only accustomed to the 'the plonk' of Poperinghe.

Hickman eased a sigh. 'Has anyone moved into Mr Murphy's house?'

'No. There's been no time, since his death.'

'Any idea of the rent?'

'I think it's about seven bob a week.'

'They tell me that I'm getting my old job back. I could afford that. What do you say?'

'Well it sounds as though that's the nearest I'm going to get to a formal proposal, so I say let's grab it.'

They held hands across the table again, grinning at each other. Then Jim said, 'I've got fourteen days before I go back to the barracks to be officially demobbed. I don't suppose you would fancy Malvern again, would you?'

Polly held up her hands in mock horror. 'What! Out of wedlock? What sort of girl do you think I am?' Then, 'As a matter of fact, I've booked it for a week from Saturday.'

Jim grinned. 'Ah. Now I know exactly what sort of girl you are.'

They were married in January of 1919 with Sergeant Martin Burgess as best man. They took a brief winter's honeymoon – in Malvern, of course – and their daughter, Beatrice (the nearest female name they could find to Bertram) was born exactly nine months later. Despite all their efforts, she was their only child but she was a feisty schoolgirl who grew up to be a beautiful young woman, with red hair ('How appropriate,' said Jim, glaring in mock suspicion at his wife) and Polly's green eyes.

When Jim's parents died they moved into their house at number 66 because it gave them a rather larger garden and room to build onto the back. Jim's career prospered in the jewellery trade until the slump of the thirties propelled him out of work, forcing him to buy an insurance 'book', collecting on penny policies, but he sold it later at a small profit and bought a small wine outlet in Aston, where he indulged himself in his new interest in French vintages. His long war and his DCM and MM had made him something of a local hero, and he and Polly – a distinguished, good-looking couple in middle and old age – became honoured fixtures at British Legion functions. In the late thirties, Jim was elected president of the local branch.

Their happiness was only blighted by the early death of Beatrice and then, tragically, that of her husband, and their three spirited daughters were brought up by Polly and Jim.

The couple made one pilgrimage to Bertie's grave in 1928. Father Picard had long since died but he had kept his word – without asking Jim for further payments – and a fine headstone, proudly carved, stood at the end of the grave under the lilac tree, now in colourful flower. The white stone stood out rather brashly from the old tombs and stones that stood around it but the couple were satisfied that it was well kept and they left a large wreath of red poppies on the grave. They also met the French lady, now in her late thirties, who had promised to maintain the grave. She had also kept her word, for the grave itself was well preserved, with fresh daffodils in an urn at its foot. Jim tried to give her a one hundred franc note but she indignantly refused. It was an honour, she said, to 'do her duty to the fallen'.

Jim was forty-three when the Second World War broke out and, although he volunteered to rejoin the Royal Warwickshire Regiment, his old wounds in leg and shoulder, together with his age, precluded him. He did, however, join the Home Guard, becoming a company commander – 'a bloody officer at last,' he crowed – and served out the war without firing a shot in anger.

The three girls all married, had their own children and left Aston, although Polly and Jim stayed at number 66, Turners Lane with Jim's treasured collection of French clarets. Polly died at the age of eighty in 1976, leaving Jim with his memories of a wonderful love, the occasional bad dream, as a relic of the Salient, and, in his later years, a determined mission.

EPILOGUE

Aston, Birmingham, August 1996

The whole street knew that this was a special day. Shortly after the milk was delivered, the buzz developed from house to house along the terrace. Front doors were opened and, despite the chill of the morning, left open for minutes as aproned housewives, most of them with dark faces more redolent of Islamabad than Birmingham, stood and chatted. Occasionally, someone would nod towards number 66, where faded bunting was draped across the dark brick, hanging like forgotten detritus of the jubilee of 1977. Later, people hurrying to work paused to direct a quick look and a smile at the house's curtained windows. Cars pulled out from the ranks that lined the pavements and sounded their horns as they passed. But here, at the epicentre of all the fuss, nothing seemed to be happening. The house stayed silent.

Until, that is, The Telegram arrived. As soon as the post office van pulled up and the postman, in his yellow traffic surcoat, sprang out and knocked on the door, a small semicircle of neighbours materialised and gathered around him. The middle-aged woman who opened the door and took the envelope from him grinned and waved it in the air.

'I expect it's from 'er,' she said. ''E ought to open it, then I'll come out and read it to you. That is, if 'e'll let me. You know what 'e's like. 'E don't want no fuss.'

The gathering nodded in appreciation. That was as it should be. A hero should be modest.

Once back inside, the woman pulled back the curtains on the parlour window that fronted the street and shouted up the stairs, 'Telegram for you, Grandpops. Time to get up anyway. Lots to do today. Come on. Get out on parade. The car will be 'ere in just over an hour. Show a leg, love.'

A querulous but loud reply came from up above. 'Bugger it, gel. I'm up. Just going to the bathroom. That thing can wait.'

Shaking her head in mock exasperation, Linda Grantham put the telegram on the table and hurried to the kitchen to put the kettle on. Then she laid the table with cornflakes, orange juice, bowls, knives and spoons. No cooked breakfast this morning, for by the time ex-Sergeant Major Jim Hickman, DCM, MM, lowered himself down that narrow wooden staircase, the bloody car would be here waiting. Well, let it wait! This was *his* day. He shouldn't be bullied. Mind you, it was just as well she'd packed his overnight bag last night. There was no way the poor old love could hurry these days.

The doorbell rang again and she opened it to admit her two younger sisters, Lilly and Amy, also plumply middle-aged. They all kissed quickly and Linda waved to the little knot of neighbours still gathered outside. 'Sorry,' she called. ''E's still not seen it. So don't 'ang about. I suppose it always says the same thing, anyway.'

'Yes, but it's a great thing to have a telegram from the Queen,' said Mrs Patel from number 70, flashing her teeth in a wrap-around smile. 'Perhaps we could see it when he's gone?'

'Okay,' Linda nodded affably. 'We're off in about three-quarters of an hour. One of the girls will show it to you.'

Inside, Lilly and Amy had gathered at the bottom of the stairs. 'Happy birthday, Grand-pops,' they called up in unison. Then Amy shouted, 'What's it like to be a hundred?'

'Bloody awful. Mind out. I'm coming down. Don't want to fall on the pair of you.'

Linda carefully laid out her grandfather's pills on the kitchen table as she listened to each heavy but faltering step on the stairs. At last he appeared at the kitchen doorway with his other two granddaughters. The three gathered together and kissed him in turn.

'What sort of night did you have, love?' asked Amy.

'Can't grumble.'

'No. You never do.' Linda gave him a second hug, pulled back and with her handkerchief removed a tiny scrap of shaving soap from below his right ear. Then she looked him up and down. Her grandfather was still a tall man with broad shoulders but he stooped heavily now and his hair was reduced to a few grey strands, carefully combed back. His face was long and thin and, despite the jowls, retained the regularity of features that had drawn comparison with Gary Cooper years before. Linda looked approvingly into eyes that were as brown and gentle as her own.

'You'll do, Grandpa. Now, sit down and eat. It's going to be a long day. Oh, and for goodness' sake open your telegram. The neighbours want to know what it says.'

Hickman removed his glasses, gave the lenses a slow histrionic polish, replaced them and read aloud: 'Hello, Jim boy. Are you up for a bit of bonking tonight? It's convenient because Phil's away. Let me know. All love, Liz.'

A howl went up from the girls. 'Oh, Granddad, really!' Linda snatched the telegram away, read it and passed it round. 'It's very nice of her to send you birthday greetings. She must 'ave quite a bit to do without thinking of you.'

'She didn't. You told her.' From under lowered brows, Jim's eyes twinkled up at her in thanks.

Linda gave the telegram to Lilly. 'Be a good girl and show the bloody thing to his groupies outside, or they'll be there all day. I'll go and get our things. The car will be here soon.'

Jim swallowed his pills with the orange juice but didn't linger long on his cornflakes, even though Linda had sliced banana on them, which he loved. He was not at all sure how he viewed this day, but it had been long in preparation and he wanted just to get on with it now. His hand trembled as he sipped his tea and shot a glance at the black and white picture of Polly on the

407

mantelpiece. Taken when she was sixty, she still looked good. Those cheekbones always helped in photos. What, he wondered, would she make of all this fuss now? There was no merit in living so long. In fact, it was bloody inconvenient for all concerned. The girls should have been able to sell the house and split the money between them when they most needed it – when they were young and starting up in life with their own young families. But he had hung on long after Polly had gone – and, of course, Bertie.

Ah well. He slurped his tea and blew his nose. He had said goodbye to the great-grandchildren last night and there had been all that fuss at the service last Sunday at Aston parish church, just by the Villa ground. Although today, of course, was the real anniversary of the start of the First World War, or the Great War as they used to call it until the other one came along. Funny that his birthday had coincided with the beginning of that bloody great mess. Ah well again. He pushed back the chair and rose unsteadily to his feet.

'Hey, Lyn,' he called up the stairs, 'don't you be carrying those bags down the stairs. The girls can do that. They're younger than you.'

'I'm doing it. Shan't be a minute. Can you get your coat?'

He tossed his head in annoyance. Of course he could get his bloody coat! He wasn't that doddery. A car hooted outside. The thing had arrived and Lilly came bustling back. 'Car's here, love. I'll get your overcoat.'

'No, for goodness' sake … oh, never mind, then.'

Amy adjusted his tie. 'I hope Lyn packed your passport. I had enough trouble organising it.'

He sighed and inwardly smiled. Amy was just establishing the fact that she too had played her part in arranging the Great Day. She wanted a little credit. He gave her a kiss. It had been necessary to take out a passport for him, for this would be only the second time he had travelled abroad since 1918. 'I'm sure she has, love,' he said. 'She's packed everything else: fourteen pyjamas, twenty-seven shirts, seventeen pairs of shoes, three walking sticks and the fire irons.'

He was interrupted by Lynda clumping down the stairs, her own bag under her arm and his on an extended handle, thumping down stair by stair behind her. Lilly held out his overcoat so that he could lower his arms through the sleeves. Amy wrapped a scarf around his neck and knotted it under his chin.

'Come on, Robert Redford,' called Lynda. 'You'll 'ave to fight your way through your fans outside.'

The car had pulled up outside. It was a long, low, black, highly polished limousine and, Jim thought, had last been used for a funeral. Might as well park it round the corner and keep it handy for when his time came ... but everyone was cheering. The driver held open the car door, sprang to attention and gave a smart salute.

'Happy birthday and congratulations, Sarn't Major,' he said.

'Oh, bloody 'ell,' muttered Jim. He thought about telling the smart young man that you didn't salute a sergeant major, then thought better of it. The knot of people outside number 66 had now swelled into a small crowd and someone began singing 'Happy Birthday to You'. For a brief moment the mind of the old man leaning on his two sticks went back to a very different birthday when the song was sung to him as he lay against the side of a shell crater in the Salient. Then he raised one of his sticks and the crowd fell silent.

'Very kind of you,' he said. 'I shall be giving out money on my return but will you kindly now disperse and go back to your work? The economy is in a bad enough way without you buggering it up further. So please go and put your shoulder to the wheel and your arses to the whatsits for the common good. Thank you very much.'

'Oh, he's always been such a wag,' Mrs Patel confided to her neighbour. 'Enjoy yourself, Jim,' she called and waved her miniature Union Jack.

Jim waved his stick again and stooped to get into the back of the limo. Then he straightened up suddenly, his face full of concern. 'The letter,' he cried. 'My bloody letter. I can't go without it.'

'What letter, love?' asked Linda.

'The letter ... you know ... the one I had been waiting for. It's important. The whole bloody point will be lost if I... You know, it's that one that came for me from the Ministry of Defence.'

'Well no, as a matter of bloody fact, I don't. Where is it anyway and why is it so important?'

'It's ... er ... personal. I think it's by the side of me bed. Get it, there's a love.'

'Oh, very well. Get in the car, then.'

The driver, smart in his grey suit and matching cap with gleaming black peak, helped him into the car and Jim half lay back, his sticks thrust before him as he watched anxiously for Lynda. Eventually, she came, waving a buff-coloured envelope and sat, panting, next to him. She handed him the letter.

'Is this it?'

'Aye, lass. That's it.'

'Looks like an income tax demand to me.'

'No, it isn't. Why are you puffing so?'

'Look, Grandpops, just because you can nip up and down them stairs like a two-year-old, doesn't mean to say I can do it. I'm a fifty-three-year-old widow now, you know, and fat with it.'

Jim smiled sourly. She had gained weight rapidly since the death of her husband three years before and moving in with Jim to look after him. She interpreted looking after him as ensuring that he ate the gargantuan meals she cooked for him and the result had had a markedly greater effect on her figure than his. Now, they waved their hands at the car window like royalty as the limo slowly drew away.

'It's Elmdon airport, isn't it, miss?' enquired the driver.

Lynda looked at him sharply to detect any impertinent irony but the driver's gaze in the mirror seemed innocent enough. 'Yes, please,' she said. 'And it's missus. You should get your eyes tested, young man.'

He gave her a nod and a grin. She returned it and grasped her grandfather's hand. 'Mum and Nannie would have loved this, you know.'

Jim nodded but did not reply. His eyes had suddenly become moist. Two hours later their aircraft touched down at Brussels. It had been his first flight – he and Polly had never needed an aeroplane to reach Bournemouth or Rhyl on their annual summer holiday – and he had spent the time with his eyes closed, trying not to think of the past. The next couple of days would be bad enough and he mustn't get emotional. Neither Polly nor Bertie liked fuss.

At the airport there was a long, black Renault waiting for them, flying a British Legion flag. 'Sorry we couldn't get a Rover or a Jag,' explained the grey-haired Legion official who met them, 'and I'm afraid that Legion funds don't run to a Rolls.'

Jim nodded but said nothing.

'It's good of you to take care of us so well,' said Lynda hurriedly. 'The Legion has been so good in arranging it all. We're very grateful.'

'Oh, the least we could do. It's an honour to have Sergeant Major Hickman with us.' He held open the door. 'Very few veterans left now, I'm afraid, only–'

'Don't call me sergeant major,' Jim interrupted. 'I haven't been a warrant officer for nigh on eighty years. Me name's Jim. Any Warwicks here?'

'Sorry, Jim. No, I'm afraid not. There are only four others. Of course they get smaller every...' His voice tailed away as he realised the solecism. 'No. No Warwicks. A bit of a mixed bag, really.'

They all climbed into the Renault. 'What's the plan, then, Mr ... er...?'

'Robinson, call me George. Well, it won't take us long to drive to Ypres. Incidentally, the Belgians call it something else now, but it sounds roughly the same. The ceremony takes place every evening at five at the Menin Gate, of course, but on this anniversary it will be a bit longer. The mayor will be there, and Jim and the other four veterans, and there will be a few speeches in French and English. The British military attaché from Brussels will be on parade and lots of attention, of course, will be on the five of you – photographs, press interviews and such.' He smiled. 'You're the senior chap there in terms of age and rank, Jim, so they will probably focus on you a fair bit.'

Jim gave him a sharp look from under a white eyebrow. 'Lot of fuss. I didn't realise there'd be that much fuss.'

Lynda turned on him. 'Oh, come on, Grand-pops. You knew what was involved. Don't be grumpy about it. It's a great honour.'

'Humph!' Jim immediately felt guilty. 'Sorry ... er ... George. It's just that...' His voice tailed away, then grew stronger. 'It's okay about tomorrow, isn't it?'

'Ah yes. You want to go to, where was it again?'

'Place called Oostbeke. Can't remember where it was 'cos I went by train, but it was our old Divisional HQ.'

'Ah, yes. You can keep the car, of course, and the driver will know where it is. Now, about tonight...'

He droned on but Jim closed his eyes and pretended to snooze. He had never wanted to get involved in all this anniversary pomp, only to go back to Oostbeke and complete his mission. The two had coincided, however, and the local branch of the Legion – his old branch – had been so insistent. Ah well, never mind. It would soon be over.

They arrived at their modern hotel in Ypres in time for him to take a proper nap. The town, of course, was quite unrecognisable, although he was told that they had rebuilt the centre more or less exactly how it was, with a Grand Place and a new Cloth Hall. Trouble was, he couldn't remember how it was before the Germans had shelled it to bits. Now, Pop – he could remember that! No time to go there, though. Maybe just as well...

He and Lynda were taken early to meet the other veterans and be filmed and photographed at a British War Graves cemetery just outside Ypres. There, Jim looked with awe at the rows of white stones – remarkably similar to that which he had had made for Bertie so long ago – and then with an even greater sense of wonder up to the east, up the gently sloping ground to the blue-fringed line that formed the distant horizon beyond which lay the village of Pass-chendaele. What was once the Salient, a place of death, destruction and horror, was now smiling farmland, intersected with green hedges and dotted with terracotta-roofed farmhouses. Apart from the cemeteries and the place names – Hellfire Corner, Geluveld, etc – there was no sign that this was once the most concentrated killing field that Europe had ever known, the place where he had watched Black Jack Flanagan drown... He jerked his head back and did his best to answer the banal questions of the television interviewers. What was it like to be back? It was fucking awful, that's what it was like. But he didn't say that.

Later, at 5 p.m., he and Lynda were among the veterans who were cordoned off under the huge white stone pillars of the Menin Gate to hear the Last Post sounded by the blue-uniformed buglers of, bizarrely, the Ypres Fire Brigade. Thank God they were allowed to sit during the interminable speeches by the mayor, other local dignitaries and a bemedalled British major general. Then they were given dinner at a restaurant – Lynda loved it because she sat next to the major general – and Jim had to confess that the food wasn't bad, although too much for him at his age. There was, however, a splendid light Fleurie, of which he drank too much, making him feel very queasy during the night.

Nevertheless, he was up early the next day and, much to Lynda's disgust, was standing waiting and shivering in the car park as the Renault drew up. He pretended to doze again on the journey, because he did not want to talk about why and where he was going. Why should he? It only mattered to him, Polly and Bertie, and now, only to him. He knew Lynda had some idea of where they were going, of course, but not about The Letter.

It took some time to find the little church because Jim could not remember its name and it had been nearly seventy years since his last visit. But eventually they found it for it had not changed, except that, instead of old cottages, it was now surrounded by new municipal housing.

'We're going to see the grave of your old comrade, Granddad, I suppose?' asked Lynda, who had been discreetly silent throughout the journey.

'That's right, love. Bertie Murphy. He used to live two doors away in Turners Lane.'

'Just a sentimental journey, then, is it?'

'I suppose it is, but p'raps a bit more than that.' He looked about him, remembering a dark night when Bertie had been unknowingly escorted by the military police on his last journey. 'I think it's down there in that far corner. The driver needn't come.'

He and his granddaughter moved slowly through the churchyard to the far corner. When he walked he jettisoned one of his two sticks and hung onto Lynda's arm. The lilac tree had gone but, heart-warmingly, Bertie's headstone stood out well, although its colour had darkened. The grass had been cut on the grave itself and some wild flowers had been recently cut and put into the urn at the foot of the grave. Someone was still looking after it, although the French widow must surely now be dead.

At the grave, Jim turned to Lynda. 'Don't think me rude, love, but I would be grateful if you would leave me alone here for a bit. Do you mind?'

'Of course not. I'll go back to the gate. Don't try and come back by yourself. Just give me a shout and I'll come and get you.'

'Thank you, lass.'

He waited until she had moved away and then, balancing on his sticks, looked at the headstone. The carved lettering did not stand out as clearly as he remembered, but he admitted that was to be expected.

'Hello, old lad,' he murmured. 'Sorry it's taken such a time to come back and I suppose this will be my last visit. But I've got a bit of news for you, that I just had to come here to tell you. Listen to this, son.'

Hooking one of his sticks over his arm, Jim fumbled for his glasses, adjusted them and then took out the buff-coloured envelope, opened it and took out the single sheet of paper within.

'This is addressed to me, Bertie, and it's from the bloody Minister of Defence no less. Listen, he says:

'Dear Mr Hickman,
906372 Corporal Bertram Murphy, 1st Bn Royal Warwickshire Regt

I know that you have been corresponding with my ministry for some considerable time over the case of this soldier, who was convicted of cowardice and desertion in the face of the enemy and executed in 1917.

As you know, this case is only one of many that have been brought to the attention of the Ministry of Defence over the years, but you have been at great pains to point out the outstanding unfairness of Corporal Murphy's conviction – the prejudice shown against him by the president and other officers at the court martial, his exemplary record right up until his arrest and the extreme likelihood that he was suffering from shell shock when he left his post in the line.

We are currently reviewing the whole question of soldiers executed in the Great War but this, inevitably, is taking some time. In view of the strength of the your case, your own involvement as prisoner's friend and your age, I am, however, writing to you now to say that I have decided that Corporal Murphy will be pardoned immediately. I have written to his regiment asking that his name should be included in the regimental records and in other appropriate memorials.

I hope that you will be pleased by this news and I do congratulate you on your persistence in this matter and your loyalty to your old comrade.

Yours sincerely etc etc.'

Jim removed his spectacles, put them in their case and replaced them in his pocket. 'What do you think about that, then, you old bugger? Bertie, lad, you are no longer a coward and a deserter – not that you ever were – and I am only sorry that it has taken so long.'

He stood for a moment longer, with his head bowed. Then, very, very slowly he bent down so that he was kneeling at the side of the grave by the headstone. With his fingers, he made a small hole in the grass and then the soil underneath it. 'Here, Bertie. You have this. You deserve it.' And he carefully folded the letter and slipped it into the hole, covering it with the displaced soil. Then he hauled himself up by the headstone and regained his feet.

He called, 'Lyn, can you come and get me?'

Jim Hickman died seventeen days later, in his bed at number 66 Turners Lane, the house he had lived in for most of his life. He had caught a cold in Belgium – the Salient had claimed him at last – and it had developed into pneumonia. Lynda was by his side, holding his hand, as he passed away and she immediately called her sisters from their tasks downstairs.

They rushed up and all three knelt by the side of their grandfather, tears trickling down their cheeks.

Amy eventually looked across at her elder sister. 'Did he say anything before he went, Lyn?' she asked.

Lynda sniffed into her handkerchief. 'Yes,' she said. 'It was only a whisper but I caught it. He said, "Ah, starshine." Wasn't that a funny thing to say?'

AUTHOR'S NOTE

Virtually all of the characters mentioned in this book are fictional and bear no relationship to any soldiers who fought in the First World War. Field Marshal Haig and the politicians Asquith and Lloyd George are the obvious exceptions.

Bertie Murphy's number, 906372, I plucked out of the air, although, to give it some veracity, it bears some resemblance to those of soldiers court-martialled for desertion in 1917. I apologise if, accidentally, I have stolen that of a brave man of the period.

I grew up in the thirties with the Great War, as it was called, hanging over the heads of me and of my family like some retrospective thundercloud. My father was the youngest boy in a late-Victorian working-class family of fourteen – seven boys and seven girls. All of the boys went off to fight in the trenches, they were all rifle and bayonet men, not support soldiers, and, miraculously, all of them survived.

My father, Leonard Wilcox, went over the top as an infantry sergeant on the first morning of the Battle of the Somme and was almost immediately severely wounded by a shell burst, which riddled his body, particularly his lungs, with shrapnel. He spent hours in a shell crater and those wounds eventually turned into tuber-culosis – then incurable – and he died in 1945.

My Uncle Ernest won the Distinguished Conduct Medal, like Jim Hickman, and became a temporary Regimental Sergeant Major at the ridiculous young age of twenty-four, 'because there was no one else left.' Uncle Bernard, also a sergeant, lost an eye but won the Military Medal, also like Jim.

Uncle Alfred, the oldest of the quartet and yet only a lance corporal, came back to a shattered marriage but wearing the medal of the highest decoration in the British Services, the Victoria Cross.

The reader will understand, then, that the First World War has haunted me, not only as a boy wondering about whether he would have had the courage, like his father and distinguished uncles, to have gone over the top unhesitatingly into the German wire and machine-gun fire, but also as a latter-day novelist, writing about the wars of Empire in the late nineteenth century. I felt unable to write about the Great War earlier for various reasons, but now I am happy to have done so. The monkey, so to speak, is off my back.

Three hundred and six British and Common-wealth soldiers were executed by firing squad during World War I, usually for desertion and cowardice. My own necessarily brief dip into the files of such cases at the Public Records Office in Kew, London, showed that many of those shot were genuinely 'hard cases' who had absconded before. It should also be said that the commanders-in-chief, Sir John French, and later Field Marshal Haig, who always had the last word on such matters, commuted the sentences of no less than 899.

Nevertheless, the story of Bertie's trial and death is not so out of the ordinary. James Crozier, from Belfast, was just sixteen when he was shot. Before his execution, the boy was given so much rum that he passed out and had to be carried semi-conscious to the execution post. Private Abe Bevistein was also aged sixteen when he was found guilty of deserting his post. Just before his court martial he wrote home to his mother:

We were in the trenches. I was so cold I went out (and took shelter in a farmhouse). They took me to prison so I will have to go in front of the court. I will try my best to get out of it, so don't worry.

The edict of the Duke of Wellington that courts martial should be considered as a form of deterrent was very much adhered to during the war and, on 13th January 1915, General Routine Order 585 was issued which basically reversed the civilian code of being considered innocent until found guilty. Under the Order, a soldier was guilty until sufficient evidence could be provided to prove his innocence.

At the end of the war, however, there was a general feeling of unease about courts martial and the Darling Committee was set up to investigate the system. It reported that 'we consider ... that the work of courts martial during the war has been well done.' It tinkered with peripheral improvements but no fundamental changes were recommended.

As the years passed and more was learnt about shell shock, that disquiet increased. It culminated on 8th November 2006 when the Labour Government included in the Armed Forces Act a retrospective pardon for all those army personnel executed in the 1914–18 war. I anticipated this, in Bertie's case, by ten years in what I hope is a pardonable piece of poetic licence.

A more outrageous piece of time distortion, however, – at least to those who know their British musical history – has been indulged in by me in terms of Bertie's (and my mother's) favourite musical, *The Maid of the Mountains*. It opened, in fact, in Manchester on 23rd February 1916 and then, after some rewriting, re-opened for a long run at Daly's Theatre in London on 10th February 1917. Bertie could not therefore have seen it with Polly in 1915. However, I so desperately wanted Bertie and his girl to go there together for his first leave that I have created the deliberate time-warp. I hope that making this confession here and explaining the reason will excuse me for perpetrating this solecism.

Starshine is a novel, a work of the imagination, but in pursuit of accuracy I have loosely based several, although not all, of the action sequences in the story on the experiences of men who fought in the war and who put their own tales down on paper at the end of it. My description of Jim Hickman's attack on the machine-gun post and his 'bombing up the trench', for instance, parallels in many ways the citation that accompanied Alfred Wilcox's award of the Victoria Cross in 1918.

Any inaccuracies in the tale, however, are my responsibility alone.

–J.W. Chilmark, 2012.

ACKNOWLEDGEMENTS

I owe a debt to my father and my six paternal uncles who all fought in World War I – as related in my Author's Note – for what they did, but the debt does not extend to the modesty which accompanied them in later life. For none of them talked about their experiences to the family, not even Uncle Alf, who won the Victoria Cross. That was no help at all to a novelist, but they weren't to know that I would become a scribbler, for they all died well before I was an adult.

Nevertheless, those experiences hung around them like some indefinable aura and as a boy I read everything I could grab about that tragic conflict. Much of that sank into my brain and, although the titles of the books have long been forgotten, the stories remained and I have drawn on them, to some extent, in writing this novel.

More to the point, however, I refreshed those memories with more contemporary reading and I must thank the authors of the following books for providing much of the detail of the campaigns and the fighting:

They Called it Passchendaele by Lyn
    Macdonald; Michael Joseph, London, 1978
Somme by Lyn Macdonald; Michael Joseph,

London, 1983

Voices and Images of the Great War, by Lyn Macdonald; Michael Joseph, London, 1988.

Ypres, the First Battle of 1914, by Ian F.W. Beckett; Pearson Education Ltd., Edinburgh, 2004

Goodbye to All That, by Robert Graves; Jonathan Cape, London, 1929

On the Front Line, Foreword by Malcolm Brown; Robinson Publishing, London, 1997

For Love and Courage: The Letters of Lt. Col E.W. Hermon from the Western Front 1914–1917, edited by Anne Nason; Preface, London, 2009

A Whispered Name, by William Brodrick; Little Brown, London 2009.

I must also, however, thank the staffs of the London Library and the Public Records Office at Kew, who helped me to dig back into the past. So, too, did my old friend Jim Farrand, to whom this book is dedicated, who drove and walked through much of the old Salient to the east of Ypres with me, as we both tried to imagine how such a fertile and rural area could have been so horrific a killing ground for four years, less than a hundred years before.

Let me also express my gratitude to the editors at Allison & Busby for picking up and remedying so many of my sloppy errors of detail. And, as ever, I must record my thanks to my wife Betty, loyal and loving proofreader and research assistant and, for her constant support, my agent, Jane Conway-Gordon.

The publishers hope that this book has given you enjoyable reading. Large Print Books are especially designed to be as easy to see and hold as possible. If you wish a complete list of our books please ask at your local library or write directly to:

Magna Large Print Books
Magna House, Long Preston,
Skipton, North Yorkshire.
BD23 4ND

This Large Print Book for the partially sighted, who cannot read normal print, is published under the auspices of

THE ULVERSCROFT FOUNDATION

THE ULVERSCROFT FOUNDATION

... we hope that you have enjoyed this Large Print Book. Please think for a moment about those people who have worse eyesight problems than you ... and are unable to even read or enjoy Large Print, without great difficulty.

You can help them by sending a donation, large or small to:

The Ulverscroft Foundation, 1, The Green, Bradgate Road, Anstey, Leicestershire, LE7 7FU, England.
or request a copy of our brochure for more details.

The Foundation will use all your help to assist those people who are handicapped by various sight problems and need special attention.

Thank you very much for your help.